# The SEA PRAYERS

## A CAROLINA COAST NOVEL

# The SEA PRAYERS

## A CAROLINA COAST NOVEL

### NORMANDIE FISCHER

Sleepy Creek Press

ALSO BY NORMANDIE FISCHER

CAROLINA COAST NOVELS

Becalmed

Heavy Weather

Twilight Christmas

Sailing out of Darkness

ISAAC'S HOUSE NOVELS

From Fire into Fire

Two from Isaac's House

*For my beloved husband, my best friend and sailing partner. Michael makes me laugh, lifts me up when I am down, and reveals to us all what sacrificial love means when he takes care of the old folk in my life. I am so grateful.*

*My sea prayer…*

*When you pass through the waters, I will be with you; and when you pass through the rivers, they will not sweep over you…. For I am the LORD your God, the Holy One of Israel, your Savior…*

— Isaiah 43:2-3

*Be still and know that I am God…*

— Psalm 46:10

1

---

AGNES

L ocked-away memories belonged to the dark, not streaking like fireballs into the middle of a shimmery day. Hadn't Agnes rendered any bugaboos powerless under layers of to-dos and long lists of what-ifs?

She'd tucked them away. Far away. And so she responded to the postman's whistle like metal shavings to a magnet. She dropped her sponge and hurried toward the front of the house, immune to thoughts of overdue notices that showed up with awful regularity. She could hope, couldn't she, that today good news would appear in her mailbox—a check, an invitation, a validation of some sort?

Link's tail swished across the hardwood floor, and he snuffled to get out. "Stay," she said, extending her hand, palm out, as she stepped onto the porch and let the door close behind her.

"Hey, Ms. Jones. How's it going?"

"Billy." She focused on the stack of mail in his hand. "I hope you're well."

"Doin' great, thanks." The round-faced septuagenarian, who acted younger than some in their thirties, held up an envelope that seemed innocuous enough to keep her excitement brewing.

"You need to sign for this one." He handed her a certified mail receipt. "Something important'd be my guess. California. Los Angeles." He winked. "Maybe Hollywood's come calling. Maybe they discovered that little beauty you got living with you."

"Maybe," she said, signing and handing back the receipt.

"You have a great day, ma'am."

"You, too."

The envelope weighed heavily in her hand as she stared at a return address she didn't recognize. D. Evermire in Los Angeles. She squinted. Who did she know in California named Evermire? Named D-something Evermire?

The realization smacked her like a slap to the face, stinging and sending shock waves all the way down her spine. And there it was. The *him* of her past.

But he *couldn't* have found her.

Darlington Evermire. *Dar...ling...ton.* The syllables separated, marbles clicking against each other.

She was going to faint.

She never fainted.

Bracing herself against the porch rail, she scanned the front yard and the street beyond her wooden gate as if he might be lurking behind a hedge or in one of the cars crawling into town. Oh, maybe not *him*, but someone, some hireling who'd located her. How had he ferreted her out when no one in Beaufort, North Carolina, even knew?

"God, please." She whispered the words to a heaven she'd railed against ever since... ever since that night. And its aftermath.

She pressed a fist against her stomach as if to hold back the bile. How had her accidental sperm donor—or, to be more precise, her rapist sperm planter—found her?

When her knees threatened to buckle, she clutched the railing with suddenly sweaty palms. Sweaty was a trick in fifty-eight degrees. It had been seventy-one yesterday, but now cold was scurrying in. Scurrying down to her belly, too, in spite of that sweat.

Agnes pushed away, turned, and stepped blindly into the front hall. The screen door slammed behind her, and she locked herself in before dropping the bulk of the mail, minus the poisonous letter, on the hall chest. Link pressed against her thighs, offering his head for a pat. She gave it absently and as absently plodded, one foot in front of the other, slowly up the wide, curved staircase to the second floor, the dog one step behind. At least no one other than Link was near enough to hear her sharp puffs of breath, the creak of that loose board on the fifth stair, the slide and slap of her faux-Uggs as she followed the path of the Oriental runner past a guest-room door to her own room, and then into her bathroom. With the door locked, she slid down the wall to the floor, raised her knees, and laid her forehead against them.

It all came back. The noise, the smells, the sloshing liquid and sloshed pretty people hadn't been what she'd expected when she'd agreed to go to the club that night. It just went to show what she'd known about pretty much anything outside of classes.

She'd been so stupid.

During the years between his first oozy smile and now, she'd done her best, her very best, to forget that Darlington Evermire —Darling to his adoring fans—had ever lived. She would have managed it except for a certain expression in her daughter's eyes, a certain tilt to Brisa's chin—or maybe it was Brisa's toffee-colored skin and the lush curls of her black hair that reminded Agnes of the man who'd stolen her innocence and changed her life forever.

She splashed water on her face, dried it, and then carried the offending letter back to her room, where she tucked it out of sight in her underwear drawer, away from prying eyes. Not that her daughter normally came into her room.

If only Agnes could burn the letter, but she'd signed for it,

3

giving proof it had come into her hands. She wished she could wipe it, him, from her thoughts, but once seen, always remembered. The ability to hold onto images and words had been a gift during her student days; it was useless now. And, no, she wouldn't consider that the letter's words might be benign.

Not if Darlington Evermire had penned them.

2

HENRY

A wave slapped the sailboat's transom, drowning Henry's whispered words. "To midnight," he said, announcing an ending and a beginning, yesterday gone, today inching relentlessly toward dawn. He had no watch hours to keep, but he recognized the hour's advent in spite of having silenced his ship's clock. He'd sat through too many midnights when he'd longed for sleep that wouldn't come.

He turned up the collar of his foul-weather jacket to ward off a late-March chill and settled deeper into the cockpit seat. Stars winked, and the full moon climbed slowly, a celebratory moon to take the place of birthday cakes or fireworks, although Eric had offered those and more.

"You still could take him up on it," Hen told himself and the now silent anchorage.

He could, but he probably wouldn't. He'd never liked birthdays.

His cell phone rang, vibrating into a dance across the marble-topped table below. He might have been able to ignore the ring, but the skittery buzz and bounce was too much. He imagined the small phone hopping over the edge and to the floor, cracking open, dying. He'd already lost one to the sea through carelessness. He couldn't afford to lose another.

Besides, who but Eric would call at this hour?

He set his water bottle on the deck and eased down the companionway stairs. Grabbing the phone, he answered as he climbed back outside. "Hey."

"I saw a light," his twin said. "Figured you hadn't gone to bed."

"Just too lazy to move."

"Well, happy birthday, little brother."

"Little? I'm an inch taller than you." His effort at humor sounded more petulant than amusing.

Eric chuckled anyway. "And I'm six minutes older."

Henry heard the old taunt hidden in his brother's laugh, or maybe it only existed in his self-pitying mind. Those six minutes had never been funny. Instead, they'd made all the difference— or had the difference been crafted already in the womb? Genetics had certainly carved the hole in his lip, but there was other blame, wasn't there?

"I'm also richer," Eric said.

This time, Hen heard only the humor, and he grinned. "There is that."

"I wouldn't be if you'd let me release some of yours."

Boy, that shifted the conversation. Nothing to laugh about now, with Eric putting on his older-brother-trustee voice.

"It's time, don't you think?" Eric said. "Call it a birthday present. You could fix up that boat of yours in no time. You could actually be in the slip next to mine, and we could chat across the dock instead of across the channel."

"There is that, too." He hoped the flatness of his voice would end a discussion he didn't want to have.

Eric was one of his trustees because, of course, their father hadn't trusted his younger son to manage anything, much less wealth. Of course, he hadn't. And Hen was the first to admit he'd have squandered it. The thing was, now he wanted no part

6

of his trust fund because it had come through their father. He wanted to earn his own way. To show everyone, especially his dead father—and wasn't that absurd?—that he was capable of going it alone. Of fixing up *Harmless* through his own efforts.

And he preferred living at anchor instead of in close proximity to neighbors as Eric did. Besides, he could take off when he wanted. Go where he wanted.

As soon as he finished the repairs.

"It's here for you," Eric said now. "Any time."

"You feeling guilty again?"

"I suppose I am," Eric said. "I have so much."

Hen could picture his twin lounging in his comfortable cockpit or down below in his luxurious cabin, wearing the perfect togs for whatever he was doing, while he, Henry, made do with his sloppy boat-repair clothes and a few walk-into-town khakis/shirt combos.

Hen supposed he could change up, if he wanted to. If. "Choices, bro. Choices. You made good ones. I didn't."

Eric said something that sounded like "If only that were all." His brother's voice had grown soft, and Hen wasn't sure he'd heard correctly.

But, then, they both knew the truth.

"Thanks for calling," Hen said. "Here's to us." And he lifted his water bottle high. "Happy birthday, big brother."

"May this be a year of great things." Eric's normally cheerful words sounded almost sad this time.

Hen cleared his throat. Eric was never depressed, never.

He put as much cheer into his voice as he could. Easter would be here soon. New birth, new hope. "Yes, sir. A year of very great things for both of us."

They disconnected. And Henry Donato Houston felt moisture hit his cheek for the first time since he'd stood beside his mother's casket.

Minutes later, he tucked the phone securely under the flap of his pocket and drew his legs up onto the cockpit seat. The

7

incoming tide and slight breeze joined to ripple the water's surface, turning the moonlight to glitter on black. Better to watch light dancing and dodging than to think of birthdays and the years when he'd been—as he was now and ever would be—an addict, years of too many tossed moments, thrown away and unremarkable. For him, not Eric. He was the wrong twin, the maimed one, and until recently, the lost one.

But.

Thank God for that huge *but*. He, that same Henry, had been clean two years, seven months, and fifteen days. *That* was a date to celebrate. Freedom from self-destruction, the rebirth of a man who planned on giving thanks daily, hourly.

He lifted his water bottle and said, "Salut," to Eric, to the town, to life, as he toasted himself and his brother at this half-decade mark. Five years from forty was old for having accomplished nothing. But that was on him, not on his twin.

He needed to let the past go. For tonight, he'd shift his thoughts from pasts and presents and, just for a moment, allow himself to contemplate futures.

He pictured Agnes of the haunted eyes. Agnes, who sometimes cast a surreptitious glance at him with an expression of longing that might have, just possibly, mirrored his. Agnes, who kept her shoulders back and her spine straight in spite of a weight she seemed barely able to carry, and not merely the weight of her waitressing trays.

He longed to lift her burdens. For the first time in his self-absorbed life, he wanted to help someone other than himself.

But wanting and being welcome to do it were two very different things. Wanting and being *capable* of doing it, instead of pulling her down with him, were hugely different issues.

He couldn't imagine Agnes wanting a broken-down him. Besides, she had a daughter to raise. And a huge house to manage. And he had years of terrible decisions to overcome.

Including the bloody knife and the threat of jail that had finally driven him to sobriety.

# 3

## AGNES

Patrons began to fill the tables and booths at *Agua Verde* for their martini-night fix and the elegant food that went with it—small plates, large plates, and *un poco de sabor*, a little spoonful of flavor designed to tease the palette. The restaurant's setting was intimate, with raised booths along two walls, tables in the middle set with linen tablecloths and napkins, and the bar to one side. Yes, it could get noisy, but Agnes only minded noise when she had to bend close to hear a soft-spoken guest and feel as if she were invading the stranger's space.

She tucked a stray hair behind her ear and scribbled orders. She poured water and carried wine and cocktails while the image of that underwear-buried missive drilled holes in her thoughts, scattering its debris like a corkscrew spewed bits of dried-up cork. She smiled, always polite, always careful and thorough and in control when delivering food and removing empty plates, although her lips felt as if they'd crack from the strain and leave a bleeding mess against her teeth.

When a momentary lull allowed her to relax, she leaned against a wall between the bar and the kitchen, out of sight, she hoped. Only, Henry must have noticed. He popped out of the kitchen and looked down at her with those long-lashed dark-blue eyes, smiling the sweetest smile she'd ever seen.

"You okay?" he whispered. His strong shoulders almost begged to be leaned against, his strong hands to be touched, his strong chin to be…

"Agnes?"

Oh, right. He'd asked a question.

"Yes," she said, smiling back with an ease she hadn't felt until that moment. Nothing was hard when Hen tilted her world upright.

Oh, he didn't mean anything by it. He'd never really seen *her*, of course. He was kind to everyone, but a man that beautiful? With a woman so *not* beautiful? The sweetness of his spirit woke a hope in her and melted all the anxiety she stored inside.

By the end of the evening, they'd exchanged several more words, always accompanied by his gentle smile. After work, he even walked her as far as Front Street.

When they had to go in opposite directions, he said, "Good night, Agnes," and she chose not to imagine any particular warmth when he spoke her name, any particular desire to prolong the moment. He turned with one last touch to her arm. "See you tomorrow."

She felt his hand's warmth through her long sleeves and tried not to let him hear the yearning in her "Goodnight" or in the whispered "See you" she gave his retreating back. Or the *see you* she repeated silently.

She wouldn't have been able to walk home alone late at night back in Jersey City, not on her street and not without a saber at the ready. What an image, her wielding a sword against anyone. She grinned, even as needles of cold off the ocean hit her face and the shush-shush of waves lapped at a dock across the street.

Brisa would be asleep. Agnes longed to be the one—instead of the caregiver—who made sure her child had eaten her vegetables, completed her homework, and taken her bath. Eleven was such a hard age.

Especially, Agnes decided, if you were bi-racial and fatherless in small-town South, in a place where the elderly black couple from just down the way lived over the garage and not in the big house. Granted, she and Brisa had only been in Beaufort a little over a year, and she'd spent most of that time trying to keep their home together until her mom's estate settled, but she had eyes, didn't she? Brisa and that old couple seemed to be the only people of color living on Front Street.

The gate creaked on its hinges as she opened it, and she lifted it to dampen the sound when she pulled it closed. Brisa could wake at a whisper.

Of course, hadn't Brisa been harder to rouse lately? Eleven sneaking up on twelve was supposed to be childhood, not adolescence.

She unlocked the door, stepped into the big hall, and stopped. At the base of the stairs two suitcases declared that someone was either coming or going, and in her house, it had to be going.

She followed the lights from the hall toward the kitchen, where Sally Ann, her boarder and Brisa-watcher, nursed a cup of tea with an expression of sorrow on her youthful face.

"Hey, Agnes." Even Sally Ann's voice sounded beaten-down.

Agnes pulled out her own chair. "What's up with the bags?"

"My mama. The cancer's come back with a vengeance. I've got to go home."

"Oh, honey, I'm so sorry."

"I'm that sorry to leave you and Brisa. I know you need me."

"Your mama needs you more. When do you have to go?"

Sally Ann carried her cup to the big double sink. Over the running water, she said, "I thought I'd head out now. My daddy's a mess."

"You okay to drive?"

"I like to travel at night. Not so many folk on the roads."

Agnes took a deep breath. "Come on, then. I'll help you load up."

"I let Link out just before you got home." Sally Ann followed her outside and climbed into her car. "He's with Brisa."

As her tail lights headed down Front Street, fear settled in its habitual place in Agnes's stomach. She didn't have a single back-up plan.

Inside again, she hit the light switches before climbing the wide stairs. At Brisa's door, she peeked in. Link raised his golden head from the other side of Brisa and then laid his chin on her hip. "Good night, my angel," Agnes whispered into the dark room, ignoring Link, who'd long ago won the battle to sleep on his favorite human's bed.

After stepping out of her black pants and pulling her shirt over her head, she folded them both and set them on the stuffed chair by her bed. By rote she completed her nightly routines until all that awaited her was bed.

Oh, and the letter in her drawer. With *his* name above a California address.

It couldn't be good news. He'd become hugely successful, making music, making records. Singing of love from a frozen heart.

And there was still the question of how he'd found her. Maybe she'd read his words tomorrow. Or the next day. Or never.

Right now, her quiver was full of broken arrows. She didn't need to add another one.

4

DARLING

Darling glanced around his huge open living room and then across at Arthur. A sense of anticipation rose in him for more reasons than the one that had brought his best friend and manager here. Outside, the sun slid toward the Pacific Ocean, and, on the plain below, the sprawling city of Los Angeles readied itself for a night of indulgence. That was fine by Darling; it could indulge without him. He had too much else on his mind tonight.

He cracked his knuckles, first the right hand, then the left, before checking his nails. The one on his left thumb had a nick in it, which meant he'd need another manicure before Lisette returned. He made a mental note to have his houseboy set it up. His beautiful wife liked his hands smooth. Liked his nails groomed, polished, perfect.

She was gonna have herself an Easter present to beat all. Better than the rubies—tacky, but her favorite gem—he'd showered on her. His little lady wanted herself the girl child she couldn't have.

Well, it seemed he had one he could give her.

Darling aimed to keep Lisette happy 'cause that little gal

knew how to turn him to putty, and my, oh my, but she had the sweetest swish and sashay...

He'd better cut that out. Otherwise, Arthur was going to notice just where his thoughts had flung themselves. Still, when that gal of his got home, he was gonna have some of her.

And, yes, his thoughts had taken a turn into the vernacular of his childhood.

Arthur shifted back against the multi-colored throw pillows Lisette had bought to brighten both white couches, his grin spreading. Darling shrugged. Who cared what his best friend saw or knew? Wouldn't be the first time.

"She on her way back from Paris?" Arthur asked.

"Gets in late." Darling pictured her, that long blond hair flung back over her shoulders, those lips parted. He slugged back his rum and got up for a refill. From the ebony-topped bar, he asked over his shoulder, "You need another?"

"Still working on this one."

Darling carried his drink to the long, west-facing windows. "I assume you found out something more." The beginnings of a sunset lit the sky in yellows and oranges. He'd been in this house five years, on the West Coast fifteen, and he still had trouble with the idea of the sun going down over the water. Back east, the sun rose over ocean and set over mountains. Here, mountains were east, sea to the west. You'd think he'd get used to it. Once, he'd been so out of it, he'd like to have driven off into the sand while trying to get to a party in the hills.

Returning to his seat, he sipped his drink. "Thanks for the rum."

"Duty free on my way back last trip," Arthur said, raising his glass to study the liquid in it. "Been saving it for you."

"You have a special reason?"

"Photographs." Arthur set aside his drink and lifted his briefcase to the table between them. "Delivered this afternoon. Don't know about the letter yet."

Darling leveled his gaze at the black leather case. "I'm going to like them?"

"Yeah." Arthur snapped open the latches and pulled out a large envelope. "You won't believe how like you she is. Just as promised."

Darling sucked in a breath as Arthur slid the first photo across the table. "This is Brisa?" He traced a finger over the shiny surface, across a face that could have been his at twelve.

Tears welled. It was okay to show tears in front of Arthur, the man who'd taught him how to create them at will. They played well at concerts, Arthur'd said.

They did. But these weren't concert tears.

He scanned an image of his daughter sitting on a big porch next to a red-haired child and a very blond boy, another of them racing around a yard, and a third of her skipping beside her mama. He didn't want to think of Agnes Jones. She existed as a means to an end. Besides, she'd be compensated. He'd made her a good offer, could up it, if necessary.

The doorbell rang. Arthur raised a brow. "You expecting someone?"

Darling shook his head. No, and he didn't want anyone either.

"I'll get it," Arthur said, wandering over to open the heavy paneled door. RJ stood there, dreads hanging down his back, his big tattooed biceps popping out of a rolled-sleeved tee.

"Hey, my man." RJ rocked on his heels, no doubt with a smile ruined by a glassy, furtive expression in his eyes.

Arthur moved to block his entrance. "You're high. I told you not to come near Darling like that."

"No, man, I'm fine. Just came to see how my bro's doin'." RJ pushed past Arthur and sauntered in to flop down on the couch. His unlaced runners looked as if they might fall off his feet and trip him up.

Disgusted, Darling turned away to study another picture of Brisa. His daughter's smile and bright eyes nearly did him in.

15

"Whatcha got there, bro?"

He didn't answer. RJ scooted closer to the table and picked up one of Brisa with her mama. Darling snatched it back.

"Hey, man, why you bein' that way?"

Darling gathered the photos and put them back in their envelope before asking, "You need something special?"

"Nah. Like I said, just checkin' on you."

Sure he was. Darling scowled. "I'm fine. You've checked. Now tell me why you're really here. Because I don't like you showing up high, either here or on stage."

RJ's fingers drummed on his knees, and he glanced around the room. "I'm not. Swear to God."

"That's a dangerous thing to do, swearing to the Almighty unless it's truth." Darling poked his brother's bicep to focus his attention. "You know what I've told you. Arthur, too."

"Sure. Sure I do."

"Then you ought to pay attention and remember."

"I do." RJ pulled a bandana from his pocket and wiped his leaky nose. Then he nodded at the envelope. "That little girl in there. She sure looks like you."

Darling couldn't help the smile. Yeah. She sure did.

Instead, his half-brother looked a lot like their father. Nothing like him—or Brisa. The main thing Darling had gotten from his black half had been skin tinted the color of toffee, or maybe it looked more like the creamed coffee Lisette liked. Stuff made him gag, but she liked to climb on his lap, nuzzle his neck, and whisper how cream made her sweeter. Cream and sugar. Well, she was sure a sweet one.

He needed to corral those thoughts. Soon, though. Soon.

Arthur poured himself another drink and resumed his seat. "You two gonna be ready to roll tomorrow?"

RJ's fidgets increased with one knee bobbing and his fingers now picking at his shirt. "Sure, man. Count me in."

Darling reached over to stop the knee.

"I'm sorry, bro," RJ said. His voice held the hint of a whine. "I just needed to see Arthur." He shifted his gaze to the other man. "Your maid said you were here. Thought you could help me, you know, with just a little."

Darling shook his head. "Arthur told you, I told you, no more. You can't do that stuff anywhere near me."

"Yeah, I know. And I quit. Really, I did. Only then we played Denver, and there was this party, and…"

"Daddy said—"

But RJ cut him off. "Daddy told me whatever it took. That's what he said."

"He wouldn't do that." But when Darling glanced over at Arthur, his friend settled it with a quick nod.

Squeezing the bridge of his nose, Darling thought about Brisa and getting a judge to give her to him. How he had to be clean. They all had to be clean. "It's not going to work this way. It can't."

Arthur stood. "I'll get him out of here and take care of him. It won't come back on you."

"It will. You know it will."

"No." Arthur tapped RJ on the shoulder and waved him forward. "The mother's powerless. She's barely keeping things together. According to my source, she doesn't have any friends and will probably lose the house she inherited. You won't have any problems from her end." And to RJ. "Come on. I'll fix you up and get you home. The bus leaves at noon. That gives you tonight to get your act together. Are we square?"

"Yeah, man. Totally."

"I'll drive on my own," Darling said.

He didn't want to be trapped in a bus. He wanted the freedom to dream about his daughter. His gift.

Darling focused on the envelope after the others left. He was barely conscious of the phone ringing before the answering machine came on, and Lisette's voice told him the plane was delayed. She wouldn't arrive until day after tomorrow night. When he'd be gone.

He pressed his palms against his thighs and rubbed them back and forth against his tense muscles. He needed her here. With him.

Now.

5

## HENRY

H en's footsteps shuffled softly on the asphalt as he crossed to the waterfront. The Beaufort Town Docks provided transient space to the pretty boats, the big and fancy and shiny yachts or the equally spit-and-polished smaller ones, all belonging to the other half, to those who liked shore comforts and could pay for them. His half, those who couldn't or wouldn't pay slip fees, anchored or tied up in the mooring field across the way. Among his cohorts were world cruisers on a budget, boats from Scandinavia or South Africa, all sizes, all designs, but uniformly sail powered.

Nothing was better than life on a boat.

He checked the short pier where *Escape,* his brother's Tayana sailing sloop—newer than his hulk by a couple of decades and many thousands of dollars—bobbed in its slip, dark now, meaning Eric was out somewhere or he'd already gone to bed.

Probably the latter. A live wire, his twin.

"Hen!" A voice called from the darkness behind him.

He turned, and Eric walked into the light of the street lamp.

"Out late tonight?" Hen asked.

Eric leaned against the wooden rail that separated the

19

boardwalk from the dock below. "Dinner at the home of one of the partners. He's trying to introduce me to potential clients."

"Things picking up or are you mostly working on the great American novel?"

"You must have been spying over my shoulder. Seems like paying clients only want a lawyer whose daddy's name was on the door first. Leaves me high and dry."

"It'll happen, soon as they get to know you better. If you'd stayed in Charleston, you'd already be there, wouldn't you?" At Eric's shrug, Hen nodded toward the water. "Haven't seen you on the docks much."

"Busy pretending to grow a practice here and writing that book," Eric said. "But I do long for a really warm day to take the boat out. You could go with me."

Hen glanced past the dock lights to the gleaming hulls taking up slip space. Fine, whatever. His brother meant well. "Thanks, but my free time's absorbed in working on *Harmless* or in the kitchen, learning."

Eric placed a hand on his arm. "I get it." The old protective sympathy was there.

Hen wished it didn't feel so necessary to him. "You need to come in again, sample some of the new menu items." He heard the eagerness in his voice and knew the burden it placed on his twin. His brother to the rescue... always. If only he could figure out how to even the scales, to be the one giving instead of taking. But Eric's life had never once fallen apart.

"Sounds great," Eric said. Then, with a wave toward his boat, "It's kind of late. You rowing out now?"

"Yeah. I'll see you later."

"Sure," Eric said. "Keep warm. And I'll make a reservation soon."

"Or drop in. There's always room at the bar." Hen waited at the head of the pier as Eric descended the ramp. His heart ached. When had their relationship become stiff and formal? Even slightly uncomfortable?

Had it been when he'd come out of rehab for the second time, making everyone wonder if there'd be a third? When he'd left the halfway house and found this job? When Eric-the-trustee had told him they were cutting off his income until he could show he was trustworthy? But Eric had offered to release his funds now, so why should there be anything but their boyhood bond?

Hen was trying desperately to prove himself. He would do this on his own, and he would not be defeated by addiction again. He would not.

He fit his watch cap down over his hair, climbed into his dinghy, and began rowing out to his boat. The row wasn't long, and the only time he minded it was when a strong wind blew against him or rain sneaked in under his jacket. Those times, he could choose to bunk with Eric. "You've always got a place here," his brother had said more than once.

He loved the old clunker he was restoring, bit by bit, inch by inch as he sanded teak, worked on systems, glassed interior areas where rot had tried to take over. Soon, *Harmless* wouldn't clunk or leak. Soon, she'd be seaworthy, her two masts straight and tall, her sails filling—although soon was a relative term. Until then, she kept him busy. Sweat and busyness kept many a demon at bay, according to Father Stanley. "Besides, the work gives you time to pray. Prayer is your way out of the cycle, son. And your way to stay out."

It had been. As long as he kept it up, Hen found a modicum of peace, but he couldn't let down his guard, ever.

A weak wind pushed low waves to slurp and slap against the hull as his oars dipped and pulled, his efforts moving the small wooden boat across the channel to the mooring field. He tried not to feel the cold climb up his open cuffs or slip down his neck. At least the moon still shone brightly in tonight's sky.

As his muscles worked, he let his thoughts return to Agnes and the wistful look he'd surprised from her at the restaurant tonight. What had it meant?

He didn't think she knew how beautiful she was, how her

large eyes captured her emotions and displayed them, how the wisps falling out of her bound-up hair and across her cheek made him long to tuck them behind her ears. Her tiny waist accented her curves, curves she tried to hide when almost any other woman would have displayed such abundance for all the world to see.

If only.

If only what?

He grinned. Admit it. Admit you'd like to be the one seeing her curves up close and personal.

Hah. As if she'd be interested in him if she knew the whole of his past. Sure, she knew—all the staff knew—the outline of it, but he'd never filled in the blanks for anyone outside his circle of Eric and Father Stanley.

He glanced over his shoulder, checking the distance as he neared. At a yard or so out, he stowed the oars, drifted closer, and grabbed the line he left at the ready to tie up the dinghy once he boarded.

Folk with fancy dinghies and outboards couldn't just tie up at night. They did, and the next morning they'd find their tether cut and their boat and motor gone. His old wooden dinghy, with its peeling paint, bobbed safely behind *Harmless*, night after night, unwanted by any but him. In preparation for a northeaster, he'd once sunk the dinghy so she wouldn't flip in the wind, then used a winch and halyard to bring her up after the storm passed. He didn't want to lose her.

Now, he unlocked his companionway doors and descended into the cabin, his way lit by a little battery-operated LED lamp. Dropping his backpack in its place next to the settee and shedding his jacket, he walked into his compact galley, where he lit his oil lamp and filled a glass with water from the jug he kept tucked away.

Something eased in his chest. After the chaos of the restaurant kitchen, he rejoiced at finding everything in its place, lined up, squared off, symmetrical.

It constantly amazed him, how much difference order made to his sense of well-being. If only he'd discovered this when he'd been younger and living in the messiness of others after he'd left home. He remembered that childhood house, manned by a staff who kept things polished to his father's exacting specifications. His mother, cowed and haunted when she wasn't putting on her social face, had barely existed for her sons—until she hadn't at all.

He could picture his parents dressed in formal stiffness, returning from some gathering and separating in the hall like strangers, wordlessly. His father would enter the library and close the door to pour a glass of something. His mother would mount the stairs, not noticing that her younger son knelt on the floor, peering through the banisters, as she focused only on her door and her room. The housekeeper, Mrs. Dally, would point him back to bed before knocking softly on his mother's door and slipping in to help her.

Mother wouldn't appear downstairs the next day. If he visited her in her room, she'd be bleary-eyed and mumbling, on her bed, barely conscious. He now knew she'd been drugged, prescription mood enhancers that Mrs. Dally regulated on the evenings she had to make an appearance outside the house.

Hen wondered what she'd been like at those events, standing like a statue next to their father. Did she speak or smile or carry on a conversation? Could she? Her mandated appearances had ended abruptly, as had her life, shortly after his—and Eric's—sixteenth birthday.

Perhaps she'd deemed her duty done, and she'd just quit.

He supposed he'd come close to quitting a time or two.

He ought to stop indulging in these memories. Father Stanley reminded him often enough that hanging onto the past was a sure way back into the pits. He needed to remember what he'd done in therapy: he'd looked at all that had happened and forgiven those who'd rejected him. Or he'd tried to. It had been mandated.

He needed to keep them—his parents—in the "I forgive you" box and not take them out and dust off their hurtful behavior again and again.

Easier said than done. Still, when the darkness of those years threatened, he had to remind himself of his freedom. Of the good place he'd found for himself. Of the God who had never given up on him.

"Thank you, Lord," he spoke aloud. "Thanks for the moon and this home and my brother and my job. And thanks for hope."

He would not look back. He would keep his thoughts focused on the good, he decided, as he flopped back on his settee. The days of self-pity had to be gone, wiped from his slate. He was here, in his own small space, with no messiness to confuse him and no emotional holes to suck him in.

*On your knees*, he told himself. But he felt too unsettled. Best to make the call first.

He reached for his cell phone, punched in a number. When Father Stanley, Anglican priest and mentor extraordinaire, answered, Henry said, "It's me."

"How are you?"

"I had the dream again last night," Henry said.

"Was it as always?"

He sighed. "The bloody knife was in my hand when I woke, and I was convinced I'd been so out of it I couldn't remember plunging it into that man."

"Ah. But you hadn't, had you? The police and your brother proved you hadn't."

"But what if?" Because they hadn't exactly established how the knife got into his hand, just that he hadn't been the one to kill the dead guy, who'd been garroted two feet from where Hen had been sleeping off a high.

By the time they'd found the real culprit, Henry'd been inside that jail cell for four long, sleepless nights. Four nights while his newly minted lawyer-brother got in the face of some police friends and pushed them to look harder and deeper. Five days, four nights.

Eric had gone to that place, seen the filth, and still he'd believed, even when Henry hadn't. When they let him out, Henry had promised to get help, get off, get clean... and stay clean. And he'd done it. He'd had to do it—in case one day the nightmare became a reality again.

For almost three years, he'd been clean. *I am who I am who I was who I will be.*

"You chose freedom after that, didn't you?" Father Stanley said.

He had. Yes, he had. The knife had been the catalyst for change. Because of that *what if.*

"And let's not forget that young girl who calls you a hero. What was her name?"

"Beth. But I wasn't a hero." *I am who I am who I was who I will be.*

"Looked like it to me. I was there, son. I saw it. She was under that bridge, curled up, petrified. And you were the only one who stepped off the path, picked her up, and got her to the hospital. You showed her a way out of the place evil men had put her, and you offered her hope. I don't think she'd be alive except for your intervention."

"You'd have done the same thing. Lots of people would."

"But I didn't. And no one else did. We saw only a young woman who seemed to be sleeping off the effects of drugs or alcohol. We didn't look closely enough to see her fear. We didn't bend down to hear her whisper, to take her hands, to lift her up. You did."

"Too bad I don't dream about her instead." He tried to put humor into his words.

Neither of them laughed.

"Is there anything else?" Father Stanley asked.

"Words. I keep hearing words that don't make a lot of sense.

Even now, while we've been talking. *I am who I am who I was who I will be.*"

There was a momentary silence from the other end. "There's truth in that, you know."

"I suppose."

"You are your past, your present, and your future. And God sees all of those at once, because he is eternal."

"What about free will?"

"Think about it," Father Stanley said. "The you of your past helps determine the you of today and tomorrow, but it's not bound by circumstance or even sin. You have the power to shift your future based on how you handle your present and how you allow your past to affect you. What you do with your sins."

"The definition of repentance, then."

"Exactly. Turning away from your sin. Rejecting it and changing."

Henry knew this stuff. He'd read it, said it, tried to walk it, but sometimes, when doubts slammed against belief, he needed to hear someone say it. "Thank you."

"Let's pray," Father Stanley said.

Prayer and then sleep. *Please.*

He finally disconnected and headed up the companionway steps to make sure all was shipshape and tied down. He was who he was who he had been and who he would be.

There was good news in there someplace. The *who he would be* was the part he had to work on. The part he needed to perfect.

# 6

## AGNES

Sleep had failed Agnes, except in snatches when her mind settled long enough for exhaustion to claim it. By the time she stumbled from bed, gray light had begun to filter through her sheer curtains.

The dark hole in her gut from fear and worry felt as if it had grown overnight, claiming more of her with its destructive acid. *Breathe,* she told herself. *Let it go.*

"You've been here before. You fixed it then. You'll fix it now."

She had. She would.

But her words bounced back from the tile walls of her shower. If only she could wash disasters off with a little shampoo and hot water.

Gently, she lifted her plush towel from a rod that listed to the right, its anchors barely hooked to the wall. If only she had money, she'd redo what her mother hadn't had time for before dying and making Agnes a transplant to the South. She'd also undo some things that made her cringe, like the gold (had to be faux) faucets in the downstairs half-bath and in the guest bathroom on this floor. In hers, floral wallpaper remained, water-stained from old roof leaks, and the faucets were chrome. She longed for simple. Cream walls. Re-caulked tiles. Fixed towel

27

rods. And a massaging shower head to work out muscle kinks from hustling too many drink-and-dinner trays. She could usually ignore the needed upgrades, but not today.

Dried, combed, and wrapped in her big terry bathrobe, she headed to Brisa's room. Slugabed Link glanced at her, then stretched himself into an arch and bounded to the floor. She patted his head and spoke to her daughter. "Time to get up, sleepyhead."

"Un-unh." The sound was muffled by her pillow.

"Yes, ma'am. You need to eat a decent breakfast before school." Although she wasn't sure what she had left in the cupboard.

Link padded downstairs. Agnes opened the back door for him and made sure he went directly to "his" plot beside the old shed. The coffeemaker bubbled, hissed, and gurgled but offered no comfort, not even with its promise of a caffeine lift.

Childcare was first on her to-take-care-of list. She couldn't call in sick, because no tips would mean a shortfall and more unpaid bills. A place for Brisa to hang out might be a temporary solution, but who'd want an extra kid at their house the hours she worked?

No one had told her how hard it would be to move into a small town and infiltrate cliques formed in childhood. She saw those women, heads together, gossiping or sitting down to a meal with their husbands, maybe two couples, the men talking golf or fishing, the women going on and on about some group they were in, some charity event, their children, their club.

They weren't her people. Not her tribe.

Then, she'd never really had a people, had she? Not even in school.

The carafe filled, and she poured the brew into her mug, added milk, and carried it to her kitchen's small wooden table with its polished oak surface and the four elegant chairs tucked under it. She sat down, sipped her coffee, and tried to enjoy the sun shining through the over-the-sink window.

Taking a banana from the fruit bowl, she studied the brown spots that had accumulated overnight, and the idea of eating palled. Still, a cup of coffee on an empty stomach wouldn't do her any good. She peeled off the offending skin and took a bite.

She sort of knew Tadie, Jilly's mother. Jilly was Brisa's school chum and playmate. Through Tadie, Agnes had met Hannah and Annie Mac, and they were all married with families.

"You do what you have to," she said in the direction of her mug.

So, maybe Tadie would know someone who needed a room in exchange for Brisa-watching. Or she could ask Hannah. Hannah Morgan seemed to know everyone.

Link gave one bark, his signal to be let in. When she opened the door, he scooted past her legs to sit expectantly next to his bowls.

"It's not your dinner time, you fraud." But she gave him a biscuit as reward for not leaving the yard and turned to make herself something else to eat, popping two slices of wheat bread into the toaster and opening a jar of peanut butter, her protein of choice in the economy of singleness. The honey jar was almost empty, but there was enough. She should be grateful for enough.

"You only have to hang on." And trust that the real *enough* would come in time.

Bare feet slapped across the hardwood, and a sleepy-eyed Brisa gave her a half-wave and Link a tug on the ear. "It's cold down here."

"You need slippers."

"I don't have any I like."

"The bunny ones?"

"Mo-m." Brisa rolled her eyes.

"Well, you liked them when you got them."

"That was *then*. I'm older now."

"Fine, but at least a pair of socks?" Agnes waved toward the laundry room. "On top of the dryer."

Brisa padded into the small room off the kitchen and came

29

back with socks on her feet. At the refrigerator, she opened the door and stared inside as if she'd find a secret stash of something yummy instead of the same contents that had been there the last time she'd looked. Link settled close to the table, all unmet expectations.

"Don't stand there with the door open—and don't feed the dog. The vet said he's getting fat, so it's one meal a day only."

"What can I have?"

"I'll go to the market today, but for now there's juice and peanut butter on toast. You can have one of these already made," Agnes said. "Get a plate of your own."

Brisa moved over to the cupboard to get what she needed. "Where's Sally Ann? Her room's empty." She stepped over Link and took the closest chair, accepting the toast.

Agnes told her about Sally Ann's mother. Brisa swallowed and washed the bite down with juice. "Cancer? That's bad."

"It is. And now I have to find someone else who'd like her room."

"I could stay by myself. I'm old enough."

"Not an option. I'm not having you turn into a latch-key kid."

"What's that?"

"A child who comes home to an empty house, unsupervised."

Brisa's eyes lit. Agnes could almost see the wheels churning with visions of unlimited access to television and junk food.

"Not happening, kiddo."

"Aw, mom, I'm old enough."

"Not in my book."

Actually, the law might allow a twelve-year-old to stay alone, but the law wasn't Brisa's mother. Agnes didn't really know this town, these people. Although Beaufort seemed tame, seeming tame and being tame were two different things. And wasn't she the poster child for that truth?

"But Rachel had her own key back home," Brisa said in a voice filled with longing. "She was only eleven."

"If I remember correctly," Agnes said, "she stayed with the next-door neighbor until her mother got home."

"I miss her."

"I know, honey. I'm sorry we had to leave." Although that wasn't strictly true. She liked this house. And *Agua Verde*. And... but no, she wouldn't think of Henry. "What about Jilly? Hasn't she become a good friend?"

"Yeah. I guess so."

Agnes set the plate in front of her daughter. "I thought I'd ask Jilly's mother about possible sitters."

"Okay," Brisa said around a sticky mouthful of peanut butter.

"Drink some milk to wash that down. You don't want to choke."

Her daughter's eye roll was best ignored, wasn't it? Getting Brisa through puberty was going to be such fun.

"You'd better get dressed for school as soon as you eat that. I'll make your lunch." Agnes poured the dregs of her coffee into the sink. "I have just enough for a ham sandwich."

She fixed and wrapped the sandwich, added an apple and the last of the chocolate chip cookies to the lunch bag, and set it within Brisa's reach.

"Don't dawdle," she called before heading back upstairs.

Rifling through her closet to find something even remotely attractive, she repeated her mother's litany aloud. "It's not what you look like, it's how you act. Beauty comes from the inside." Right, Mom, thanks so much. Her mother's assurance that she had more brains than any of the other girls hadn't made Agnes feel better or more beautiful. Intelligence certainly hadn't helped her fit in.

How often had she heard words meant to cover her mother's disappointment—and her own—as it became obvious to everyone that she resembled the father who'd died when she was five and not the mother whose tall, willowy form, highlighted hair, and lovely face turned heads. Agnes had her father's short stature as well as his dark hair and pale complexion. And her figure? Her too-early endowment had made the boys ogle and her mother insist she wear loose shirts to hide an embarrassment of riches.

Four years after her daddy's death, her mother had married Richard Ware, a good man and a good step-father. Maybe not soft and cuddly, and maybe a little strict, but he'd treated her kindly and had paid for that year of college. And then he'd retired and moved with her mother down here to his family's home. And then he'd died.

Agnes winced at the memory of her mother's relief on moving away from Jersey City, the scene of her daughter's shame. Once the supposedly "brainy" daughter announced she was pregnant without a husband, her mother hadn't even had Agnes's supposed intelligence to use as a balm. "How *could* you?"

How *could* she? She hadn't exactly asked for the sex that had created a baby. She'd woken to feel the mess between her legs, the bloody residue of her lost virginity, and the confusion that went with finding herself in a strange hotel room, alone, too ashamed to tell anyone how stupid she'd been, taking that drink, excited that *he* had offered it. As if he'd actually found her attractive as he'd whispered her real name.

Why did her thoughts keep harping on his use of her name? She was no longer Agnese. Now she was Agnes. Plain old Agnes, hard-edged and no longer vulnerable. Do you hear that, self? No longer *weak*.

But back then, on that morning after, she'd cleaned herself up and waited too long. By the time she'd recovered enough to tell anyone what had happened, she'd recovered too much to be tested for rape. Anyway, who would have believed *her* against *him?*

And when she'd come home with news of her pregnancy, the response had been, "Well, then, get *rid* of it."

Agnes had stared hard at her mother and moved out permanently. That had been the end of her college career.

So what? Really, *so what*? She had the most gorgeous girl child anyone could want, and normally the sweetest. Although there had been a change or two since they'd moved to Beaufort, a new whininess that made Agnes want to go into hiding until her once gem-like daughter returned.

Buttoning up her cherry-red blouse and smoothing a darker-hued sweater over it, she told herself it would have to do. She was who she was, and she'd never be anyone else.

And no letter, no matter what it said, would change that.

Once Agnes had seen Brisa off to school, she filled her mug one more time and headed to the back porch to let Link sniff around while she studied her unkempt yard and sipped her coffee. She couldn't manage the Food Lion without that caffeine lift.

The morning chill would soon burn off. Scents from the early spring growth next door and her own forsythia bushes and honeysuckle mingled with the dew-laden greenery taking over her yard. She loved mornings, but the beauty of this one was almost lost under her load of worry.

She'd seen that old couple who lived at the end of the Merritt's driveway lumbering up the outside steps, looking as if they'd appreciate an elevator. What did that say about Jilly's parents, the ones who owned the property? Did Tadie think black people—even half-black or a quarter-black—belonged above the garage and not in the house? It wasn't as if there were other non-white residents living anywhere along this stretch of waterfront concrete.

Who knew? Tadie *had* let Brisa play with her daughter, so maybe Agnes was just overthinking this. And maybe she was just tired. She may have lived in Beaufort these many months, but she didn't know much about the people or the place, other than what she'd seen from behind her serving tray.

Tiredness had to be it. She was tired of not having answers, tired of her step-father's step-children (the judge had been married to their mother for a measly few years) saying they deserved the house Agnes's mother had inherited from him and passed on to Agnes. She was tired of trying to figure everything out on her own.

She would not be run out of town. She had never, ever been a quitter. She found herself in trouble, she fixed it—or did her best to make something from nothing, a life for her child, no matter how small or constricted that life was with a mother whose income put her in the lower quadrant of the working class.

Why on earth did Ralph and Lorraine, the step-steps, imagine they had any right to what Richard Ware had owned? They weren't his blood relatives any more than she was, but at her mother's death, they'd filed an injunction to stop the estate from settling, *her* mother's estate. And that was just wrong. They'd supposedly found some document from their mother saying she'd put $10,000 into renovating the kitchen, which, the lawyer said, gave the judge's ex-wife—and now them—an interest in equity.

Agnes knew her own mother had overseen those renovations, not theirs, but she hadn't been able to locate any bills or receipts. She needed to research the issue. In a town this size, someone had to know something about the workers who'd put in the new cabinets and appliances. And when they'd done it.

With a sigh, she rose. "Come on, boy. Let's go see to the laundry. Then I need to talk to Tadie and get to the grocery store."

Well, that had been a dud. She'd gone to shift the laundry from washer to dryer, only to find the washer still full of soapy water.

She needed her now-sopping uniform slacks before she went to work, which meant she had to get the washer fixed, which meant she had to call for help, which meant she had to wait around for the repairman.

By the time he'd come and gone, she had only ninety minutes to get to Food Lion and back before meeting Brisa's bus and heading to Tadie's. After that, she'd have very little time to find somewhere for Brisa to stay before she went to work.

She looked up Tadie's phone number in the list of places Brisa played. When her neighbor answered, Agnes asked if she'd be available to chat when the girls got home from school.

"Of course. Stop on by."

"Thank you."

It was hard enough asking someone she barely knew for help, but doing it over the phone would be worse. At least face-to-face would let her gauge Tadie's attitude. She shut down the thought that showing up might force Tadie to take pity on her; she didn't want pity, but she did need help—a suggestion, a name, someone who needed a place to stay as much as she needed a Brisa-watcher.

And if worse came to worse, she supposed Brisa could go with her to work this once. There was a small locker room with a couple of chairs and a table, a place where employees could take a break. It didn't sit well with her, imposing on the staff like that, but she figured Margaret would prefer she plant her daughter there than call in sick and leave them short a waitress.

She didn't try to stop her daughter's back-and-forth rocking as they waited for someone to answer the Merritt's door. Her own insides were doing a jitterbug.

Jilly, the cute little redhead, grinned at Brisa when she saw her. "Oh, hi! Did you come to play?"

Agnes answered with, "Is your mom around?"

"She's just getting my little brother up from his nap. He has to be changed." Jilly opened the door all the way. "You come on in. She won't be long."

Tadie's house was the way hers could be, if only she could afford to get rid of the pretentious and uncover the homey. She got why her mother had wanted to look like she went with the house. Before Saundra Jones had married Judge Ware, she'd supported herself and Agnes on her paralegal's salary and the pittance from Agnes's father's insurance.

"Come on back," Jilly said. "We like the kitchen best for hanging out when it's just us. It's cozy." And then the child's hand flew to her mouth. "I didn't mean to say that. I mean, you're company and all, but I just figured since Brisa's my friend, you're not *really* company, not like you'd need the living room. I mean, I know Mommy invites some of the ladies in there, and they drink tea, but not Miss Hannah or anybody close. Not real *girlfriends*." She took a breath and grinned from one to the other, then grabbed Brisa's hand. "Is that okay? I mean, you're not upset or anything, are you?"

Trust a child to banish awkwardness. Agnes smiled. "I'm flattered you're treating us like friends instead of guests."

"Good! You want some tea? Mommy's got a pitcher all made. If you want something hot, you'll have to wait for her."

"Cold would be fine. Thank you, Jilly."

Footsteps sounded on the wooden floor, and Tadie stepped through the doorway, dressed in jeans and a man's blue-and-white striped shirt with the sleeves rolled up. Her dark, thick hair was pulled back in a ponytail, and her smile was her usual infectious one. "Well, hey there, Brisa, Agnes. I see Jilly's been playing hostess."

"I was just getting tea, but the pitcher's kinda full," Jilly said. "Can Brisa come upstairs with me?"

Tadie nodded and smiled. "Maybe you girls can relieve your dad, Jilly. I left Sammy distracting him from work."

"Sure."

"That'd be cool," Brisa said, her smile brightening. "He's cute."

"He's a boy. And he's two." Jilly's hand wave said it all.

Tadie watched the two girls dash toward the stairs. "World weary at their age. Are you seeing that with Brisa?"

"Her birthday's coming up, and she imagines it's her fifteenth instead of her twelfth."

"You sure you're okay with iced tea? I keep it for Will, who's a recent convert."

"Sure, thank you."

"Lemon?"

"Please," Agnes said, relieved. "Several slices, if you can spare them. I'm still getting used to your state drink."

"I don't make it very sweet, so you're probably safe." Tadie's grin widened as she led the way to the other end of the huge country kitchen where there was a seating area with a chintz-covered sofa and two armchairs covered in slipcovers of complementary greens and blues. Agnes chose one end of the sofa, and Tadie the other.

"Your house is so comfortable and welcoming," Agnes said. "I love this space."

"My mama insisted on having a place where she could be in the center of things when she couldn't actually cook anymore. It's my favorite spot, too. Works really well when the kids are eating, and I'm tuckered out but need to stay nearby."

"I need to redo a lot of my house. I mean, I love the kitchen remodel my mother did, but it still doesn't feel very homey."

"Speaking of your house, how are things coming? I heard the judge's step-kids are pushing for a settlement that includes them."

"I'm still trying to find proof that my mother was married to the judge when the renovations happened. It all hinges on that."

"Have you asked Matt Morgan if he knows anything? Morgan's supplies most hardware and lumber around here. Someone there would know who did that job."

Why hadn't she remembered that? Or her mother's lawyer should have remembered. He was a local and well-connected. "What a good idea. I need my mother's estate to settle so I can afford the taxes, if nothing else. And then there's insurance coming up."

She hadn't seen much of Hannah and Matt since the Morgans adopted the young girl with Down Syndrome and her younger brother who'd made himself his sister's guardian. She should check in with both Hannah and Matt, see how they were doing.

Glancing at her watch, she brought the conversation around to the reason she'd come. "You met Sally Ann, didn't you?"

"I did. And I like her. She seems great with Brisa."

She finger-combed wisps of hair back from her forehead. "Her mother's cancer is back, and she had to leave last night." She paused, tamping back the discomfort.

"I'm so sorry." Tadie looked right at her. "So now you need to find someone else to take her place."

"I can't lose my job." And, yes, heat rose in her cheeks.

Tadie glanced toward the hall. "I think Jilly would be really glad if you let Brisa stay with us when you're working."

"Oh, no," Agnes said, stricken. "That wasn't what I meant at all. You barely know us, and besides, some nights I'm really late."

"Then she can go to sleep on the kitchen couch until you can pick her up."

Agnes wasn't sure she could even speak in the face of such generosity. "Maybe for a night or two? I was thinking maybe you'd know someone else who needed to live-in, as Sally Ann had. You know, in exchange for being there for Brisa." She glanced out the back door at the sound of a car pulling up.

"I'll ask around. In the meantime, Brisa has a place that's safe here with us." When Agnes started to go collect her daughter,

Tadie said, "No, you go on. There's no call to take her home only to bring her back."

"Thank you. I'll get her as soon as I can."

"Don't you worry. I'll put the key under the planter out there." Tadie pointed to a pot with small shoots emerging from the dirt.

"I can't tell you how grateful I am."

This was good, all was well. Just because she was a single mother and a waitress who needed help, that didn't make her less. And tonight, she'd see Hen again. Maybe he'd walk a ways with her. Maybe their hands would brush accidentally.

Maybe.

Work was a disappointment. Not only were tips low, but when it was time for her to leave, Hen was too busy in the kitchen as assistant chef to walk her to Front Street. She headed off alone to pick up Brisa at Tadie's.

Poor baby, having to wake up to walk the block and a half home. Agnes found the key and tiptoed into the house. She roused her daughter with a nudge, then folded the blanket and sheet and set both on top of the pillow Brisa'd used.

"You okay?"

Brisa nodded and let her mother help her into her sweater. The evening wasn't cold, but the temperature had dropped since morning. Brisa clung to her arm as they headed down the street. They didn't talk, which was just as well. Sounds traveled in the night, and most of the houses on Front Street were already dark.

A wiggling, enthusiastic Link met them in the hall. "Hey, boy," Agnes said, and then, "I'll let him out. You go on upstairs."

By the time she'd seen Link out back and waited for his return, Brisa was in bed and ready to snuggle with her dog. "Come on, boy," she said, curling around him. "I had so much fun. Jilly's daddy is going up tomorrow to check on their big boat, and Jilly showed me more pictures from when they were all sailing. I'd love to go to the Caribbean. You think we could someday?"

Henry owned a boat. Maybe someday he'd invite them, her, to see it. Maybe go out on it. They were friends, weren't they?

"That sounds like fun." She spoke with a fake lilt to match a fake smile. She was too exhausted to deal with this. With any *this* or that or his or hers.

Tired and not at all herself. At least, she hoped this wasn't her real self. If she'd fallen to this level of self-pity, she'd better hurry up and get back her moxie, the *her* who'd gotten them both this far.

She smoothed her daughter's hair back. "You and Link both need your sleep."

"Jilly said they'd invite me to sail with them," Brisa said, unwilling to drop the subject. "I'd really like to go."

"I'm sure you would." Not that this landlubber mother knew anything about it, but if you were almost twelve going on twenty, a big boat would sound like great fun. She didn't want her daughter to know the limitations she'd experienced.

"I really like Jilly's daddy."

"He seems nice."

Brisa pulled one of her curls toward her face, twirling it near her mouth, a sign she had something on her mind, probably something Agnes wouldn't like. "Jilly's so lucky, having a daddy." The child peeked up at her mother as if to gauge how that had gone over.

"She is."

Maybe Brisa heard something in her mother's tone because she dropped the curl and said quickly, "Not that you're not the greatest. I mean, you are. It's just…"

"I know." Agnes leaned over to kiss her daughter's forehead. "I wish things had been different for you, baby. Now, go to sleep."

She turned out the light and crossed the hall to her own

room. It took no thought to head to her bathroom, change into a gown, wash her face, and brush her teeth. But then she stood, immobile, staring down at the basin.

The wind had come up in the few minutes they'd been home. Behind her, the window rattled in its sash. A storm was coming, or it had begun.

Too wired to sleep, she headed down to the kitchen to brew herself something soporific. She filled the kettle, distracted by the scrape of a low branch against the back of the house. It needed to come down before it damaged the paint.

Too much scraped at her that night, threatening damage. She'd brought the letter downstairs with the idea of tackling it during the day, and now it jeered from beneath the pile of bills.

She was such a coward, afraid of words as if they had the power to leap out and sting her. Darlington could do nothing. *Nothing*. Finding her, writing to her, didn't confer power to him. He was no one. In spite of his fame and fortune, in spite of a physical beauty that lied.

She tore open the thing. And read.

Then she dropped the thin sheet and scrubbed her hands on her gown as if his soul's poison had leached onto the paper and would seep in through contact with her skin. She'd imagined it a poison-pen letter. She'd been right.

Darlington Evermire, that soul-stealer, wanted to *buy* Brisa. He offered money for her *daughter. Her* daughter. Not his. Never his.

Bile scored her throat. He thought he could take Brisa for $50,000. As if her precious girl were for *sale*. This from a man who'd drugged and raped and, by accident, contributed sperm. Was he out of his mind?

He had to be. No sane man could imagine such a thing. No sane man could *ask* such a thing.

She bent to pick up his letter, longing to rip it to shreds. But she wouldn't. Oh, no. She'd find a way to use his words against him. She was *not* going to be looking over her shoulder for the rest of her life, waiting for the creep to pounce.

*You let him in, Agnes. Remember, you're the one who brought this on yourself.*

"So I took the stupid drink. I was a kid."

*And out where you weren't supposed to be. Breaking the law.*

Agnes scowled. If her mother'd hated her so much, why had she left her everything? Would her mother's last letter, unopened and hidden away, provide answers or only more accusations?

*Read it.*

Not yet. The voice in her head was bad enough. On paper? The thoughts in her mother's voice she could override. But a visual reminder added into the mix?

*But what if my letter isn't what you imagine?*

How could it not be?

The taunts hadn't changed in more than twelve years. The help had never come.

# 7

## AGNES

A gnes's running shoes slapped concrete as she forced one foot in front of the other. Determined to exercise her way to a good mood, she pumped her arms at her sides and pressed forward. Her enemy was the sidewalk beneath her feet, the heavy air she sucked in and let out, but she kept her rhythm, in/out/swing/breathe. Sweat trickled between her breasts, off her forehead, under her arms, leaching out the toxins that accumulated due to worry and, yes, anger.

The sun glinted low on the water to her right, diamond shards that hurt the eyes if she stared at them. She hadn't remembered sunglasses, a fashion necessity on days like this. She turned at two miles and slowed to a walk.

Back home, with only Link for company until after Brisa's school let out, she drank a full glass of water and trudged upstairs to shower. She dawdled under the water, letting the heat of it ease the knots in her stressed muscles. Then she dressed and went downstairs to the waiting stacks of bills—two stacks, one the most pressing, the second less so.

She picked up her checkbook and a pen. Her calculator stood ready to help her decide how much to apportion where. She couldn't keep procrastinating, but she hated this. Hated owing money to anyone, hated the dithering, the excuses.

The doorbell rang. With a sigh of relief, she blessed whoever'd shown up to distract her.

Link's single *woof* and wagging tail would never scare off anyone. "Some guard dog you are," Agnes said. At least he knew how to sit.

She opened the door to a slim woman whose bright smile and smooth skin seemed so like Brisa's that Agnes responded with a smile of her own and a quick hello.

"Hey," the woman said. "I'm Rita Levinson, a friend of Tadie's. We've seen each other—Christmas, wasn't it?—and I've met your daughter a number of times." Her eyes darted down to Link, who'd pushed forward to sniff this new visitor. "What a gorgeous animal," she said as he sidled close enough for her to pet his soft coat.

"That's Link."

"Well, hey, Link." Grinning, she looked up. "I was hoping to speak with you for a few minutes."

Agnes backed out of the way. "Of course, come in."

"Thank you. I trust I'm not interrupting anything."

"Not at all." Only a pity party. "I've had my quota of coffee for the day, but I'm always up for a cup of tea. May I fix you one?"

"That would be lovely."

Agnes led the way past her embarrassment of a bill-laden dining table and into the kitchen where she set the kettle on and got down two china cups and saucers from her mother's collection. "I have English Breakfast and herbal."

"Anything's fine."

Link slid to the floor as Rita eased herself onto a chair. Agnes focused on the tea cups, on pouring water over the tea bags, and on bringing the sugar bowl within reach of her guest when she set a cup in front of her.

This was probably a Southern thing. Fulfill the niceties before you got down to business. No self-respecting person from Jersey City would bother.

"Thank you." Rita added a sparse spoonful of sugar and stirred. "You must be curious why I'm here." She looked up with a smile. "I stopped in to see Tadie a little while ago, and she told me you're in a bit of a bind with your daughter."

"Yes." Agnes took the seat across from her guest and waited.

"Tadie asked if I knew anyone who could take Sally Ann's place to help you out. You see, I'm a lawyer with the women and children's center in Morehead, and I'm acquainted with a lot of folk."

"And do you?" Agnes asked, trying to keep her surprise from showing. "Know anyone, I mean?"

That hadn't come out the way she'd meant it to.

"As a matter of fact, I may," Rita said. At least, she was still smiling. "My mama mentioned that one of her church ladies, Mrs. Becca Barnes, doesn't have enough to keep her busy and is looking for extra work. You've met Annie Mac and Clay Dougherty, haven't you?"

Agnes nodded.

"I don't know if you've been told Annie Mac's story," Rita said, "but it wasn't too long ago that her ex almost beat her to death. Hannah, Clay, and I had to help with her kids and figure out where they could stay when she got out of the hospital. Mrs. Barnes moved with Annie Mac's crew out to Clay's house. She still works for them some."

"I'm sorry about that happening to Annie Mac. It must have been horrible." She'd heard something about the abuse, but never with any details. "I can't pay for someone to work here, though. I can only offer a room and modest meals."

"That's not a problem. Becca Barnes has retirement income and what Clay gives her and says she has all she needs. Except more to keep her busy." Rita paused. "Especially now her daughter's back living with her."

Ah. "And Mrs. Barnes is hoping to be needed elsewhere?"

Rita laughed. "Exactly. If you're interested, I could call her."

"You know this isn't a wait-on-me job, don't you?"

"Sure, but Becca's going to want to help out. She likes to be needed and doesn't like being idle."

Sally Ann's contribution had been to feed Brisa and herself dinner and clean up after them. She hadn't even washed down her shower or cleaned her own toilet. The idea that Mrs. Barnes might tackle a few of the household chores almost made Agnes giddy.

Then she imagined Brisa's reaction. "Is Mrs. Barnes black?" A woman of color who knew how to help and who was liked by friends of Brisa's might prove a good influence on a young girl still trying to find her place in the world.

"She's about four degrees blacker than I am," Rita said, her voice chillier than it had been, "but she's good people."

"Oh, I didn't mean... I wasn't talking about... You know my daughter."

"Color is an issue for some folk, daughter or no. If you have problems with our race, then it's good to know that right up front."

"That's not what I meant at all." She'd done it again, opened her mouth before thinking.

"No?" Rita's cool tone had ramped to frigid.

"I don't think I'm prejudiced against anyone, certainly not against people of color." Although, she had made judgements, hadn't she, when she'd reacted to the old couple struggling up the garage stairs back of Tadie's?

Rita pursed her lips. "A lot of transplants arrive with a whole set of prejudices about how we do things down here. I hear it all the time, how we just need to change to be like where they came from."

Had Rita read her mind? Of course, it sounded as if Rita might have her own issues with people from the North. Agnes took a deep breath and tried for conciliatory. "If I have any, I'm sorry, but assumptions are what make the news."

"Yeah, well, only stupid people take the news for gospel."

"Fine. Color me stupid."

Rita answered with a wide grin. "I will."

"Good." Agnes lifted her cup, sipped, and set it back down. "I let my tea get cold. How's yours?"

"Tepid doesn't bother me."

"I'd rather have hot." She set the cup in the microwave and pushed the thirty-second button. Then she turned to her guest. "Brisa and I are still going to have to get used to the idea of someone helping out around the house. My middle-class self is going to feel awkward if someone else cleans for me." Then she pictured Brisa. "Well, maybe not my daughter."

Rita's laugh sounded melodic and brought an answering smile from Agnes. "Oh, she'll love it," Rita said. "As for you, I'll give you a week. After that, you're going to wonder how you ever managed without another pair of hands in this big place."

The microwave binged, and Agnes retrieved her cup, but she didn't sit back down. Leaning against the counter, she said, "You're probably right." Everything about her life in Beaufort ran counter to her expectations—and to her history.

Rita toyed with her cup. When she glanced up, her grin had widened. "You imagining yourself playing mistress to Becca's kitchen maid?"

Was she? "I may be. But I can't see myself watching while someone works around me." Wouldn't it make her feel as if she always had to be busy, too? She'd never be able to relax over a cup of tea alone—unless she sneaked upstairs and hid in her room.

"You think you might be taking yourself a tad too seriously?"

"Mmm" was all Agnes said in response. Still, she did need help for Brisa. "Maybe you could call Mrs. Barnes? Just to see if she's available to meet me."

Rita dug her phone from her purse and searched through it as she headed toward the front of the house. "Be right back."

It wouldn't hurt to meet the woman, Agnes told herself.

NORMANDIE FISCHER

Make a decision in person instead of based on her fears—which seemed absurd after she'd spoken them aloud. She rinsed the empty cups and put away the box of tea bags. By the time she'd cleared the table, Rita's heels were clicking on the hardwood floor of the dining room.

She waved her phone as if in triumph. "Becca's going to come by tomorrow after she goes to morning prayer meeting with the church ladies. How does eleven o'clock sound?"

"That would be perfect."

"I'll bring her by. Introduce you. You can figure out the sort of questions you want to ask her, but do try to relax. She's a lovely person. She even won over Annie Mac, who'd never in her life imagined someone waiting on her and was doubly skittish because she had a broken leg and a messed up face and two children she couldn't take care of on her own."

The hours blurred once Rita had gone, and her busyness involved everything but bill-paying—or dealing with that letter from *him*. Her house was going to look guest-worthy, while she left well enough alone when it came to Darlington.

*Well enough?* Nothing was well, and his letter certainly wasn't well enough. She'd had a lawyer here and could have asked for advice, but they'd gotten off to a rocky start. So, maybe she'd figure out the rest tomorrow. Or the next day.

---

That evening, Hen's smile seemed particularly sweet when he passed plates to her. Once, their fingers touched, and fire zinged through her. She glanced up quickly to see if he'd noticed, but his smile remained friendly, kind.

As she carried food and set it before her customers, she tried to slow her pulse. Would her thoughts ever line up with the facts of her single-dom and stop aching for more, stop yearning to be one of two and for the other half to be this dear man with his repaired lip and the kindest eyes she'd ever seen?

He caught up with her after work. She bent her head to hide her sigh at the thought of him there, next to her. Of him, making conversation. And, no, she would *not* swoon.

He shortened his stride to match hers, and she searched for something to say. Her tongue felt tied. She finally blurted, "Things going well in the kitchen?"

"They are. I'm grateful for this chance to prove myself."

She longed to touch him. Failing that, she put sympathy into her voice. "Is there anything I can do to help?"

"You are. You do. Just by being my friend."

"Always."

She stopped at the Merritts' walkway. "I go in here. Thanks for walking with me."

"I'll walk you both home."

"You sure?"

"Of course."

He followed her to the back door and waited outside while she woke Brisa and led her sleepy daughter down the steps. Brisa raised her head and stared at Henry.

"Honey, you remember Henry Houston, don't you? From the restaurant?"

"Yeah," Brisa said. "Hi."

"I thought I'd walk you two ladies home."

"Mmm" was her only response.

He offered them each an arm in an exaggerated gesture. "To keep any of us from stumbling on the cracks."

"You think you might fall?" Agnes asked.

Hen said, "Not with you two to hold me up."

They laughed, all three of them. Amazing.

Link whined when she turned the key in the lock.

"Seems you're expected." He waved them inside. "Good night, lovely ladies. See you."

And there it was, her nightly longing encapsulated in those same two words: *see you.*

His rubber soles muffled his footsteps as he headed down

49

their walkway. Brisa was already in the hall, and so Agnes didn't watch the black silhouette that was bound to show against the soft light of street lamps.

She didn't have to. She could imagine.

8

AGNES

Agnes sat in her sunny kitchen, sipping her morning coffee as her overtired mind flitted from image to image, landing eventually on a delicious fantasy involving her father's sister's husband, Massimo Something-or-other. Massimo had connections. Yes, *those* connections. The kind of connections you'd call on if you hoped to involve guns and cement-anchored bodies in the Hudson River.

Agnes let out a quick bark of laughter. If only she could hint Massimo in Darlington's direction. And then she imagined a smelly jail and Brisa having to petition to visit.

Too bad she couldn't opt for murder, the unforgiving part of her said. Find a lawyer, the more practical part retorted, and then send a scathing letter in response to Darlington's. Not the lawyer handling her mother's estate, though, because he charged a fortune per hour.

Brisa wandered into the room, her hair tumbling around her face, her pajamas looking as if they'd been buttoned willy-nilly in the dark. She opened the screen door to let in a piteously whining Link, who acted as if he'd been separated from her for weeks. She stooped for a hug full of doggy kisses.

"Morning, sleepyhead. Saturday pancakes?"

"Can I have cereal?"

"In the cupboard." Agnes stirred a dollop of milk into her second cup of coffee. "Mrs. Levinson—you remember her, don't you?"

"Yeah. Miss Rita."

Of course. The Southern way of showing respect. "She's bringing someone by who may be able to help out evenings. A Mrs. Barnes."

"You mean the lady who helps out at Ty's? She's cool. Ty and Katie really like her."

Ty, who often hung out with Brisa and Jilly after school, seemed like a good kid, as did his little sister, Katie.

"Good to know," Agnes said. Very good to know because the prayer-meeting thing had given her pause. She hadn't crossed a church's threshold since Darlington had crooned his country gospel songs on the way to drugging her, talking God from the stage and then stealing her innocence in a hotel room.

When Brisa upended her bowl to drink the last of the milk, Agnes said, "Dishwasher, please. And your room. Make sure it's presentable because they're bound to want a tour of the house."

"'kay." Brisa rinsed and loaded her dishes, and then she was off, Link at her heels.

Agnes picked up a sponge to wipe down the counters, then made sure clean hand towels hung in the downstairs powder room—where she doubted anyone had kept or used powder in this century.

———

She ushered the two women into the house and smiled in response when Rita introduced Mrs. Barnes. The older woman had tight gray curls, ample curves wrapped in a plaid dress, and black tennis shoes, but what grabbed Agnes's attention were her twinkling eyes, small dark irises that captured the light and were surrounded by a myriad of laugh lines.

"How d'you do?" Mrs. Barnes said, oozing *happy*.

Brisa, who'd come downstairs at the sound of the doorbell, reassured Link and grinned up at their guest. "I know you. You used to take care of Ty and Katie."

"Still do, some. Good folk, the lieutenant and Miss Annie Mac. And me and those kids, we get along just fine. Always have."

"You've become family to them," Rita said.

"That's the truth of it. And them to me." Mrs. Barnes smiled down at the dog. "You gonna introduce me to that fine animal?"

When Brisa did, Mrs. Barnes extended her hand so he could sniff it. "Link. That mean he's your link with the rest of the world?"

"I suppose… I suppose he is," Brisa said, seeming to like the idea.

"Well, it's a good one." She looked around. "Mighty nice, all this light coming into your hallway,.

Liking light was another good sign, wasn't it? "Let me show you the rest of the house. Brisa," Agnes said pointedly, nodding toward the stairs. Brisa scurried back up with the dog.

"Her bed need making?" Rita asked.

"At least that. She's had all morning." Agnes stopped at the arched entrance to the living room, with its large furniture and fireplace.

"It's the age." Rita stepped into the room, smiling.

"You keep a neat house like this," Mrs. Barnes said, "she's gonna be learning, as long as you make it about her helping too."

"Oh, I do." Agnes thought of how difficult that could be. "It's not always so easy."

"That's the truth. Only if you let them off, thinkin' how much easier it is just to go ahead and do it yourself, they'll never learn."

"You'd know, wouldn't you, Mrs. Barnes?" Rita's grin made Agnes wonder what secret they were sharing.

Mrs. Barnes only laughed. "Oh, honey, wouldn't I just?" And to Agnes, "It's my daughter. I was real young when I got married and had my girl, and before my husband lit out, he spoiled that girl so much, it turned her head. She was about Brisa's age and had a mouth on her something awful. But instead of being the mama in the household, I just fussed under my breath. Bad rearing ain't the child's fault. It's the parents'."

"I'm sorry." Trite words, but, really, what else could she say?

"Well," Mrs. Barnes continued as if telling her deepest secrets was what she did on meeting new people, "she ran kind of wild, my girl did, and got herself in trouble. Pretty soon she came on home, tail-tucked, so I'd fix her mess. By then, I'd learnt me a few things. My pastor, he set me up with a deacon's wife who come alongside to mentor me, teach me how to be a mama. Between us and God, we turned my girl around. And turned me around, too."

Why, then, did Mrs. Barnes want to leave her house to her daughter and come here, unless the turning around hadn't lasted? But that wasn't a question Agnes could ask.

Ushering them past the closed door to their left, she couldn't help wondering how this was supposed to work. "That's the library, I guess you'd call it. Behind it, there's a small room that looks like it was an office. Nice rooms, but with only the two of us, I keep them closed off. Now, come on back." She waved toward the powder room and another smallish room opposite it. "I don't have a clue what that one was used for, but here is the dining room, and beyond it, a pantry, and then the kitchen. Keep going on back, and there's a laundry room and another pantry. The porch is out there. It's a big house, meant, I suppose, for a big family."

"Keepin' some rooms closed off's bound to help with the electric bills," Mrs. Barnes said.

"I hope so. I go in the unused rooms every so often and pretend to dust. You know, to keep the spiders at bay."

"Good idea. *Very* good idea," said Rita. "I'm not a fan."

"A broom," Mrs. Barnes said. "Pull 'em down, shake 'em outside."

There was a lot of oohing and ahhing and appreciating the character of the place during the tour. Between the second and third floors, Mrs. Barnes paused to catch her breath. "My daughter's always telling me I need to go to that workout place with her. This house? It's a workout just going from top to bottom."

"Is it too much for you?" Rita asked. "You don't have heart trouble or anything?"

"Not a thing wrong with me other than I have a little too much padding stuck on from too much food. Won't hurt me none to get rid of it."

Several storage rooms and what had probably once been servants' quarters made up most of the third floor, and along the front was a larger room with a tiny bathroom next to it. "Oh, my, look at that view." Mrs. Barnes bent to peek out as she sighed audibly. "Yes, ma'am. I imagine a body could sleep well here, listening to the water sounds, not much traffic."

"There's no air conditioning up here," Agnes said. "I wouldn't recommend it."

"I won't pay that no mind." Mrs. Barnes turned from the window. "No air conditioning in my house either, but we get along fine. Seems to me, we get those windows to open up to the breeze off the water, a person would hear the music and smell the smells on warm days."

Warm days didn't worry Agnes, but hot ones would turn the room to an oven. Still, the woman seemed so determined—about everything. How would that work, the two of them in the same, albeit large, house? Sally Ann had barely made her presence known, except during Brisa-watching hours, so it hadn't been an issue.

Perhaps they should both take time to think about it? Or maybe do things on a trial basis. No hard feelings.

She opened her mouth to speak, but Mrs. Barnes spoke first.

"You need me, Miss Agnes. I'm going to say I see how much you need me here. Now, I know I said some things made you uneasy today, but I said them to a purpose, so you could see me as someone who has made her share of mistakes and has learned from them. My girl and I, we've got ourselves to a good place, only it took some work, mostly on my part."

Agnes wasn't used to someone speaking so openly. But there was something appealing about the large woman with the wide smile and the eyes that glinted along with it.

Besides, Rita liked her. Oh, and Ty.

She took a deep breath. "I do need help."

"I know it. And I think we'll do just fine together. I'm goin' to have a few things to settle between me and my daughter about my own house and her keepin' it up, so it may be several days 'fore I can get here. I've got some figuring to do. Rita here said Sundays and Mondays you wouldn't be needing me, so I'll plan to go to church with my daughter and spend time at my house then. Be stayin' here Tuesday through Saturday, 'ceptin certain mornings I might go help out Miss Annie Mac, should she be needin' me. That work for you?"

Agnes nodded. "Thank you. I think Brisa's going to go into Jilly-withdrawal when she doesn't get to stay there evenings."

"Tadie said your sweet girl can come anytime," Rita said. "There's no rush from her end."

"She's very kind."

"Well, I'll be headin' on back." Mrs. Barnes extended a slip of paper. "Here's my cell phone number. You have a question for me, you just call. I think we're going to do fine."

They descended the stairs, passing Brisa's closed door and the blaring sound of country gospel coming from inside. "She's going to be deaf before she's twenty, the way she plays that music." What Agnes didn't say was that Brisa was playing *his* music. Hearing it made her hands itch to throw something breakable against something hard.

The other women didn't comment, which was probably a good thing.

"Rita, could you stay just a little longer?" Agnes said. "I've something I'd like to show you."

"Certainly."

After seeing Mrs. Barnes out the door, Agnes led the way to the kitchen and out of earshot if Brisa left her room. "I need advice. I mean, I know you don't owe me anything, and I can't pay you right now, but could you... I mean, if it's not an imposition."

She shouldn't have asked and was about to take it back when Rita touched her forearm, saying, "Relax, Agnes. You're never going to be an imposition. Friends help each other. That's what we do."

"Thank you," Agnes said, trying to hide her surprise at being called a friend. "You want water, anything else?"

"No, I'm fine."

She pulled a kitchen chair over to the refrigerator and climbed on it to reach the letter tucked behind some cookbooks. "Would you read this please?" she asked, sliding the chair back under the table. She couldn't sit. Not yet. And she couldn't watch Rita's face as she scanned the words.

Outside, the grass still looked like the back forty in need of a harvester—as if she knew anything about back forties. She needed to get that mower working. She'd meant to mow and weed and trim and mulch. She might even enjoy getting her hands in the dirt, planting, caring for something that was hers, but her life had seemed too tenuous to make the effort.

And now she faced this.

"Talk to me," Rita said.

At Rita's words, she turned and sat down in the empty chair. And then she talked.

When she'd finished, Rita asked, "You have proof of the rape?"

Agnes shook her head. "I was too ashamed. By the time I told anyone, it was too late."

"And you never told him about Brisa?"

"He had no right to know."

Rita smoothed her hand over the sheet of stationery as if to iron out the creases. "The court may not see it that way, absent proof of rape. On your side is the fact that he never contacted you after that night, although he may claim you were a groupie who offered yourself to him."

Agnes sank onto her chair. "I didn't. My crime was in sneaking into the club in the first place and then in being flattered when this gorgeous singer offered to buy me a drink. In taking it."

The fake ID had looked enough like her that she'd passed inspection from a bouncer who didn't check specifics. She remembered the noise, the lights, the press of bodies, and the initial thrill of it all. Then the most beautiful man she'd ever seen, who'd been at the mike on stage, had asked what she'd like to drink. She'd wanted to seem older and, for once, attractive, desirable. Wine had sounded sophisticated and less dangerous than a mixed drink.

She didn't remember stumbling out on his arm or entering a hotel. Or anything that happened before she woke alone in that bed with an ache between her legs.

"He will not get Brisa," Agnes said.

"You want me to draft a response?"

"Would you? One that'll make him go away?"

"I can't guarantee his reaction, but I'll make it as forceful as I can."

"Whatever I have to do, I'll do it to protect my girl."

Rita took a small pad from her purse. "Here. I need your full name and other particulars—where you lived, the name of the club, your age then, anything you can think of. Do you have a middle name?"

"Only Agnes, except my given name is Agnese. I quit using it after that night, except on legal documents."

"It's a beautiful name. It carries a certain dignity, don't you think?"

Agnes barked a laugh. "Look at me. Nothing dignified is going to work on someone like me."

"Don't undervalue yourself. You just be proud, honey. You're a lovely woman."

Agnes felt the heat rush to her cheeks. "Aren't you nice. A liar, but nice."

"I don't lie." In spite of a smile, Rita's voice was stern when she said, "It's no good judging ourselves by what some folk think. You imagine I'd have made it as far as I have if I'd believed shallow-minded people? Nope. I listened to my mama and daddy. And it was Tadie's daddy—a white man of the South, a good white man who happened to be colorblind— whose encouragement sealed it. I told you he put me through school, but it bears repeating. It was Tadie's daddy who expanded my world by giving me access to his library. We need to believe the real truth about ourselves, not the fashion-plate or small-minded lies." She paused, pointing a finger at Agnes and gesturing from her head to her toes. "That's the outside of you. It's good and true and lovely. But the inside of you? The one that raised your precious daughter? It's pure beauty. And don't let anyone tell you differently."

Tears welled. Agnes brushed them back and held her voice still. Otherwise, she'd bawl all over Rita.

*Good people, that woman.*

She had to agree with her mother. But the phrase *good people* didn't sound like the mother she'd known.

*Honey, I died a Southern woman, remember.*

Oh, right. As if one could slide on a different persona just by changing addresses. She shut down the voice in her head.

Rita tucked her notepad away. "If this goes to court," she said, "I'm going to have to help you find someone who does trial work. There's a relatively new lawyer in town, Eric Houston, who has helped me some with a couple of cases at the center. He's the one I'd pick."

"Eric Houston." Agnes felt heat crawl up her neck. "I've met him at the restaurant. Henry, his brother, works with me."

---

A couple of hours after Brisa'd left to see if Jilly could play, she returned with Henry in tow. Wiggling and whining, Link headed toward the voice. Agnes dropped the sponge she'd been using to wipe splatters of water from the counter and patted her hair, hoping she didn't look a fright. "Hi," she said when she stood in front of him, unable to stifle a grin.

He returned the smile. "Your daughter found me wandering the streets in search of a new hat. My ratty one gave up the ghost today. Heartbreaking, as I've had it for years." He held out a beige, brimmed hat and set it on his head, its drawstring hanging loose. "The new one."

"Looks great," Agnes said.

"As long as it keeps the sun off my skin. Too much exposure when I was younger."

She pictured the sun reflecting off the water, bronzing his skin, including those newly shaved, slightly bronzed cheeks. "A hat works," she said, shutting down thoughts that didn't belong.

Brisa sidled up, a big smile on her lips and in her eyes. "Mr. Henry said he has to go to work now on account of them trying out some new menu items for tonight, and he said I could come and be a taster, you know, to see if I like anything. So, can I, Mom? Can I go?"

Agnes raised skeptical brows. "Really?" she asked Hen.

"It'll be fun. I'm sure Chef won't mind. It's relaxed with just the two of us there."

It would be good for Brisa, wouldn't it, to feel a part of something different? To give her a peek into Hen's world for an hour or two? "You'll stay out of the way, won't you?"

"Oh, Mom, I know how to behave. I'm not a baby anymore."

Agnes sighed. No, she wasn't, but she wasn't fully grown either. "You'll be staying with Jilly again tonight. And I have to go in early for set-up."

Henry rested a hand on Brisa's shoulder. "We'll be finished in plenty of time. Maybe Brisa can grab what she'll need, and I can make sure she gets to her friend's by"—he checked his watch —"say four o'clock? You'll be coming in shortly after?"

"Yes. Okay." But she still felt full of sighs, and she wasn't at all sure why.

---

She'd hoped to get the mower started and tackle the long-neglected grass, but all she ended up with were questions. A little investigative work unearthed the manual and the need to add oil as well as gasoline, which necessitated a stop at the hardware store before work.

She was ironing her black work slacks when the phone rang, and Henry's cell number popped up. But it was Brisa who spoke. "I had so much fun! And Chef was great, but Mr. Henry is such a good cook. He made some amazing things, and I got to try bites of a lot of them. Anyway, I wanted to let you know we were heading to Jilly's when we met up with her, so Mr. Henry wants to know if it's okay for me to hang with her and then go to her house."

"Hang with her? What does that mean?"

"She's supposed to pick up some pickles at the Taylor's Creek Grocery. That's not far."

Jilly seemed to have the run of the town, which meant Brisa often tagged along to the ice cream shop or around and down to *Samantha's*. It was a freedom her daughter reveled in, and, after all, this was Beaufort, not Jersey City. Everyone knew Jilly and her family. The shopkeepers looked out for them. But she didn't want them roaming while she was at work.

"Okay. But don't go further downtown than the grocery. And do everything Jilly's parents say."

"I will. I have been."

"Good girl. Okay, then, I'll see you tonight."

"I wish I could just stay over. I'm really tired of having to walk home in the middle of the night."

With a sigh, Agnes said, "We're imposing on them enough as it is. I'm sorry, honey, but Mrs. Barnes will be here on Tuesday, and there'll be no more middle-of-the-night walks home for you."

"The Merritts are great." Brisa sounded wistful.

"I know you've had fun, but it's time to give them back their kitchen couch."

Brisa ignored her attempt at humor and only said, "Okay. 'Bye, ma."

*Ma*? That was new. Perhaps it was twelve-year-old Southerners slang?

She shook out her work blouse. It looked fine, so she tucked the ironing board and iron out of the way and dressed for the evening, which also meant twisting her hair up and hoping it would stay there.

She took care of Link and then headed out the door. She was a few houses from Tadie's when she heard her daughter's voice, easily recognizable, harmonizing with someone in the backyard. Wouldn't you know it? They were singing Darling Evermire's ballads.

Her feet wouldn't move until at least one breath let go and filled her lungs. Then she bit her lip and pressed on toward the hardware store and her pre-work errand. After all, Brisa liked to sing and she liked Darling's songs. She listened to them far too often, as did a lot of other people.

If only.

But it would be okay. Everything would be okay.

*Deep breath.*

9

DARLING

A rthur followed Darling down the low steps that separated his home's front entrance area from the sunken living room. "I have both the investigator's report and the concert reviews. You want the bad news or the good news first?"

Darling waved his manager toward the drink cart and eased himself down onto the circular couch. "Where'd the good news come from?"

"Beaufort." Arthur carried his filled tumbler to the couch section across from Darling. It didn't take him long to down half the contents.

"Then that first."

"Seems the mother is shuttling Brisa to stay evenings with a friend while she goes to work. That means during the school year the girl is away from her all day and then every evening— except Sunday and Monday when the restaurant is closed."

"So, we might have a case for neglect if she won't take the cash offer?"

Arthur raised his glass to his lips again. "Your daughter runs off down the street—unattended—to play at the same neighbor's house where she's staying evenings. Her mother doesn't pick her up until the middle of the night. That's cause enough, in my opinion."

Excitement skittered across Darling's skin, almost better than the snowflake he'd once used with none of the drug's downsides. Having a little girl who looked like him? Lisette was gonna settle right down, and life would be good again.

As if Arthur read his mind, he asked, "Where's the little woman tonight? You seen her since you got back?"

"Yeah, but this morning one of her girlfriends got sick. Said she needed Lisette to come keep her company."

The look Arthur gave him needed to be wiped right off that snarky face. Still, he'd ignore Arthur's nasty innuendos and remarks. Arthur would see. It would all come out right before too long.

"What else you got for me?" he asked.

"Reviews weren't too great."

"We may have to drop RJ. Won't make my daddy happy, but the boy's hurting us."

Arthur stood, waving his glass. "You mind if I refill?"

"'Course not."

Arthur took his time heading to the drink tray, filling his glass, and wandering back. Instead of returning to the couch, he headed to the wall of windows that overlooked the lights of L.A. Darling waited patiently for his friend to speak.

Finally, Arthur turned around. "Those reviews? They didn't mention RJ. Or your back-up girls, except to say they like the tall one's sound."

Darling set his glass on the table in front of him before looking up. "Meaning?"

"Meaning they think something's off with you. You didn't seem to be giving it your all."

"So, it wasn't my best performance. An artist is allowed a few fails, isn't he?" He snapped his fingers. "I'm why fans come."

"And they like your songs."

"Yeah, well, as long as we sell tickets." He tried to sound

upbeat, because he didn't want Arthur returning to bad news, but when he felt a scowl wrinkling his forehead, he smoothed it away with his fingers. Wrinkles weren't allowed.

"Back to those reviews," Arthur said, as if reading Darling's mind. "You know this business, Darl. You put in a few bad performances, you get a few bad reviews, and, pretty soon, you're no longer the singer commanding the big venues—or the big bucks."

Darling had done his best, was doing his best. So what if some snooty reviewers couldn't see past the warts on their nose? Myopic, that's what they were. All of them.

"This thing with Brisa making you edgy?" Arthur asked.

Was it? "Think it's more the thing with Lisette."

Arthur merely returned his focus to his glass.

Darling knew he ought to keep his mouth shut, but the words slid up, craving release. "She came home smelling of sex. And it wasn't sex with me."

"Ah."

Surely, Arthur could be trusted if anyone could. Darling plowed his fingers through his long hair, so like his white mother's. And who cared what that prejudice said about him? He'd drawn enough scorn from blacks who taunted him for having a white mama. He'd yet to meet a white woman who had trouble with his half-ness. They claimed to love his skin color, his hair, his looks… his talent.

So, he'd milked it. Maybe set his mind to preferring the shades and shadows of his wife.

"You're thinking Brisa's going to keep Lisette at home?" Arthur interrupted his thoughts.

Darling flashed his friend a look of resentment. "She wants a child, but she can't have one. So, yeah. I give her Brisa, you don't think she'll be grateful?"

Arthur steepled his fingers over his whiskey tumbler. "I'm not so sure about that. Brisa will never be hers biologically."

"Yeah, but we adopt, who knows what the kid will look like.

65

Lisette wants a beautiful girl child, but one who's different enough so no one's going to compare them."

"Because, of course, comparisons are almost always invidious."

"Quit trying to one-up me."

Was that a smirk Arthur tried to hide by raising his glass?

"I mean," Arthur said, "they're usually unfair, but against Brisa, Lisette would still be the shiny blond, so she could parade around happily with this new daughter." Arthur took another sip. "Assuming Brisa's mother will give her up."

"I'm the father. I have rights." He stood and began pacing.

"Do you?"

Darling glared. "What do you mean by that?"

"Your way of going about impregnating her mother."

"I was a kid," he said, waving away Arthur's words.

"Who took no responsibility for his actions for almost thirteen years."

"I didn't even know about a child. Not until you told me," Darling said. "Whose side are you on, anyway? Aren't you the one who told me to try that stuff, put it in her drink? You and RJ?"

Arthur ignored his accusation. "Just playing the devil's advocate."

"Well, stop." He didn't need a naysayer around him. Certainly not one who was paid to be on his side. "You got any more news, or should we call it a night?"

Arthur stood. "I'll leave these reports here."

Darling pointed to the sheaf of papers. "Take the reviews with you. I'm not interested in what jealous fools have to say."

"Suit yourself. But I wouldn't be so quick to dismiss them."

He waited until the door shut behind Arthur before he picked up the latest report from the investigator. This had to work. It just had to.

Refilling his glass, he looked around at the empty room before retreating to the opulent bedroom he shared with Lisette.

His fingers rested lightly on the silver brush he'd given her on her last birthday, and he willed her to come home, to want him again. Opening her closet door, he let his gaze run the length of the small room before he strode in, drew one of her lovely dresses toward his face, and breathed in the scent of her. His bright and shining star. *His.*

He would not lose her.

And then he sat down in the chair by the bed to await her return.

## 10

## HENRY

Henry carried his mug of coffee to the deck, along with gloves and sandpaper. The images that greeted him when he looked across the water to land were ghostlike behind an early morning mist. Until the fog burnt off, he'd spend a couple of hours sanding on the forward hatch, getting it ready for its first coat of varnish. Then church. Then on to the ferry with Brisa and her mom.

Brisa had been a good sport yesterday when he'd presented her with samples of dishes that were slightly more sophisticated than most girls her age would tackle. She'd even approved the marinated squid—until he'd told her what it was. After that, they'd laughed because it had been too late to take back her praise.

She'd asked about his boat, and he'd shown her where *Harmless* was moored. "Why *Harmless*?"

He'd thought how to tell her without saying too much. "Given my history and how I tended to go after things that weren't good for me, I looked at all the work she needed and all the sweat she'd require, and I figured she was one thing that couldn't do me harm."

Her eyes had grown round. "Really?"

Maybe that had been too much truth for a kid her age. Finally, she'd whispered, "Thank you." He still wasn't sure what she'd meant.

"Maybe," she'd said later, "you could take Mom and me out someday. You know, when you finish."

"Maybe to Cape Lookout. Have you been there yet?"

"My friend Jilly has. She said it's beautiful."

"It's supposed to be really warm tomorrow."

"You mean, we could go?" The rounded eyes had all but glittered with excitement.

"By ferry. At least to Shackleford to see the ponies. If your mom wants."

Agnes had wanted. "I'll pack a picnic," she'd said when he'd mentioned it last night.

Something to look forward to, he decided as he scraped the sanding block across the teak. He wouldn't imagine it could be more.

He wouldn't.

---

They were waiting for him at the ferry dock when he showed up later, Agnes with a small cooler in one hand and bag in another. Brisa carried her own beach bag.

"Sunscreen? And long sleeves to cover up on the way back?" he asked. "I brought water."

"In the bag," Agnes said, holding it aloft. "Hats, too."

"I really want to see the ponies," Brisa said.

"Bound to." He hoped so, at any rate.

It had turned into a gorgeous day, sunny, warm, with very little wind. Brisa sat at the ferry's rail, watching the boat slice through the water to create a bow wake. Even this early in the season, people were enjoying what the area did best—water, boats, and adventures.

Leaning forward, the breeze streaming her hair, Agnes said,

"Thank you again for letting Brisa be a taster yesterday. She couldn't stop talking about the food, and she was *very* impressed with herself for liking the squid and the stuffed mushrooms. She hates mushrooms. I assume you cut a slice off so she didn't recognize the dish?"

"I didn't want to prejudice her palette." He smiled down at her.

"Well, it worked. You were a hit."

The ferry dropped them off on the sound side with a return scheduled in a few hours. Brisa raced across the dunes toward the waves.

"Shoes off!" Agnes spread a blanket on the sand and held it down with the cooler at one corner and her shoes at another.

He kicked off his and followed her to the edge of the water, where they stared out at the ocean. "We're looking almost directly south toward cerulean seas and tropical islands."

"I love imagining what's out there. I always wanted to travel."

"I've dreamed of taking *Harmless* voyaging. As I varnish woodwork and fix leaky places and faulty wires, I let my mind wander to places I could go. If only."

"If only what?"

He shrugged. He didn't want to tell her that going solo seemed dangerous—not physically, of course. His peace of mind had been hard won, and all that alone time felt, well, risky.

"Standing here," she said, "I can imagine believing in a creator. Because of the vastness and yet the detail put into every small creature that lives in that ecosystem."

She was certainly right about the vast emptiness that was so full of life and not empty at all. "I know," he said.

Sails appeared on the horizon. One day, perhaps. He could hope, pray. *Lord?*

Speaking of God, thinking of God, felt like a prayer. Maybe it wasn't. Maybe it was.

Brisa walked up the beach, looking down at her feet as they kicked through the shallows.

"Do you want to follow her?" he asked. "See if there are any shells worth collecting?"

"I don't have a bucket."

"Ah," he said, pulling a plastic grocery bag from his pocket. "I have this."

Agnes bent to check out the treasures the sea had dropped. It wasn't long before Brisa came running up, her hands filled with shells, among them a small conch, a Scotch Bonnet and a Cone shell. "Excellent finds," he said.

She grinned happily and dropped her collection into his bag, then turned to look at the low dunes in the distance. Banks ponies nibbled sea grass. "Look," she whispered. "Horses."

He never tired of seeing them. But ponies weren't the only wildlife out that day. A pod of dolphins cavorted a short way off shore, and, later, as the ferry took them back to Beaufort, they caught sight of a sea turtle gliding along the surface.

"Such a perfect day," Agnes said as they left the ferry and strolled toward her house. "I can't thank you enough."

"It was my pleasure." And perfect for him, as well.

At their walkway, Brisa turned her full-wattage smile on him. "I loved it. Thank you, thank you!"

"You're both very welcome."

He hated the day to end, hated to go back alone to his boat. It wasn't late…

"Would you," he started, "I mean, if you're not too tired…"

"What?" Agnes asked.

"Would you like to row out to *Harmless* with me?" Where had that come from? He hadn't meant to ask yet, had he?

"Me, too?" Brisa asked, her expression hopeful. "Because I'd really, really like to see your boat."

"You can't expect much. I mean, I still have a lot of work to do on her."

"Well," Agnes said, "it would be fun to see a work in progress."

"Why don't you put your things inside," he said, "and I'll go order pizza?"

"Just pepperoni for me," Brisa said.

The smile on Agnes's face thrilled him. "Most anything works for me."

"Meet you at the dinghy dock in thirty minutes?"

"Perfect."

Good thing his slightly obsessive compulsion toward order meant his boat would be ready for its first non-fraternal visitors. He'd seen the care Agnes took of her home.

By the time he emerged from the restaurant with pizzas in hand, Agnes and her daughter awaited him on the sidewalk at the head of the dinghy dock. "Ladies, this way." He ushered them to his old wooden dinghy. "Good thing we're not going very far. I don't have lifejackets for either of you. You can swim, can't you?"

"Of course," Brisa said. "I'm not afraid."

"Good girl."

He tucked the pizzas under the seat, helped Brisa board, and reached up a hand for Agnes. Once they were settled, he took up his place at the oars. "Will you uncleat us, Agnes?"

She raised a brow.

"Untie the line at the dock, then push us off."

She did, brought the line onboard, and gave a shove.

"Brisa," he said, "you remember which boat is mine, don't you? Perhaps you'd point me in the right direction."

"Because you're sitting backwards."

"That's it. If you see we're headed too much to the right or left, you can say so. Keep me from having to turn around and look all the time."

"Okay!"

This should be interesting. It wasn't in his nature—or experience—to trust anyone other than himself. But he'd try.

11

## AGNES

A gnes went first up the boarding ladder, followed by her
daughter. Henry aimed their feet so they didn't miss a
rung and told them where to place their hands to grasp the most
secure hold.

While Brisa scoped out the deck, Agnes bent to pick up the
pizza boxes and headed back toward the seating area. Henry
followed, letting the dinghy drift back with the current.

"Welcome to my home," he said.

Brisa held on to the wood rail and looked around. "It's
wonderful."

"May we have a tour?" Agnes asked.

"Of course," he said. "We're in the cockpit now. Look." He
drew Brisa toward the wheel and stood with her behind it. "This
is where I steer. And under those covers are the instruments that
tell me the water's depth, the wind's speed, and the boat's
direction and speed."

"And that?" she asked, pointing to a stainless-covered ball.

He opened the cover. "That's a compass so I can know which
direction I'm heading."

"Oh."

He laughed at her puzzled look. "I'll give you a lesson

someday."

"Oh, yes, please." Brisa pointed at the masts. "You have two."

"I do. This small one is the mizzen; the taller is the main mast. Having two gives me options for different kinds of wind."

Agnes listened to the lesson as she rubbed her hands along a varnished rail, imagining what the boat would look like when all the teak parts shone like this one.

Then Henry led them below, down what he called the companionway steps, to the salon. "A fancy name for the living area," he explained.

There were two sleeping cabins and two bathrooms, or *heads*. Brisa thought it hilarious that a person had to pump the toilet by hand, both to fill it with water and to empty it. When she asked where everything went after it was pumped, Henry told her about a tank under the floor. "There's a small boat that comes around to pump it out right here, without *Harmless* having to go to a dock. Boats for living aboard need to be self-contained— water in tanks, sewage treatment, diesel for the engine, batteries to work the lights and other toys."

Brisa giggled and was delighted when he let her look under the floorboards at the engine and the tanks. She stood on the other side of his u-shaped galley—or kitchen—counter to watch him get plates and napkins.

Agnes wandered out onto the deck when the image of Henry cooking in that space, everything in reach, tidy, organized, perfect, assailed her with a longing to be part of this world, too. Which was just stupid, considering the big house she owned with its yard and its space... and its overwhelming responsibility.

Laughter filtered out to her, and her heart warmed. Her girl and this man. It was what Brisa needed, a man who'd show her kindness and strength. He'd have to be strong in more ways than the physical, wouldn't he, to live alone at the whim of storms on a sea that wasn't always calm?

Brisa stuck her head out the companionway. "Here you go, Mom," she said, passing plates out and following with napkins. They settled down to feast on pizza and watch as the day ebbed.

"Tell us what it's like, living on a boat," Agnes said, thinking about those storms and uncalm seas.

Henry took a long drink of water. "There's good and bad about it. Good, in that I have freedom to change my backyard whenever I want. Bad, in that there's constant maintenance just to stay afloat and be able to move. Although that can be a good thing. Boredom doesn't exist out here." He winked at Brisa.

"It must be a lot of work," Agnes said. "What about people who don't have your skills?"

His eyes danced. "They'd better have a credit card and a cell phone. Of course, I can't imagine they'd opt for an old boat in need of a lot of work."

Brisa wiped a smear of tomato sauce from her lips. "Unless they're rich."

"Yeah, but a rich guy would probably buy a new boat, don't you think?"

"I guess." But she seemed more interested in her food than in the discussion.

Agnes heard the sound before she felt it, the loud noise that indicated someone with too much testosterone behind the wheel of something. Instinctively, she reached out just as Hen said, "Grab hold and hang on."

He circled an arm around Brisa, and Agnes wrapped her fingers around a vertical post—a stanchion, he had called it—just in time to keep from falling off the seat when the motorboat roared past, creating a wake that bucked *Harmless* up, over, and down again in an ungracious dance. Although Henry held Brisa close, she still bobbed with the motion, and down below something banged and clattered as it obviously hit the floor. Creaks and groans came from nearby boats, and a couple of shouts followed the reckless boater who soon vanished out the channel.

When things settled, Hen asked, "You both okay?"

"That was fun!" said the child who liked rollercoasters.

Agnes hated them. "Really?" She hadn't thought it fun at all. "What if that happened when you were in bed? Would it knock you off your bunk?"

Henry laughed. "No. When I go to sea—if I ever go to sea—I'll have lee cloths for protection."

"What's a lee cloth?" Brisa's eyes were still shining from the excitement.

"I have netting that can be attached top, bottom, and sides on the bunks to let air in and keep stuff, including people, from falling out." He stood. "Speaking of falling, I'd better go see what the noise was. Be right back." And he disappeared below.

They waited, she and Brisa, she enjoying the calm, Brisa staring at the other boats as if waiting for some other madman to rock *Harmless*. When Hen returned, Brisa said, "I saw a boat with a pirate flag. Are there real pirates on the sea?"

"In some places," Hen said, "but none around here."

"Some places like where?" she asked suspiciously.

"You worried about them?"

"What if you sailed where they are? I mean, you could get robbed or hurt."

He laughed. "I could, but I doubt I'll ever sail in dangerous areas. I'll do my best not to."

"But what about storms? And hurricanes?" Brisa's brow wrinkled now with worry.

Agnes thought to deflect some of it. "Good questions, honey. I'm sure Hen is taking care to avoid those."

"Indeed. I have no wish to be in the path of hurricanes," he said. "Besides, people who live on land also have to deal with them."

"Yeah," Brisa said, "but our house has been fine for a really long time, and it's really strong. But a boat isn't. And what if you were sailing some place and the storm just hit you, like they do sometimes?"

"*Harmless* is a lot stronger than you imagine, and there are ways to manage a storm at sea."

"I bet you'd be scared," Brisa said, this time scooting closer to her mother. "I would."

Agnes draped an arm around her daughter's shoulders. "I imagine Henry won't go near any dangers without being fully prepared. Right?" she asked him.

"You can count on that."

"I certainly hope your boat's name is truly indicative of your future on her," Agnes said.

Henry grinned. "I do, too."

Brisa still seemed worried. "You really like living on a boat better than on land?"

Hen's gaze shifted from her daughter to her and sobered. When he finally spoke, he said, "For now, yes." And Agnes was left to wonder what the *now* meant… and if it meant anything at all.

She didn't want the evening to end. Brisa sat curled against her, chatting sleepily with Henry until the child began to make no sense at all.

"I think there's one person here who's longing for her bed," Henry said.

"Not s…leepy," Brisa mumbled.

"Right." Agnes grinned over at him. "We should get her home sooner rather than later." She shifted from under her daughter. "Come on, baby. You need to wake up so you can climb down into the dinghy and not fall overboard."

"Please, yes," Henry said.

It took a little shake to wake Brisa fully. "Up you go," Agnes said. "We've had a lovely time, but now we'll say goodbye to Henry's big boat and let him row us back in his little one."

He raised the lid of one of the cockpit seats and drew out a lifejacket. "We'd be wise to tuck her in this." He handed it to Agnes. "While you're doing that, I'll ready the dinghy."

She got Brisa strapped in and to the boarding ladder. Henry had not only shut up the boat, but he'd also set up red and green lights on a pole. "Regulations," he said. "Navigation lights."

"Ah," she said as if she understood exactly what that meant. "You ready for us?"

"I am. Brisa, back down, honey, just the way you climbed up. I'm right here to guide your feet and help you settle."

Agnes climbed down on her own and gingerly stepped to the seat next to her daughter. The wind had stilled to nothing, and they glided across the pond-like surface, the sound of oars sliding in and out of the water and barely noticeable against the backdrop of a busy waterfront.

Seeing the restaurants and revelers from the water gave her a new perspective, as if she were one of the privileged who traveled by boat. She'd seen them, the cruisers tying up a dinghy and going inside one of the fancy places for lunch or dinner. She'd wondered, often, about their life, where they'd come from, where they were going.

Henry drew them to the dinghy dock and, after tying up, helped them out before offering an arm to each. "You don't need to," Agnes said, but he responded with "Of course, I do."

Their end of town was empty of people, and their footfalls sounded clearly against the cement sidewalk. No one spoke. Brisa was exhausted, and Agnes had much to think about.

Her dreams of sailing off into the sunset had taken a beating when they'd spoken of storms at sea, and yet now she found herself again on land where turmoil abounded. Perhaps the storms of life could never be outrun, but the courage to reach out and explore new things had to be grasped, didn't it? Henry had done that, changed course and plucked courage from the ravages of his life.

She needed to do the same.

## HENRY

*Agua Verde*, like most restaurants in town, was closed on Mondays. That morning, Henry spent a couple of hours replacing a bilge pump that was acting up and then washed and dressed for the dinghy ride to town. The row in was quick and easy, and he tied up, climbed out, collected his small backpack, and began walking toward town. And then he turned in the opposite direction.

A block down, and he was climbing to Agnes's front porch. Before his knuckles hit wood, the door opened, and Agnes regarded him in surprise. "Henry?"

Hearing only his name might have been discouraging, but he'd noticed a glad light in her eyes before she'd lowered the veil. "Are you heading out?" he asked. "Is this a bad time?"

"No, not at all. I thought I heard the mailman coming onto the porch, although he usually whistles."

"I don't."

"No, I see that." She grinned. "Still, I'm Pavlov's dog at the thought of mail. Always the optimist."

"Ah." Interesting thought process. He wondered what she looked for so optimistically.

"I came to help," he said into the momentary silence.

"Help?"

Brilliant, Hen. Just brilliant. She didn't have a clue what he meant. "You mentioned having someone, a caregiver for Brisa, coming tomorrow. I just wondered if you needed anything moved... or whatever. My help."

"Oh."

He shifted from one foot to the other. "But maybe you don't. I'm sorry to bother you." He'd begun to turn away when she stepped back, making room for him to enter.

"No, I do. You just surprised me. Please, come in."

He was in. One hurdle down.

She nodded toward the stairs. "I could use some muscles around here. Mrs. Barnes wants the upper-floor bedroom, and it's not quite ready to be lived in."

Agnes stopped on the second floor to grab linens from the closet. "I want to thank you again for yesterday. We had so much fun."

"I did, too." Now might be a good time for eloquence, but it didn't come naturally. He followed her as she made her way to a room at the top of the house.

"I have no idea why Mrs. Barnes picked this of all the available rooms," she said. "Maybe she likes her privacy?"

"Nice view." The window looked out across Front Street to Taylor Creek, where only a few boats were moored this far east between town and the islands of the Rachel Carson Reserve.

"And it does get the ocean breeze from that one window. If you could help unstick the swollen ones, there'd be some cross ventilation. And I need to move the bureau from across the hall. And the clothes tree."

He followed her to the smaller room and looked around. "Big house." Not as big as the one he'd grown up in, but large for a small woman and her daughter. Large and leaky, he'd guess.

She laughed. "Says the man who lives on a boat."

"Well, yes." He returned her grin.

He spent the next half hour moving furniture while she made

up the bed and set out towels. Then he checked the windows. "You have a crowbar or something I could use on these? Even a putty knife might help."

"Maybe outside in the shed?"

He wandered down the stairs, through the house, and out the back door, avoiding the longest patches of grass in case a snake wanted a piece of him for lunch.

Sure enough, the shed held all the tools he needed, lined up on and above a work table that made him itch to get his hands on some of them and this place. A layer of dust covered everything. He shook his head at the neglect.

Although maybe he could help out with that mower. Dust it off, get it running.

Be the friend she seemed to want.

By the time he'd returned to the top floor, crowbar and putty knife in hand, Agnes had set up a box fan in one window. He went to work on another.

"You don't make much noise when you walk," she said. "How is that?"

He glanced back and out the door. No noise?

Ah, yes. Of course. But she didn't need to know why, especially because it wasn't something he talked about outside his conversations with Father Stanley.

"I never wanted to be heard," he said, surprising himself as the words he wasn't going to say tumbled out. "I'd get in trouble if I disturbed my mother's sleep."

Her brows shot up. "Does your brother tiptoe around, too?"

"No tiptoeing needed. But, yes, we both learned the art of walking softly, although I don't know if he does it now there's no need."

"But you still don't want to be heard."

"Guess not." He turned away so she wouldn't see the red creeping up. Why had he opened his mouth?

The image of his young self skulking past closed doors

resurrected memories he'd rather bury. He certainly didn't want them disrupting his time with Agnes.

He ran the putty knife down the edge of the window frame and then worked at its base with the crowbar, a nudge to the right, a little to the left, in and push, until a satisfying crack broke the seal. Once he'd manhandled the window open, he moved to the next one.

For years, he'd blamed both his father's wrath and his mother's tears on his disfigurement. He remembered whispers first, then sighs and curses. Kids had pointed and asked what was wrong with his face. Grown-ups had spoken in his hearing about his gorgeous brother, and wasn't it too bad about Henry. Too bad they hadn't been identical. It was really too bad.

Yeah, it was. And, yeah, he'd reacted badly to the differences during his teen years, which had tilted sideways into his twenties. Since that day almost three years ago when he'd heard the metal door clanging shut with him outside and not in, he'd never taken his freedom for granted, not with two backslides into rehab in his history. Instead, he stayed connected, focused, and working on becoming the man he'd been created to be.

He tried to shake off the memories, but as he forced the next window open, his thoughts slid back to the wealthy father who'd wanted—no, demanded—perfection from his sons. Robert Eldrich Houston had found it instantaneously in Eric but had needed to call in the surgeons to manufacture a new lip for his second-born. At least, the senior Houston used to say, it had only been the lip cleft and not the entire palette. Several operations later—because the one done in infancy had been botched or incomplete or just not up to his father's specifications—and several years of speech therapy later—because there'd been a slight stutter as a result of who knows what—he'd declared Henry passable. Not lovable, of course. Never that. But the fixed Henry would do. He wouldn't have to be hidden away any longer.

*Rah, rah.*

The final window seemed to be glued shut. Hen pounded around the edges with the side of his fist. Then he used the putty knife. Finally, he worked the crowbar in and levered it, freeing one side a couple of inches. The other remained stuck.

"That one not cooperating?" Agnes's words jolted him out of his memories.

Wiping sweat from his brow with his forearm, he blew out a sharp breath and sat back on his heels. "Afraid not."

"There's cross ventilation now. That might be enough." She nodded toward the hall. "Come on. Let's have some iced tea."

"Thanks." He stood up and shook out his left knee, stiff from resting on a warped floorboard. At some point, there'd been water intrusion up here.

She led the way downstairs to the kitchen, where she filled two glasses with ice and tea. "It's unsweetened. You want sugar?"

"No thanks," he said, accepting a glass.

He glanced around at the upgraded appliances and cupboards. The remodel had been well done, keeping with the period of the house while making the space more conducive to food preparation. Knives hung on magnet bars, two rows of them near a large cutting board and the double sink. He noted the orderliness of it, clean and neat, everything in its place. He found that comforting and studied Agnes covertly before gazing out the large over-the-sink window that gave a view of the backyard. He'd only noticed the unkempt grass before, contrasting that now with the orderly indoors. She must be overwhelmed.

When he stood to take his glass to the sink, he saw that there'd once been a vegetable garden out there. "You like to garden?" he asked, turning slightly to look at her.

"I'd like to learn. I've never had much time to work outside, and now I'm going to have to get that mower started so I can actually make it look like someone lives here. I had to let Denny go last September. He liked to ride his dad's mower, but I couldn't afford to keep him on."

"Denny from work?"

"Yeah. He ended up doing just the front." Her smile had shifted sideways. "To keep up appearances."

"Ah." The upkeep must be enormous. She'd said something about the estate being held up by legalities. That had to be hard. "I can help. At least look at your mower."

"Could you really?"

"Come on." He led the way back out to the shed, opened the door, and hauled the mower out to level ground. He checked the gas, the oil. "You have any oil?"

"I do."

He found a funnel in the shed and took the oil from her when she returned. The liquid gurgled as it flowed into the small hole.

"Okay," he said, "let's give it a try." He pointed to a lever. "You close the choke here, like this." He showed her. "Then hold this safety bar close against the handle, grab the starting cord here, and pull in a long, smooth stroke. No jerking."

It started on the fifth pull.

"Here's where you adjust the throttle," he said over the noise.

"Throttle."

"The thing that sets the engine speed."

"So, if I set it wrong, the thing will drive off without me?"

He laughed at the image she'd painted. "Not likely."

He adjusted it until the engine ran smoothly and waved her out of the way so he could push the mower forward and cut a swath. He had to ease the blades up and over what were mostly weeds.

She called when he'd turned from the second row. "You don't need to do this. I can get to it."

"The yard's not that big. Why don't you fix another tea?"

He used to help his father's gardener, a weathered Mexican-American whose friendliness had been a gift for a lonely boy during the summers Eric spent at soccer camp and baseball

camp and most-popular-everything camp. Eric had said he
didn't want to go without Hen, but that hadn't stopped him
from climbing in the back seat and waving goodbye, while Hen
hid from mirrors and from groups and from anything that might
draw attention to his less-than-perfect self when the first surgery
had to be redone. Juancho, though, had liked him and listened to
him and taught him about tools. And lawn mowers. And fixing
things that needed fixing in the yard of that big Charleston
house. Only, Juancho hadn't shown him how to fix himself.

Hen ducked into the small downstairs bathroom to wash his
hands and douse his face and neck with cool water. By the time
he'd come out, Brisa was calling the dog from the front of the
house. Link passed him in a scurry of fur and nails clicking on
the hardwood. "Back here," Agnes called to her as Hen reentered
the kitchen.

An excited Brisa started chattering before she got to them.
"Mom, Ty was at Jilly's after school, too, and we got to go fishing
on Jilly's dock 'cause it was so nice out and there were a bunch
of guys trying for crabs down the way, but Mr. Will didn't think
we could get many fish, on account of it being the wrong time of
day, only we did! A whole bunch." She skidded to a halt inside
the kitchen and noticed him. "Oh, hi!"

"Good afternoon." He grinned. "I used to love fishing off a
dock."

"We got a whole mess! Miss Tadie said she's never seen so
many at one time, but maybe she was just being nice. I mean,
they're kinda little, but she said they're big enough to eat. Seems
like we just *hauled* them in, like they were waiting for us right
there. Miss Tadie said we should have a party, on account of the
weather cooperating. Only, if it rains, we might have to use the
inside, but that's okay because they have a big house, too, even
bigger than this one. Mr. Will's going off to get hushpuppies and

salad stuff, and Miss Rita's coming, she said with food to fill in the gaps—I don't know what she meant, except maybe because there won't be a whole lot of fish for everybody, on account of them being smallish. Plus Miss Rita's mom and dad will be there —and Miss Tadie said that meant some really good food would be showing up—and Miss Annie Mac and Mr. Clay, and I don't know who else. *And* they want us to come." She barely stopped long enough to breathe between words. "And I bet they'd be real excited to have a chef there," she told Hen. "Maybe you could cook something to add in. You think? Because most everybody's bringing something."

"I can't just show up," he said. "I don't know any of them, other than Lt. Dougherty."

"If I can go," Agnes said, "you can, too. We'll scrounge for something to take."

"How much time do we have?" he asked, thinking it was already almost five.

Brisa said, "I don't know. An hour, maybe? Everybody has to get there."

"I'm kind of sweaty. Not exactly company material."

Agnes leaned over and sniffed. "No problem. You'll dry."

Brisa giggled. "Mom!"

Hen grinned from Brisa to her mother. "Then let's see if you have the makings of Spanish Flan. If not, I can run to the store."

"Flan would be fantastic," Agnes said. "What do you need? Eggs, milk?"

"And vanilla, sugar, the rind of an orange."

"I just went shopping, so I have all except the orange. I think Brisa took the last one a couple of days ago."

"But I forgot to eat it!"

Agnes laughed. "Then go get it, honey, and we'll do some cooking in this fancy kitchen."

His gaze snagged a large bag of apples. "Wish we had time for apple pie."

"I can slice some for finger food. Brisa loves those."

When Brisa returned with the orange, he asked, "Would you be willing to help?"

Her eyes widened. "Yes, sir!"

"I need someone to gather the ingredients first."

"I'll do it!" That girl's grin was going to slay hearts someday.

---

Henry stopped at the edge of the Merritts' garage. People milled about. Some sat in chairs or stood near tables or beside one of the two grills. Some wandered toward the other side of the house, where the grass ended and a small wooded area began. Agnes marched on ahead into the chattering melee carrying the flan while Brisa dashed off to join the younger ones.

He wasn't hanging back because he hoped to be noticed. Oh, no. He was searching inside himself for the courage to walk forward as if he belonged in such a crowd. They looked so happy, so normal, as if all were right in their world.

Agnes set down the dish and returned with a man she introduced as Will Merritt, their host. "And that's Will's wife, Tadie," Agnes said, nodding toward the woman headed their way.

"Heard you brought us my favorite dessert," Will said, before turning to his wife. "Honey, you hear what Henry made? Do we have to share? I mean, how often do we have a chef in our midst?"

"And another sailor," Clay said, coming up with his hand outstretched. "How's your boat coming along?"

"Slowly," Hen said, shaking the other man's hand. "I did get a first coat of varnish on a good portion of the teak."

"Good thing the weather's supposed to hold a while longer once we get past tonight's squall," Will said. "Shouldn't be much."

"That's what we want, short squalls," Clay agreed. "I haven't seen your brother in a while. How's he doing?"

"Eric's fine. He'd like to get more sailing in."

"What about you? You think you'll up anchor and get yours moving this year?"

"Good question. Work and weather dependent. If *Harmless* sits around much longer, she'll need to be hauled just for new bottom paint."

"Boy," Will said, "I know about weather and work. The *Nancy Grace* ended up in the yard during a hurricane—"

"And was in worse shape after another boat fell off the stands and holed her," his wife added.

"Of course," Will said, snagging an arm around her waist, "it kept me in town long enough to let me fall for this lady here."

"Yeah, right." She grinned and tucked in close to her husband. "Being in town had nothing to do with it. It was all Jilly."

"It was, wasn't it? Great discernment, that girl of mine."

With her eyes alight, Agnes said, "It sounds as if there's more to this than you're telling. What sort of bribe is required for us to hear the full story?"

Another woman approached behind Agnes. "I'm Hannah Morgan. My other half is that balding guy with a spatula in his hand."

Hen grinned. "Henry Houston."

"Pleased to meet you." She flashed a smile at Agnes. "If Tadie and Will are teasing you about how they met, I'm the one you ought to bribe. I was there for the whole thing."

"Really?" Agnes asked.

"Absolutely. Happy to give you all the juicy details for my very own custard. I adore flan."

"Sorry, Hannah," Tadie said. "Henry here is the chef, not Agnes. And I don't think he cares about our romance."

"But," Hen said, "I do want to hear all about your boat and its adventures."

Will looked smug. "So *we* get the flan."

Hannah sighed loudly. "I'm dying here."

"Come on, Hannah, Agnes." Tadie looped arms with the two women. "Let's go check on the rest of the food. And Elvie Mae would probably like a break from Sammy-chasing."

As they wandered away, Clay winked at Will. "Good general, that Tadie. Always has been."

"Yes, sir. Best just to tell her 'yes ma'am' at all turns."

"Always a good idea with our women folk," Clay agreed.

Hen laughed. "You think?" And then he sobered. "Not that I have any women folk to yes-ma'am."

Clay glanced toward the women as they walked away. "But I'm thinking you may have one on the hook. If you're interested, that is."

"Ah, yes, well…"

"Leave the poor man alone, Clay." Will slapped the lieutenant's back. "He's not used to us yet."

"True. But I remember a whole passel of busybodies trying to make things happen between me and Annie Mac."

"Yeah, and how well did that work?" Will asked.

Clay sighed. "Not nearly as well as I'd have liked. Took the fool woman forever to figure things out."

Hen raised his brows. He must be missing years of context here.

"Someday," Will said, "we'll share a beer and bring you up to date."

"Tea," Clay said.

"Oh, right." Will gave a quick nod. "Forgot."

"Me, too. Tea, I mean." Hen studied the other man. So, Clay didn't drink either?

"Drunk driver killed my dad," Clay explained. "I was in the truck."

"Addiction issues," Hen said. Why hide the truth?

"Ah." That was Will. Clay merely nodded.

"So," Will said, drawing them toward the group. "Where do you have your boat?"

Hen told him, and then they were surrounded by others, and

the evening became one of good food and good conversation, with more talk of boats and sailing. Hen couldn't help envying the trips to exotic places the Merritts had taken before they'd moved back to Beaufort. And wasn't that something, the way Will had taken his little girl, Jilly, with him cruising when he'd been a single dad? It made a guy long for other, didn't it? Other than the way he'd lived. Other than the choices he'd made.

So why did he feel deflated as he walked Agnes and Brisa home after the picnic?

Agnes stopped at her walkway and extended a hand. "I really appreciated your help today. Especially the lawn."

"It was my pleasure."

"And your flan was a huge hit."

"I have other recipes." He tried to rein in his eagerness. "Perhaps I can make something else for you another time."

"Sure," she said. But she was looking over her shoulder at Brisa. "I'd better go. Thank you again."

"You need anything else, please call."

He waited until she walked up the porch steps, unlocked her door, and ushered her daughter inside. She was already speaking to Brisa and didn't see his last wave. And then she closed the door and shut him out of her world. Maybe last waves weren't in her vocabulary of friendship.

He pressed the heel of his hands to his forehead. No, no, and no. He would not let self-pity in. It was disgusting—and he knew better. Hadn't Father Stanley warned him of its devastating effects? Hadn't he seen it himself?

He was strong. He was true. He was fine. God had set him free, and he'd stay free.

*Really?* the whisperer said. *You think you can? You think God really cares about one puling little soul?*

"Yes," Hen spoke his words to the air and to the voice in his head. "God cares. I *am* free. And I am loved."

*You're a broken mess.*

"I am a broken mess. But I am loved."

*Sure. Go on, lie to yourself.*

"I will not listen to a defeated liar. My God has won." But his assertion sounded weak to his ears. Faltering.

*Help!* That time the cry was his.

He scuffled forward, heading back to quiet and order where nothing was out of place, everything was neat and ship-shape. Heading back to nothingness.

"Hen!" Eric's voice came from across the street.

Hen stopped, waiting. Relief washed over him. "What's up?"

"You just heading back to the boat?" Eric spoke in his friendly, unconcerned voice, which usually meant he'd been worried. They may have been only fraternal twins, but they knew, didn't they, when one or the other was in trouble? "Where've you been?"

"I helped a friend move furniture around, and then we joined a few others at the Merritts'."

"I met them. Last Christmas when I visited their church. More sailors."

"Good people from what I can tell."

"And the friend?" his brother asked.

"Agnes Jones."

"Ah, yes. The waitress."

"A good woman."

"So, tell me about her."

Why should he? Hen waited a beat before asking, "What do you want to know?"

"Don't get defensive."

"You sounded like my-brother-my-trustee instead of my-brother-my-twin. Besides, it's late. I still have to row home."

"You sure you don't want to stop at my boat first? Chat a while? Have a cup of decaf?"

"Another time. It's been a really long day."

Eric cocked his head, giving him the Look. His pause lasted a long minute, and then he said, "Sure. See you."

Hen walked toward the dinghy dock. The temptation to

wallow in self-pity sucked the air from him, but he mustn't let it win. He turned, called to his brother's retreating back. "The invitation still good?"

"Always."

He heard the smile in his brother's voice. He was obeying Father Stanley's admonition that he call for help if the voices grew too insistent. That he not be alone.

*Escape* welcomed him, all varnished warmth and polished teak. He followed Eric below and accepted Eric's offer of decaf coffee.

"Hope you don't mind if I don't join you?" Eric asked. "I had a cup after dinner and would prefer water."

"Don't brew any on my account."

But Eric had already put the kettle on to boil and gotten a bag of coffee beans down from a cupboard. He took out a grinder, added beans, and waited for the whirring blades to stop before he said, "I love the smell of freshly brewed, don't you?"

"I do. I don't have a big enough battery bank to grind beans on my boat. Not at anchor."

"One of the reasons I'm dockside and hooked up."

Hen sighed. His brother could afford to dock here. He, on the other hand, would have to content himself with languishing at anchor unless he made more money.

Eric would say that was due to his own stubbornness. Fine, he was stubborn. But he needed to be.

Hen studied Eric's bookcase, filled with nautical books both fiction and non-fiction, searching for a distraction, something he could borrow to read when sleep eluded him. Before he'd settled on a title, his brother slid the mug across the galley counter. Hen accepted it, saying, "Thank you for asking me here."

"Looked like you could use a break."

Hen sighed. "Maybe."

"It's supposed to storm tonight. Around one."

"As long as it's pretty tomorrow. I have another two coats of varnish to apply."

"You have everything you need on board? How's your anchor chain?"

"You imagining I'd skimp on that?" Did his brother think he was an idiot? "Just because I can't afford new and spruced like you can?"

"Sorry." Eric had the grace to look apologetic. "It's just, I keep offering to loosen my hold on your funds."

"I'd rather earn my keep, if you don't mind."

"Stubborn," Eric said. "You always were stubborn."

Hen flinched as his brother's words replicated the ones in his thoughts. "No. I wasn't stubborn enough. I didn't fight hard enough." Hen stood and set his mug on the galley counter. "If I'd been stubborn enough, I wouldn't have gotten myself in all that trouble, would I? I'm trying to learn how to hold myself to standards I ignored too often."

"But you've been clean for years. Why won't you take control of your own money?"

Hen snorted. "And have all that temptation at my fingertips? You know better than that."

"Would it be?" Eric plowed his fingers through his hair, a sure sign of agitation. "Would it really be temptation?"

Would it? Hen was so used to believing he couldn't handle the wealth he'd been left that it had become a challenge to see how well he could manage without it. He slid back down onto the settee and sighed. "I hate that it was his. That I got it from him."

"We both did. But Dad got it from the General. And the General was a good man."

Hen knew that. Before their grandfather had died, he'd been considered a military oddity by some of his peers, so genial, convivial, and charitable. He'd actually played with his grandsons, letting them take turns riding on his knee, lobbing balls toward their plastic bats so they'd have a good chance of getting hits.

"What made our father so different?" Hen asked, not for the first time. They'd puzzled over it, he and Eric, as their father's anger had escalated, and not only toward their mother.

"I don't know. Maybe something happened to him in his childhood that turned him into a mean and angry man." Eric rinsed Hen's mug and turned it upside down to dry. "Perhaps our grandmother was the mean one."

"Perhaps." They'd never know. She'd died when their father had been in his twenties, but by then she hadn't been living with the General. No one had ever said why, but Hen remembered asking, only to see his granddad's face close up with what seemed like sadness. All he'd said was that she'd been an unhappy woman.

Unhappiness plagued Hen's family. Or it had until Eric had broken free.

Now Henry was trying to do the same. Break free of destructive behaviors. The behavior part was a whole lot easier than the thought part, but those went hand in hand, didn't they? One compelled the other.

"I'd better get on back," he said. "Thanks for the coffee."

At the companionway stairs, he added, "And for being here."

"Always," Eric said. "Remember that, will you? You're never completely alone."

He wasn't, of course, and not just because of his brother.

## 13

## AGNES

The storm's ferocity kept Agnes awake as lightning streaked the sky and thunder rumbled. She half expected Brisa to come padding in to join her.

Eventually, the world stilled, and, eventually, she slept.

She woke too early, but sleep wouldn't return, and so she rose and pulled on her robe. The view out a southeast window stopped her. A mist of purple-gray hovered over the creek making it look like pewter. As the sun inched up toward the horizon, the colors began to flame, all oranges and brilliant pink behind now-purplish clouds. Out over the Atlantic, heavy gray-purple hovered, but the yellows were breaking over them, and the higher clouds reflected heaven's paintbrush, pink and orange and a lightening sky of blue-gray above.

Stunned, she stood, enjoying what greeted her when her windows didn't face brick or aluminum siding, when space existed between neighboring homes and a yard fronted on a view of water and boats and an island.

She felt energized and got to work before Brisa needed rousing. She actually managed to pay all her overdue bills and had ten dollars left until her next check. She wouldn't go anywhere or buy anything. She had enough milk and eggs, along with a new supply of cheese, peanut butter, bread, and cereal. And she had a couple of meals in her freezer, along with frozen veggies. They'd manage. She could do this, even if she had to feed Mrs. Barnes beginning tonight. Cheese omelets?

She climbed the stairs and stepped into Brisa's room. "Honey, it's time. Get dressed and come on down. And you've left a mess on the floor from your letter writing, so that needs picking up before school." Brisa waved her away.

Agnes tried not to worry. Her daughter had stayed up to finish writing a letter to her friend Rachel, saying she had to tell Rachel about the fish and the ferry ride. But it wasn't like Brisa to leave papers strewn on the floor.

She let Link out, then began breakfast preparations, but when her daughter hadn't come downstairs by seven-thirty, she headed upstairs again. Brisa lay curled on her side, facing the far wall. Link followed her in and nosed Brisa's back.

"Are you ill?"

"Leave me alone." Brisa sounded angry, not sick.

She touched the child's forehead. "You don't have a fever. What's wrong? Can't you go to school?"

Brisa shook her head and repeated, "Just leave me alone."

Maybe it was an intestinal upset. Or a headache. Maybe she was experiencing hormonal issues. She probably wasn't too young for those.

Was she?

Who could remember?

"I'll check on you soon." Agnes left Link to guard her daughter.

There was still no movement from upstairs when she went to see if Brisa would be able to get up and go to school at all. Brisa excelled in her studies—unless something had happened that Agnes didn't know about. Had someone been cruel? If Brisa *was* ill, Mrs. Barnes' arrival this afternoon would be timely. Agnes couldn't let her daughter near Tadie's family to risk infecting the baby. She readied a breakfast tray and carried it up.

"Here you are," she said, pushing open the door with her shoulder. "A little toast and juice."

Brisa's expression when she turned brought Agnes up short. "I'm not hungry."

Worried now, Agnes pushed books out of the way and set the tray down on Brisa's desk. Then she lowered herself to the bed. "Talk to me, honey. Tell me where you hurt. Or did something happen at school that made you want to stay home?"

There was only silence.

"I can't help you if you don't tell me what's wrong."

Brisa rolled over, glaring and waving a folded letter. Agnes recoiled. For a moment, she merely sat there, staring at Brisa's hand and what it held. She swallowed back bile that filled her throat. "You dug through my papers?"

"Don't turn it on me, Mom. I was looking for an envelope so I could address my letter to Rachel. You didn't do such a good job hiding this."

"I guess not." She should have burnt the thing instead of putting it in her desk after she'd shown it to Rita. At the very least, she should have buried it beneath her underwear again.

"You said you didn't know anything about my father. Like, you didn't know where he was. That was a lie, wasn't it?"

"He's not a good man. I didn't want you to know anything about how awful he is."

"You mean *was*. You don't know what he's like now. You always say people can change." Brisa squinted suspiciously. "Or have you seen him? Did you just decide not to let me have a daddy? I don't even know what he looks like."

"Oh, honey."

Agnes closed her eyes. Brisa listened to the man's music… and hadn't that nearly sent Agnes over the edge when she'd first discovered the CD Rachel had brought to share? But Brisa hadn't connected a singer named Darling with a letter writer named Darlington Evermire. Nor had she noticed her resemblance to the man who was both.

Brisa shrank away from Agnes's outstretched hand before drawing a pillow over her chest. "You know how much I've wanted a daddy. All these years. You've known."

"I have. Of course, I have. And I've longed for you to have one. Just not this one."

"Why? Why not my *real* dad?"

How could she tell Brisa the truth about her conception? Agnes cringed at the image of Brisa's horror if the child knew she was the product not of love but of rape.

"I need you to trust me on this, honey. And not ask more questions."

"He wants to meet me." Brisa waved the letter. "He wants me to come see him."

Agnes closed her eyes on a sigh. "No, honey. He wants to *buy* you. To take you away from me. Read his words more carefully."

As Brisa scanned the letter again, her expression didn't soften. She glared at her mother with a scorn Agnes never expected to see from her sweet child. "He's offering to help you, Mom. You need the money so you can buy real food."

"I buy real food. I just don't buy luxuries."

"Well, he doesn't say he'd take me forever. He just wants to know me and let me know him. What's so wrong with that?"

Agnes reached for the letter. "Do you see the word 'custody' there? Custody means keeping. He's saying he wants to have custody of you, and he's offering to pay for the privilege." It was hard to keep the bile from rising. "As if you were something for sale."

"I guess he thinks it's his turn. 'Cause he never got to see me before."

"Yeah, well, that's not how it works." Refolding the letter and tucking it back inside its envelope, Agnes searched for appropriate words. Good parenting of this precious girl meant she had to hide the horror of her daughter's conception, didn't it? With that truth ruling out anything else, what could she say that would convince Brisa to let the matter drop? All she could manage was the repetition of "Your father is not a good man."

Which no child wanted to hear.

"I don't believe you." Brisa's pout ruined her normally sweet expression, and her eyes blazed anger.

Agnes wasn't going to be able to wipe off either of those with the promise of a treat. If only she had a magic wand or the conviction that prayers worked.

"You're just saying that because you don't want me to know him," Brisa said. "He didn't want you, so you're mad." And with that, her daughter crawled deeper under the covers and drew them over her head. "And you're mean."

"Brisa." Agnes drew a deep breath, finally releasing it, but slowly. She didn't want to speak in anger, not the anger that raged in her—anger at him, at herself, at her daughter. "I don't appreciate either your words or your attitude. I understand your disappointment, but this isn't negotiable. No man who behaved as Mr. Evermire did should expect to buy his way into our life. You are not for sale."

Brisa reached out with one arm to pull Link close.

Agnes's heart constricted. Her sweet baby. Her sweet, wounded girl. And on that thought, the anger dissipated, leaving only regret. "I'm so sorry, honey. I wish things could be different."

Brisa threw the sheet off her head long enough to say, "They could be. You could say yes. I could *see* him." And then she buried herself again. "I just want to meet him," she whined, her words muffled. "That's not too much to ask, is it?"

It was, of course, and knowing that made Agnes feel even more helpless. Absolutely, completely helpless.

And like the worst mother in the world.

If only she had someone to call. Someone who'd listen. And care. And maybe give her advice.

Although Hen's kind eyes came into her thoughts, she knew she couldn't go there. She couldn't burden him with this.

She walked out the door and into her room, unwilling to continue the fight. Brisa should get up and go to school, but Agnes didn't have the will to fight about that, too.

She was a horrible mother.

---

She leaned against the back-porch rail and stared out at her yard while Link did his business. Somehow, she and Brisa had managed to get through a silent morning and afternoon. Brisa had finally eaten the toast and a sandwich Agnes had taken upstairs, but she'd done so out of sight of her mother.

How long could she sustain silence and anger?

Shrugging off that thought, Agnes checked her watch. "Come on, Link, inside." Mrs. Barnes was due to arrive in ten minutes.

She arrived in seven, along with two bags, a grocery sack, and a one-person electric kettle. "For a cup of tea once I've finished my morning prayers. And this here?" Mrs. Barnes said, setting the plastic sack on the hall table. "I brought some things I hadn't gotten around to fixin' at home. Hope y'all like stew and biscuits."

"Sounds delicious." Agnes grabbed the handle of the larger bag as Link stuck his snout between them to sniff the goodies. "Leave her alone, Link." The dog turned away but stood ready if needed. "As for tea, you know you can use anything in the kitchen whenever you want."

"Yes, ma'am, but this is just my way."

Agnes started up the stairs, trying not to frown at the image of the other woman puttering around in the attic. As they passed Brisa's closed door and the still silence behind it, Link sniffed and whined. Agnes let him inside.

The slight huffing as the heavier woman climbed from the second floor to the third didn't sound good. At the top, Mrs. Barnes paused to catch her breath. "Honey," she said, her eyes twinkling, "one good thing about having my teapot up with me is that it will save me the trek down and up just for a calming cup of tea to go along with my scripture study. You won't be minding if I plug this in my room, will you?"

"No, not at all." Assuming the wires up here could handle it. She really did need to find out who'd done the work on this house and ask a few questions.

Mrs. Barnes stepped into her room and set down her bag and kettle. "Oh, my, you've gone and fixed it all up. You didn't have to do all this."

"Of course I did. Anyway, I had help."

"Well, that's a good thing, it truly is. Friends to help, I mean."

Agnes tried to see the room from her new housemate's perspective. "If you need anything else, there's a linen closet off the hall bath downstairs. But are you sure you want to be way up here? With those stairs to navigate regularly?"

"It'll be good for me. Doctor's always sayin' I should get myself more exercise, and seems to me, stairs is a good way to get it. Gotta lose the weight so I won't get problems later."

"If you're sure. You can always change your mind if you find this is too much, or if you want to get cool."

"Thank you, Miss Jones."

"Agnes, please."

"Thank you, Miss Agnes. And you just call me Becca." She hefted the suitcase up on the bed. "I'll get myself unpacked, then maybe you can show me around your kitchen, help me get the lay of the land, so to speak, so I can know what kind of meals that girl of yours will be expecting."

"But you don't have to…"

"Now, missy, I told you how I need to keep busy. Seein' as how I love to cook, this will be one of the best ways you can use me. And," she said, the twinkle turning into a momentary grin, "if'n you haven't had a batch of my biscuits or my cornbread, you just haven't eaten good, even if I do say so myself."

Still, Agnes hesitated. It seemed like too much, so much more than she'd imagined.

"Of course," Mrs. Barnes said, "if I'd be intruding on something you'd prefer doing yourself, you need to say so. This is your house. I don't want to be upsetting any routine of yours."

"I love cornbread," Agnes said. "And I'd love to have you helping with meals, but I don't want to take advantage of you."

"Oh, honey, you won't be. Having folk to cook for—because now my daughter's been on her own with her own kitchen, she moved home and took over mine—well, being able to do this will put a smile on my face every time."

"Then, I'll let you get unpacked. I'll put the groceries away and have water on for tea when you're ready."

As she headed back downstairs, Agnes told herself she shouldn't worry. This would work. Surely, it would work. Besides, with all the other worries crowding her thoughts, she didn't need one more.

---

She slid Becca's cup of tea across the table. "Sugar?"

"Yes, ma'am. Thank you." Becca glanced around the kitchen. "When will your girl be home?"

That was the question, wasn't it? Brisa might have been in the house, but she wasn't home.

"She's upstairs in her room."

Becca frowned. "She feelin' okay?"

"Other than being furious with me? She's fine."

The last thing Agnes wanted was to explain everything to anyone else, but if Becca were going to live here, she'd need to understand. When she got to the part about her daughter waving Darlington's letter, her insides matched the chill in the teacup she lifted to her lips.

Finally, Becca spoke. "My daughter, she listens to that man's music. I can see the pull of his fame when it comes to your girl, along with the pull of wantin' a daddy of her own. This is gonna be hard."

*Hard?* Agnes stared at the other woman. "I don't think she put his full name together with the singer she listens to. Not yet, anyway. She's been holed up in her room all day, barely eating. That's not normal for her."

"Maybe I can tempt her out with my biscuits. Most folk really love them straight from the oven. If'n your girl doesn't come out before you go off to work, I'll see what I can do." Becca tapped a finger to her forehead. "Maybe we can plan together to get her mind off that letter and being mad at you and onto good things to eat."

Agnes noticed the time. "I'd better get ready for work."

"You do that. And don't you worry about us none."

"Easier said…"

"I know," Becca agreed. "A whole lot easier."

## 14

## DARLING

D arling knew himself to be a patient man, but to have two women jerking him around? Lisette had claimed to have caught the flu from her friend, which meant she'd have to recuperate before she came home. But tonight should be the night. If she kept putting him off, he'd find her and know the reason why.

And Agnes?

Seems she'd hired a lawyer. He slapped the letter across his palm and cursed. Agnes Jones. She was *nothing!* A nobody. A speck of dust in time, and he would wipe her away with a flick of his hand.

He'd tried to be nice. He'd offered her enough money to make her comfortable. To get her off welfare, if that's where she hovered. Arthur'd had the authority to up the ante to a full hundred grand, but had she accepted? No. The fool woman.

It was possible Arthur hadn't had a chance to raise the offer. Darling pursed his lips, moving away from the windows and toward the sunken couch. "A lawyer." He spoke aloud as he lowered himself onto the soft leather, because it didn't make sense. How could Ms. Nobody afford to pay a lawyer to draft a letter?

He didn't want to imagine some secret bank account Arthur's investigators hadn't discovered or her having enough cash to thumb her nose at him. No. He needed her dependent and ready to grovel. Otherwise, he'd have to ruin her, which shouldn't be too hard. He was Darling Evermire, and she was nobody.

He pushed a button on the table next to the couch and waited. When the knock sounded, he told his man to enter. "I'll have dinner in here tonight. Something light."

Todd nodded and backed out. Quiet and efficient, perfect. Just as his cook was because he could prepare a menu that suited his boss's requirements, no matter what those were. Although he was pretty sure "something light" was always at the ready.

While he waited, Darling thought of his next step. If Arthur's letter offering even more money failed, he'd have to go to Beaufort himself. It was time, past time, for him to meet his daughter, his Brisa, face-to-face in that hick town she called home. It shouldn't be hard to convince her she'd be better off with her rich and successful father than with her loser of a mother.

"A waitress." He gave the word the disdain it deserved.

From the pictures he'd seen, Agnes Jones was just as nondescript as his slight memory of her. Her small stature coupled with those large breasts had been enticing, and her shy smile had lowered the barriers enough for a one-nighter. She'd obviously wanted him. But look at her now, aging way too fast. She and her Beaufort could never compete with L.A. and him.

He dug his phone from his pocket and hit speed dial for Arthur. When his manager answered, Darling said, "You written to that woman's lawyer yet?"

"Sending it off in the morning."

"If that fails, I want you to book me a ticket so I can go see Brisa. Get her on my side."

"Let's wait for an answer. In the meantime, you've got a new drummer to interview. And Las Vegas is coming up first of next week."

"When'd you set it up with the drummer?"

"Tomorrow, three o'clock."

"Put him off for a couple days. I want this thing with Brisa settled. No reason I can't talk to her now."

"It's not going to be settled in the next few days, not unless you plan to snatch the girl." Arthur cleared his throat. "Which I'd advise against. A kidnapping charge wouldn't play well with the public. Or the courts."

As if he'd do that. "Fine. I'll see the drummer and fly out after. We like him, he and the band can figure out how to make music while I'm away."

He could almost hear Arthur's teeth grinding against each other. "Fine."

But it wasn't fine at all, was it? Nothing was fine right now.

---

Darling heard the soft click of the door closing and her soft footfalls on the floor. Sitting in the dark, staring out at the moon rising over the mountains, he waited.

Where had she been this time?

Perhaps he should set an investigator to follow her. But what would that say about him, a man who had to send someone to follow both his wife and the mother of his child? A man who couldn't keep his wife satisfied and had no contact with the one and only person who carried his genes into the next generation?

She walked... no, glided... over to the bar and poured herself a drink. The liquid sloshed into the glass. He saw her contours outlined by the soft glow of moonlight coming through the windows. He saw her lift her glass. Savor the taste.

He kept his voice low as he spoke. "Welcome home."

She almost dropped the tumbler when she jerked. "I did not see you."

"I know."

She carried her drink to the couch that faced his. He waited until she was seated. "Good of you to visit."

"I was not well."

"So you say."

"It is truth, cherie. My friend, she had the nasty stomach illness. I caught it."

"Conveniently."

"You are not being kind to your Lisette." Her voice went from petulant to cajoling.

The game. This was it, always the same, pushing him to the brink and reeling him back. He was growing sick and tired of the repeat.

"I'm not feeling very kind right now." And then he let loose a deep sigh and remembered Brisa and his reason for wanting her.

"Come here," he said, patting the cushion next to him and then leaning over to snag the lamp switch.

When she snuggled close to him with her hip, he noted that she smelled merely of soap. Perhaps she had been ill and not with some other man. He drew the envelope of pictures closer.

"Ah, *mon amour*. I have missed you." Lisette traced one of her long nails down his cheek.

Man, he had missed her, too. So, yes, he would do it. He would show her.

Maybe it would help her stay put.

He lifted the envelope onto his lap. "I have a surprise for you. An Easter present of sorts."

"Ooh, Darling, *vraiment? Pour moi?*" Her eyes sparkled in the lamplight.

Slowly, he slid the pictures out and onto her lap, one at a time.

She rounded her lips, then bit the lower one. "And this? Who is this?"

He waited a moment before setting the close-up on top of the others. It was a little blurry, but it was good enough to show the likeness.

*"Mais, c'est toi!* It is you!" She drew it closer. *"Une jeune fille."*

"Yes, a young girl who looks just like I did at her age."

*"Je ne comprends pas.* This I do not understand."

"It seems," Darling said, "that once upon a time, I made a baby."

Lisette squinted from the photo to him. "How? How is it that you did not know this before?"

"I barely knew the woman." He shrugged. "Better to say, I didn't know her at all. She came onto me at a bar, and so…" He let his words trail off.

"You together made a baby."

He wiped the tears that spilled over onto her cheeks. "I don't want it to hurt you, my love. It was long, long before I met you."

*"Oui.* That I can see." She sniffed and took the handkerchief he offered. "But, *tu comprends,* this does not make it the easier thing. For you to have a child I did not make."

He cleared his throat. "I thought perhaps if you had her, she might help fill the gap. Instead, you know, of adopting a child whose parentage was uncertain."

"But we do not have her!" And then Lisette's head snapped around, and she looked at him hopefully. "Or is it perhaps that she has no mother? *Sa maman est morte?"*

"No. Her mother is alive, but she's poor. She has debts, and Arthur has offered to help her out of her difficulties if she'll allow Brisa to come to us."

"Ahh…" She took his hand in hers. "Tell me all."

He created a story for her, a story that made her yearn, as he did, to have this girl child as their own. He could almost hear her mind conjuring images of herself petting a daughter, doing for her, making her into a child she could adore. Because this one would never be able to compete with Lisette's blond loveliness, and yet Brisa would do her credit.

Oh, yes, this would be perfect.

This way he'd keep his wife by his side and his daughter close enough to mold into someone like him. Not like her mother.

## 15

## AGNES

Brisa dashed past her mother's open door and down the stairs toward the kitchen where Mrs. Barnes manned the pancake spatula. A day and night had passed, and she still hadn't relented.

Agnes squared her shoulders. She needed to be strong and vigilant.

Rita had sent her demand letter to Darlington, and Agnes would make certain Brisa didn't get hold of another of his. She hoped Brisa hadn't noticed and written down the return address, because there'd be no stopping her if she had access to that.

*You see? Rebellion creeps into the next generation. We pay for what we sow, don't we, Agnes?*

"Yes, Mother," she said aloud. After all, there was no one else to hear. "But when does it end? Did you have any sowing to pay for?"

Agnes closed her dresser drawer and stared at the mirror. No other face glared back at her, although she half-expected to see her mother's eyes reflected from somewhere. Her imagination was really working overtime. Unless...

No, she didn't believe in anything else. She wouldn't.

*You still have my letter waiting for you.*

She walked out of her room because, suddenly, the idea that she was conversing with a crazy voice in her head—and what seemed like a double-minded voice at that, turning and twisting away from the truth as this one did—made her wonder on which side of sanity she stood.

She'd prided herself on her intelligence, hadn't she, in spite of having failed to use it to avoid bad choices? Still, she'd comforted herself. She could think. She could reason. She had an excellent vocabulary from her years of reading.

She might not have a university degree or a great job, but she had her books and her thoughts and her dreams. And she wasn't stupid.

No, but she might just be certifiable.

*Stop that.* She wasn't. Absolutely not. Because crazy would allow Darlington to win.

And that was not going to happen. She wouldn't listen to the voice in her head ever again. She'd drown it out. Put earbuds in and listen to her iPod.

When the phone rang, she answered, and Matt Morgan from the hardware store said, "Hey, Agnes. Good to see you and Brisa last Monday."

"You, too." Pleasantries always came first.

"I looked up the information you wanted," he said, "and I came up with a couple of names for you. You have a pen and paper?"

"Hang on." She grabbed a pen from her everything-drawer and used the back of an envelope. "Ready."

"Far as I can tell, it was James Long who did the cabinets in that kitchen remodel for the judge and your mother. I've got his number here. And the plumber was Harding Bros., probably Frank. I'm not sure about the general contractor, but James will know."

She scribbled down the names and numbers as Matt read them. "I can't tell you how grateful I am. Wouldn't it be incredible if I could actually get this thing resolved this year?"

"It would indeed. I've already told James you'd be calling."

"Thank you so much."

She stared at the number after she disconnected and wondered why she hadn't thought of asking Matt earlier. All this time and all that fretting.

She couldn't get through to James Long, but the plumber at Harding Brothers said he'd look up the paperwork, see what he could find. She thanked him and tried Mr. Long again. This time she left a message.

It was a start. She was a lot closer than she'd been yesterday to finding out the truth.

And she wasn't homeless.

# 16

## DARLING

Darling thanked the steward who'd served him on the chartered plane and, without glancing around, descended to a steamy tarmac. Then he wandered into the general aviation terminal. At least it had air conditioning to combat a humidity that was going to have his shirt sticking to him in about four seconds.

How could the locals stand it? He was used to higher temperatures, but none of this pore-clogging heaviness.

He'd chosen not to have the pilot land the executive jet in Beaufort, where word might spread about a black man with more money than most of those hick-town locals had ever seen or ever dreamed of. New Bern, though? He doubted anyone here would even notice him or his plane, especially as he didn't plan to hang around longer than it took to pick up a car, which should be waiting outside for him.

It was. After sliding behind the wheel of a sleek black SUV, he let the GPS guide him out of town and east, down a highway littered with gas stations, straggly-looking houses, billboards, and pines. He saw evidence of a nearby military base in advertisements for reduced rates at tattoo parlors and check-cashing services. He hadn't planned to stop for food, but then a sign for barbecue flashed before him, and he pulled into the drive-through lane to order.

North Carolina barbecue and sweet tea reminded him of Mama Bea's Sunday afternoon feasts. Not that she'd served this exact menu. There'd been cornbread and molasses to go with the fried chicken, plates filled high with good things, and plenty of sweet tea. Mama Bea was his daddy's mama, the woman who'd raised him when the woman who'd borne him had up and died without much, if any, family left. Mama Bea'd tried to turn him into a Southern, church-going boy until Daddy'd come for him.

Since he'd been in L.A.? Better food, healthier food, but none of the comfort Bea had offered against her ample form. She'd never written, which had hurt more than he'd wanted to admit. Daddy'd told him it was just her way of not dealing with reality, but that didn't fix the hurt, the feeling of loss he'd experienced in between his gratitude for being offered more.

He remembered what she'd told him along with her last hug. "Remember, my lamb, you've always got a home here and folk who love you. And your daddy may try to run Jesus out of you, but you belong to the Lord, and he ain't finished with you. Never will be."

He needed to let memories go. Not remember them now, certainly. A ways up the road, traffic nearly came to a standstill in the right lane heading across a bridge to the beach, but he kept on going through that town and on across one high-rise bridge and then another. A right turn, a straightaway, and he was in Beaufort.

The GPS found Agnes Jones' house. Why did his surprise at what he found come in Mama Bea's voice? He heard her say as she had about a lot of things, "My, oh, my. Lookee there."

Agnes Jones lived across from the water in a big house. How'd she manage a house that grand? Why hadn't Arthur mentioned it?

He pulled over and parked where he could watch for her and

for his girl. He ought to have brought Arthur along, have him do some digging.

No matter. Unless that investigator had it all wrong, saying Agnes Jones didn't have money. Seemed she had a house but no cash.

Lucky for him, he, Darling Evermire, had millions. And these days, those millions might actually be billions.

The thought of his houses and cars and investment accounts filled him up with the sort of pride that brought on a slow grin and heat to his belly. Oh, yeah. He just wished Mama Bea were here so he could show her how little worth came from following her God and how much came from following his.

Oh, yeah.

He was basking in the comfort of being right when the front door opened and out stepped a woman dressed in black slacks and a long-sleeved shirt, a sweater folded over one arm and some sort of tote on the other. Looked like Agnes had filled out some since that night, but she wasn't showing any of it off. No extra flesh there, for sure. Yeah, you could tell she had curves, but she needed to be about a foot taller to compensate for those breasts and hips if she wanted to come anywhere close to his notion of elegant.

He figured she was headed off to work, but who was staying with Brisa?

If that woman went off and left his girl alone... Oh, he'd milk that. Yes, indeed. One more nail in her coffin.

He leaned further away from the window as Agnes marched on down the walk. Last thing he wanted was for her to spot him and get on her high horse. No, he'd bide his time and see.

He waited while she crossed one street, another, until other pedestrians blocked her from view. Then he checked himself in the visor mirror, took a deep breath, and got out of the car.

The doorbell's peal echoed inside, as if the sound had shot out of a little bell and bounced on its way to other parts of the house. Footsteps sounded on the stairs, and the bell had nothing on the clatter of a voice calling out that she'd get it.

A woman's face showed momentarily in the sidelight, a black face, with the look of Mama Bea, except this woman was bigger than Mama. Had Agnes found herself a nanny? The door opened slowly and not so wide as to seem welcoming. "May I help you?"

He chose to confront her coolness with his most winning smile. "Hello, how are you? My name is Darlington Evermire, and I'd like to see my daughter."

The woman straightened. A dog's nose poked beside her leg, and the dog growled. The woman smiled at that. "Yes, sir, I figured that's who you was, and I don't think you're welcome here. I happen to know the lawyer who wrote you, and I happen to know some of the things she told you. So, before coming here to bother decent folk, you just go give her a call." She began to close the door.

He extended a foot and planted it on the sill. The growl intensified, but the dog looked like a Golden. Probably taking his cue from the woman, so Darling kept his tone level. "I have the right to see Brisa. I'm her father."

"Well, that's what you say, but whatever proof you have needs to go to the police or to Miss Agnes's lawyer. I'll be happy to open this door if one of them comes saying so. Otherwise, you just go on now. Seems to me, you, sir, are trespassing."

With a sigh, Darling rubbed his forehead. He'd traveled a long way, and now this woman, this stranger, was standing between him and Brisa. He'd like to shove her out of the way and gave it serious consideration for a moment, but then what?

Someone, probably this beefy black woman, would call the police. This was the South. The South took care of its own.

And… he didn't have proof except his looks and Brisa's, and he didn't have a court order, and he was trespassing.

He took out a card and scribbled his cell number on it. "Give this to Agnes, please, and tell her I'm staying at that inn down the street. I'll meet with her whenever she is free."

"Contact her lawyer." The woman didn't take the card and only glared at his foot.

He moved it. She shut the door, and what sounded like a deadbolt clicked into place.

# 17

## AGNES

Agnes didn't keep her cell phone turned on while she was at work, but Brisa and her caregivers all knew to phone the restaurant in an emergency. So, when the hostess motioned her over, Agnes knew a moment of sheer panic.

Becca Barnes was on the line. "You maybe need to know. That man came to the door, that Mr. Evermire."

"He's *here*?"

"In the flesh. Came asking for Brisa."

"What did you tell him?" Her voice had hiked, drawing attention from patrons nearby. She lowered it and turned her back on the room. "Did he leave?"

"He sure enough did. I told his sassy, sorry self he could just take himself off and call your attorney. No way was I letting him in without he had a court order or the sheriff along with him ordering me to."

"That won't happen." Agnes wanted to spit the words out, but Mrs. Barnes didn't need to hear her anger. "Brisa didn't hear him, did she? She doesn't know he's here?"

"I'm hoping not. She was headed up to her room when he got here. She's there now."

"Keep an eye on her? Just in case?"

"Yes, ma'am. You can count on that."

"I'd better get back to work. Call me if anything else happens. Oh, and could you call Rita? Let her know? I can't do it from here."

"Soon's I hang up from you."

"Thank you." Agnes closed her eyes and reminded herself that she had a job to do, a job that left no room for panic. After all, the crisis hadn't reached critical yet.

And it better not.

---

She deserved an Academy Award on that busy night. She'd kept her fake smile fixed, her voice modulated, her order-taking and food delivery smooth and on time. No one seemed to notice she was dying inside.

Except perhaps Hen. He came 'round from the kitchen once and leaned toward her as she waited for an order to be filled. "You okay?" he asked quietly.

The shaky smile she turned toward him may have had something to do with his nearness, because she hadn't lowered her guard once in the last hour. Until now. "Fine. I'm fine."

His gaze was appraising. "You need anything, you'll tell me?"

"Absolutely. Thank you."

He didn't touch her, but she felt the caress of his smile before he went back to food prep. If only... If only.

She glanced at the phone and then picked up her tray, willing the phone to remain silent and wishing it would give her an update, some positive word. But the only really positive word would be the promise that Darling had left and would never return.

In a perfect world, he'd never bother her or Brisa again.

# 18

## DARLING

A knock sounded at Darling's inn-room door. It had better be the maid, bringing more towels. He couldn't believe this place, with its sorry excuse for everything. So small town in the South.

Thank the stars for Hank Evermire, a name in the music business with his very successful record company. Mama Bea had hoped to keep him close, but how'd she imagine those tactics would work against the powerhouse who was his daddy? No sir. Darling'd been saved, though maybe not the way his granny had wanted.

He grinned at that thought as he opened the door and spied not a towel-laden maid but his flesh and blood, staring up at him with eyes the shape and color of his own. Taking a deep breath to rid himself of the shock—because he'd pictured this moment, but not with him still unshowered and less than perfectly groomed—he stepped back and ushered her into the room.

They stared at one another, not speaking. At first, Brisa seemed just as appraising and confident as he. Then he looked closer. A flutter of her lower lip was the first sign. And her hands. She tucked them in her pockets, and her shoulders

120

hunched slightly. Her eyes lost their intensity, and her lashes lowered.

Look at those lashes... Any woman'd kill for lashes like those. Lisette only had them when she applied fakes. This daughter of his? Not a speck of make-up or anything other than pure natural beauty. Just about took his breath away.

He barely heard her words first time she spoke. Then she raised her head. "You're Darling." There was a stunned expression on her face.

He smiled. "Yeah, I am." He waved her in and closed the door behind her.

"I found your letter," she said, glancing around the room as entered, "but it never occurred to me that someone named Darlington was *Darling*."

Listen to that voice. Pure, sweet. He wondered if she could sing. Wouldn't that be a gift? A daughter on stage with him?

"You like my music?"

"Do I... do I *like* it?" Her expression was priceless, all eager and unbelieving rolled up together. "How can you be my father? I mean, you're famous."

"Famous people can have kids."

"Yeah, but... I mean, how do you know my mom?"

"We met at a club in New York City, a long time ago."

"But..."

He touched her cheek. "Just look at the result. A beautiful daughter."

"Then why didn't you ever write or visit me?" she asked, but he was busy studying her features. "Why?" she asked again. Her face seemed to have closed off.

"I didn't know about you. Your mama never told me."

She shook her curls, silky hair that hit her shoulders. "Then how come you know about me now? How'd you find out?"

"We ought to sit down." He motioned her toward one of the two awkward-looking chairs stuck under a round, faux-wood table, then scooted the other back so he could fit his length onto it.

He could tell by her long legs that she'd end up tall, too, a female version of him instead of a copy of her small mother. Again he thanked the gene-pool genie for blessing him like this.

She plopped down, little-girl like, and curled her fingers around the edge of the plastic-upholstered seat, waiting.

He should have practiced his lines, figured out how much to say, how much to leave out. "It seems a friend of mine, my manager, didn't bother to tell me I had a kid until just recently."

"How come?"

Arthur'd said he was protecting him when he kept silent. Brisa's mother hadn't come looking or demanding anything, so why should Darling have been bothered?

Yeah, he'd have agreed with Arthur if he'd known, but he wasn't about to tell this girl-child he'd hadn't given his encounter with her mother a backward glance or a second thought after Arthur'd fetched him from that room and cleaned up after him while the girl slept.

Why should he have cared? He'd done her a favor. She probably wouldn't have found someone like him willing to give her the time of day otherwise.

Although he hadn't actually meant to take her like that. He'd been drunk himself. And he'd never had—or tried—to use a sex drug before, not until his brother had agreed with Arthur, saying its use enhanced the pleasure. In retrospect, Darling admitted the drug had made her easy, but it hadn't made the sex better.

Still, if this little beauty was the fruit of that, neither her mama nor he should be disappointed. No, sir.

"How come?" Her words came at him again.

What had she asked? How come what?

Oh, right. "I don't know. Guess he thought you were better off with your mama."

"I always wanted to know about you. She knew. She knew,

but she never told me. I asked." Her tone had flipped to petulant.

Twelve. That must be it. Of course, he'd have been really pissed if his grannie'd kept him from knowing about his daddy.

Still, he had to be careful what he said. "I'm sorry we didn't keep in touch." Giving her what fans called his trillion-watt smile, he reached again to feel the smoothness of her cheek. She didn't flinch.

"But I'm here now," he said, "and we can start from this point, can't we? There is so much I want to share with you—my life, my world. Would you like that?"

Her eyes said yes, but her mouth formed a pout. "Mom would never let me. If she knew I was here, she'd kill me."

"How did you know where to find me?"

"I heard you talking to Mrs. Barnes. I didn't let on, though."

He checked his watch before leaning back in this butt-numbing excuse for a chair. "I know she doesn't want to let you go, but we'll work on her." He winked conspiratorially. "Between the two of us, we can do it."

She shook her head. "You don't know my mom."

"No, I don't. But I'd like to." Not in this lifetime, but no need to let her daughter know that.

Brisa's smile shone. *His* smile. Glory. The kid would be worth millions on stage, even if she couldn't sing.

He thought about his next move. It was possible, no, probable, that the mother would block any more contact with Brisa when she found out about this visit, and he'd like to avoid legal hassles if he could. Sure, he'd probably win at least visitation rights, but better if he could figure how to get Brisa to California so he didn't have to mess with North Carolina laws and the court's probable snail's pace. A father's rights might hold water in this backwoods place, and they might not.

He reached behind him to where his wallet rested on the room's low dresser. He extracted a business card, scribbled his cell number and his personal email address on the back, and handed that to her. "You can call me or write any time. You need me, I'll be here."

Her lips parted. "Really?"

"Really. It may not be immediately, not if I'm on the road, but I'll get to you as soon as I can. You have an email address of your own?" At the shake of her head, he slid one of his eight credit cards across the table. "How about a credit card? You ever used one of these?"

She eyed it. "No."

"It's always handy to be prepared for emergencies, and this one will work for whatever you might need. You can buy clothes with it or even a plane ticket to visit. When your mama says a visit's okay." Keep it legal, no enticement. Not so he could be charged, anyway.

"Really? How?"

He told her how to use the card. And then he said, "But let's just keep this between you and me, okay? I'm not sure your mama would like you having such freedom."

Brisa clutched both cards to her chest. "She'd hate it. She still treats me like a baby."

"You're certainly not that," Darling said.

No, and she showed such promise of beauty. So much promise.

# 1 9

## HENRY

Agnes had told him she was fine, but when Hen glanced up from chopping leeks, she lifted the phone to her ear again. Although he couldn't hear her words, it didn't take a detective to recognize that something was very wrong.

The waitstaff had already cleared the first two seatings, and a few booths remained empty, which was probably why the restaurant manager only seemed worried about Agnes, not about the disruption from the second phone call. Hen had to turn his back on the room to slide the leeks into the skillet, but as he stirred, he checked again and noted the manager's nod when Agnes spoke to her.

His hands were too busy for him to reach out and touch Agnes as she hurried back to grab her purse. She didn't pause to speak, and he couldn't, not with Chef next to him, waiting for those leeks, waiting for Hen's next moves. As she scurried out the door, Hen longed to follow and ask what had so obviously frightened her.

Was Brisa hurt? Had something happened?

Of course something had happened. But he still had leeks to soften and vegetables to chop and food to plate. He couldn't leave. Not until closing and clean-up.

He shifted his thoughts back to the job in front of him and by rote did what needed doing. The minutes passed, and he kept busy, Chef kept busy, the world kept busy.

What about Agnes?

"You worried about her?" Chef asked, his gaze focused on the two plates in front of him and the horseradish garnish he was spooning in small dollops.

Hen stopped what he was doing. "How did you—?"

"What? You think you can keep a secret in this small kitchen?" Chef looked at his watch. "Go. I can handle the rest."

Hen shed his apron. "I owe you."

"You do."

"Thanks, man."

## 20

## DARLING

The high ground. Take the high road and play the long game, that's what Darling told himself. No matter how much he'd like to whisk Brisa away with him.

And face kidnapping charges.

No thank you.

Time to get this daughter of his—and that still amazed him—back to her mother before that mother noticed her absence and called the cops.

"Give me a minute." He held up a finger, grabbed clean slacks and a decent shirt, and closed the bathroom door behind him.

When he came out, he felt able to face a furious mother hen if he had to. "Come on. Your mama must be frantic with worry."

"She wasn't home when I left."

"Who's that staying with you? The black lady?"

"Mrs. Barnes. She's living with us so there's somebody to take care of me when Mom works. Not that I need anyone. I'm old enough to stay alone."

Of course, Agnes Jones would be the sort to keep the kid guarded, only that hadn't worked out so well this time, had it?

"Well, let's get you home before she arrives. Or before your sitter misses you. I assume she doesn't know you escaped?"

"I climbed out the back window and shimmied down a big tree."

"Enterprising and unafraid." He grinned.

He caught a glimpse of her smile, but she was looking down, as if suddenly shy.

He led the way outside and down to the street. Brisa scuffed her feet, so he tried for upbeat. "We'll work on your mama, get her to let you spend time with me. But you know, we'll only get her to agree if we toe the line. You get that, right?"

"I guess."

"She gets super mad at me, she's not going to cooperate. Right?"

"Yeah."

Beyond the streetlight it was too dark to see her expression, but he could tell she was looking up at him. He touched her head. "You just keep that credit card hidden and at the ready. Remember, there's power in it. And if I have to get back to California without seeing you again, you just remember what I told you. Call anytime."

She reached out a hand. Startled, he took it and held on.

When they got to her porch, she said, "Thank you. I hope she lets me see you again."

"I hope so, too. But we'll work it—"

The front door opened as the porch light snapped on, and Agnes stepped out. "Brisa, in the house. Now."

Brisa scurried up the steps and dashed around her mother. She paused to wave back at him.

"*Now*, Brisa." Agnes waited for their daughter to close the door behind her. "What are you trying to do, Darlington?"

He stuck his fingers in his front pockets as he approached the porch. "I had no idea she'd come to the inn to see me, and I brought her right home. You have to admit, though, by refusing to give me access to her, you've made me a whole lot more attractive. Seems the girl has been longing for a daddy."

A loud poof came from Agnes's pursed lips. That overhead light didn't accentuate her better features—if she had any left. Curves, yes, but for the rest? He must have liked something about the woman thirteen years ago, something that had made him single her out for his attentions. Unless it had merely been her obvious fascination with him.

That didn't seem like enough of a reason. Lots of young women fawned over him. Still, she was the one he'd chosen that night.

Oh, well. He wasn't going to regret it, not when it had given him that gorgeous daughter. Who wanted to be with her daddy.

Oh, yeah. And her daddy wanted to be with her.

Agnes was trying to shoo him away like he was a stray dog she didn't want coming too close. "Listen. You haven't shown interest since that night. Not a word. No curiosity. Nothing. So what makes you think you can come waltzing into our life now? What are you hoping to get out of it?"

"I didn't know about her. I had no idea I had a daughter."

"You might have known if you'd bothered to ask. You know, after you raped me." She spoke that last in a lowered voice that had gone gravelly and sounded as if she were spitting the words along with rocks she'd probably like to throw in his face.

Yep. The porch light amplified what he could only describe as a snarling, mad-dog look.

"You're exaggerating," he said. "It wasn't rape."

"And you're delusional. I was drugged."

"Honey, you wanted me."

"I was a teenager. I wanted your smile, your attention, not your body. Sex never occurred to me."

"Yeah, well, you looked eager enough that I was convinced."

A car pulled into the drive. Darling turned as a man climbed from a Jeep. "Agnes, you okay?" the man asked. "Mrs. Barnes called, said you might need some help."

"Hey, Lieutenant Dougherty."

The man approached, took out his badge, and flashed it toward Darling.

Darling extended a hand. "Darling Evermire. My daughter came to find me at the inn up the road. I just brought her home."

"It's kind of late for a child Brisa's age to be out on her own visiting a stranger."

"That's the problem, isn't it, detective? I'm a stranger to her, and she wants to get to know me as much as I want to get to know her."

"I understand there's some question about your right to do that, Mr. Evermire. Seeing as how you've been absent from her life all these years."

Darling waved that away. "Only because no one bothered to tell me she'd been born—or even that Agnes was pregnant. I'd have been there, certainly would have been involved financially, if anyone had mentioned it."

"Well, I'll tell you what's going to happen right now," the detective said. "This isn't the place to be holding this conversation, so why don't you go on back to your hotel room, and Ms. Jones' lawyer can get in touch with you tomorrow. Maybe you two can work out something amicable that will protect the interests of Brisa." The detective glanced at Agnes and then back at him. "I assume she's your primary concern?"

"Of course," he said.

"You need a ride back?"

Darling shook his head, turned, and headed down the walkway toward the street. That policeman. Smug son of a...

But Darling dropped the curse word. He'd been trying his best (see, he'd curbed himself there, too, sticking in a namby-pamby word like "best" instead of the much stronger d-word) to clean up his language, and that meant he had to get his head in line, too. He'd been real sloppy with cusses since he'd left Mama Bea's, but he knew the South, and when it came to custody, no respectable Southern judge was going to give him the time of day if he presented himself as a foul-mouthed partier from Tinseltown.

21

AGNES

Agnes waited with Clay as Darlington sauntered off. "Come on in," she said finally. "I know it's late, but I might as well give you a cup of coffee or something now you're here."

"Water's all I need." He was already stepping through the door when he spoke. "Hey, Becca. How's it going?"

"Fine, Mr. Clay. That man gone?"

Clay grinned at her. "He is."

"For now," Agnes said.

"I'll get that water," Mrs. Barnes said. "You need anything, Miss Agnes?"

"Nothing, thank you."

The other woman headed toward the kitchen, and Agnes led Clay to the living room. "Have a seat," she said, indicating one of the big leather chairs. She perched on the edge of the couch. "Your coming was timely. Thank you. I thought I'd die when Becca called to say Brisa was missing." At least the call to the restaurant hadn't come during a busy time and she'd been able to leave without a huge hullabaloo. "Becca was in a state."

Becca Barnes handed Clay a glass. "I went up to check on Brisa, like I'd promised, and the child didn't answer my knock.

So I peeked in. Soon's I opened her door, I knowed something was wrong. Link was waiting there, whining, so I checked other rooms. The wide-open window told me she'd gone runnin'."

"By the time I got home, I was so angry I wanted to spit nails."

"I wasn't far behind you, Miss Agnes. That man had the *gall* to sashay up to this door!"

Clay's laugh was not contagious. "Easy for you to find humor in this," Agnes told him, "but I wanted to kill him."

"Can't blame you." Clay glanced around the downstairs. "Where's Brisa now?"

"I'm sure she stomped off upstairs."

"Does she know the truth?" Clay asked.

Agnes took a step back. "Do you?"

"Only that there had to be a reason you didn't tell the father about his daughter—and he's obviously her father."

"Obviously. And there's a very good reason I never told him —or her."

"I assume Becca and Rita know the full story," he said and waited for her to nod. "If you think I can help you better by knowing what we're up against, I'd be happy to listen."

"Fine." He was a policeman, after all.

"You need me?" Becca asked.

"You must be exhausted."

"I'm okay. Just don't want to intrude."

"Then sit down. You aren't intruding."

Mrs. Barnes sat at the other end of the couch, her pose restful. Agnes wished she could relax into any of this. She hated letting people know what a fool she'd been, and this man? This police lieutenant with eyes that held such compassion?

She glanced toward him and cleared her throat. A knock sounded on the front door. Whoever it was hadn't chosen the doorbell.

"You expectin' anyone?" Mrs. Barnes asked.

Agnes shook her head. "But don't you bother getting up," she said, with a wave of her hand as she stood.

Clay ignored the wave and followed her to the hall. It comforted her, having a policeman at her back.

And there, on the other side of the door, stood Henry. "Agnes," he said.

Clay spoke over her shoulder. "Henry, hey."

"Clay." Hen glanced behind her and then returned his gaze to her. "Everything okay here?"

"Come in," she said, stepping back so he could enter.

They stood, the three of them, in a loose circle in the wide hall, just inside the door. Hen cleared his throat. "I was worried about you, the way you dashed off."

Heat crept up her neck to flood her cheeks. "I was about to explain everything to Clay. Mrs. Barnes is here, too. Have you met her?"

"I don't think so," Hen said.

Once they returned to the living room, Agnes made the introduction and tried to tell her story. She got as far as the club bar and her fascination with a world she'd never let herself enter. She mentioned the other girls and the fake ID.

The rest stuck in her throat because she saw again the gorgeous caramel-colored face smiling at her, stunning her with his thousand watts of charm. As if his smile wiped her brain clean of all its stored intelligence, she'd forgotten words of warning when his fingers slid a glass of wine her way, when his voice said something like "A lovely vintage for a lovely woman."

She hadn't been lovely, but for a moment he'd made her believe that perhaps, just perhaps, he thought so. For that moment.

She couldn't admit those thoughts, the reckless abandon that had overcome her scruples and allowed her to thank Darling Evermire for the drink and for his kindness. Henry watched her with a look of compassion on his face, and she couldn't speak the sordid details of her messy past. Instead, she pressed her palms against her eyes and bent her head.

Hen seemed to read her mind. "It's okay. You don't have to continue." He stood. "If I make you uncomfortable, I'll leave. I just wanted to be sure you were okay."

She shook her head. She didn't want him to leave. She really didn't.

And yet a part of her really did and was nudging her to get up and usher him right out the door. "Please stay."

He raised a quizzical brow and waited. When she added a quick nod, he returned to his seat. Agnes needed to grease her throat and her lips and let the story slide out. It wouldn't take long.

Not if she could get going.

She closed her eyes, pulled in a slow, deep breath, and almost laughed at the image of grease and slippery words.

"It was like this," she began again, and this time the words came, and the story unfolded.

And in the end, it wasn't so bad.

Not really.

———

She should have offered Henry something to drink, but should-haves meant very little right then. She was talked out, and whatever words remained needed to be directed at her daughter.

Hen spoke softly as he stood. "Thank you for letting me hear your story. It must have been hard to tell. May I call you tomorrow?"

She nodded and loosed her best half-smile, first him and then at Clay as she showed them out. Mrs. Barnes had already gone to the back of the house, saying, "I'll get the lights."

Heading up the stairs, Agnes sighed. Now that Brisa knew who her father was, keeping them separated was going to be like scaling the overhang of an ice cliff where she'd have no traction at all—and nothing to grab onto if she wasn't willing to tell Brisa about the rape.

She didn't bother to knock on the door. As she hit the wall switch, Brisa yanked the covers over her head, and Link looked up. Agnes pulled out the desk chair and turned it so she could sit looking at her daughter without touching her. "I suppose I'll have to put bars on that window if you plan to use it as your preferred exit route."

Brisa mumbled from under the sheet. "You can't do that."

"Oh, yeah? And who says so?"

That got the sheet down and a glare from those dark eyes. "You just can't. It's wrong. Child endangerment or something. If there's a fire."

"What's wrong is that you disobeyed me and sneaked out of the house without permission."

"I didn't disobey you." Brisa sat up, propping herself against the headboard. The glare had morphed to cunning. "You never said I couldn't go see him at the inn. And you never said I couldn't climb down the tree."

"Those come under the heading of not being sneaky. Of obeying the spirit of the law."

"Ha! You were sneaky and lying all my life, saying you didn't know anything about my dad. You knew who he was all the time."

"I also knew what he'd done to me. And that he hadn't cared about you."

Brisa looked down as if studying her hands as they clasped the coverlet. "That's not true. He didn't know about me."

"I'm not going to talk to you when you're being disrespectful," Agnes said, standing again. "But don't you dare sneak out that window again. You try it, and the bars go up."

Her daughter's head shot up. "You're a horrible mother! I hate you!"

On those words of cheer, Agnes let herself out of the room

and into her own. There was nothing more she could say, was there?

Yes, there was. And she would have to do it. Knowledge was power. A description of date rape and drugs had to enter this conversation.

Agnes closed her door and leaned back against the wooden surface. And then, with tears filling her eyes, she whispered, "God, are you there? Because I've got a kid who hurts, and I'm not doing so great either."

Agnes had heard thunder offshore in the early hours of a sleepless night, but it was still dry when she stepped onto the back porch, her mug in hand, and wandered toward the now-barren fig tree that had madly sent out new growth last summer. And figs, although she'd only picked a few. She should have gathered them to share. She should have. So many should-haves.

What was she going to do about Darlington and the ache in her gut? With the cat out of the proverbial bag, she couldn't very well keep Brisa locked away from him forever.

Her daughter had refused to get up when Agnes had gone in to rouse her for school, and Agnes had backed off, because she didn't have the energy to fight this morning. Besides, based on yesterday's performance, Agnes wouldn't bet on Brisa actually staying in school, not with the temptation of Darling just down the road.

No, it would be better to keep the girl here and under her watchful eyes.

A soft song wafted through the partially opened kitchen window as Becca worked to the rhythm of her own music. The sound was soothing enough that Agnes lowered herself to the top porch step to finish her coffee.

It was an old hymn, one she remembered from her childhood

when they still went to church. And just like that, she had to blink back tears.

Because the other woman sang about an old rugged cross. Who knew what Becca'd come back with after she went to church. She'd promised to pray and get her church praying, which was a good thing, wasn't it? Prayers couldn't hurt.

Agnes just hoped they helped.

She waited until nine to call Rita. In the background at Rita's house, someone laughed, ostensibly Martin. Agnes hoped she wasn't interrupting anything, but the humor in Rita's voice when she spoke made Agnes imagine a shared joke. Or a shared something else.

"I'm sorry I couldn't get there last night, but at least Clay did. I have a call in to the inn, and I'll make an appointment to see Darlington this afternoon."

"Thank you."

"I need to tell you, Agnes, North Carolina law only allows a restriction of parental rights if the father has been convicted of a rape that resulted in the pregnancy. As you have no conviction—and didn't even report the rape—Darlington is within his rights to seek custody, presumably joint, or at least visitation."

"That can't happen." *Please, no.*

"I'm afraid it can. We can delay it by insisting on a paternity test, but that's not going to take long. And then he'll have to hire a lawyer and petition the courts for his parental rights. Justice is never speedy, and that could delay it again."

"But you're saying he will win. And I can't afford a court battle."

"Then let's see what we can manage through negotiation."

"Oh, Rita." She couldn't. The idea of that man having her girl, even for a visit, made her sick to her stomach. "He's a horrible man. I don't want him to have any hold on Brisa. I don't!"

Those last words screamed on repeat in her head. *Please. Oh please.*

She used the excuse of food to knock on Brisa's door. When she didn't get an answer, she turned the knob and entered. Her daughter lay curled around Link, who'd come back up for his morning nap. Link opened one eye, decided she posed no threat to his comfort, and closed it again. Brisa didn't move, which meant she was probably feigning sleep.

Agnes sat on the edge of the bed and patted Brisa's hip. "Aren't you hungry?"

"Un-unh."

"Well, we need to talk."

Her daughter grunted.

"Can you please sit up? I have something I need to tell you about your father."

"No." The word wasn't spoken softly or deferentially, but with anger.

Taken aback, Agnes stared at this foreign entity who looked like her child, had the voice of her child, but spoke with a new defiance.

"Excuse me, but yes." Agnes waited a moment. "Now, Brisa. Turn around and look at me."

Brisa didn't move.

"I said *now*."

Slowly, Brisa shifted until she faced her mother, but she kept her focus averted.

"The story isn't a nice one, and I wasn't going to tell you," Agnes said, "but now I think I must. For your own protection." She paused and took a deep breath. This was so hard. "I was very young, and I did a foolish thing. I went to a place where they sold alcoholic drinks before I was legally allowed."

"You *broke the law*?"

"I did." Maybe she shouldn't have begun with that tidbit. She could imagine it coming back to haunt her.

Oh, well, no unsaying it now. She steeled herself for what would come next.

Describing the scene was difficult, the handsome singer approaching her, offering her a drink. "I was so flattered he seemed interested in me, and I said yes." That much had been her fault, her stupidity. These rest was on him. "If it had only been a glass of wine… but he'd added a drug, a very dangerous drug. I was too young to know about such things. They weren't talked about in my world."

Agnes wondered if they were spoken of in high schools here. They should be. All girls should be warned. "The drug was the sort that makes a person forget what happens. It sort of wipes out memory."

She took another deep breath as Brisa stared, wide-eyed.

"Once the drug began to take effect, he took me to a room in a hotel. As I said, I don't remember what happened next. I only know that when I woke up, I was alone in that room, and I was pregnant with you."

Her daughter sat up and wrapped her arms around her bent knees, her eyes uncomprehending. "How? You went to sleep and woke up pregnant? That doesn't make any sense."

Agnes wanted to reach out and touch her daughter, this too-young girl who should never have had to hear this story, but she held back. "You know how babies are conceived. It's a lovely thing when the parents are married and they both want to be together in that way. When they're not—"

"Sex. You're talking about sex. You had *sex* with my father."

"But I didn't have it willingly. I was raped."

"Raped? *Raped?*" Brisa shook her head vehemently. "No, you're lying. He wouldn't do that. My daddy's a good man, and he'd never *ever* hurt anyone."

Agnes sighed. She'd known this was going to be hard. "I'm afraid that night he did hurt me."

"Nope. No." Brisa scooted past her off the bed. With her hands braced on her hips, she leaned forward and almost spit the words. "You're just making that up because he didn't want you. You never even *told* him about me." She shuffled one step back. "You kept it a secret from him and from me, even though you *knew* I wanted a daddy and he would have *wanted* me if you'd told. He would have *loved* me." Choking sobs broke from her. "You... you k...kept him from me... because he didn't love *you*." Swiping at her eyes and sniffling, she said over her tears, "He loves *me*. He would have *always* loved me. And I won't let you ruin this. I won't!"

And, finally, through her bathroom door, she wailed, "I *hate* you!"

## 22

## DARLING

Darling picked up his order of a steaming latte and carried it to the table where the lawyer sat. He'd been surprised to see a woman whose skin was a mere shade darker than his own. She was lovely, really, and he might have shown his appreciation if she hadn't worn a ring on her finger—and if she weren't representing the woman he'd come to believe his enemy.

He'd done some research last night, following up on what Arthur had sent, and it would take very little for him to establish his rights for visitation. But he didn't want that. He wanted his daughter to be his. His and Lisette's.

"Now," he said, easing his length into the chair across from her, "how can I help you?"

She didn't smile. "You can stay away from my client—and her daughter."

"My daughter also."

"That's yet to be determined."

"Happy to submit to a paternity test, but all you have to do is look at Brisa to know for certain."

"My client wants nothing to do with you."

"Counselor, that's not worthy of you or the situation."

She looked affronted. And she did the look well. "What is it you want? Other than to buy your daughter."

"Really? *Buy* her?" He pasted on a sad expression. "I thought of it as missed support payments."

"Which would be a whole lot more than that fifty thousand you offered my client. Think more like nine hundred thousand."

He hiked his brows. "Are you now offering to sell my daughter for that amount?"

"I am, as you know well, merely stating that if you'd been paying a mandated child support in New Jersey all these years, you'd have paid a lot more than the measly figure you offered."

He plowed his fingers through his thick hair. "Help me out here, Rita." He tried for sheepish. "May I call you Rita?"

"I'd prefer Mrs. Levinson."

"Okay. But feel free to call me Darling."

"Let's keep it professional, please. I'm not here to be your friend. I'm here to help my client."

He sighed. "Mrs. Levinson, surely there's a way we can work this out so everyone's happy. I didn't know about my daughter for the first twelve years of her life, and I want to spend time with her. You can understand that, can't you?"

"And I'm sure you can understand my client's reluctance to allow you near her or her daughter. Your behavior almost thirteen years ago did not endear you to Ms. Jones. You, in fact, raped her."

He moved his hands to his lap so she wouldn't see the fists he made as he told himself to calm down, keep cool, smile. He gave himself a minute to regain control. "I'm sorry, but that allegation is patently false. Your client approached me at the bar and obviously wanted the encounter that happened between us. It was consensual."

"And then you deserted her and never contacted her to find out if there were consequences of the rape."

"Counselor, that assertion will not hold up in a court of law, not after all this time. Did your client report a rape?" Thank heavens Arthur'd coached him after talking to their lawyer. "Did she get a rape kit? Was there evidence, other than her word, all these years later?"

The lawyer cleared her throat. "We are fortunate to live in a time when sexual predators such as yourself are being exposed for what they are and what they did. There's no statute of limitations on rape. I am convinced that the media would have a field day with my client's assertions. They don't seem to need proof, do they? And my client was a young, impressionable college student with excellent grades who was preyed upon by a semi-celebrity who got his way through a date rape drug."

"Now, now, Mrs. Levinson. Agnes will come off looking ridiculous. I'm a happily married man with no blemishes on my character. And when Brisa was conceived, Ms. Jones and I were both young and foolish. I'm older now. I've changed, and I'm eager to get to know my daughter." And he'd read the law that said he had rights here. Neither this lawyer nor *Ms.* Jones would be able to keep him from seeing Brisa. *His* daughter.

"Have you?" the lawyer asked. "Because it looks from here as if you're still living the same life—although perhaps on a larger scale—and that life offers all the wrong messages to a young, impressionable girl. Because of the manner in which Brisa was conceived and because of my client's stellar character, she and her daughter live a quiet, conservative life."

"Commendable, of course, but it doesn't speak to my right to know my daughter or her right to know me."

"Also," Mrs. Levinson continued as if he hadn't spoken, "in our culture, Brisa has a mark against her because she is illegitimate."

Darling snorted. "In today's world? Illegitimacy no longer carries a stigma."

"Maybe not where you come from, but here? It matters. And if you disrupt her life and try to introduce a vulnerable child to your affluent lifestyle, what do you think it will do to her? It will ruin her life. And what happens to Brisa when you lose interest?"

He cracked his knuckles, first on one hand and then the other. Anything to keep from pounding the table in front of him. This woman, this *small-time, small-town* lawyer was judging *him* and *his* lifestyle?

*Breathe*, he told himself. Take a step back. She was just doing her job.

But he'd crucify her in court.

"Mrs. Levinson," he finally said, "I don't appreciate being judged by you when you have absolutely no idea how I live or what I might bring into my daughter's—*my* daughter's—life. And if that's the best you can do to try to negotiate with me, then I'll see you in court."

She stood. "I'll look forward to it. You have my phone number and address. I'll expect to hear from your legal counsel." At the side of the table, she paused. "In the meantime, Mr. Evermire, keep your distance from my client and her daughter."

## 23

## AGNES

B risa remained tight-lipped all morning, but just before noon, she came into the kitchen and announced she wanted to go to school because she didn't want to miss her spelling test. "Will you take me?"

"Sure."

Brisa was a good student, so not wanting to miss a spelling test made sense. And she'd want her grades up so spring break, which coincided with the Easter holidays this year, wouldn't have to act as a reset button.

Becca walked in and overheard this request. "Since I'm going out to run some errands, I'll drop you off."

"Thanks, Becca. I'll write a quick note."

While Brisa ate a bagel slathered with peanut butter and jam, Agnes went upstairs to draft an excuse for her daughter's tardiness. She kept it general, merely saying that Brisa hadn't felt well enough to get up that morning but seemed fine now. She wanted to tell the school secretary to guard her daughter with her life. It was terrible when you felt as if you needed an ankle monitor to know where your child was at all times.

After she'd seen them off, she cleaned up the mess Brisa'd

left and wiped down the counters. Then she sprayed them and wiped again, because her hands needed something to do other than open the refrigerator again—in case there might be something to tempt her toward food. Those nerves had clamped around her stomach again, shrinking it to fist size. The flesh on her belly hadn't shrunk, just the stomach beneath.

It was two o'clock before Rita called to report on her conversation with Darlington. Agnes was on her second cup of coffee, and she stared out the kitchen window as she listened.

"I'm going to file a Complaint along with an Order of Protection," Rita said. "I also think you need to consider charging him with rape. Even if it can't be proved, it will give you the advantage of filing the first complaint. The way the press seems to be on the side of women who come forward, even years later, can work to our advantage."

"Okay."

And then she thought of it, the press, the mess, Brisa. And she said, "I hate thinking of people here reading about Brisa's conception in the local papers—or Brisa seeing herself named in the media next to Darlington."

"I know. But who is going to tell the press, what there is of it here? It's not like he's a media sensation in downtown Beaufort. I'm going to call Eric Houston and talk to him. He may be better able to give you good advice than I. He had experience as a trial lawyer before he moved here."

Eric Houston. Hen's brother.

This was the problem with small towns. Everyone seemed to know everyone else, which meant privacy didn't exist. Agnes sighed and asked, "He'll be bound by confidentiality, won't he?"

"Of course. You don't need to worry about it getting out."

But she did. Too many people knew. Far too many who weren't sworn to secrecy.

Next, because the Darlington issue wasn't her only concern, she spent an hour trying to track down workmen who'd dealt with her mother's repairs. She'd left messages last week. She left them again now.

And the day dragged. She wanted to scream.

It wasn't until she'd seen a still-unhappy Brisa off to school on the next morning that she gave up waiting for the workmen to call back and phoned the law office handling her mother's estate. If she had to fight in court to keep Brisa here, she would need money.

She'd left messages for Mr. Gillespie, telling him about the information she was trying to uncover, but she still hadn't heard back from him. Nobody seemed to return calls around here. It was killing her. Finally, the receptionist answered and transferred her call to a Mr. Matthews, who seemed surprised no one had told her of Mr. Gillespie's illness or the fact that he'd retired because of it.

"I'm sorry for the silence at this end," he said. "It's been hectic around here. Anyway, based on your last message, I set an investigator on the case. He found the general contractor for the kitchen remodel who has promised to come forth with relevant receipts."

"Really? That's wonderful."

"As soon as I have all the evidence, I'll draft a letter to opposing counsel based on the fact that repairs happened long after the petitioners' mother divorced the judge."

"That's good, isn't it?" Agnes asked. "That will take care of all of this?"

"It will. But nothing runs swiftly in this business, so it may be a while before we can actually settle the estate. I'm petitioning the courts to allow me to release funds for your use in the meantime."

"Oh, thank you! That would be fantastic."

"That's a lot of house for you to maintain on your own. I'm only sorry it's taken this long. With Winfred Gillespie in the hospital off and on, I've had a lot to do to pick up the pieces he left."

And hers obviously had seemed the least important. "I understand."

"Still, someone should have been doing something to help you out. I do apologize."

"At least things are finally happening. I should be grateful for that." And she had made it to this point. She'd survived. That was something to be grateful for—and to feel good about.

Her mother hadn't been there for her thirteen years ago, but Agnes supposed she'd tried to make up for it by leaving her the house.

*My letter, Agnes?*

Agnes waved a hand as if to shush a real person standing nearby. Her head was what needed hushing.

Things were moving forward. There'd be money to pay for the house soon. And perhaps enough to fight Darlington.

At least enough to delay the inevitable while Brisa grew a little older, perhaps a little wiser to the ways of the world. *His* world.

Agnes managed to destroy both thumb nails as she fretted through the day. She was picking at the left one when Henry called and she told him about her talk with Brisa.

"You'd better not come over," she told him. "She's giving me the silent treatment. It doesn't make for a pleasant atmosphere."

"Do kids her age even know about the silent treatment? I thought they had temper tantrums and then got over it," Henry said.

She appreciated him trying to lighten the mood. "Those are boys. And two-year-old girls." She paused. "That child used to be so sweet. Cuddly, loving, obedient."

"She'll be that again. You just hit her with a lot."

"I did. And I have no idea if it did any good, other than to make her think she hates me."

"That will pass, and you've armed her with the truth."

"Pray?"

"Of course," he said. "Call me if you need company."

"Thanks."

## 24

## DARLING

According to Arthur, it had been a productive day in California, which meant they'd both accomplished something. Arthur had been in touch with the lawyer Daddy'd recommended, and the man was preparing a Complaint against Agnes Jones. "You're the Plaintiff—don't you love that? Plaintiff? —and you're attesting to the fact that you and Agnes Jones had a consensual one-night stand. After that, the Defendant, Ms. Jones, failed to tell you she had conceived a child. We're willing to submit to a DNA test to prove you're the father of Agnes Jones' child, which gives you the right to shared custody."

"Good. How soon will that be ready?"

"By Monday, is my guess. We file here and then we deliver papers to NC. Somebody there, a process server of some sort, delivers them to Ms. Jones."

"That'll wake her up."

"In the meantime, you get that pilot to bring you on home. We're not cancelling the concert just because you have this hanging over you. The band has been practicing with the new drummer, but they can't manage without you."

"Fine. Heading back tonight unless I hit a glitch. At any rate, I'll be around tomorrow morning."

After meeting with Agnes's lawyer, he'd bought a cell phone, which he'd added to his plan. He'd discovered Brisa's bus route and the time she normally got off as well as the route she took home. It shouldn't be that difficult to make the transfer someplace in those four blocks.

Then, she'd have a phone and a credit card. He'd be surprised if a smart child such as Brisa failed to figure out how to use both to get her own way, mad as she was at her mama for keeping him a secret.

---

He parked where he could see the school bus drop off the kids, and when Brisa headed off on her own, he put the car in gear and followed slowly. Her hair bounced as she hurried along the sidewalk while other kids hung out in a group near the bus stop. He smiled and drew his car up beside her. She turned.

"Daddy!"

He loved that she called him daddy. "Hey, honey. I wanted to say goodbye. I've got a concert I've got to go home for, but I'll be back to see you when I can."

"I was afraid you'd already gone. You sure you have to leave already?"

"I do. But I bought you something." He held out the small box. "It's all set up. The passcode to get into the phone is the day we met. You can remember that, can't you? Yesterday's date, using six digits? And I've put my phone number in it, so you can call or text me whenever you want. You don't have to worry about the cost. It's yours."

"Mine?" Her eyes brightened as she took the box.

"I don't think you ought to show it to your mama. Can it be our secret?"

"Of course!"

"Good. There's also a small zipper pouch for it so you can get rid of the box. I leave, you just tuck it all in your backpack, okay? Oh, and don't forget to keep it charged."

Her head bobbed excitedly. Good girl.

He noticed her little redheaded friend, the one he'd seen in those pictures Arthur'd given him, coming up behind. "Looks like you've got someone wanting to walk with you. Just take care of the phone and remember the card I gave you. Anytime you need something, you use it."

"Oh, thank you. Thank you so much!"

"We'll talk soon, okay?"

"Yes, sir." She clutched the box to her chest. "Oh, and good luck with the concert."

"I think my luck is all going to be good from now on, honey. All because of you."

Her eyes looked suspiciously damp.

Good. The hook was in and set.

## 25

## AGNES

B risa dashed up to her room after school, only taking time to yell, "I'm home!" The behavior seemed odd. She normally came straight back to the kitchen to raid the refrigerator, even these days when she wasn't speaking to her mother.

When she still hadn't come down ten minutes later, Agnes headed up and knocked on her daughter's door.

"Just a sec," Brisa called.

Agnes turned the knob, but the door was locked. Brisa's door was never supposed to be locked, a rule her daughter knew well. She knocked again. "Brisa, unlock this door. Now."

The knob turned, and Brisa opened the door.

Agnes stared at her. "What's got into you? Why the lock?"

Brisa didn't answer until she was sitting on her ruffly yellow bedspread, her knees up. "I need privacy. I'm not a baby anymore."

"What are you talking about? You have plenty of privacy without locking your door."

"I didn't want anyone just barging in."

"No one barges in. No one has ever barged in. I knock. I've always knocked on a closed door." Well, except the night Brisa sneaked out of the house, but that didn't count. A mother did what a mother had to do.

"Yeah, well, maybe Mrs. Barnes wouldn't."

Agnes blew out a loud breath. "Mrs. Barnes? Can you imagine her doing anything at all rude?"

When Brisa merely shrugged, Agnes glanced around, her eyes narrowing as she tried to imagine what her daughter might be hiding. Her white desk held schoolbooks. The chair Brisa's grandmother had covered in pink and yellow chintz was empty. But there had to be something.

"No, you can't imagine it," Agnes said, pulling her attention back to a pouty Brisa. "So, I'll ask you again. Why do you need this extra privacy? What's going on?"

"Nothing."

Obviously, this wasn't nothing, but Agnes couldn't force her daughter's confidence. On a loud sigh, she said, "I have to go soon, but Mrs. Barnes is making a delicious dinner. I want you to help her with clean-up. And be polite."

"I am."

It was true that she always used to be, Agnes admitted. But now, since the advent of that man into their world? Brisa was a different girl.

And didn't that put the fear of some vague something in her? She was convinced it had to do with Darlington. She'd phoned the inn just before leaving for work and discovered he had checked out. While that should have set her mind at ease, it didn't.

She served customers, but her smile was forced and she kept checking her watch. Once, she shook her wrist, sure the thing had stopped.

But, no, only time had, or rather, time marched as if it had glue on its soles.

Hen caught her as she waited for a drinks tray to be filled. "How are you doing?"

"Okay. Managing."

He leaned toward. "You need to talk, I'm here."

As he returned to the kitchen, she smiled slightly, her lips a tight line to keep them from quivering. The dear man. The very dear man.

And so she got through the evening.

Saturday morning, Brisa slept in and then, still non-communicative, asked if she could go play with Jilly. Agnes wanted her sunny-tempered daughter back and hoped that a morning with Jilly would do the trick.

She was on her way upstairs when Becca returned from her prayer meeting and announced she was about to go off to the Food Lion but wanted to check in, make sure Agnes didn't have anything else to add to the list.

"I don't think so," Agnes said. "You got my credit card?"

"Yes, ma'am, I do. I'll bring back the receipts."

Of course, she would. Becca was scrupulous with her bookkeeping and her purchasing. The woman was a godsend.

Agnes had reached her room when her cell phone rang. Tadie's number appeared on the screen. "Good morning," Agnes said. "Did Brisa arrive?"

"She did. The girls are out back while Sammy's napping. Do you have a minute?"

"Of course. What's up?"

"It may be nothing, but Jilly happened to mention that Brisa stopped to talk to a man in a black car on the way home from the bus stop yesterday. She also accepted something from him."

Darlington? Of course, Darlington. Brisa wouldn't speak to a stranger.

"Did she ask Brisa about it?"

"Brisa said it was nothing. But Jilly didn't think it was nothing."

"No, it wouldn't have been. That would have been her father."

"Her father? I thought she didn't know who her father was."

"She didn't. Now she does. He's Darlington Evermire."

"Darlington Evermire," Tadie said. "Why does that sound familiar?" She was silent for a couple of beats while Agnes waited. "Are you talking about *Darling?* The singer? *That* Darlington?"

"The very one."

"And you kept this a secret. Why?"

"I'd been hoping Brisa wouldn't have to know how she was conceived."

Then she told Tadie the story. All these years of keeping quiet, and now she'd shared it once, twice, three times in just a few days. What a strange turn of events.

"How can I help?" Tadie asked. "I'd be happy to do whatever you need."

"I don't know. Brisa's so angry…"

"We'll pray. Will and I will definitely be praying."

When Agnes hung up the phone, she imagined the knife she'd plunged through her daughter's heart when she'd explained that the father Brisa thought she adored was a man who could rape a drugged victim and never look back.

And then she saw the knife her daughter had plunged right back in this mother's heart when she'd rejected the truth and instead picked the man, the fake daddy.

---

She entered Brisa's room and rummaged. Somewhere in here, Brisa had hidden the thing Darlington had given her. Unless she carried it around in her backpack. Had she taken her backpack to Jilly's?

No, there it was. She searched it and found nothing unusual. There didn't seem to be anything out of place in her drawers, but that wasn't much of a surprise. Agnes checked behind the shoes in the closet, on the shelf, behind Brisa's books in the bookcase. Link joined her when she got on her knees and looked under the bed, but she found nothing except a stray sock and a dusty pencil.

She stood up and circled the room slowly. Under the mattress? She lifted first the head, then the foot, running her hand under it as she moved. Finally, her hand touched something. She extricated it and unzipped the pouch. Inside rested a neat little cell phone and its charger.

Darlington would have wanted a way to talk to Brisa directly. Secretly. Of course, he would.

She straightened the spread, erasing evidence of her investigation, and returned to her room. Then she hit the power button and waited. It needed a passcode. What would be the passcode?

Brisa's birthday? Darlington would have set it up, and did he even know the date she was born? Okay... Agnes tried to imagine something both he and Brisa would know, something important to both of them.

What about the day he'd met her, a birthdate of sorts? They'd remember, and so would Agnes, but for her it would never be a fond memory.

She keyed in the numbers, and just like that, it came to life.

There was only one name in the contacts list, his. He'd called himself *Daddy*.

A bullet would be too good for him. Agnes shuddered as she imagined all the things she'd like to do to make that man suffer. If only she were the sort who could carry out any one of them.

The haze behind her eyes morphed to full scarlet, and she bit the side of her cheek before curling her fingers into fists. The pain of her nails digging into her palms was salutary. Although she still imagined murder.

2 6

AGNES

Twelve seemed so far in Agnes's past and so obscured by her later messes that she could barely conjure a memory to go with the age. All she had was textbook authority when considering her daughter's moods and behavior. Twelve was on the cusp of teendom, and that felt too scary to consider, especially now that Brisa was pushing her way out of childhood so quickly. There would be hormone rages soon, along with an entirely new vulnerability.

Agnes had never been much of a rebel, not until that one night when she'd gone to a club and then taken that one risky drink. But she'd never not known her parents... or her step-parent. She'd never felt truly orphaned until she'd left home rather than abort her baby. At almost twelve? Well, when she'd been a preteen, she'd spent all her free time reading and studying. All of it.

What did she know about dealing with a child when all that child wanted was a daddy? Into that longing had slithered a handsome, famous father offering Brisa her own moon.

They had to come to an understanding before they held the as-yet-unplanned birthday party, before vacation began, and before they needed to get ready for Easter. Would this be the year she and Brisa faced off against each other in the silence of her daughter's anger and her own inability to fix things?

Agnes wished she could push her child back to babyhood. As hard as it had been with a toddler underfoot and barely sleeping, those days were nothing compared to this.

Nothing.

She carried a cup of tea into the living room and sank into one of the judge's two leather chairs. Her mother would have been swallowed by either, just as she was, and yet right now it cocooned her.

Until the angst-ridden cause of her worst worry barreled into the house, dashed up the stairs, and slammed her bedroom door. Agnes waited for the inevitable eruption. When it didn't come right away, she wondered if Brisa had discovered the phone's disappearance. Was she only biding her time? What was going on in that pre-teen brain?

Agnes didn't move. Perhaps if she stayed where she was, nothing more would happen to disrupt the stillness of the living room. Mrs. Barnes wouldn't be back until right before Agnes left for work, and as she was scheduled for clean-up and not set-up, that wouldn't be for another hour. Still, she was sorry Becca wasn't here yet. She'd like to pretend to civility with someone, preferably an adult who'd been through storms of equal ferocity. And Becca Barnes had.

The tea had cooled in her cup, but she sipped it anyway. It gave her hands something to do.

Upstairs, the stereo in Brisa's room blared, the volume raised so her mother would hear Darling's songs through the door, down the stairs, and into the living room. The child would go deaf if she kept it that loud for long.

But Agnes only winced and waited.

She had things she ought to be doing. Laundry to fold. Ironing. She should be planning a birthday party for her daughter, but that needed the daughter's involvement. The daughter who'd just stared at her when she'd mentioned it a week ago. Stared and shrugged and finally said, "You know what I want, but you won't give it to me."

Her father. She'd wanted her father.

Agnes felt the weight of that, ten pounds, at least, added to each shoulder, ten more to her gut. Thirty extra would bend her over until she became hunchbacked, stooped and old. And no good at all to anyone.

"Stop." Her voice said the word, but her ears couldn't hear it over *his* music. So she only thought the next admonition.

Get up, get busy, forget about anything other than doing what's first.

She needed to iron a blouse for tonight. She headed to the laundry room, got out the ironing board, plugged in the iron, and found the newly washed blouse on its hanger. She had just sprinkled it and was letting it sit for a moment when the first scream came from the top of the stairs. The second one resembled an agonized howl, followed by "What did you do with it?" as Brisa thundered down the stairs and toward the kitchen. Then the person who had once been her sweet, innocent daughter was in her face, tears of frustration streaming from her eyes, her expression contorted in fury. "How could you! How dare you!"

Agnes spread the blouse on the ironing board, waiting a long minute before she looked up at her panting child. "I am your mother."

"That doesn't give you the right to take what's mine!" She looked like she was about to stomp her feet in frustration. "It was given to *me!*"

"As a matter of fact, being your mother gives me every right to protect you and to keep you from harm." Don't react, Agnes told herself. Be the adult.

"*Harm?* What harm? He won't hurt me. He's my *father.*" Brisa's voice brimmed with angry frustration. "He *loves* me."

"Okay, it's time for you to calm down." Agnes modulated her

tone, keeping her voice low when she wanted to sledge-hammer the words.

"Calm down? Calm *down*?" Brisa flung her hands up. "How do I calm *down* when my own *mother* sneaks into my room and *steals* from me? When you hide who my daddy is, then you lie about him because he didn't love *you*, and then you go hunting for the phone he gave me only so I could *talk* to him? You had no *right!*"

"Brisa, you are my daughter, and I love you, but you may not speak to me in that tone of voice." Agnes waited. "Do you understand?" She'd never imagined such an ugly glare coming from her child's beautiful face.

"You're a horrible mother!"

Brisa fled. Moments later, her door slammed.

Sliding onto the nearest chair, Agnes stared blankly. How had they come to this place, her beloved daughter and she? Brisa, the child of her heart, hated her.

It was all his fault.

His fault. "His fault, his, his, his…"

That last was a whisper wrapping her in a ghost-like sibilance.

---

The evidence that Becca had already been in the kitchen greeted Agnes from the counter: a clean mug, a pot of coffee, and a tin of bran muffins. The scents kicked her more fully awake, and she poured a cup, doctored it, and took her mug and a muffin to the back porch.

The sun shone, bright and warm. The lawn looked so much better, but she hadn't pulled a weed in months, and didn't they seem to know it, popping up uninvited everywhere she looked. The worst offenders faced the street, where her mother had once planted flowers in front of a line of azaleas. Now that the pinks and purples of those bushes were grabbing attention, the messy weeds were, too. She could yank them up while she waited out the morning's silence from upstairs.

Her clothes were grubby enough for yard work, but still she dawdled as she finished her breakfast, added her plate and mug to the dishwasher, and wiped down the counters. Eventually, though, all she had to do was unearth gardening gloves and a trowel from the bin at the back of the pantry. Those found, she squared her shoulders and headed outside. "You're going to be so proud of yourself."

Like Brisa's friends, hers, including Becca, had gone to church. Her still-silent and sullen daughter remained tucked in her room after one foray into the kitchen to grab a bowl of cereal. Agnes only knew that because, when she'd gone inside to grab a glass of water, she'd found milk splashes on the counter and an unwashed bowl in the sink.

Poor Brisa, miserable and neglected with no one available to listen to her moaning. And, yes, her mother was being sarcastic, although Agnes admitted she'd like a listener of her own. She, too, had moans aplenty bouncing around in her mind.

She dug and yanked at green shoots she was pretty sure didn't belong—at least, she hoped they didn't—ignoring street noises and the sounds of pedestrians on the sidewalk. Tourists would be out today, enjoying Beaufort, so she didn't notice the footsteps coming up her walkway until a voice said, "Looking good."

She sat back on her heels and turned to see Hen grinning down at her. "Thank you."

Sunlight glinted off his dark hair and put his eyes in shadow, emphasizing only the lines at their edges. Her heart sped to a glad dance.

"I came to ask if you'd like to go for coffee," he said, "or lunch, if you haven't eaten."

"Really?"

He laughed. "Yes, really."

She glanced back at the house. "I wish I could, but Brisa has shut herself up in her room at least until Jilly gets home."

"Ah, then may I sit here a while and watch?"

She stood, took off her gloves, and grabbed the trowel. "I don't need an audience, thank you."

"I thought maybe you'd like a weeding coach, you know, so you don't pull out any more flower bulbs."

"I didn't!" She bent over her nearest pile and squinted. Nothing looked suspicious. "Okay, big shot, where's the flower I supposedly murdered?"

He picked up a small bulbous root and dangled it by its green shoots. "*Et voilà.*"

"And what is that exactly?"

He brought it closer to his face. "Beats me." And then he sniffed it before tossing it back to the ground. "Onion, or its cousin."

Laughing, she said, "You had me for a moment. I thought you knew what you were talking about."

"I thought I did, too."

"Come on inside. I should be able to find something we can eat." She led the way to the kitchen. There were muffins and… What could she offer him? Ah, the leftover stew. "Becca made beef stew. You interested?" she asked as she washed her hands, handing him the soap when he stepped up.

"Perfect."

She turned the burner under the stew pot to low, and he said, "Point me to the glasses and bowls."

"Cupboard behind you."

Meanwhile, she stirred the soup and laid cutlery on the table, along with a plate of muffins.

"Butter?" he asked, opening the refrigerator door and finding it.

With her back to him, Agnes smiled. She'd never had a man in her kitchen, and this one fit perfectly. She served the stew and passed him a bowl, then set one down for herself.

He held out her chair and slid it in when she was seated. This time, she focused on her plate to hide her smile as he went around to his seat. "Such chivalry," she said when she lifted her head.

"We try."

Hen's long forearms rested on the wooden surface as he reached across with open hands. "Shall we thank God for this bounty?"

Agnes nodded and set her hands in his, thinking as he spoke his prayer that this was almost too perfect, this man, this moment, this feeling of rightness. When she opened her eyes, she tried not to stare at his strong shoulders, his squarish jaw, the slight stubble of beard, the stray hair falling on his forehead, the tan of his skin. She gazed at his eyes instead.

"Tell me," he said, dipping his spoon into the stew. "What's been happening?"

"I told Brisa about the rape," she said. "Now she's furious and has convinced herself I made up the story of her conception because I don't want her to have a daddy."

"Ah. That's hard."

She lifted her glass, but she didn't drink. "She may actually decide to believe me but want a relationship with him anyway. I mean, what if she shrugs off the idea of date rape because of all the things she sees around her, the music, the ways kids probably talk at school, everything out there? Maybe she'll think rape is no big deal. The world has such ideas. Wrongs are made to seem right and right is made to seem wrong."

"I know." He probably did.

She imagined he'd experienced a lot of that. "We hear enough about soap-opera lives at work, and I imagine it's the same in school, with kids too immature to understand."

"Especially when so much drama is played out in front of them. As for what's discussed, people ought to be careful who's listening," he said. "It's a lesson some boaters ought to learn. I had a transient boat anchored not too far from *Harmless* last week. I don't remember where the couple had come in from, but they yelled at each other from the moment they dropped anchor."

"Oh, my. Sounds do travel across water."

"Even when they weren't yelling, I could hear snatches of conversation Although," he said ruefully, "it wasn't exactly conversation. It was more like racquetball with words."

"Do you think it ever works well, people, couples, living in such small spaces?"

His shrug was swift, as if he couldn't decide how to respond. "Your friends, Will and Tadie, seemed to have enjoyed cruising together."

"Yes, and Jilly can't stop talking about it with Brisa, who wanted to go sailing until Darlington became her primary interest. I don't imagine an offer of a trip to Tahiti would satisfy her at this point or make her hate me less." She studied her half-full bowl before looking up again. "Do you ever think you'll head to faraway places?"

"I'm not sure I'd want to go alone. I think I might be just as happy taking smaller trips once *Harmless* is ready. I probably need to be tethered to a place and to people with whom I'm comfortable." He smiled, but without humor. "Because of my history."

"Does it bother you still? The pull toward addiction?"

"Only on dark and dreary nights."

"And yet," she said, "Anne Frank claimed '...a single candle can both defy and define the darkness.' I prefer that to Poe's words about peering into darkness."

"Well-read, are you?"

"I happen to remember things I read. It's no huge feat. I didn't finish college, so I've had to create my own path to education. I always frequented libraries."

"I prefer to work on things, building or fixing." He paused to take a bite of stew. "When my hands are occupied, there's less chance of negative thoughts taking hold. And when it comes to things dispelling darkness, I like what Psalm 139 has to say. 'Even the darkness is not dark to You.' Knowing that God watches over me even in the darkness has brought me great comfort."

"Beautiful. I'm glad you have that."

"The psalmist also says that God knew me before I was conceived. When you're born with a mouth like mine—really, with any infirmity—it takes a lot of reminding that anyone formed you on purpose. I've had to grow into that truth."

"Oh, Hen. You're beautiful." Did she actually say that aloud?

For a moment he stared at her, seeming as surprised as she. "But I'm not. I'm horribly flawed."

"I don't see it. I see strength and beauty."

Was he blushing? She'd never seen a man blush. She bit her lip and felt a little more courageous. Every woman needed a boost of courage, didn't she? Especially when disasters loomed large in her world.

He traced fingers over her skin. She breathed in and slowly released the air.

"Remember, truth is always the right choice," he said, obviously harking back to the discussion about Brisa. "She will remember, and it will protect her."

"You sure?"

His smile was a little lopsided. "Well, it's what I'd like to believe."

She bit the inside of her cheek. "I suppose you felt constrained to add that qualifier, didn't you? I'd have preferred you lie and tell me you're positive."

That elicited a bark of laughter. "And you'd have believed me?"

"Maybe. Maybe not. But I'd have wanted to."

27

DARLING

Santa Ana winds whipped up, rousing dust swirls and ruffling the hoary manzanita and ragweed, the scrub oaks and eucalyptus, as Darling accelerated up the hill road leading to his home, his beautiful home, which he'd bought after his first album went platinum. Remembering that, the heady knowledge that he, a kid from Georgia, had gotten a place in these hills on his own, brought a smile to his lips.

He turned into his drive, punched in the numbers for his security gate, and then hit the garage door opener. His black Mercedes fit neatly into its space among his other cars. He couldn't wait to get inside, to pull Lisette into his arms, and to tell her about Brisa.

He'd been unable to fly out until today, some issue with the pilot of the chartered plane, but at least he'd spent the night in a decent hotel in New Bern. He'd walked the docks, studied the bigger yachts, had a couple of drinks on the hotel terrace, and dreamt of showing Brisa the Pacific Ocean.

He didn't expect to hear from her right away, but she'd call. She wouldn't be able to help herself. That thought made his smile pop to a small laugh. Oh, yeah. She wouldn't be able to resist the lure of a daddy, especially a famous one.

Now, he slid his key card across the sensor and entered the garage elevator. On the ride up the hillside, his insides picked up their own jitterbug.

The lightness in his stomach rocketed to his brain the moment he entered the living room. Because there she was. He stood, staring at her, and she looked back, her eyes direct as if there'd never been doubt between them. "Lisette," he whispered.

"You have seen her? This girl?" The hopeful note in her voice charmed him.

He'd been right to go, right to do this thing. "I have. And it won't be long. She'll be here."

"You know this of a certainty?"

He didn't answer her question. Instead, he said, "She is just like the pictures. And very sweet."

"She wishes to be here? To have me as her *maman*?"

"She does." He wouldn't admit he hadn't mentioned his wife to Brisa. There hadn't been time.

But there would be. When Brisa called, they could talk. They could spend hours talking.

*"Je suis contente."*

If Lisette was content, so was he. Now, to keep her that way.

"Come," he said, taking her hand and leading her to the big room they shared at the back of the house.

Todd had seen him arrive, and he stepped into view long enough to ask what they'd like to drink. "And perhaps something to eat as well?"

"The moment calls for champagne, I think," he said, "and something light to accompany it."

"Immediately."

Todd wouldn't need to be told to serve on the terrace. He'd find them.

"Come, my love," Darling said. "Let's see if there's a sunset awaiting us."

They'd toast his trip, watch the sun set, and then he'd take her to bed. Keeping her happy, keeping him happy.

Lisette had fallen asleep immediately after sex, but he hadn't. He still couldn't. And so he climbed out of bed, wrapped himself in his midnight blue silk robe, and wandered into the living room where he fixed himself a rum over ice. Then he stepped out onto the terrace.

The black of the sky was dulled by city lights, but he never tired of the view below him. Up here, he felt like king of the mountain. Beneath his feet and behind him was the house his wealth had bought, inside, the beauty his fame had enticed into his life. And soon there'd be more.

He didn't know why Mama Bea's face came to mind just then. Maybe a small part of him wished she could see him now. Wished she could meet her great-granddaughter.

He'd been six when his mama'd died, gone to heaven, Mama Bea'd said, where no more troubles existed and where she could rest in the arms of Jesus. Mama Bea had taken him up in her ample lap, drawn his head to her soft chest, and crooned.

He hadn't thought of Mama Bea's singing in a while now, her contralto lifting in worship and drawing him with her. He'd believed back then, hadn't he? Believed right along with her, her foolishness sucking him right into that net.

Only it hadn't felt like foolishness. It had felt like comfort. Like peace.

Why was he thinking this now?

He shook his head, trying to let it go, but the words kept playing in his head, the softly repeated, "Jesus, Jesus..." The lilting "my Savior God to Thee..."

He'd sung those songs, too, hadn't he? And then he'd let his daddy sell him as a black country singer because there was a place for him, a market for him, for the songs that made listeners bleed tears and with their tears, money.

And now he had all this, including his beautiful Lisette and—

soon—his beautiful Brisa. He was one blessed man, although maybe not the way Mama Bea'd imagined blessed.

When sleep finally overtook him, he dreamed. He was back at the front of the small Georgia church, singing, while Mama Bea played the piano and the choir belted out a gospel song behind him. His daddy's kinfolk all went to that church, where the preacher wore a purple-and-black robe. He remembered the Mothers, as they were called, in their white dresses, white gloves, and white hats, sitting off to the right. He was never quite sure what they did, but they were revered, those ladies.

As dreams went, this one appeared fairly benign, although he couldn't seem to get through the song without having to start over again and repeat, start, repeat, stop, until he finally awoke. He had no idea what the dream meant or why it had picked this particular night to visit him. Except that Mama Bea had sneaked into his earlier thoughts. He supposed that made sense.

He glanced over at his wife snoring slightly at his side. Even in sleep Lisette was beautiful. He turned away and tried to recapture drowsiness, but it eluded him.

He didn't reenter the dream, but he continued to think of that time, those people, that place. His mother's had been the only white face in that congregation of various shades, but they'd welcomed her and loved her. When Beverly Lucas had married Hank Evermire, she'd found a new family, a darker family than any she'd come from, and folk who loved up on her, as Mama Bea called it. Only, once Hank left to go make it big in the music world, it hadn't taken her too many years to fall apart. And then she'd died.

And Mama Bea had taken over, along with the church and the music, and had taught him gospel. First, he'd had a little boy's voice, then a man's croon, and it had all been for the Lord

Mama Bea worshiped so fervently, the God Mama Bea'd pushed on him.

All of it.

Until Daddy'd come to fetch him.

Just as he would do for his little girl. Fetch her and make her his. Make her a star.

## 28

## DARLING

It was Monday when the text message came in, but he didn't notice until he got home from a local club.

*Mom found my phone and hid it. I got it back. She'll be mad. Help.*

Darling grinned at the picture of his resourceful daughter.

He typed back. *Sorry it's so late. Just got your message.*

It had to be the middle of the night back east. He laid his phone on his nightstand and turned out the light.

Then he turned it back on and wrote: *Jot down my phone number and keep it hidden in case you lose the phone again. Better delete these messages too. You know how to do that? There's something that looks like a trash can on your phone. Tap on that.*

*And don't forget that card I gave you. Keep it safe. Use it whenever you want for whatever you need. Don't worry about the cost.*

*I can't wait to see you again.*

Maybe, just maybe, the child was smart enough to take the hint and figure out how to get here.

With great effort, he controlled his eagerness, but Lisette must have noticed because she demanded more of his attention. And when he told her about the contact, she demanded even more.

Arthur was thrilled. "You've got a winner there, Darl. Obviously your choice to visit her was a good one."

Yes, it had been. A very good one.

# 29

## AGNES

Other than Brisa's "No" when Agnes asked if she wanted breakfast, their only communication came when Brisa phoned from a school friend's house after school, saying she'd be home by dinner time. Maybe that was better, the two of them taking a break from staring contests. Maybe it would give Agnes time to figure out how to speak the truth to her daughter.

She headed off to work, and by the time she was ready to leave the restaurant, the temperature had taken a beating from a northerly blowing down the coast. The wind danced around town, hooking onto a storm sitting right out there in the Atlantic.

Henry walked out with her. "Whoa. Turned chilly on us, didn't it?"

She hugged herself. "Forgot my sweater."

"Neither of us is prepared, but I do have a foul weather jacket for my row out." He dug into his backpack and pulled out what looked like a blue rain jacket. "Put this on." He draped it over her, and they both laughed. It swallowed her.

She shrugged it off. "I'll be fine. Home isn't far."

He slung it over his shoulders and pulled her to his side. "Then let's share body heat."

Agnes bit her lower lip to keep from swooning right there. Her breath quickened, as if she were a giddy schoolgirl holding hands for the first time.

"This okay?" he asked.

She nodded.

"I'll walk you home."

"Oh, but you don't need to. It's out of your way."

She felt his shrug, felt the movement of his arm, although she didn't look up. He said, "I want to."

And those simple words brought a smile to her lips. He wanted to.

As they walked, a little awkwardly because of how much longer his steps were, her thoughts went straight to the warmth of his body, the firmness of his arms, and she longed to slide her fingers up and onto those muscles. Instead, she squeezed the hand draped over her shoulder. He squeezed back.

A giddy teenager, that's what she was. But then, she hadn't dated since... No man had touched her since... *Get hold of yourself.*

At her walkway, she slipped out from under his arm, but before she broke away completely, she reached a hand to stroke his cheek and whispered, "Thank you."

He leaned down and kissed her forehead. She wished he'd move to her lips, but why would he desire her? She was a catastrophe waiting to happen—a catastrophe that *had* happened.

Taking her hand again, he held it in his, and the warmth of his touch was better than any jacket. They walked the remaining steps to her porch. "Thank you again, for the walk and the company."

"It was my pleasure." He paused. "I know you're still worrying about Brisa, but remember that she has your love to fall back on, her memories of all you've done for her."

Would Brisa remember, though? That was the question

Agnes took with her up the stairs, the one she held onto when she peeked into her daughter's dark room and saw two sleeping forms.

All she came away with was a maybe. Maybe Brisa would remember. And maybe not.

## 30

## DARLING

He was heading home from Las Vegas when the call came through. He'd taken to driving himself to all their gigs so he wouldn't have to share the bus with his brother or any of the groupies, including the back-up singers. Usually, the girls traveled alone and only the guys in the band had bus privileges. Usually. But he wouldn't put anything past RJ.

He punched *Accept* and answered.

Her voice was low, as if she didn't want to be heard. "I did what you said, but if she finds the phone again, she'll be so mad. I'm already on restriction for yelling at her."

"Too bad."

"*You* wouldn't put me on restriction, would you?"

He grinned, then turned the grin into a low laugh so she'd hear it. "I wouldn't need to, would I?"

"Never."

"There you go." He thought of something. "You have a computer?"

"Unh-unh."

"Access to one?"

"At school. Maybe one of my friends."

"Good. Then you can link to my webpage and follow where I'm singing next. It will help us stay connected."

"Really? I will. I'd like that."

"It's on the card I gave you. You can access it from your phone, too."

"Really?" she repeated, sounding excited. Her response made his heart soar. She said, "Maybe I can find someone to help me. There's a girl I know. She's good at stuff."

"Just be careful. That's a real small town you're living in."

"I will. I'll be very careful. Now I gotta go."

It was going to happen. He could feel it.

He broadened his smile and tapped his hands on the steering wheel, finally loosing a *woohoo* like one of the country western boys he sometimes emulated on stage.

She'd come, he'd get her some stage garb—and he'd let Lisette buy the girl clothes that didn't come from Goodwill. Something fitting for *his* daughter.

And Lisette's.

## 31

## AGNES

The days passed at a snail's pace, with Brisa refusing to talk to her. Agnes had allowed her off restriction on Thursday to work on a special project for school at a classmate's house, Maddy someone, Brisa said. Snail's trails left a gooey mess, and from Agnes's point of view, the week was full of gooey emotions that remained just under the surface, unexplored and unspoken.

She did what needed doing around the house, which was very little with all Becca did, and she exercised by walking around the far end of town until it was time to get ready for work. Becca left her alone, spending her free time elsewhere. Agnes thought she'd mentioned helping someone from her church, and Agnes was glad the other woman had other things to occupy her because Agnes's own house had never looked so clean.

Work was work, nothing special except for knowing Hen was nearby while she served tables. Special, too, because of the time she got to spend with him when he walked her home.

Eventually, Saturday came and with it the chance to sleep in. She found it amazing how tired she felt by week's end.

She woke slowly as sunlight streamed in her window. The air was still, the promised storm long blown out to sea. She slid her feet into socks and then slippers, pulled on her fleecy robe, and padded downstairs. She'd heard Becca stirring earlier, but now there was only silence.

She was surprised to find Link lying on his cushion in the kitchen. "Becca let you out, boy, before she went to her meeting?" He gazed at her, but didn't get up.

She brewed coffee by rote and by rote fixed a bowl of oatmeal, listening for sounds that meant Brisa was awake. Surely, they'd be okay and be able to have the real birthday party they'd talked about, one with more than Jilly participating. Last year, they'd gone for pizza and taken Jilly along to make it festive. But Brisa seemed to have made other friends this year, maybe not ones she brought home with her, but she'd mentioned a couple of other girls from school, and she'd spent yesterday afternoon with that other classmate, working on their project. A party wasn't out of the question.

Agnes let herself daydream about Brisa happy again. Brisa bouncing around with a bunch of kids, enjoying her life. Back to her old self without the specter of Darlington.

While she continued to let Brisa sleep, Becca returned, and they figured out the next week's menu. Becca volunteered to do the shopping. "Don't need much, Miss Agnes. Just thinkin' of makin' a pot roast for dinner tonight. There's a sale on at Food Lion, good deal on the meat. Some green beans to go along. And we got short on milk."

Agnes checked the time as she handed her credit card to the other woman. It was almost eleven, closing in on lunchtime, which meant the child needed to get out of bed. Sleeping in on Saturday was one thing, but to laze the entire day away?

It was quiet in the hall, quiet in Brisa's room. Agnes knocked and, not hearing a response or any of the normal grunts that meant "leave me alone," she opened the door and checked the silent space.

The room was empty, the bathroom light off. The bed was rumpled, but no one lay in it. Clothes were strewn on the floor, clothes that hadn't been a jumbled mess when she'd looked in last night.

She wouldn't panic. She turned on the overhead light so she wouldn't miss any clues and looked for a note, for something that would give her an idea when her daughter had sneaked out and where she'd gone.

*Sneaked out. Gone.*

Those words ricocheted in her thoughts and set her pulse to hammering. *Please, oh please, no.*

She dashed to her own room and tossed sweaters out of the way. The cell phone box she'd stashed back there was empty. Which meant her daughter had taken the phone back and probably used it.

Used it for what? To call Darlington? To *vanish*?

Agnes plopped down heavily on the bed and stared at the floor, unseeing. Help. She needed help. Hanging onto vestiges of control, which threatened to shatter if she moved too quickly, she picked up her own phone, checked her contacts for Clay's number, and punched it in. "She's gone, Clay. Brisa's gone."

"What do you mean, gone?"

"She's not in her room or the house, and she took the cell phone he gave her."

"I'll be there as soon as I can. Where is Becca? She with you?"

"She went to the store."

"Call her. And Rita."

---

Agnes left a message on Rita's phone and punched in Hen's number. She couldn't sit still as images of what might have happened to Brisa flashed through her thoughts. Her girl, her innocent little one on the brink of puberty, was out there with potential monsters? *Oh, God, please no.*

Hen picked up. All she'd had to do was say Brisa was gone. "Heading out now," he said.

She called the restaurant and asked for the night off and was engaged in the unfruitful process of pacing from the kitchen to the living room and back when muted footfalls approached the front porch. Henry called her name as he opened the door and stepped inside. Brisa must have left that door unlocked. The image of her girl sneaking off into the dark made Agnes's gut clench.

She ran straight into his arms. "Oh, Hen," she cried on a sob.

His long fingers caressed her head, brushed down over her shoulders. "Hush, love," he whispered over her tear-filled gulps.

Finally, when she'd quieted, he said, "What do you know?"

She stepped back, dashing her fingers over her cheeks to dry them. "I'm sorry. I soaked your shirt."

"Doesn't matter."

She took a deep breath to steady herself. "She didn't leave a note, but the cell phone he gave her is missing from the back of my closet."

"You think he took her?"

"What else can have happened?"

A knock sounded. Clay and Rita stood framed in the doorway. Rita came immediately to her side. "Tell me. Did he take her?"

3 2

DARLING

I t was four in the morning when the beep of a text woke Darling. He stirred, reached to turn on the hotel's awkwardly placed lamp, and read it. "At airport. Is that OK?"

What airport?

He dialed Brisa's phone. It only rang once before she answered. "Hello?"

"Where exactly are you, and where are you headed?" He let the eagerness show in his voice. He'd received an alert yesterday that she'd used the credit card for a purchase and had taken a cash advance of three hundred dollars. Now he had confirmation.

"I'm in Raleigh. The big brother of that friend from school brought me. Remember, I told you about her?"

Had she? At four in the morning, he was a little foggy. "What friend is this?"

"I told you how I know someone who can do computers, Maddy. She's real smart, probably smarter than anybody in my school. She helped me figure out how to buy a ticket with the credit card and how to use it to get cash. Only we found out they'd say I needed a parent along, some kind of permission thing. All except one plane that goes out of Raleigh."

"That's not very close to Beaufort. How'd you get there?"

"Well, uh, Maddy's brother, only that's not the whole thing. I hope you're not going to be mad, because it gets real complicated. Maddy was kinda nervous they might want an ID, even though the airline people said I didn't need one because I'm not 18, but just in case, Maddy gave me her sister's birth certificate and wrote the permission letter about her. Maddy signed her mother's name. She said she has a lot of practice doing that." Brisa lowered her voice to almost a whisper. "I'm supposed to be Charlotte Evers. Charlie. She's 14. I don't really look 14, but the person who checked my papers didn't pay too much attention. Probably because it was so early, and he was sleepy. That was the scary part. I mean, it's lying, and I'm not supposed to lie. Ever. Only I really want to see you, so do you think it will be okay? I mean, I won't go to jail or anything, will I?"

Darling wondered if he'd had too much to drink last night and so wasn't processing very well. His not-yet-twelve-year-old daughter had found a friend—a classmate, so another kid—who knew how to do all this? And who obviously practiced forgery. Amazing, and maybe not in such a good way.

"Ok..kay," he said, still processing it all. "No, you won't go to jail." Maddy might, he thought, if she kept this up for another few years. "Tell me again how you got all the way to Raleigh?"

"Craig. Her brother. All I had to do was give him some money." She hesitated.

"How much did he want?"

"I hope it's okay. It was kind of a lot." Another hesitation. He waited.

Her voice was a little quavery when she said, "He wanted two hundred dollars. He said for gas and his time."

Really? Interesting that she sounded more frightened about the cash outlay than about the forged letter.

"How old is this kid?" He almost called the boy a punk but

185

stopped himself just in time. No need to make Brisa feel bad. What was two hundred to him anyway?

"Um, seventeen." Another pause. "I didn't like him very much. He doesn't talk. He picked me up down the street from my house in the middle of the night. It was scary being out there so late, but it was the only way, or Mom would have stopped me. Anyway, Craig, the boy, drove all the way with his music blaring. I don't think he has very good taste in music."

"Didn't play mine, I take it?" Darling chuckled.

"No. Riding with him all those hours was real scary."

He sat up, on the alert now. "He didn't touch you or anything, did he?" No way could he keep the worry out of his voice.

"No, nothing like that. It's just, I've never been in a car with another kid driving before. And it was night. I was real sleepy, but I stayed awake. I watched, just in case, you know? I mean, sometimes people fall asleep when they drive at night. I didn't want him to do that. He drank a lot of cola."

"Okay, what time do you land? Oh, and where are you landing?"

"Um, my friend read your website and said you don't have a concert this weekend. I mean, none that showed up. So she said I should fly to Los Angeles, on account of you living there. And I won't have to change planes. Is that okay? I mean, will you be around?"

"I have a show tonight in San Diego. At a club," he said. "When do you land?"

"Um, this morning. Like at around 10:30. Maddy said it was on account of the time change. But I can wait. I can hang around. I guess."

"No, you can't." This wasn't good. This wasn't good at all. "I'll find someone to pick you up. Can you text me the flight number?"

"Yeah."

"You at the gate now? Where your plane leaves?"

"I'm supposed to board kinda soon."

"I'll have someone meet you. You just need to follow the signs to Baggage Claim. I'll have someone waiting, holding a sign with your name on it—no, with that other girl's name, I suppose. Charlie Evers? You just look for her name. Can you do that?"

"Sure. I can read."

"Of course you can."

"And I can follow signs."

Snippy, was she? He took a deep breath. Fine, she'd been awake all night, and he doubted she was used to that. He'd give her this one.

"I'm so sorry I can't meet you myself, but you'll be fine at my house. And I'll be home in the morning."

"Can I come to your concert?"

"No. It's in a club. They won't let you in."

"I want to see you."

She could. He could have her brought to his hotel. That would work.

"Okay, let's do this. I'll have the driver bring you to my hotel. If your plane is on time, he could get you here in a couple of hours. We can spend time together before I have to be at the club." That could work. "How does that sound?"

"Good." The relief in the young voice brought a smile to his face. He wasn't used to thinking in kid terms, but this was much better. She'd be frightened. Maybe he'd see if Lisette wanted to meet her and drive down in the same car.

"I'll have my phone with me if you need to reach me once you land. Just remember to turn the phone off when you're on the plane."

"Okay." Her voice suddenly sounded small.

"This will be great, Brisa. I can't wait."

"Yeah. Me too."

Loudspeakers boomed announcements as she signed off. And he was left with the knowledge that everything was about to turn around in his world. Wasn't Lisette going to be over the moon?

He checked the bedside clock again. She wouldn't be up for another several hours. Then he'd call her, arrange for a driver, and life would start to make sense again.

## 33

## AGNES

R ita nodded at Becca and Henry before glancing around. "Where's Link? She didn't take him with her, did she?"

"No," Agnes said. "He's on her bed, waiting for her, I think. He was in the kitchen when I came down this morning."

"I assume you've already checked her room for clues?" Clay asked.

"I have, but feel free."

Rita turned, her hand on the banister. "I'll go with him."

Hen sat near Becca and, like her, bowed his head. Agnes stifled the urge to follow Rita and Clay. Becca mumbled something. Hen's hands were clasped between his knees, Becca's in her lap. They were obviously praying.

*God, please…*

She couldn't sit, and so she paced, hoping, yearning for God to listen to her friends—especially if her pleas didn't count because she'd doubted and ignored him for years.

*Please.*

She turned when descending footfalls sounded on the stairs. Rita entered the living room first, shaking her head. "Clay's thorough, but we didn't find anything that pointed to where she went or how she got there. The papers I filed haven't reached Darlington's hands yet."

"What does that mean?" Agnes asked.

"He hasn't accepted service of them."

Agnes didn't have time to ask what happened next before Clay said, "I'll head back to the station to get the word out, and I'll see if the LAPD can find out where Mr. Evermire is, if he actually left the area and if he left alone. Best if they contact him."

"I confiscated the phone he gave her, but Brisa found it again. She's been able to talk to him."

"Do you have the phone number?"

She shook her head.

"I'll try to get a court order to look through his accounts." He nodded to them and headed toward the front door. "I'll be in touch."

All she could do was nod before turning back to the room. Hen had come up behind her. Now, he draped one arm over her shoulder and pulled her close. "We'll find her. Clay has resources."

Her throat constricted, and she couldn't speak. Hen's warmth comforted her. He was so big, so tall... so warm. Afraid to move and scare him off, she remained still, waiting.

And then Rita broke the spell. "Does Brisa have friends other than Jilly and Ty?"

Agnes twisted toward her to answer. "She visited some girl from school several times, someone named Maddy. I don't remember her last name, because Brisa was barely speaking to me by then. She always promised to be home by dinnertime."

"Was she?" Rita asked.

Agnes checked with Becca. "Yes, ma'am," Becca said. "And last night, she ate my dinner, then she headed upstairs. Said she had homework she and her friend hadn't got to. Before I went up myself, I checked on her. She was about to go to sleep, she said."

"She was in her bed when I got home," Agnes said. "She must have sneaked out during the night. I guess that's when she left Link in the kitchen, because I didn't hear him."

Rita sighed. "You think Jilly might know who Maddy is?"

Agnes shrugged. "We could ask. I normally check the homes she's going to, but it's been walking on egg shells around here. I was just glad she was making other friends." She sighed. "Stupid of me. Negligent."

"Don't beat yourself up, Agnes. She'd have found a way to do what she wanted even if you'd been diligent and checked all bona fides. I'll head over to Jilly's now." Rita gathered her purse. "Talk to Tadie, too, see if we can get Jilly to tell us anything. If she can't, there's Ty. Maybe someone from school knows something."

"Any chance," Hen said, directing his words to Agnes, "that Brisa has the ability to figure out what to do on her own?"

"She could have gotten out of the house, but the rest? Where would she have gotten the money to go anywhere?"

Rita finished buttoning her sweater. "I'll call Clay, see if he can look into Darlington's credit cards. It's possible something will show up there."

"Will he need a warrant?" Hen asked.

"In a case like this," Rita said, "he'll be able to get one right away. In spite of it being Saturday."

"Good to know."

Rita headed toward the door. "One of us will call you as soon as there's any new information." She looked past Agnes and Hen. "Becca, see you at church tomorrow?"

"Yes, ma'am. I'll be there. Gettin' my ladies to pray for sweet Brisa, too."

"Amen," Rita said. "We'll get the word out."

Becca stood as Hen walked Rita to the door. "You need me to stay with you tonight, Miss Agnes?"

"No, of course not. You go on home to your daughter."

"Best I start rallying the prayer warriors. We gonna pray that girl home, don't you doubt it." She laid her large hand on Agnes's. "And you just remember that God sees your baby. She's not gone out of his sight, not for a minute."

If God had been watching, why hadn't he stopped her girl from getting sucked in by Darlington? Why hadn't he woken anyone in the house to stop Brisa leaving? It seemed instead as if he'd turned his back. Just as he had thirteen years ago in that bar when she'd been stupid enough to believe a gorgeous man paying attention meant something good... and not the end of everything she'd know, everything she'd imagined for herself.

---

Hen's fingers smoothed over her bent head. He tilted up her chin and wiped tears from her cheeks. "Honey, don't," he whispered. "Agnes."

She shook her head, shook him off. And then wondered why she couldn't, wouldn't accept his comfort.

"It's going to be okay," Hen said, even as she turned from him.

"How? How can you say that? We can't know. She could be anywhere. He could have taken her *anywhere!*"

And on those words, the leaking tears turned to sobs. Her baby... gone. Maybe kidnapped. Maybe petrified.

Maybe glad to have left the mother who'd made her so angry? Maybe *glad?*

This time, when Hen pulled her against his chest, she clung. If she let go, she'd probably collapse, a puddled heap on the floor.

When she'd calmed, which may have been minutes or hours later, Hen suggested they do some research of their own while they waited to hear from Clay and Rita and before he had to head in to work.

"You have a computer?" He pulled out his phone.

"I used to. It quit months ago." And she hadn't had the

money to replace it. She dropped her head to her hands. It should have been a priority. It would have been, once Brisa hit high school, but they'd needed to eat, hadn't they?

"I have one back on the boat, but we can use this." He brought up the web browser on his phone. "Kind of small for doing much but better than nothing."

She sat on the edge of the couch, watching him as he punched some buttons and thumbed a few keys. Moments later, he showed her the screen.

"Darlington Evermire—Darling—doesn't have a concert this weekend, but if you scroll here" —he touched the screen —"you'll see that he's performing in a club in San Diego tonight," Hen said. "And there's no mention of him cancelling. My guess? He wouldn't've had time to kidnap Brisa."

Time? Why would anyone rich have to worry about time? He could pay for anything, hire anyone. "Maybe he got someone else to do it. Could she be out there?" This was bad. Imagining a hired kidnapper, a criminal, was so much worse than she'd imagined. California. Her little girl. With that man.

She swiped her hand down her face, as if the movement would wipe away her fear and give her back yesterday. The day before. Some other reality.

"I thought telling her about him would make her wary," she said. "Maybe twelve isn't old enough to be wary."

"Or maybe his charisma and his daddy-ness was bigger than the truth you gave her," Hen said. "Let me call Clay."

They had Clay on the phone very quickly, and Hen put him on speaker as he explained what they'd discovered about Darling's schedule.

"Good," Clay said. "I'm still waiting to get a court order so we can access the phone records and credit cards. We're rushing it, because of Brisa's age."

"Have you heard anything from Rita yet?" Agnes asked.

Someone had to know something.

"Nothing. She'll probably call you first, don't you think?"

193

"I hope so."

"I'll keep you posted," Clay said. "I'll call LA again. They're taking this seriously, and we have folk checking with buses and airlines."

"You think she could have boarded a plane?" Hen asked. "By herself and at her age? Would they even *let* her?"

"She's never been on a plane," Agnes said. "It's not like vacations by air were in our budget. And don't they have rules?"

"Hold on," Clay said. "I've got to set the phone down for a sec."

She reached for Hen's hand and held on tightly. He squeezed back, but gently. "It'll be okay. We'll find her."

"Here we go," Clay said. "I just checked. American and Delta, the only ones that fly out of New Bern, have strict rules. She wouldn't be allowed on by herself without a parent's permission. You'd have to show up with her birth certificate and then sign papers and tell them who would meet her at the other end. Plus you'd have to fork over a good chunk of change for an escort. My best guess? She didn't go to the airport there."

"And a bus would be too... too hard," Agnes said, the image of drug addicts and escaped criminals or perverts catching a bus out of town making her words catch. "There'd... there'd be all those changes, all those days of sleeping in a cramped seat with no food. She'd be scared to death."

Hen squeezed again. "Maybe she's just hiding out at a friend's house. She's not quite twelve. Even twelve isn't likely to go too far from home."

Unless you were talking about a furious almost-twelve.

## DARLING

A rthur stood outside the suite door. "You rang?"

Darling grinned. "I want you to meet my daughter."

He'd have liked to photograph Arthur's stunned expression. "Here?"

"Sure. She arrived at the L.A. airport this morning." He waved Arthur forward. "Lisette met her and Donald drove them both here a couple of hours ago. We fed her and sent her in for a nap."

Arthur squinted at him. "How'd she get on the plane? How'd she manage to fly here?"

"Come on in. She's still in her room, and Lisette is in ours, so we can talk."

Darling led the other man into the plush living area and waved him toward the sofa while he took the cushy armchair. "It seems she managed to board a plane all on her own."

"She's too young to fly alone. How'd she pay for it?"

"Oh, I left her a credit card when I was out there. For clothes, expenses."

"Did you tell her to run away? Did you explain how to do it?'

"Of course not. I just told her I couldn't wait to see her again."

Arthur walked to the bar that had been set up against one wall. He poured himself two fingers of whiskey, swirled it in his glass, and turned to face the room. "You're going to have to report her presence to her mother, and then we'll have to call Paul to see if he can petition a judge on your behalf for temporary custody. Because no way will a judge let you keep a runaway if you played a part in luring her here and then you hide her." He gulped a long swig and coughed. "All right. We can't do anything tonight. You have to go on stage in a few hours. And then you have to drive home tomorrow."

"Fine."

"Let's get through tonight. I'll call Paul. And we'll see." He paused as he took his seat again. "So, how's Lisette doing with this?"

"So excited. She couldn't keep her eyes off Brisa. And Brisa? Well, you can imagine. Everyone loves Lisette."

One of the bedroom doors opened slowly. Darling stood and waved to Brisa. "Come on in, honey. This is Arthur, my manager. I wanted him to meet you."

Brisa looked shyly at Arthur, who watched over the back of the couch. The man wasn't going to stand up for his girl? Darling glared at him and walked toward his daughter. Taking her hand, he drew her forward.

The other door opened. Lisette stood in the entrance in a very intentional pose. Darling let his gaze travel from her tilted head to her hand poised on the door frame. She could have come straight off a Hollywood poster of a glamour girl. He grinned at her. "Look who's come to meet our daughter."

"Arthur," she purred.

His manager stood. "Lovely to see you," Arthur said in Lisette's direction, his tone a little too enthusiastic for Darling's taste.

Lisette nodded and glided up to Brisa. "*Ma petite,*" she said, raising one palm to caress Brisa's cheek. "You have rested?"

"Yes, ma'am." Brisa's smile seemed shy, her eyes adoring.

Shy and adoring were good touches, Darling decided. Just the right ones when speaking to Lisette.

*"C'est bien.* Come now, and let us sit together. Arthur," Lisette said, fluttering a hand at him, "you must take a chair. *La petite* and I, we will sit together there, on the couch." She pulled Brisa down with her. "And we will plan our evening. You two?" Another flutter. "You go do your singing thing. We will shop."

Arthur raised a brow. "Shop? In San Diego?"

"Ah, pooh. What do you know? I will use my online. And my dresser, she will be available. She will help us find just the right clothes for this, my new daughter. They will deliver." She looked at Darling. *"N'est-ce pas?"*

"Anything you wish."

Arthur angled his head toward Darling's bedroom.

"Excuse us for a moment?" Darling said and followed his manager into the other room.

"We have phone calls to make," Arthur said when they were alone.

Darling stared at the street below as Arthur made his calls. When he finished leaving a detailed message for the lawyer, he punched in another number, waited, and then spoke. At his first words, Darling turned to look at him. Arthur had called Daddy Evermire.

"Yes, sir," Arthur said. "Yes, we've got something here we might need your help with. You remember the situation back east we discussed? Yeah, that one."

Darling scowled. Had Arthur been talking to his father? Behind Darling's back?

"It seems your granddaughter caught a plane out here—yes, all on her own... yes, sir. Intrepid of her, I agree." Arthur nodded, as if Daddy Evermire could see him. "No, the mother doesn't know where she is yet... I have. I've done that. Put in a call to Paul first thing... Saturday night. Yes, I know." Another pause. "Thank you. I was hoping you might be able to do something... You'd like to meet her. Of course." He glanced up at Darling, but he didn't wait for Darling to do more than nod. "Yes, Darling wants that, too. Lisette? Oh, she's ecstatic."

Darling held out his hand. "Give me the phone."

Arthur shook his head, held a staying hand in Darling's direction. "I know. We'll be on stage at eight." He listened.

Short of grabbing Arthur's cell phone out of his hand, Darling could do nothing. Anger bit at him, but he pushed it down. His father and Arthur... They'd always done this, run his life, his and RJ's. They'd found Lisette. Arthur'd found Brisa. What else had they conspired to do and kept from him?

He was thirty-five. Fine, he'd been a stupid almost-kid when he'd made all those mistakes, but now he was grown. An adult. A huge success. Making them all piles of money. Why should they try to manage things without his input? Why didn't they actually let him manage them?

Arthur said, "Yeah, I get that. Who do you think should make the call?... Really? You sure about that?" He covered the phone and whispered, "He wants Lisette to call Brisa's mama. What do you think?"

Oh, so now Arthur was asking him? His daughter. His wife. His...

*Calm down.*

He had to calm down and remember that Arthur was just looking out for him. Doing his best. And if he got Daddy Evermire involved to help fix it, well, that was the way it was. Always had been.

He could picture his father, his afro so big it looked like he might topple from its weight, his face unlined, full of smiles, but not a one of those smiles lit his eyes. Never had. Everybody called him Daddy, from the lowest of his employees to his friends in high places. Came with having a lot of money, a lot of power, and a cold heart.

"Yes, I agree," Arthur said back into the phone. "She'd

probably be a good one, mother to mother. Only, don't you think Brisa's mama might not want her girl bonding with another woman? I mean, not right away?" Silence. "You may be right, Daddy. If she'll do it. You want to talk to her or you want Darling to?" Another pause. "Fine. Let me get her for you."

## 35

## HENRY

Henry watched closely as Agnes answered her cell phone and immediately stiffened.

"She's there? She's in California?" Her voice had hiked an octave, maybe two. "Who are you again?" A pause, then, "Let me speak to her."

There was more. She reached for his hand as the person on the other end continued speaking, and he recognized a foreign accent when she put it on speaker. He heard, *"Bien."*

What was good in this situation?

What else the French woman said he didn't know because Agnes took the phone off speaker and said, "I don't care if you're Darlington's wife or not. You have my daughter, and I want her back. I need to speak to her." And then Agnes started jabbering back in French as if she were a native.

Where had she learned to speak a foreign language fluently? He didn't think she'd traveled abroad.

"I want to talk to her," Agnes said, in English again. "I don't care if she's too tired or asleep. You want me to contact the police? Charge you with kidnapping her?"

He placed a hand on her back and spoke a prayer under his breath.

She stared at the phone in frustration. "She hung up."

Agnes leaned into him while she made three other calls, one to Clay, and one each to Rita and Mrs. Barnes. Clay promised to get word to the California authorities, Rita wasn't in, and Mrs. Barnes said she'd continue praying.

He checked his watch. He should have already left for work.

Finally, he was able to ease her down onto a couch. Five minutes. He'd give himself that long. After all, he could run, make up the time.

"What did Darlington's wife say?" he asked. "What's her name?"

"Lisette. Her name's Lisette, and she said she'd take good care of Brisa if I would let her stay for a visit. How can I leave my daughter there? How? She said Brisa would call me tomorrow. How can I know anything if I can't even speak to her? How do I know she's fine?" Her face crumpled as she burst into tears.

"Come here." He drew her close and let her sob against his chest. He couldn't believe how well she fit.

What a thing to think when she was hurting. She probably wouldn't have cared whose shoulder offered itself as long as she had the comfort of arms around her while she wept.

But he wanted them to be his arms, now and forever. He tightened his hold even as he told himself to let it go, let her go. Besides, work waited.

When he pulled away, he wiped his fingers over her cheeks. "I'm so sorry I can't stay."

She swiped at her still-dripping eyes. "I know. Don't worry about me."

"May I come back after we close?"

She nodded.

"If you change your mind, just turn off the lights down here. I won't bother you." And then he left.

As he sprinted down the sidewalk, he prayed harder than he

ever had for mercy and kindness to flow upon her, for peace and rescue.

# 3 6

## AGNES

Agnes was bereft after Henry left. If only she had a plan, a way out of this horror. Brisa, so far away, in the hands of a rapist...

Darlington was *not* daddy material. And what about this French woman, this wife who had no children of her own? Who was she?

Brisa would never want to come home. She was the daughter of a star... and a waitress. Star... waitress. Waitress... star. Bright lights, applause, what was probably a fantastic home, along with a French step-mother who seemed delighted to have her?

Yeah, Agnes knew which her vulnerable almost-teen would pick. What child wouldn't?

Her stomach spasmed, and the bile rose. She dashed to the powder room where she threw up the little she'd eaten—the nothing, really—and then sat on the floor and lost it again.

She was still on the bathroom floor when she heard a knock at the front door. She didn't want to move.

But what if it was Rita? Slowly, she rose, splashed water on her face, and went to answer the door.

Rita held out a piece of paper. "Sorry it took me so long. Jilly went with her daddy to check on their boat, the *Nancy Grace*, up in New Bern, and Will didn't listen to his messages right away. Anyway, I just spoke with Jilly, and I now have the name of the girl Brisa's been getting chummy with recently. Madeline Evers is incredibly smart, Jilly said, and was thrilled that Brisa wanted to be her friend."

"Why?" Agnes asked. "I thought Brisa and Jilly were best friends."

"It seems right after Brisa discovered her father's name, she wanted to figure out how to find him. Jilly didn't know, but this Maddy did. They'd made plans to get together to do research, but before they could, Darlington actually showed up here. Anyway, Brisa made new plans with Maddy, and that's where she's been going."

"Jilly doesn't know what those new plans were, other than after-school meetings?"

"No. She said Brisa was really quiet about it. She's worried Brisa discovered she'd told her mom about the phone, which actually exonerates her. Still, she's upset."

"How do we get in touch with this Maddy?"

"Well, we can send Clay or one of his officers there, or we can go ourselves."

"Let's go." At least she could do one thing.

She grabbed her purse and led Rita out the door. And then she stopped. "I should freshen up."

"No, you shouldn't. That child needs to see what you're going through."

Agnes sighed, but she locked the door and headed to the passenger side of Rita's car. The visor mirror revealed just how horrible she looked, but all she could do now was comb her hair and add a little lipstick for color.

The house wasn't far away, just a couple of blocks further along Front Street and then another couple to the left. While Rita rang the doorbell, Agnes stared at the peephole in the middle of a blue door that had paint peeling and cracks radiating around an indentation that looked as if something had tried to poke a hole in it.

She imagined someone staring out at them. Rita rang again.

This time, the door opened slightly. A young girl with big glasses peeked out at them.

Rita spoke, her voice coaxing. "You must be Maddy. I'm Mrs. Levinson, and this is Brisa's mother. May we come in and speak to you?"

Maddy shook her head and closed the door on them.

Rita rang the bell again. They could hear voices raised inside, the sound of a chain lock sliding. The door opened, and a woman in a housedress asked if she could help them.

Again, Rita introduced herself and Agnes. "We understand that Brisa has been to visit your daughter, and we'd like to ask her a few questions, if we may."

The woman turned to her daughter, fists on hips and a scowl wrinkling her face. "What have you done?"

"May we come in, Mrs. Evers?" Rita said. "We won't keep you long."

Mrs. Evers backed out of the way. The small living room was filled with old, slightly tattered furniture, but it was tidy and seemed clean. What looked as if it had once been a dining room, now held a couple of desks and computers. An older girl sat at one, her mouse clicking as she worked. Maddy had returned to another, but her head was bent and her hands were clasped in her lap.

"Maddy," her mother said, "you come on over here and talk to these ladies. You tell them what they need to know."

Maddy complied. She was probably a head shorter than Brisa, not particularly attractive, but she didn't cower when she stopped in front of them.

Rita bent closer and spoke softly. "Honey, do you know where Brisa is?"

Maddy nodded.

"Can you tell us? Her mother is worried."

"She flew to California."

Agnes dug her fingernails into her palms. She also bit her lower lip before asking, "How did she get there?" She was proud of herself. She'd kept her voice level, non-threatening, when what she wanted to do was scream.

"She bought a ticket."

"How?" This was from Rita.

Maddy looked over her shoulder at her mother. Her mother nodded. "Answer the ladies. You know something, you answer."

"We did it online. She had a credit card."

Brisa had a credit card? Where had she... no, Agnes didn't need to ask that question. He'd given it to her. Probably told her how to use it.

"Rita?" Agnes asked.

"I know. I'll call Clay." And then Rita spoke again to Maddy. "Didn't Brisa need a parent's permission to fly? And how did she get to the airport?"

"There are flights that don't need parents. She got one of those. Direct." Maddy looked uncomfortable here.

"Really? And which airline let her do that? Which airport?"

"One in Raleigh."

"Raleigh?" Rita asked.

Agnes couldn't speak. Or imagine it. Her eleven-year-old daughter had gotten to Raleigh on her own and taken a flight across the country? Light-headed, she backed up so she could lean against the wall.

Rita glanced at her. "You okay?"

"Not really. But I'll live."

"Maddy, how did Brisa get to Raleigh?" Rita asked.

Maddy just shook her head.

"I know you helped her," Rita said. "You're smart. You figured out how to get her a ticket."

"She's my friend."

"I'm glad. But how did your friend get from her house to the airport in Raleigh? That's not exactly next door. That's a three-hour trip." Rita paused as if to let that sink in. "You must know."

"Maddy," her mother said, "you know, you say. It's only right."

"Craig." Her voice was a whisper.

"What'd you say?" Her mother's voice had sharpened.

"It was Craig, Mama. Craig took her."

"Your brother drove to Raleigh? By himself with a girl your age? Where is he? I'm going to scalp him." Mrs. Evers voice rose until it was almost a shout. "He knows he's not s'posed to go roving anywhere in my car." She went to the window and peeked out. "Car's there. Where's he?"

"I don't know, Mama, but Brisa, she paid him. She gave him money, two hundred dollars." Maddy pleaded with her mother. "It's not like he used the car and left it empty. And you're always wanting us to make money. It was a job."

"How old is Craig?" Rita asked, probably thinking how much trouble he might be in—with the law and with his mother.

"Seventeen. He's seventeen, and he ain't got the brains of a twelve-year-old. Maddy's s'posed to have them, so's her sister over there. Seems only the women in this family know anything, and Maddy just showed us how her knowing got drained by her wantin' to please your girl. I'm real sorry. I thought they were doing homework."

Agnes was sick. Or she'd soon be. She pulled away from the wall. "Let's go," she said to Rita.

"One more thing," Rita said. "What about an ID? Didn't she need to show something?"

Maddy shrugged. "I don't know."

Agnes squinted at the girl, but spoke to Rita. "It wouldn't be hard to find out, would it? Because if she needed an ID and didn't have one, she couldn't have flown across country, could she? And we know she did fly."

"Maddy," her mother said.

"She borrowed Charlie's."

"Who's Charlie?" Agnes asked.

Maddy jabbed a thumb behind her toward the other girl at the computer who kept her head down and her focus on the screen in front of her. "Charlotte."

Mrs. Evers threw up her hands. "Can't believe you did that, Maddy Evers. How're we gonna get another one for your sister?"

"It was just her birth certificate," Maddy said. "You can get new ones easy enough."

"Lands, what will you think of next?"

Rita settled a hand on Agnes's back. "At least we know. We'll call Clay from the car. Let him deal with this." To Mrs. Evers and Maddy, "Thank you for explaining things. I hope you'll never help another underage girl run away from home or put another one in danger. I'm sure you'll be hearing from someone about this."

"I'm sorry," Maddy said. "I just wanted her to like me."

"Yeah, well," Rita said, "she probably does. But friends don't let friends do dangerous things. They just don't."

Unless you're eleven. Unless you don't know any better. But Agnes kept quiet.

She waited until Rita had buckled her seat belt before speaking. "I can't believe it. That young girl—she doesn't look over ten—figured out how to send Brisa across country. What do you think they do with those computers, those two girls, besides helping my daughter run away?"

"I wondered the same thing. Seems like the older one was glued to hers. She barely looked up." Rita buckled up and drove away. Her fingers beat against the steering wheel. "I imagine Clay's going to want to look into those computers, but at least now we know how Brisa got on the plane. And that she arrived safely."

"Now we just have to get her home."

---

"You want me to stay with you?" Rita asked.

Yes, no, yes. "Thank you, but I'll be okay."

"You sure?"

"At least she seems to be temporarily safe."

"She arrived; that's huge. And we'll be working on getting her back. I'm sure Clay has already been in touch with the authorities in Los Angeles. I'll pursue other avenues."

"What if he gets some kind of temporary custody order? What if he gets to keep her? He's powerful. He has money. "

"We'll apply for one here. I'll see if I can find out why he hasn't been served." Rita reached over and touched her shoulder. "And we'll fight anything he tries. You're her mother."

"Oh, Rita."

"Hang on." Rita drew a pad and paper from her voluminous bag. "We're going to follow through on that charge of rape."

"I guess, but…"

"We need him on the defensive, and he's not going to want to face this charge even if he imagines it won't stand up in court. It probably won't, because it will be your word against his. But this MeToo Movement has powerful men on the run, and all it takes is one accusation—true or not—to get folk trying to unearth other accusers. If Darlington drugged and raped you, who's to say he didn't try the same thing with other women?"

"Maybe he did."

"I'll draft a demand letter saying Darlington should return Brisa immediately or face criminal legal action. We'll allege First Degree Forcible Rape with the condition that he, the rapist, was aided and abetted by someone. I know we can't prove this, but we can charge him with it and see where it goes. I'm hoping he'll want to avoid the sort of media frenzy that we've seen plaguing all those celebrities recently."

"You think that will work?"

"All we can do is try. I'm sorry the order we drafted got stuck in the court system, but we'll keep working on this." She put the pad away and said, "I need to get home. But you call me if you start to worry and want talking down off the ledge."

"I will. Thank you."

As Agnes closed the door behind Rita, a single bark came from upstairs. Link. She'd forgotten Link.

"Poor baby. Come on down." He lumbered down the stairs and sat at her feet. "Let's get some dinner for you, and maybe a trip outside?"

He followed her to the kitchen, but he didn't look any more joyful than she felt.

# 37

## DARLING

D arling thanked the crowd and stepped off the small stage, but the whole club gig felt like a waste of time. Arthur had booked it. Said he needed the exposure of a more intimate setting, back to his roots.

He'd earned his pay tonight, and he hoped that would satisfy both Arthur and Daddy.

The idea of a conspiracy between those two gave him the creeps. He'd thought himself Daddy's number one—the one who made him proud, the one he promoted and pushed and cheered. Maybe Darling had been wrong.

Maybe he was just a number on a ledger, appreciated as long as the revenue poured in.

It was late when he let himself in the suite. All was quiet. Both Lisette and Brisa seemed to be asleep, so he crossed to the bar and poured himself a whiskey.

And then he sat back in one of the wide chairs and pondered his next steps.

---

He was sitting at the suite's long table the next morning, sipping coffee and waiting for the women to emerge. He'd left Lisette lounging in the large tub when he'd poked his head in to tell Brisa breakfast was ready.

She'd pulled her curls into a fluff at the back of her head, wore a new and lovely dress in some shade of pink, and had a smile on her face that brought out an answering one from him. "Hungry?" he asked.

She nodded but approached the heavily laden table carefully. "All this is for us?"

"It is. I ordered some of everything because I didn't know what you liked." He waved toward a plate. "Fill up with whatever you want."

She spooned fruit into a bowl and forked a couple of blueberry pancakes onto her plate. "Can I have a donut, too?"

"Sure. Which kind do you like best?"

"I don't know. We don't get donuts like this at home."

"How about the jelly filled? I used to love them. And the chocolate."

She grinned. "I'll try the jelly."

When Lisette emerged fully dressed in one of her flowing dresses, Brisa watched her movements with rapt adoration. Lisette patted the girl's cheek and took a chair next to her. Darling went to the coffee bar and fixed her a small cup of espresso. *"Merci,"* she said, smiling up at him.

He bent to kiss her forehead. "My beautiful ladies."

Interesting what pinked cheeks looked like on his daughter's skin. Lisette took the compliment as her due.

"I have made arrangements for us to fly back to Burbank and my car to be delivered to the airport for our use. Can you both be ready to leave in two hours?"

Lisette gave a very Gallic shrug that was mostly facial. Brisa said, "Oh, yes, of course."

"Then that's settled. I'll let the pilot know."

The private jet enchanted Brisa, and she almost bounced in her seat. Lisette sipped champagne and smiled indulgently. Arthur spent time in the back of the plane on his phone.

Darling assumed they were business calls—to lawyers, perhaps. His lawyer, about custody of Brisa. Then Arthur approached.

"Daddy asked me to bring you all to his home for dinner tomorrow," Arthur said. "He has a few other guests coming, but he'll see you first. He wants to meet his granddaughter."

Darling stared at his manager. And then he shrugged off his disquiet and watched his daughter. She had a tall glass of lemonade in her hand and a plate of small sandwiches on a table next to her. She seemed unable to stop grinning. "You like the plane?"

"So much!"

"If you want anything, you just tell the attendant."

"I'm fine, thank you," Brisa said.

It seemed Agnes had done a good job teaching his daughter manners. That would be a plus when he introduced her to Daddy.

Arthur smiled across the aisle at Brisa. But his smug look bothered Darling. Something was brewing, and he wanted none of it. Control, that was the issue. Who had it—and who didn't.

Darling tried to imagine what Arthur was up to as they flew and then as they landed in Burbank. Of course, as soon as the door to the plane opened and the stairs were lowered, he understood. He glanced over his shoulder with his brows raised, but his manager merely shrugged.

Darling was the first off, his eyes protected by sun glasses, his smile firmly affixed as the cameras rolled. But the smile didn't reach his eyes. Arthur had no right, not without asking him first.

At the bottom of the steps he turned to offer a hand to his wife, who was waving and smiling brilliantly. No one liked cameras as much as Lisette. Brisa, on the other hand, stood with wide eyes. Arthur, just behind, bent forward to whisper something in her ear. Arthur seemed to be doing his best to shrug off Darling's trust, if not his friendship, without a single move of his shoulders.

Cameras and microphones pressed toward them. Darling upped the amperage on his smile and waited on the tarmac for Brisa to reach his side so he could draw her close. Voices cried out, the questions slapping them from all sides.

Arthur stepped forward. "Yes," he said to their audience, "as you've heard, Darling and his wife received a surprise visit last night from this lovely young girl. Look at her, won't you? Isn't she the spitting image of Darling? Brisa is indeed Darling's daughter, although he only recently discovered her very existence."

More questions flew. This time, Darling raised his hand to stop them.

"It seems that in my youth, I had an encounter with a young woman, and that encounter resulted in a pregnancy. Mistakenly, Brisa's mother did not feel I had a right to know I was to be a father. I am so pleased that my manager, Arthur Ames"—he waved toward Arthur—"was able to discover this beautiful young girl and tell me about her. I regret the years I was not allowed to know my precious daughter or to help take care of her, but now Lisette and I have this incredible opportunity to get to know her. I hope you will rejoice with us in our good fortune."

Several reporters asked where the mother was, what her name was, and how Brisa had come to be there, considering he'd mentioned this was a "surprise" visit.

Arthur stepped forward again. "It seems the mother is reluctant for her daughter to spend time with or even talk to her daddy. We are taking steps to seek a court order that will allow Brisa to visit with her father. Brisa, being a highly intelligent and resourceful young lady, found a way to get here on her own—"

"You mean, she ran away from home?" shouted one man. Darling didn't recognize him.

"She wanted to be with her father. She hadn't known about him for the first twelve years of her life," Arthur admitted. "When she landed, she was able to contact Darling because he'd given her a cell phone, and his wife, the beautiful and talented Lisette, met her at the airport."

Lisette stepped forward with a regal nod. "I was so very thrilled, *vous comprenez*, to meet *ma belle-fille*. Is she not the image of my beloved Darling?"

Darling squeezed Brisa closer. "We are indeed thrilled she has come to visit us." He smiled down at her. He wouldn't mention a permanent change.

"And you, Brisa?" another reporter asked as cameras clicked throughout the crowd. "You must have been frightened to come all this way on your own."

"It's okay," Darling told her. "You may speak to them if you wish."

"Um, I was a little, I guess. But I knew my… um… my daddy would take care of me. He'd promised."

"That's all folks," Arthur said, easing himself in front of the others to create a path for Darling to lead his wife and daughter to the waiting limo. "I'm sure you'll be hearing from Darling and Brisa again soon, but for now, they're tired. It's time he took his daughter home and got her settled."

"Thank you all for coming," Darling said, waving even as he ushered Lisette into the backseat.

He helped Brisa step in next. Arthur was the last to settle in the car. He tucked his briefcase at his feet. "That went well," he said. "By the way, your car is waiting for you at home. Daddy suggested the limo. Looks better."

Brisa grinned. In spite of how it had come about, Darling had to agree this impromptu news conference might have been a brilliant move.

"You didn't warn me. Why?" he asked his supposed best friend.

"Just following orders."

"Daddy." Suddenly the great marketing move made him want to puke. When would they treat him like an adult? An adult who'd made them both richer than they'd ever been and who just might be able to think for himself?

He was no longer the seventeen-year-old hick Daddy had snatched out of one world and into another. He wasn't even the nineteen-year-old Daddy handed over to the up-and-coming Arthur.

He was grown, successful, and able to take charge of himself and his family.

When he might have been sucked deeper into the sludge of anger, he glanced up. Brisa was gnawing on her lower lip. "Hey," he said. "You okay?"

"Who's Daddy? You said 'Daddy.'"

"Your grandfather." Darling let his smile spread at the thought of Daddy being anyone's grandfather. He remembered the grandfather back in Georgia, all big laughs and big pats. His own father? Hah.

"Oh," Brisa said.

"Everybody calls him Daddy Evermire."

"Will I meet him?"

"You will indeed. He's already invited us to his house tomorrow."

"Oh." The child looked slightly overwhelmed. "That's nice, isn't it?"

"He'll like you."

He did not mention that she'd like him, because no one *liked* Daddy. Not even his wives. They'd liked his money and his power, but when those wore thin, they'd left. Hadn't bothered Daddy much. He just replaced them, although he said after the last one left that he thought he might just bed the next and forget about marriage. "Four's enough."

Darling couldn't imagine. He only had one, and that was all he wanted. But Lisette seemed focused on the passing scenery of cars and more cars. He wished she'd turn back and engage with them. Engage with Brisa.

He patted Brisa's hand. "We're going to have a great time."

---

By the time they'd dropped Arthur off and Darling had had the pleasure of Lisette's megawatt smile directed at him the rest of the way home, he'd relaxed into the moment. He would let Arthur and his father figure out the legal thing of keeping Brisa here, and he and his family would settle in.

The driver carried their bags into the foyer, and Darling followed Brisa as she wandered across the living room to the windows overlooking the city below and the sea beyond. She stood mesmerized, her bottom lip again between her teeth. He waited a few moments while Lisette plopped down on the sunken couches and lit a cigarette.

"This is all yours?" Brisa asked, almost in a whisper. She glanced up at him, her eyes shining.

"It is. Do you like it?"

She nodded. Her smile widened. The kid was gorgeous.

"It's incredible," she said.

"Would you like a tour?"

"That would be great."

He looked over at Lisette, but she'd picked up the television remote. He hated having a TV in the living room. After all, they had a media room. But she'd insisted they install a large one here. "I do not like to be so far away from you, *mon amour,* cooped in a room like a theater."

He and Brisa had just entered the hall toward the first-floor rooms when he heard his name mentioned. He turned her around and went to watch.

There they were, on the screen, the four of them, as the announcer talked about him and his secret daughter. Brisa drew in a sharp breath.

"That's us," she said. "I'm on TV."

He pulled her to his side. "You are. You're going to be famous."

"Oh, wow."

"Come, *ma petite*. Sit here with me. There is time enough to show you the house and your room." Lisette patted the couch, and Brisa dashed down the three steps and to her side.

So, it had begun. The campaign.

3 8

AGNES

"Turn on your television," Tadie said when Agnes answered
her phone.

"I don't have one. What's going on?"

"Brisa. She's on the television with Darling and his wife. And
some other man. They just got off an airplane, looks like some
fancy private one. Okay, now they're getting in a limo."

"How does she look? How does she seem?"

"Well. She looks well. Fine."

"Tell me the truth, Tadie."

"Think about it. She's being interviewed for the first time in
her life. They were talking about how she got there all on her
own, making a case, I guess for the fact that she wasn't
kidnapped, but she'd just wanted to see her long-lost father."

"You think it'll be online?"

"Bound to be at some point."

"Okay." But it wasn't okay, was it? Agnes shuddered.

"What can we do? Anything?"

Agnes sighed. "I guess you could pray."

"Oh, honey, we are. Our whole church is. They remember
Brisa from the Christmas pageant. Jilly, all of us, were hoping
she'd join us for the Easter one."

"Yeah, well, Darlington got in the way. Thank you for letting me know about his latest strafing run."

"Strafing? What's that?"

"When a fighter plane goes in low at high speed with guns blazing."

Tadie laughed. "You are a surprise, Agnes. How do you know about that?"

"I read. You wouldn't believe all the things I've picked up in my years of library visits."

"You've changed how I'm going to look at this man's interference forever." She laughed again. "I've got to tell Will."

"Yeah, you go on and do that. Thanks again for calling."

"You need distraction, come on over. Anytime."

"I appreciate it. I just may take you up on it. At the moment, Brisa's dog and I are commiserating together."

After disconnecting, she patted the sweet dog's head, then wandered to the window to stare out at the darkening street. Did she want to see Darlington and his wife parading around with her daughter?

Not really. But, yeah, she guessed she did. She punched in numbers for Hen's phone and waited.

"Hey, Agnes." He didn't sound as warm as he had yesterday.

"I just heard from Tadie. Brisa was interviewed with her father and his wife, and Tadie saw it on television."

"Ah." His voice was still cold. Still aloof. "What channel?" What was up with him?

"I have no idea. I don't even own a TV." She hesitated. "Are you okay? I mean, did I catch you at a bad time?"

"Sort of."

"I'm sorry. I should have asked first. I'm sure you're busy. I'll talk to you later." She was babbling. She didn't give him time to say more before she disconnected.

Maybe she should call Rita. But before she could implement that idea, her phone rang. Hen said, "How can I help you?"

"I don't know. I don't want to bother you, but I was thinking you know so much about research on the computer, but only if you have time. I'm sorry for interrupting you."

He sighed. "Look, you didn't. You want me to see what I can find and bring my computer over to show you?"

"Would that be too much trouble?"

"Of course not. I told you yesterday, I'd like to help any way I can."

An hour later, they were seated at her dining room table, the computer open in front of them. He'd brought his cell phone and said he needed to use it as a hotspot so they could go online. Whatever. The words meant little to her, but she ought to learn. As soon as the money came through from her mother's estate, she was going to buy herself a computer and get internet access for herself. Perhaps Hen would be willing to help her navigate that.

As he waited for the computer to boot up, he asked, "How are you dealing with all this?"

She *wasn't* dealing with it. She wanted to commit murder one minute, sob hysterically another, and lose yesterday's breakfast —again—the next. She couldn't eat. She couldn't sleep.

The weeping thing threatened, and she shook her head.

"I tried to come by last night. You'd obviously gone to bed."

He'd tried to come by? "Why didn't you knock?"

He stared at her for a moment. "I said I'd walk past and if all the downstairs lights were off, I'd go on home."

"Oh."

*Oh?* She couldn't be more eloquent than that? She said, "I'm so sorry. I forgot." That didn't sound any better, and when he raised one brow, she blushed. "I guess I was so upset, everything went out of my head."

"Makes sense."

He clicked on something, and there they were, her baby and

*him.* Agnes scooted closer and leaned in. So that's what the French wife looked like. Lisette. She was *beautiful*. That hair, blond, long, and those lashes, batting at the reporters.

Agnes squinted. Her girl was watching the woman and... what was that look on Brisa's face? Adoration?

Agnes was going to be sick. She was.

She swallowed against the acid and closed her eyes, blocking the images.

So what? Brisa would see through it all, wouldn't she?

*You didn't see through it, did you?*

"Mother, stop!"

"What?" Hen asked.

She looked up at him. Had she spoken aloud? "I... I..."

He laid a hand on hers and squeezed gently. "It's okay."

Leaning toward him, she felt the tears slide onto her cheeks. "I'm such a mess."

"No, you're scared. But God has this. He really does."

That straightened her spine, and she pushed away. "You think? So far, that hasn't exactly happened."

Hen smiled that sweet gentle smile. "Sometimes he's working, and we just don't recognize it. That doesn't mean he's not there."

She shook her head. "I don't have time for platitudes right now. I mean, I appreciate everyone's prayers, but I have to figure out how to get my daughter home."

## 39

## DARLING

D arling paced his carpeted office, around the desk, across to the windows that faced the hillside, back to the wall of plaques and awards, around, back, again, and again. His bare feet reveled in the plush pile. At least something touched his skin while Lisette was plagued with headaches from her monthlies.

"*Je suis désolé*," she'd said. *I'm sorry.*

She hadn't looked very sorry. Or headachy.

He forgot about her rejection when he remembered summers of running barefoot through Georgia fields, down by the river, wiggling toes in mud. He'd had a pack of friends back then, boys who worked the fields like his granddaddy and his uncles did, uncles his own daddy had disavowed when he'd gone off and made it big.

Disavowed like Daddy had done to Mama Bea. But hadn't he done the same?

Well, yes, but Daddy'd explained it all to him. The uncles and Mama Bea liked their simple country life, couldn't be expected to appreciate the finer things. Had he heard from any of them since he'd moved to California? No. Not a single letter.

Which, suddenly, didn't seem right.

Wouldn't they have written? Mama Bea had promised. But she hadn't even acknowledged the money Daddy'd promised to have sent.

He ought to visit her, see how she was gettin' on. And his cousins. He had a passel of cousins. Billy, Isaiah, Joey, and Jeremiah had been the closest. He'd thought they'd write, least ways one of them speaking for the rest.

He should check in. He'd let Daddy run things long enough.

Of course, some of Daddy's recent work had been helpful. He'd talked to the lawyer and the judge who happened to play golf with him, and who happened to think Darling had been ill-used by a woman who hadn't bothered to inform him he had a child. The Complaint had been filed on Friday, and by Monday at noon, Daddy and the lawyer were in the judge's office, presenting a Temporary Restraining Order and Temporary Custody Order, which the judge signed. Certified copies of the Complaint, Summons, and TRO/TOC were on the way to the Carteret County sheriff.

Arthur had warned him Agnes might try something, so he'd been able to avoid getting served legal papers here and would continue to do so, no matter what she tried to throw at him. Thank heavens for Todd, who knew how to keep all process servers away by just checking the outside monitors. If he didn't recognize the person, he didn't let them past the gate.

All good, Darling thought as he slipped his feet into his around-the-house loafers and headed to the living room. "Hey, ladies," he called to his wife and daughter. "What you two planning?"

Ah, there was Arthur. Darling hadn't heard him arrive.

"The birthday party for *la petite*," Lisette said.

She had insisted they host a party to show off their girl-child. "She will wear the lemony dress we bought, yes? It is not too old or too young but will be perfect. And I will wear one that is of the same color, and we will match!" Lisette's laugh was more of a gurgle of delight.

Brisa glanced up at him, still unsure.

"It sounds great," he said. "You'll both be beautiful." But why did Lisette want to dress them both in a color that matched Lisette's hair? Still, his wife was the designer. She must know what she was doing.

Arthur leaned against the foyer entry, a tumbler of something in his hand. "You think it's wise to have a big party? So soon?" He addressed his question to Darling.

"Why not?" he said, watching the interplay between Brisa and Lisette as the latter fingered his daughter's curls. "Brisa has a birthday. It'll be fun."

Arthur lifted his glass and sipped. The ice clinked as he lowered it. "How many of the invitees are going to be children Brisa's age? Do you actually know any?"

"Lisette's taking care of it." And then he thought of something else. "Will Daddy expect to come?"

"For family, of course."

He was strumming his favorite acoustic guitar and practicing one of their new songs when Brisa walked into the living room. He glanced up and smiled.

Her grin widened, and before he could say anything, she'd joined in. She was singing a song that hadn't been released yet. "You know the words and the tune." He didn't make it a question.

She was sitting on her hands now. "I do. I met the woman who wrote the song. Her grandma lives down the street from my best friend in Beaufort." She grinned. "I'm gonna see her next time she comes to visit."

He wouldn't react to that. Next time the songwriter visited Beaufort? No, Brisa would see her right here in L.A. "My manager knows her. Jeminy Buchanan, right? If you want, Arthur can arrange for her to come to your birthday party."

"What is it that Arthur can arrange?" Lisette had come in so quietly he hadn't noticed.

He patted a place on his other side. "Join us."

"I am still busy, but I heard *la petite*'s voice singing with you. Very beautiful."

"Seems she met the songwriter in Beaufort, wants me to invite her to the birthday party."

"*Vraiment?* Really? This would not be too many people?"

What was that emotion he saw in her eyes? They were hard as she looked into his.

Brisa seemed not to notice. "She's so nice! I would love to see her again."

The eyes, still uncompromising, turned to Brisa. "But perhaps she will be unavailable."

Darling could almost hear the *she'd better be* in Lisette's tone. He was staying out of this one. Lisette pouted those full lips and then lifted one shoulder in a half-shrug. "It matters not. We will have a lot of people and a lot of food, and it will be a good time, *n'est-ce pas?*"

"Of course," he answered.

He set his guitar on the table in front of him and asked, "What are your plans for this afternoon?"

Brisa watched Lisette.

"I am to see Dominique. I thought to take Brisa."

"Don't let them do anything radical to her hair. I like it the way it is."

"I'm going to keep growing it," Brisa said proudly, flipping her soft ponytail from side to side. "Mom said I look good with long hair because mine is wavy and curly."

"It's gorgeous," Darling said.

Lisette waved a dismissing hand. "I go alone then."

"I'm sorry," Brisa said. "I'd be happy to go with you if you want."

"This time, no," Lisette said, gliding toward the hall. "Perhaps the next."

After she'd left, Brisa bowed her head. "I didn't mean to upset her. I'm sorry."

Darling lifted her chin and leaned over to kiss her forehead. "You did nothing. Don't worry about it."

He picked up his guitar. "What other songs do you know?"

## 40

## AGNES

Mr. Matthews phoned as Agnes was getting dressed for work. "Good news," he said, sounding pleased with himself. "I presented copies of the receipts that date the repairs on your mother's house both to the court and to the opposing lawyer. That lawyer has conferred with his clients. They are backing down on claims to a portion of the inheritance, which will allow us to close the estate soon."

"Oh." She could hardly believe it. After all this time, all that heartache and worry, she had trouble knowing what to say. "That's great. I mean, that's really great. Thank you so much."

"I also have a check for you for maintenance of the house. It's not the full amount, but perhaps it will help you until all the paperwork is completed."

"Anything. Anything will help. Thank you. Thank you again. So much." She'd be okay. She'd actually have some cash. She couldn't take it in.

She had no idea how much would be in her mother's estate after all the legal fees were deducted, but it would be substantial. The judge had had money. There'd certainly be more than she'd ever imagined owning.

"Do you want to pick up the check, or should we put it in the mail?" Mr. Matthews asked.

"Oh, I'll come by. I'm just on my way to work now, but you're only a little past there, a couple of blocks. I can make it. It won't take me long to get to you. And the bank's on the corner, so that's good. Thank you so much. Do I need to sign anything?" She was babbling, but oh, my...

With a small chuckle, he said, "I'll leave everything with the receptionist."

A ray of light in this dark place. As she set off down the sidewalk, she whispered, "Thank you," to whoever might be listening. And then she repeated it. "Thank you."

And she was pretty sure this time she directed it toward God.

---

The next morning, she woke to a little less despair than she'd felt yesterday and a little more hope. Because the check from the estate's lawyer had been written from an account in the same bank she used, the teller promised it would clear very soon, which meant she'd be able to pay her bills. Most importantly, she'd be able to figure out how to get her daughter back.

Eric Houston hadn't billed her yet, but he would. She bet he lived in a fancy house and drove a fancy car. And she'd help him maintain his lifestyle. Yay for her.

Rita? Well, Rita had been helping her for nothing, hadn't asked for a dime. It seemed to Agnes that paying Rita—who couldn't be making much at the Women and Children's Center— would be the act of a friend. Sure, Rita's doctor husband probably made enough for the both of them, but Agnes was *not* going to take on the mindset that she was owed. That somehow folk should "do" for her without earning their fair wage.

Even Eric. Henry's brother.

She bent forward until her forehead touched the dining table. The cold of the wood felt like her heart. How could she endure this? Her daughter lost. Her baby, in his hands. The love of her life, gone.

And if one other person told her it would all be okay, she'd scream.

"We're praying," Tadie and Rita and Becca had said.

Hen had said it. Clay had said it. His wife had called with the same words. Hannah Morgan, too.

Thank you so much. They were praying.

Maybe it was time for her to take action, real action, like going to get her daughter.

Her bills could wait. They'd been waiting, hadn't they?

"Patience," Hen had said. "Rita is doing her best. And now she has my brother on the case. Eric is a fine lawyer."

*Patience?* Easy for him to say. Or for Rita or Eric. Easy, because it wasn't their child thousands of miles away. It wasn't their child who was gone—and who hadn't called home.

She was pretty sure she couldn't just march up to Darlington's front door and demand to see her daughter. Well, she could, but then what? She couldn't force Brisa to leave with her, not without a judge saying so. And if she came face to face with her sweet girl and that sweet girl told her to go away?

She'd die. She'd simply die.

Would Brisa care that they'd talked of having a party here? Not when she had the excitement of L.A. at the tip of her fingers.

Agnes raised her head and spoke aloud. "Please."

At her feet, Link whined. "Oh, Link, I'm so sorry. You're missing her, too, aren't you, sweet boy?"

He slept on Brisa's bed every night, sniffing for her, waiting. This morning, Agnes had stood in the doorway, watching, commiserating with the dog, united with him in misery. "She'll come home," she'd whispered to the room and the dog. He'd merely glanced up and returned to his post.

"If that man corrupts her, I'll kill him." But her words bounced back, unheard by anyone except perhaps the God who hated murder.

"Fine. Maybe I wouldn't be able to get close enough to pull a trigger, if I even knew how to do more than point and try, if I even had access to a firearm. But I'd want to."

That got her sitting up straighter. If God didn't like murder, maybe she could make a deal with him. "How about this? You don't want me to kill anyone, and yet you've got to know Darlington is a bad man, and that bad man has my baby in his clutches. So, will you fix it? I mean, you could kill him, right? Like you did in the Bible? I remember something about you smiting some liars, and this guy's more than a liar."

She bit her inner cheek. Caught a thumbnail between her teeth. Sighed loudly.

"Okay, okay. You probably don't slay people on a regular basis any more, but this Goliath is going to take more than a stone from me. Or even the five David had. So, maybe you could do something, send a real David into the battle? I don't know. You could make him sick—you know, boils or a plague. I doubt he has a conscience you could tweak. He sure didn't when he helped conceive her."

There was only silence once the echo of her voice died. She was a fool.

"Whatever."

When her phone rang, she ignored it. Whoever it was could leave a message, because, unless Brisa...

Wait, what if it were Brisa?

She scurried into the kitchen and grabbed her phone without looking at the number. "Hello?"

"Hey." It was only Hen.

Suddenly, thinking his name made her angry. Calling someone "Hen" sounded stupid. What man would let himself be named after a chicken? And a female one at that? He ought to be Henry.

"Hello, Henry."

"Uh, hello."

"You needed something?"

He cleared his throat. "You've never called me Henry before."

"I never thought of it, but why are you called anything else? What's wrong with Henry? It's a nice name."

"My brother started calling me Hen when we were kids in honor of one of the bantam hens Cook kept out back, a runty one who kept escaping the coop. Eric and I had great fun chasing her around the yard, which brought Cook's wrath down on us." Henry's voice held traces of humor. "Eric pointed at my skinny knock-kneed legs and flailing arms and said I looked like the chicken. The name stuck."

"I think I'll unstick it, if you don't mind."

"My sponsor calls me Henry. That will be two of you."

"Good. It fits you better."

"Thank you." He paused a moment, then said, "How are you today?"

"The same." Then, "How do I do it, Hen..ry?" Her voice broke as she damped back the tears. "How?"

"One day at a time." And then, "May I stop by?"

"I was going to try to take Link for a walk. Meet you at *Samantha's*? One of the sidewalk tables?"

He'd sit with her, try to make her laugh. He'd offer to help with whatever she needed to fix or do. Maybe he'd even distract her with a touch. A hug. Or maybe even something more.

---

Agnes put some speed into the walk to the coffee shop, swinging her hands, stretching her legs, breathing in the seventy-degree spring air. Maybe endorphins would kick in to dispel her gloom. As her mother used to say, a positive attitude went a long way toward changing a situation.

Like her mother'd walked around as Mrs. Happy. Must have been a do-as-I-say-not-as-I-do.

Agnes slowed her pace when two couples emerged from

Clawson's Restaurant without even checking to see if the sidewalk was empty. As she paused, Henry crossed the street toward her.

"Fancy meeting you here," he said, only his eyes showing the humor behind his words. "What happened to Link?"

"He refused to leave the house. He's really taking Brisa's absence hard."

"Poor boy. I wonder if you could use that in some way. Maybe try to do a video call with Brisa so he can see her—and so she can see how much he misses her."

"I call every day, but that woman won't let me talk to her. I doubt very much they'll let me see her."

"Can't Rita or Eric intervene to make them?"

"I don't know. Maybe. I hope so."

She was quiet then, lost in thought, and he didn't push her, but she was conscious of his arm swinging very slightly next to hers and of the weight of her own. She'd never realized how awkward walking next to someone could be when you weren't quite sure how close you could get. What exactly did you do with that arm, the one only two inches from his?

When he took hold of it and slid her hand around the crook of his, she almost sighed with relief.

He held the door for her into *Samantha's*. Coming here had been a rare treat since she'd moved to town. Maybe now it wouldn't have to be— once she got Brisa home and thoughts of her daughter didn't threaten to knock her flat.

"Good afternoon!" came the cheery greeting of the manager.

"Afternoon, Tootie," Henry said. "How're you doing?"

"Great, Hen. How 'bout you? And it's Agnes, isn't it?"

Agnes was surprised the young woman knew her name. "It is. I'm glad to see you again."

"What can I get you?"

"Tea for me," Agnes said. "Green, please. One too many coffees already today."

"Can you make mine a latte?" Henry turned to Agnes. "Anything to eat?"

"No thanks. I don't have much of an appetite."

"Grab a table," he said. "I'll bring our drinks."

She found a table by the window where they could watch the street traffic but be far from other patrons. Jittery, that's what she was, both inside and out. Her hands wanted to pick at something, preferably each other, and so she picked up a napkin and spread it on her lap. When he arrived with her tea and his coffee, she thanked him and said, "I got a check for the house, a little money, and I want to fly out and get her."

"Really?"

"I need to talk to Rita." Agnes cradled her cup in her hands, trying to transfer some of its warmth to her suddenly chilled core. "I'm afraid she'll say I can't, that I don't have the right to take my own daughter. Brisa will have to want to come with me, and I don't think she will, not yet."

"Are you sure?"

"She ran away because she wants time with him."

He sighed. "How much time are you planning to give her?"

"Oh, Henry, I want her home now." She bit the inside of her lip to keep the tears—and the scream—away.

He touched the back of her hand as if to soothe her. "Brisa loves you. You're her mother. I'll say it again—she'll remember all the years you've given her," he said. "All the love you've poured into her."

"What if she doesn't?" She would not cry.

He spoke softly. "Listen to me. She will. Maybe not in the next week or two, but you have to trust."

"I wish," she said in just above a whisper, "I wish I knew how to do that."

"Look, Brisa's been longing for a daddy her whole life. She's smart, and you've raised her well, with lots of love and discipline. You've given her a sense of security and self-worth that's not going to vanish just because her world has been enlarged to include a self-centered musician who happens to have donated his sperm."

That forced a bark of self-conscious laughter from her.

"She's had almost twelve years to absorb the values you've instilled in her. She won't forget."

Agnes wished she could be certain of that. All she could do was sigh.

"God doesn't promise us an easy road or a certain road, but he does promise to walk with us and to bring us out on the other side. He is right here, walking with us—if we let him in."

"I don't know how to shift from here to there. Faith like that feels so foreign to me. How can I imagine God's going to suddenly step in and fix things after I've ignored him all these years?"

Leaning back in his chair and sipping his latte, Henry didn't answer right away. Finally, he said, "Just call on him." Another pause. "The way I see it, he's either God, or he isn't. He's either who he claims to be, or he's not. I mean, I don't think he's considering this some sort of *quid pro quo,* like he's going to measure out how many prayers to answer based on what you do for him or how much you believe in him. He wants to bless you. Period."

"You think?"

"I do. Trusting him is something I've been learning daily, hourly. Without the Lord, I'd be in jail or in the hospital—or I'd be dead."

*Dead?* She slammed shut her eyes at that thought.

The ramifications of addiction had never touched her life—unless she imagined Darlington addicted to power and getting his way. What did they call that these days? Narcissism? Jenelle, the waitress who had an abusive boyfriend and a baby by him, had told her how only his truth and his wants mattered. That sounded familiar. When Jenelle's boyfriend actually hit her, she'd let the battery charge stick, so if there was a next time, he'd go right back to jail, and for a lot longer.

Wouldn't that be great, Darlington in jail? It would never happen, but she could dream. Unless he got there by hurting her daughter.

A hand settled on hers. "I lost you for a moment," Henry said.

"I'm sorry. I was imagining Darlington in jail."

Henry hooted. "Good image!"

"Yeah, but it'll never happen." She sighed. "I remembered Jenelle and her narcissistic boyfriend."

"She told you." He didn't make it a question.

"She did. It's horrible."

"It is. At least she has family at *Agua Verde*."

"Really?" Agnes asked. "Who?"

"Oh, I don't mean literally, but we watch out for her. The owners, the rest of us."

"I didn't know."

"They've been good to me, too. Encouraging and also watching to make sure the pressure's not too much."

"Is it ever? Too much, I mean?"

He smiled at that. "Not so far." When she didn't speak, he continued. "I'm one of the fortunate ones. I have my brother here, and I have my mentor, Father Stanley, who came alongside me when I did my last stint in rehab. He's still reachable by phone, and I'll be forever grateful for his insights and his encouragement, but, most of all, for his prayers."

She had nothing to say to that either, although she supposed she should be grateful if that priest's advent had helped Henry get clean—and stay clean. When the silence had thickened to uncomfortable, she pointed to their mugs. "You finished?"

"Yep." He stood.

Outside, clouds scudded across the sky, making her wonder if there'd be a storm soon. She tucked her hands out of the way in her pockets, but they were still too close, she and Henry.

"Becca said something I didn't quite understand," she said. "You know her, she's full of God talk, and she told me she'd gotten assurance Brisa will be back home before very long. Then she said all we have to do is bide." She glanced up at him. "What do you think she meant by me *biding*?"

"I can almost hear her saying it. I'm sure she meant you should trust and wait on God."

"And if I sit around, Brisa's going to magically show up at home?"

"Maybe not today or tomorrow—and not magically. Sometimes we have to wait for the answer as God strengthens our faith muscles."

"I don't have any muscles for him to strengthen. Besides, this biding thing sounds way too passive. I'd rather get on a plane and go get her. Do something besides sitting around and praying."

Henry laughed. "I get that. Waiting and trusting are always hard."

"It's not at all like biding your time, which I guess is more waiting until it's the right time to act."

"But maybe there's some of that in what she says. You know, not acting until the time is right—or until God says to move forward."

"Like I'd ever hear God say anything." She'd imagined the words muttered too softly for him to hear, but old eagle-ears nudged her with his elbow.

"You might, though. You just might."

*Ha,* but she didn't utter that aloud.

His last words to her as he dropped her at home were, "Call Rita."

---

Rita had been furious that Agnes wasn't allowed to speak to her daughter and promised to get Clay on it. "Maybe someone from the LAPD can go to the home to check up on Brisa—and take the process server with them," Rita said. "The problem is, they have no concrete evidence against him—and no record of past sins."

"Because I didn't report the rape when it happened."

"I'm only saying that this is a difficult situation we're facing with no judgement rendered and no determination of jurisdiction. At the very least I'll see if Clay can get a cell phone number for Darlington so you can try him directly instead of continuing to go through Darlington's wife."

"I can't stand not doing something. I want to go out there."

"I'll talk to Clay and Eric and be in touch."

While Agnes waited for answers, there was work, there was sleep—some—and there was another day. There was letting Link out, there was trying to tempt him to eat more than a bite or two, and there was watching him climb the stairs to Brisa's room.

She tried to comfort him, but he wouldn't be comforted.

Becca came and went and spent a lot of time talking to that God of hers.

The bank said she could access a portion of the check, enough to buy groceries so Becca could eat and she could nibble. After she shopped and put the food away, she mopped the kitchen floor. It wasn't really dirty, but she hadn't washed it in a while. It kept her hands busy. She wished it kept her mind occupied.

And then Clay phoned. "Is Eric Houston on your case or just Rita?"

Puzzled, she said, "I think both, but I've only spoken to Rita."

"Call her and see if she can come by around two. I'll meet you at your house."

"What's going on? Can't you tell me now?"

"I'll see you then."

Agnes checked her watch. She had two hours to wait. She clicked on Rita's number and left a message.

When Rita returned the call, Agnes repeated Clay's words.

"I'll be there."

Agnes made herself a salad but pushed most of it around with her fork instead of bringing it to her mouth. To take her mind off not eating, she wrote checks. She wouldn't mail them until she knew the money was safely tucked in her account, but she'd begun the process of getting out of debt.

When both Rita and Clay had arrived, Rita asked, "What's going on, Clay? Did you get the phone number we need?"

Clay shook his head. "Not yet. I'm here on another matter. I didn't want to say anything over the phone, but I happened to 'hear' that some paperwork came in from California late yesterday. I think it included a Complaint, where Darlington, as plaintiff, argues that you never told him about a child resulting from a consensual one-night stand. There's more, at least a Temporary Order of Custody. I'm not sure what else, as the sheriff seems to have temporarily misplaced it."

"Oh, really?" Rita asked, her eyes twinkling.

"Yep. I'm not sure how long it will be before he finds it again, but you may not want to waste much time thinking instead of acting."

"No, indeed," Rita said. "We've filed our own paperwork, but we need to get that TOC granted here—and we need Darlington to accept service."

"Well, that's all I wanted to say, except that I'll try to get Darlington's cell phone number for you, Agnes. I'll let you two figure out what's next on the paperwork front, and I'll mention maybe overhearing that you're waiting for Darlington to accept service of your papers—so the sheriff can make sure what he has stays hidden a while. Other than that, I don't think I want to be involved—plausible deniability when it comes to that paperwork. That okay with you?"

"Absolutely." Rita saw him out the door and turned to Agnes. "We have to file additional motions immediately, before the sheriff has to 'find' and serve those papers. Darlington's team is obviously trying to fight through the California courts as well as through the media."

"We can't let him do that."

"No, we can't. I'll head over to Eric's office now and call you as soon as I have something ready."

"Can I go get her?" Agnes asked. "I want to fly out and bring her back."

Rita touched her forearm. "I know you do. I'm right there with you. But you don't want to show up and have them serve papers on you, which is exactly what they'd do. It's a jurisdictional issue, and we want to keep custody determination right here in North Carolina."

Agnes sighed. "I know. But sitting here doing nothing is killing me."

"Let's get our papers filed and served on him, and then I'll put pressure on for them to let her talk to you. He has to emerge from his house sometime, so a little while longer. Okay?"

With another sigh, Agnes nodded. "She's supposed to be in school."

"I'm putting that in the petition for custody. Charging that he has no idea how to take care of a child while noting that Brisa is enrolled in school here and needs to come back."

"Let's hope they pay attention."

Action had been in short supply since Brisa's departure. Waiting for the courts, waiting for a judge, waiting for a phone number... It was making her crazy.

# 41

## AGNES

Agnes wanted her baby home. She wanted to hear her voice, to touch her soft skin, to press her close. To celebrate her birthday. Why hadn't she written Darlington's cell number down when she had access to it? She hadn't even thought to figure out the number of her daughter's phone.

But—and she really needed an answer to this one—why hadn't Brisa used her phone to call home? Was she still so angry? Had she stopped loving Agnes, stopped caring that she even *had* a mother? Brisa *knew* how much Agnes loved her. She *had* to know.

Where was Clay? Was he so busy keeping Beaufort free of crime that he hadn't been able to dig around for the number yet?

Lying here in bed, she studied the sunlight traipsing its way across the floor. Soon, the dark blue and rose that edged her mother's thick Chinese rug would bleach out where those rays hit.

So what? A rug was a rug.

*Stop that,* the voice in her head said. *That's a valuable rug, very old.*

"Fine, Mother, it's worth something. Who cares?"

*You should. Get up, get moving.*

This had to stop. "Leave me alone," she said to the specter that didn't exist. Imagining a voice was one step away from a straight-jacket/padded-cell asylum. She'd get up and find that letter. Maybe reading it would make the voice in her head shut up.

---

She pawed through her desk drawers, trying to remember where she'd stuffed all the correspondence she'd been given after the reading of her mother's will. Finally, she unearthed it, bound with a rubber band to the other letters, its envelope her mother's favorite pale blue with flowers decorating the flap. Agnes used a silver letter opener, also her mother's, also decorated with flowers, to slice along the top edge. And then she pulled out the handwritten sheet.

But she couldn't bring herself to do more than tuck it in her pocket where the heat of it forced her to tie on running shoes and hit the sidewalk.

Who was she kidding? She didn't have the energy to jog. So, she walked, arms swinging to propel her legs to a faster forward motion. Sweat beaded, dripped, made her shirt cling front and back. She hadn't bothered with sunscreen or a hat, and she'd pay for it if she kept this up. Besides, there were people out, too many people, and she didn't want witnesses.

A quick dash inside to grab her purse, a hat, and sunscreen, and she was in her car, waiting for cool to take the place of sweltering as she drove. She hadn't consciously chosen a destination, and yet, here she was, turning onto Atlantic Beach causeway, then left at the light.

She knew a spot where she could park, climb the dunes, and be away from the beach huggers. She left her car far from the path and made her way to the ocean, tucking the letter safely away in her purse. Standing at the top of a dune, she noticed storm clouds brewing on the horizon, but she had time, time to kick off her shoes and dig her toes in the sand. Time to let herself feel the growing wildness of the sea in front of her.

Waves crested, broke, and rolled in, leaving the froth at her feet. She longed to plunge into the water, dive through the breakers, swim far and fast and away, to somehow escape the pain of Brisa's absence and her own inability to fix anything. She'd been so afraid for so long. From the moment she'd awoken in that hotel room, she'd lost her sense of self, hadn't she?

Or had it begun before then, back after her father's death when her mother'd barely been able to cope and had been so critical of her child? Agnes had never been quite good enough. Never quite pretty enough or talented enough. Her mother hadn't valued Agnes's intelligence or her perfect grades because Agnes hadn't looked good next to her. Then the unplanned pregnancy had pounded the nail in their relationship's coffin.

And now there was the letter.

Agnes returned to her small pile on the sand and dug the letter from her purse. Taking a deep breath in preparation, she smoothed it open and read.

*My darling Agnese,*

*If you're reading this, I have succumbed to the heart issues I'd not wanted anyone to know about. You've discovered that I left you the house your step-father, the beloved judge, made sure I inherited at his death. And I've left you a sizable inheritance to go along with it.*

*I know this won't make up for the times I failed you. It won't make up for my not being there for you when you really needed me. I'm sorry for that.*

*Since moving to Beaufort, I've discovered a new faith, a new relationship with God. I'd say I discovered it again, but there's no again about the way I worshipped—or didn't—when you were young. And I've spent a lot of time with my priest, trying to work through my litany of sins, most of them against you. I wish I could have done so in life and not had to wait until death to tell you, but you wouldn't take my phone calls or answer my letters.*

*I suppose you learned unforgiveness from me, so I've no one to blame but myself. I'm praying that you will find it in your heart to forgive me finally and to accept that your mother loved you with an imperfect love, one I hope you'll finally believe in. I hope you'll find the God who makes real love possible.*

*I have one more request of you. In the attic, you'll find a box labeled* Brisa. *Will you show my beautiful granddaughter the letters I wrote to her? I didn't begin until her fourth birthday, because it wasn't until then that I realized how horrible I'd been—to both of you. Rejection is a terrible thing, and I rejected you and that beautiful girl for far too long.*

*I am proud of you, Agnese. I was always proud of you, even in the days when I failed to show you how much. I've had to live with my guilt and my failed love for too many years now. May it end with me. And may you find all the love you so deserve in the life you lead here in Beaufort.*

*I love you.*

*Your mother*

*Trying to fix things at the end.*

Tears dripped down Agnes's cheeks long before she'd finished reading her mother's words for the third time. How had she not known? Why had they wasted so many years?

She swiped away the wet and squinted. Squinted away any remaining tears as the truth slammed into her.

There was another side to this last-minute pasting on of *I'm sorry*, as if those words would fill a lifetime's worth of gaps. Because the question remained—why hadn't Sandra Jones Ware tried harder when it might have made a real difference in her daughter's life? In her granddaughter's? She could have gotten in a car or on a bus. Jersey City wasn't the other end of the universe. Her mother'd had *years* to make this right.

"Easier to have a pity party and talk the talk instead of walking the walk, right, Mom? Write your sweet letter of 'I'm so sorry' and leave it for me to find when you no longer have to face me."

Agnes stuffed the sheet of paper into her purse and pressed the heel of one hand on her belly where the acid burned, the acid and the ache.

"Here, again, you put it on me. If only I'd returned your calls or opened your letters. Great. Exactly what in our relationship might have encouraged me to imagine kindness instead of recriminations?"

Instead, there'd been so much time and emotion wasted... Could have, should have, would have. Useless words. Useless baggage. Useless, wasted years.

Longing for a freedom she'd never found.

*O God. Please...*

She headed to the water's edge, her tears falling unchecked. She waded in, calf-deep, and dropped to her knees as the sea raced in and flooded out, pulling at her, willing her to let go, collapse fully into it, be sucked out and under and down with it. In the shallow water, she let herself fall forward, her hands braced on the sandy bottom. Sobs wrenched from her, and her chin took a hit from one of the waves. Suddenly afraid of the water's power as the breeze picked up force, she scrambled to her feet, but not before her tears had joined the salty sea water on its journey in and out and away.

Stumbling, she sloshed to the hard-packed sand and dropped again to knees, then all the way down, rolling onto her back, eyes open and staring at white clouds scurrying out of the way of the menacing dark ones. A storm was coming, and she lay exposed. Longing to be cleansed, washed, made whole.

Her mother wanted forgiveness, specifically hers. And Agnes wanted the hatred gone, an end to the wasted years of anger. Unless she sold the house, reminders of that same mother would remain with her, hurting her with the what-ifs.

Maybe they'd always be with her, those if-onlys, the regrets, the rejection. She'd worked so hard all these years so her mother's painful words wouldn't break her, so she'd be able to rise above the low expectations and make something of herself.

She sucked in a breath and blew it out, in and out, the exhale whistling through her teeth. Her mother hadn't come for her.

And she? What was she doing for her own girl?

## AGNES

Agnes tried to rejoice that Becca was here this afternoon, praying, because the object of the woman's prayers was Brisa, the birthday girl, who was far away, celebrating there and not here. Becca cooked at the stove and mumbled. She cleaned a bathroom—and it wasn't even one she used—and sang softly. Then she wandered the downstairs rooms, fanning her apron and taking the prayer and the singing to the next level in both volume and force.

Link sometimes parked himself near her, and those times gave Agnes hope for their beloved dog. Becca had taken to being the one to let Link out in the morning and sometimes in the evening, too. Maybe Link saw something in Becca that reached out to his grieving self.

When Henry stopped by before work, Agnes fixed a glass of tea for each of them and let him try to make her laugh. He knew what the day meant to her, and although his efforts failed, it was good of him to try.

In a few days, Brisa would have been gone a week. A week of no phone calls, no touches, no hugs. Just that thought made her eyes fill and her nose clog.

They were sitting in the living room when Becca wandered in

from the kitchen and belted out an old hymn Agnes thought she recognized from Sunday School way back when. She liked it well enough, but to have it invade her time with Henry? She was about to get up and suggest Becca keep the noise to the back of the house when Henry did the standing up and the intervening —by opening his mouth and joining in the song.

He moved next to Becca, his tenor blending perfectly with her alto. They sang of mountains high, of valleys low, of storms and raging seas, and, through it all, of the Creator who had set all in motion and could free them from any bondage.

The words that came from the two of them, the sounds that filled her house as the sunlight streamed through the glass panels surrounding the front door and illuminating the spot on which they stood, nearly had her, Agnes Jones, skeptic, on her feet. She definitely had tears leaking and streaming down her cheeks. She felt those, but she couldn't do more than swipe at them.

"How great... how great... is our God..."

She went to work that evening, and Henry walked her home. "You try to call out there today?"

"Yeah. Clay finally found the number that's supposed to be Darlington's, but both it and the one I have for his wife continue to go to voicemail. Rita said she'll draft a demand letter. But what's killing me is that Brisa hasn't tried phoning me. She must know how worried I am."

"Maybe she no longer has the cell phone."

"And maybe she's still mad at me."

"Or, she's too afraid to ask someone if she can call you," Henry said.

"That's a horrible thought."

"It is. I'm sorry. But it can't be because she doesn't miss you. She loves you."

"Yeah, I guess." She hoped.

Their footfalls echoed in the darkness, slap-click-slap. Under the illumination of a streetlamp, he kicked at a stone, sending it off into the road. A car approached and passed, the driver taking his time as if he had no one waiting for his return.

As Henry didn't. As she didn't. Henry because he lived alone by choice. She because her daughter had been enticed away and because Becca was spending the night with her own daughter and gathering with her church folk to pray. What awaited Agnes was a too big house, full of creaks and groans—and empty of girlish chatter.

They turned onto her walkway and up the porch steps. She dug in her purse for her house keys, then turned toward Henry. His fingers found her chin, he bent, and his lips touched hers.

His lips, oh my, his lips. She forgot everything, even how to think, as sensation overwhelmed her. They were tender, those lips of his, moving over hers with a barely-there touch that had her reaching for his shirt, pulling him closer, her lips trying to take more, feel more. He gave it to her for long minutes.

And then he lifted his head, and she felt bereft.

As she tried to steady her breathing, she watched him trying to do the same. And she smiled. "Oh, my," she said.

Did he want to come in? Was that the prelude to more?

She had just begun to consider what she should say when he touched her cheek and said, "I should be going now."

"Really?"

"I'll see you tomorrow."

She unlocked her door with unsteady hands and let herself in. Then she turned. "Good night, Henry."

"Good night."

She didn't shut the door until he was down the walkway and almost to the sidewalk. And then she braced her forehead against the cold wood and whispered again, "Good night." *My love.*

She eased away and turned to climb the stairs to her room.

She passed Brisa's, and there, looking up at her with his sad, sad eyes, was Link. She approached the bed and sat down on it.

"I know, boy, I know. I miss her so much. I wish she knew how much we need her, you and I." She ran her hand over his head, down his back. When he nuzzled her palm, she tried to whisper "I know," but the words broke on a sob. Link crawled forward so his head was in her lap.

When her tears finally dried up, she headed to her room to shed her clothes, hanging up her pants and tossing her shirt in the laundry basket. She finished her ablutions, pulled on a nightgown, and stood next to her big empty bed. Her eyes felt scratchy from tears, and her mind wouldn't stop surveying her world and her days and her empty house, whose creaks and moans sounded loud in a darkness that was only slightly grayed by the filtered streetlight from outside her two front windows.

The silent room down the hall screamed accusations like a banshee on the prowl: her silence had done this, her insistence that Brisa not know, not know, not know... Then he had come, offering all that he was to a daddy-starved child.

She walked that same hall and climbed in her daughter's bed, pulling Link close. He pushed his snout under her arm, squirming like a child until he was comfortable.

Eventually, his even breathing let her find sleep. Eventually.

# 43

## DARLING

His daughter's birthday party was in full swing, but Darling had yet to see any other children waiting for the games to start or the cake and ice cream to be served.

He glanced over at the uniformly blond hair, the almost identical midriff-revealing clothes, and the samey-same expressions of a fawning group of young women who didn't seem to notice that he paid them no attention after his quick appraisal. He imagined they were vying with one another for one-upmanship, not for his approval.

His gaze shifted, and he frowned. His father stood between Lisette and Brisa, one arm draped possessively across Lisette's delicate shoulders, the other hand sliding up Brisa's upper arm as he spoke. Brisa looked uncomfortable, maybe even worried.

"They're fine." Arthur's voice cut through the babble as the young women sidled off together in the direction of the bar, shifting their focus to other prey, blond heads nodding in unison to something.

He and Arthur stood isolated near the foyer entrance. "Brisa doesn't look happy," Darling said. "Lisette was supposed to invite some kids closer to her age. What happened to that idea?"

"Yeah, it doesn't look much like a party designed for a

251

twelve-year-old." Arthur sounded unconcerned. "Lisette and my secretary worked on the list. Maybe they couldn't find any kids willing to come, you know?"

"Then they should have looked elsewhere." Darling raked fingers through his dark curls. "How come that songwriter didn't show? Jeminy?"

"Her boyfriend had another gig planned. You wanted her specially?"

"Brisa did. The two of them met in Beaufort."

"Oh, right. Well, maybe we can work something out. You didn't tell her about her mother calling, did you?"

"No, but she's bound to ask soon."

"We want those papers served first."

"I know."

"The benefit is tomorrow. No reason Brisa can't invite Jeminy to that."

Darling squinted. "You think the concert's safe enough for a child her age?"

"Sure. It's for cancer research for kids. Why not?"

"Gotta be careful what we expose her to, on account of the lawsuit."

"It's for kids. Who can say anything about that?"

Maybe Arthur was right. "You know she can sing?" Darling asked.

Arthur turned a speculative eye his way. "She can, huh? She know any of your music?"

"Most of it. Even the new song we haven't recorded yet."

With a slap to his back, Arthur said, "Perfect. If she can hold her own, we'll put her on stage for one song. Good thing there aren't any media people around tonight. Best if we keep a low profile until tomorrow night. Surprise everyone."

"How'd you keep them away?"

"I told my secretary not to let any invites go out to press. There was one who called, I don't remember if she told me his name, but the guy claimed Lisette suggested he be there. He got uninvited."

"Lisette wouldn't have invited media."

Across the room, Daddy still held her against his side. Darling squinted, but Lisette's face was turned toward Daddy. She ought to push the old man away. At least duck out of his hold.

"You sure about that?" Arthur asked, then tipped his drink to his lips.

The impertinent question had Darling pressing his palms flat against his thighs, a gesture he needed far too often these days. "What are you hinting at? You insinuating that Lisette would do anything to hurt Brisa?"

"Not on purpose. But she might have felt the publicity would be good."

"For Lisette?"

"Well, yes." Arthur scanned the room as if looking for someone in particular. "She *is* angling for that role in the new Stockton film."

Yeah, she was. And she might actually get it, if his father got involved. *Was* Daddy working to make Lisette famous? Darling stared at his father's hand, which seemed to have inched down Lisette's back. *Down. Lisette's. Back.*

What he saw as Lisette turned her face up to Daddy's had those fists of his clenching after all. She smiled at the man, the old man… the powerful, old man. *His* father. Whose hands were where they shouldn't be. On *his* wife.

"Cool it," Arthur said. His voice was low, alert. "He doesn't mean anything by it."

Arthur's words barely penetrated the fog of anger rolling over Darling. "He means it all right. He always means it."

His manager blocked his view of the rest of the room. "You need to back it down before you make a fool of yourself," Arthur said. "There are a lot of people here who can ruin you."

Darling glared at the other man. "Who? Who has Daddy not bought and paid for? And who is next?"

"That lawyer's letter and the petition they filed. The accusations. Remember how they can turn the tables on us."

Threats from Beaufort? Nobody'd believe those.

"Who else has seen the documents?" he asked Arthur.

"Your father."

"Yeah, and what's he recommend?" Daddy wouldn't want negative publicity anywhere near him.

"He said if she continues that route, he'll know how to take her down. We have the money and the clout. What's she got? A whiney complaint she can't prove."

At least his father would stand by him. He eased around Arthur and pushed through their guests to his wife's side. But it was Brisa's delighted smile that met him, not Lisette's. And Brisa he needed to take care of here, not Lisette. For tonight, at least.

The noise of the room faded as he drew Brisa aside. "This too much for you, sweetheart?"

"There are so many people!" Her voice was so soft he had to bend to hear.

"What do you say we take off, just the two of us?"

Her eyes widened. "You mean it? Could we?"

"Sure we could."

Darling turned to Lisette. "I'm taking Brisa out for a little drive. You okay here?"

His father spoke for her. "We're fine. You take that little girl and give her a birthday treat, the kind she deserves."

Lisette was watching Daddy, not him.

Darling called her name. She finally turned to him and reached across to touch his arm, the sort of touch that normally melted him. Normally. "You go," she said. "We will be fine here."

She didn't finish her sentence with "as Daddy said," but she might as well have.

He pulled out a couple of light jackets from a closet and took

Brisa's hand. They'd reached the foyer when a door opened and RJ ambled in, his shoulders and hips swaying as he walked. Three hangers-on brought up the rear, and they were followed by some of the girls who sang back-up.

"Hey, bro," RJ said, cocking his head as he studied Brisa. "This my little niece?"

Darling pulled Brisa to his side. "Who invited you?"

He regretted his tone when Brisa stiffened. "Sorry," he said to her. "That's RJ, my half-brother."

RJ grinned, bobbing his dreads at her. His watery eyes made Darling want to strangle him—or lock him up. "That makes me your uncle," RJ said. "And aren't you a gorgeous thing?"

Brisa looked from one to the other, but she didn't speak.

"Come on, honey." Darling waved the others inside. "Daddy's in there. Toe the line, you hear?"

As he led Brisa toward his car, he prayed to whatever god might be listening that no one would get wind of this party and figure out how unsuitable it was for a child's birthday.

---

When they were in the elevator, he reached into his pocket and pulled out a small box. "This is for you."

"Something else?" She grinned as she fumbled with the wrapping. "I mean, I love my new clothes. I don't need more."

"But this is special, for my girl, my daughter." He stopped the elevator and waited.

Then she lifted the lid of the velvet box, and her breath caught. "Daddy..."

"Let me," he said, lifting the necklace from its pillowed carrier. "Your birth flower is a daisy, did you know that? And your birthstone, a diamond."

"Really?"

He'd had the jeweler craft a pendant in the shape of a daisy, made up of several carats worth of diamonds. All girls liked diamonds, right? "You want me to put it on you?"

"Please," she whispered.

He fastened the clasp at the back of her neck as she held up her hair. "There."

Fingering it, she suddenly burst into tears. "Oh, Daddy, thank you," and she flung herself against him, circling him with her arms. "I love it so much. Nobody's ever given me anything like it."

It took a moment for her hug to galvanize him into returning it. "You're my girl. I'll be giving you gifts for the rest of your life."

When she broke loose, she gave him a watery grin. "Wait until I show Jilly. She'll love it."

"Jilly?"

"My best friend."

"Ah."

"I kind of wish I could call her."

"Maybe we can do that later."

He wondered why she didn't mention calling her mother but decided he'd leave that one alone. He ushered her out of the elevator and through to the bay where all the cars lived. "Take your pick. Which one?"

She chose the bright red Lamborghini. And then she oohed and aahed over the cream-colored leather interior, the real wood of the dashboard, the gold trim on the gear shift. Her eyes were huge and luminous as he drove them out of the hills and toward the sea.

She was quiet, gazing out the window at the bright lights when they hit city streets. "Where are we going?" she asked finally.

"I thought you might like to see Pacific Park. It has rides and a pier."

He smiled when he noticed her fiddling with her pendant, but then she said, "Has my mom called?"

"Not sure."

"I just figured she would. You know, because of my birthday."

"Does she make a big deal of birthdays?"

"Yeah. She always does. We were going to have a big party this year, invite all my friends." She sounded wistful.

"I'm sorry you had to miss that."

She sighed. "Maybe next year."

"That sounds like fun." A whole lot more fun than the party Lisette had organized for the child. What had his wife been thinking?

Finally, he pulled into a parking lot, tipped the attendant to watch his car and keep it safe, and then ushered Brisa toward the pier.

And then it was lights and noise and rides. She wanted to try everything, but he guided her to the ferris wheel. They rode it twice, climbing high above Santa Monica Bay as the sun dipped lower over the water. The emerging sunset smacked the sea with oranges and pinks, shading the upper sky in purples. She pointed happily. Her exuberance made him want to laugh aloud with real humor for the first time in years.

They progressed to the Plunge and the Swing—and more. Brisa laughed and screamed and snuggled close to him. And Darling had more fun than he'd ever had in his entire life.

By the time they stopped to eat hot dogs, she'd completely won his heart.

---

"That was the best," she said sleepily as he opened the car door for her.

He helped her recline the passenger seat before climbing behind the wheel. "It was. The very best. Happy birthday, sweetheart."

She sighed. "Thank you. Thank you so much. For everything." Her breathing evened out, and she slept.

Darling glanced over with a surge of protectiveness he'd never before experienced. This beautiful girl-child was his. Fine, he'd planted his sperm accidentally—or rather, it had taken hold unintentionally—and he'd gone after her for reasons that had nothing to do with love.

But what he felt now? After an evening of feeling her soft hand in his, of seeing her eyes shine into his, of hearing her laughter at simple pleasures he'd given her…

*Mama Bea, you'd love her, this great-granddaughter of yours. You'd love her.*

He swiped at unfamiliar wetness. When had he last cried over anything or anyone?

He sniffed. Well, he wouldn't start now. No, sir.

And yet.

No. *No and-yets allowed.*

Nope. No, sir. Not on his watch.

He slammed shut the memory of Mama Bea crooning over him. Of her tears flowing freely when he'd lifted his voice in that church of hers, and again when Daddy Evermire had come for him.

"Remember, my darling boy, what you've learned and what you've known. The good Lord loves you, and He'll never let you go."

Well, that last didn't seem true, at least.

---

They were fifteen minutes from the house when he hit speed dial for Arthur's phone. It rang several times, and Darling was about to disconnect when his manager answered.

"They cleared out yet?" Darling asked.

"It had thinned by the time I took off. I got RJ out of there, but that's the best I could do. Seems he'd heard about the party from Daddy."

"And been invited?"

"No. Daddy didn't look particularly happy to see him, but your father had me do the dirty work."

"Thanks for that."

"Sure. Where'd you two go?"

"Santa Monica. She had a great time."

"Much better than a party for adults. Hard to believe Lisette thought this was a good idea."

"Yeah, well, something's going on with her."

"You think she's tired of mommy-hood already?"

"I don't think it's that."

"Sorry, bro."

"Yeah, me too." Darling glanced over to make sure Brisa still slept.

"You need me for anything else?" Arthur asked.

"Nope. I'll just hope everyone else has left by the time we get there."

"Talk later."

"Sure."

Amazingly, the area around the house was free of cars by the time he approached the garage. He pulled in and leaned over to touch Brisa's cheek.

"Hey, beautiful, we're home."

She slowly opened her eyes and smiled. "Mmm…"

"I'll come around and help you."

He eased her out of the car, supported her as he led her inside. The place seemed empty and quiet. His staff had obviously cleaned up, and only Todd was still straightening things in the living room. Darling thanked him.

"Go to bed, Todd. I'll see my daughter upstairs."

"Yes, sir."

He helped Brisa to her room and flicked on the bathroom light. "You okay?"

"Un-huh."

"Goodnight, then. And happy birthday."

"Thank you. I had a great time."

He kissed her forehead and closed the door behind him as he left.

The note rested on his bureau where he'd be bound to see it. It had only been folded once.

*I suggested to Lisette that we take the party elsewhere so we could get rid of all those hangers-on someone invited. Don't worry about her. I'll see she gets home sometime. You just enjoy that daughter of yours.*

Darling stifled his immediate rage as the image of his father's hands on his wife's back came into focus. Daddy's hands and Lisette's smile.

## 44

## AGNES

Agnes let Link out the next morning into a drizzle while a cup of water heated in the microwave. Tea was all she could manage.

When she let Link in again, she held him off with an old towel she'd pulled from the laundry room. "Let's dry you off." When she removed the towel, he shook the remnants on everything around him, including her.

"Thanks a million," she told him.

Tea in hand, she retreated upstairs to her bathroom. Drying off, she made the mistake of looking in the mirror at her ravaged face. It shouldn't have been a surprise, but every time she saw herself, she was appalled. Gullies ruined her once-smooth forehead, trenches had formed around her mouth and eyes. She bent closer. Were those gray hairs? That's all she needed. Gray hairs and worry lines. She was old. Barely into her thirties and she needed Botox.

Jenelle had mentioned wanting the injections, said she'd read they could make a person look decades younger. Only, neither she nor Agnes would be able to afford a chemical youth. Besides, an injection meant needles, and needles meant pain, and pain was to be avoided. So, it didn't matter if Agnes couldn't afford them because, actually, she didn't want them. Win/win. Right?

She finished her tea and accepted the siren's call of warm covers, this time from her own bed. Rain slashed the porch roof, the window screens, the sidewalk and street. She imagined it slicing and dicing plant life. Her life.

She ran her fingers over the sheet at her side—750-count cotton, silky, smooth. She had never lain on sheets like this before moving into her mother's luxury. She didn't want to leave that comfort to get up and face the nothingness of no one here.

What would it be like if she had a husband, a man whose breath would mate with hers, a man whose body would share this big bed and these silken sheets? She hadn't a clue.

But maybe, just maybe, she would someday. And maybe, just maybe, he'd kiss her again as he had last night.

Kisses, no kisses, none of it mattered while Brisa was three thousand miles away. She'd give the legal system a few more days, and then she was going to pack a suitcase and get on a plane.

She had to see Brisa face-to-face, even if that meant rejection. And even if it messed up her lawyers' plans. The way she felt right now, she'd be willing to grab Brisa and take her across the border to safety.

A tear trickled out the corner of her eye and down the side of her cheek as the futility of it hit her once again. She couldn't do that. And she couldn't risk losing a custody battle. Brisa was hers. She was.

What was that old saying? Possession was nine-tenths of the law? And Darlington had possession of her daughter. If Brisa hated being with him, a trip out there might work in Agnes's favor, but what if her daughter didn't want to come home? Then there'd be that possession thing. And, unless she did a snatch and run, which might prove difficult based on their relative sizes, hers and his, Darlington's lawyer would have a chance to get a copy of his paperwork served on her, forcing the custody case into California courts.

At least, that was what she thought all Rita's words meant.

The acid hole in her gut was going to start bleeding if she couldn't find resolution soon.

45

DARLING

B risa's natural talent continued to amaze Darling. "You still okay with going on stage tonight, honey?" he asked as he tucked her closer. "The concert's a benefit for cancer research, for kids, and we can leave as soon as your performance ends."

"Do we have to? Leave right after, I mean?"

He gave her shoulders a quick squeeze. "You remember I'm trying to do things right and not give the courts any reason to say you can't stay here. We may have to go before a judge so your mother and I can share you. You know, some time here and some time with her."

Unless he won and got full custody. Daddy seemed to think it possible, but you never knew with judges.

He noticed a flash of something that looked like pain cross Brisa's face, but it vanished quickly. He needed to make it stay gone.

Especially since Agnes had left two voice messages on his phone in the last two days. Arthur continued to tell him not to respond. "Let the lawyers sort it out," he said. "You don't want to muddy things by allowing the mother to use emotional manipulation on Brisa. It's all going to work out. After all, Brisa came here of her own accord."

Darling put an extra dose of enthusiasm into his voice now as he spoke to his daughter. "Arthur suggested we sing the new song, the one you and I were practicing the other day. We'll keep it simple. Do you remember how the chorus goes? And the bridge?"

"I remember the chorus."

He strummed the opening chords, and she began.

*"A day long gone and a new one beginning, I see the sun reaching up to dry my tears. And you, my darlin', are the one who's waiting, waiting on the sunset to bring me home."*

She paused at the last note. "What do you think that means? The sun can't reach up to dry tears. And the sunset can't bring anyone home."

"Perhaps it's not to be taken literally. Maybe it's talking about the sun warming her enough for her tears to dry, and maybe the other person is waiting until evening, after the sunset happens, to bring her home." He smiled at her worried look. "Does that make sense?"

"I guess."

How many artists cared about understanding what they sang? Maybe he'd thought of such things back in Atlanta, but certainly not since he'd come west.

"Can we do it all, from the beginning?" she asked. "If I have to sing in front of people tonight, I want to be good enough."

"You'll be great. Have you learned the whole thing?"

"I think so, but I can look at the music, can't I?"

He pushed the sheet music closer to her. He knew she couldn't read it, not properly, but she'd said it gave her memory cues for when the notes changed. And she'd been memorizing what they all meant.

The kid was brilliant. A brilliant musician, a beauty, and with a nightingale's voice. She could do anything she wanted, be anything she wanted.

A sudden shiver shot through him, and it wasn't a shiver of excitement.

The concert organizers had sold to capacity. Probably over capacity, according to Arthur. "Word's circulated. We've got media attention clamoring to know more. Man, this is going to take you to the next level."

"I don't need a next level," Darling had said then. But now, as his crew sneaked them through the rear door of the concert hall to avoid reporters, overzealous fans, and possible process servers, he felt the familiar acceleration of his heartbeat.

He glanced down at Brisa, who was clutching his hand and looking around with huge eyes. She wore a new dress, some sort of pinkish color, that looked great—not too young and not too old. As always, Lisette had shown her sense of style in choosing it.

Arthur, Daddy, and Lisette were already in their reserved seats when Darling led his daughter to a small lounge behind the stage. The warm-up band would be on for twenty minutes, then he'd do a set, and then he'd bring Brisa on. He opened a bottle of water for each of them. "You'll be okay back here?"

"Sure."

"You only have to tell that girl, the one reading a book, if you need anything. There's a bathroom. Good idea to use it before she brings you to me." He nodded toward the young woman Arthur'd found to sit with Brisa, someone who worked for the cancer group putting on this show. "She'll receive a text message. Just go with her."

Brisa nodded. She seemed less nervous than he was for her. One quick hug, and he headed to the wings, ready to go on.

When he finally brought her on stage, she took his hand and grinned as he introduced her to the crowd. He'd told her to keep her focus on him, especially if she felt scared. Although he started them out, it soon became evident she could carry the song on her own. He nodded for her to sing the chorus, and she brought the house to their feet before he came in on the next verse. Before long, concert-goers were singing the chorus along with them. He'd never felt such a swelling of love as he did right then.

His girl. His *daughter*.

That was the last song of the evening, and he didn't even want to do an encore, but with the clamor of applause, he nodded and let Brisa pick a song they hadn't practiced. At the end, she walked off the stage with him and started shaking.

He drew her close, suppressing a sigh when her arms circled his waist. *His girl.* "You okay, honey?"

"I was so scared."

Tightening his hold, he spoke quietly. "You? You'd never know it. You were brilliant."

She backed away and looked up into his face. "Really? You really think so?"

"Magnificent," another voice said. Arthur came up behind her. "Great job, both of you."

Suddenly, the backstage erupted with the booming voice of Daddy Evermire. "Where's that granddaughter of mine?"

Brisa turned in Darling's arms but stayed close. His father grabbed hold of her shoulders and held her at arm's length. "Seems we have a golden girl here, son. Glad you showed the world the Evermires' talent didn't skip a generation."

Darling had imagined he'd enjoy his father fawning over Brisa, maybe feel pride. Instead, the image of Daddy's hands sliding to Lisette's bottom had seared itself on his brain. Considering that Lisette hadn't come home that night and hadn't wanted to make love since then… well, what was he to think?

He was sure glad he'd developed a relationship with his daughter that had nothing to do with his yearning to give Lisette a child. A curse slid into place, but he didn't speak it, not with Brisa standing six inches away from him. Lisette wanted to play him for a fool, and with his own father? Well, let her. As Mama Bea'd once said, "Nobody can make you into a fool lest you let him."

The puppeteer's strings needed cutting. Before they did damage to that next generation.

───

Lisette stood next to the benefit organizer, Bradley Dunstan, talking to a reporter, when Darling and Brisa arrived at the invitation-only after party. Daddy'd insisted they bring Brisa, in spite of Darling's skepticism. "Don't be a stick in the mud," Daddy'd said. "It'll be fine and good publicity for you and her. Bradley asked especially."

And Bradley certainly welcomed Darling and his daughter, pulling them into his small circle. "I'm absolutely thrilled with the turnout tonight." His eyes glistened, his voice rising in enthusiasm with each word. "We've topped last year's biggest seller with just this one concert. So grateful! So glad!" The punctuated words made Darling want to wince, but he kept his smile pasted in place in respect for Bradley's little brother, who had been diagnosed with brain cancer. As if that weren't enough, Bradley's long-time partner was in the last stages of AIDS. So he was a little over the top. The man had a right to his angst.

The *Evening Sun*'s reporter edged toward Brisa, but Darling deflected him, drawing Brisa out of the man's reach. Lisette took the opening and led the reporter away.

"Wise woman." Arthur followed Lisette's tactics with a grin and brought Darling's attention to him. "She'll keep him distracted and perhaps get something out of it for herself, but you don't need to see Brisa's name associated with this party. The concert, yes. A late party, no."

Darling nodded curtly and turned back to his daughter, only to see her whisked off by Daddy toward another group. A group that included the other musicians from the band. And RJ.

He did not want his daughter anywhere near his half-brother. He'd barely taken a step in their direction when Arthur grabbed his arm.

"Don't do it." Arthur's words were spoken softly enough that only he heard them. "You don't want to draw unwanted attention to them, do you? Trust Daddy to take care of your girl. He only wants the best for everyone."

"Oh, yeah? You think that's true?"

Arthur's bushy dark brows rose, but his eyes glinted with more than surprise. "What are you implying?"

"That Daddy has grown mighty possessive of what belongs to me."

"I'd be careful there, Darling. I'd be real careful."

Darling felt heat climbing up his neck. Careful? Who was Arthur to tell him to be careful?

And why?

Darling pushed his way past and headed to Brisa's side, only to be drawn up short by another reporter. By the time he'd freed himself from that man's questions, Daddy had returned to speak to him, but without Brisa.

"Where is she?" Darling asked.

"Sent her home with one of the girls. Time for that child to be in bed."

It was, but what right did Daddy have to interfere? He'd been the one insisting Brisa be here.

"Seems to me," Daddy continued, "we need to find us another safe venue for Brisa to show off her talent. That's what you ought to be thinking about."

"But the lawsuit—"

"You just let our lawyer take care of that while we make that girl of yours famous."

Darling just stared at his father. Famous? Who'd decided Brisa needed to be famous? And what would that cost?

# 46

## DARLING

Darling had been glad of the excuse to leave that after-party, even if he had resented his father for sending Brisa home. He could have done that himself, but perhaps it had been for the best. It had taken him ages to get past all those who wanted to speak to him.

He pulled into his garage and took the elevator upstairs. When the doors opened, he was surprised to hear a guitar and voices on the back terrace. Laughter, hooting. Daddy had said he'd sent Brisa back with one of the girls from the band. Had more come along to have an impromptu session at his house?

Without him?

He propped his guitar case against a side table, shed his jacket, and headed to the French doors. And stopped right there.

There must have been five girls along with RJ and two other band members. RJ was leaning over something on one of the benches, something that looked a whole lot like a line of white powder. The scent of marijuana smoke hovered over the deck like smog over an airless city. And then he saw Brisa with the girls. One was flashing her breasts, another her scantily clad bottom. Brisa stood between them, giggling, as one of the guys held a phone up, taking pictures. Or maybe videos.

For a moment, he was too stunned to move. Then he slammed his fist into the side of the picture-taker's head. The guy went down. Darling snatched Brisa by the arm, hauled her behind him, and picked up the phone off the stones. He removed the SIM card, pocketed it, and smashed the phone at his feet.

He held out his hand. "Phones, all of you. Now." Sputters of protest vanished under his glare. He pocketed the phones that would fit in his jacket, held the others in his left hand. "You can pick up these from Todd tomorrow," he said before marching over to his brother.

RJ gawked as he stood rooted in place. With one long breath, Darling scattered the powder in a cloud of white and then grabbed the baggie his brother had dropped near it.

"Hey, man, you can't do that!" RJ cried in a shocked voice.

"Can and did." Darling raised his fist. "Now, out of here. All of you." He barely controlled his rage. What he wanted to do, what he would have done if Brisa hadn't been here, was kill every one of them.

The girls straightened their clothes, giggling. RJ was the only one who spoke. "We were just having a little fun." He gathered his things carefully, wrapping what was left of his equipment and stuffing it in an oversized pocket. "We didn't mean anything, bro. Brought her home, like Daddy asked."

"She's twelve. Twelve. And you know my rules. This is *my* house. Not yours. Not theirs. If you are all not out of here in two minutes, I'll call the police. Anyone want to test that?" His gaze traveled over them. "Any of you want to land in jail tonight?"

The police were the last people he wanted with his minor daughter and drugs in the same house, but he wouldn't let those fools know. He bellowed toward the house. "Todd!"

Todd must have been standing by. "Sir?"

"Take these." Darling handed over the phones. "And watch they don't leave anything behind. Make sure it's clean out here." He still held the baggie. "You got a place to put this?"

"Back pocket."

Darling transferred it and said, "Can you figure out how to get rid of it so it's unusable by anyone?"

"Easy."

"Tell me later."

"Yes sir." Todd backed out of the way.

A good man, Darling knew, but he didn't watch to see what Todd did with the phones or how he orchestrated the departure of the unwanted guests. Instead he took hold of Brisa's arm to lead her into the house. Her lips trembled, and she stumbled, but he held her upright as they moved into the living room.

The girls pressed through the terrace doorway and paused, staring up at him. One said, "Sorry, Darling." Two others grabbed her arm, lunging drunkenly toward the front door. They were followed by the men. The one he'd decked wouldn't make eye contact.

Who were those guys? They'd better not show their face around him again. And the band members? They were replaceable. In a heartbeat.

RJ brought up the rear. "Catch you later," he said. To Darling's pointing finger, he just nodded and walked carefully out.

"I'm sorry," Todd said as the door shut behind them. "They brought your daughter, said you were right behind them. I didn't want to presume."

"Next time, presume. Brisa belongs, they do not. Ever again."

"Yes, sir." Todd reached back and closed the door to the terrace. "I'll get it cleaned up in a sec."

Darling pulled Brisa's chin up so he could look into her eyes. "What did they give you, honey?"

"Give me?" She was leaning heavily against the wall.

"What did you have to drink?"

"Juice."

"Nothing else?"

She shook her head and then pressed her palms to her cheeks as if to stabilize herself. "Swirly. Feels funny."

"How many juices?"

"I was thirsty." She giggled.

"Okay, let's get you to bed." He half-carried her down the hall to her room. Under his breath he said, "This is not good. Not good at all."

She plopped down on her bedspread and moaned. "My head. Dizzy."

"I bet."

He removed her shoes and pulled a comforter over her. Then he collected a towel, placed it on the floor next to her bed, and went to ask Todd for a big wide bowl. This he placed on top of the towel, remembering what Mama Bea'd set up when he'd had a stomach bug.

By now, Brisa was asleep. He hoped if she woke up sick, she'd be able to find the bowl—or make her way to her bathroom. Leaving the bathroom light on, he left the room and pulled his cell phone from his jacket pocket.

He tried Arthur first, then Lisette, and finally his father. Not a one of them answered.

Not a one.

The message he left with each was "We've got to talk."

They didn't call him back, and Lisette hadn't come home when he turned out his light around one.

He was on his own.

---

He'd left both bedroom doors open so he'd hear if Brisa needed him. An hour later, she did.

Her moaning woke him. Granted, he hadn't been sleeping all that soundly, and he'd been expecting something, either Lisette to come home or Brisa's stomach to reject whatever they'd put in her juice.

It was the latter. Poor kid. He pulled on a silk robe and headed in to see if he could help.

She lay curled on her side, her knees up, her hair damp around her face, in agony. A moment after he sat down and touched her forehead, she opened her eyes, gave him a panicked look. He had just enough time to bring the bowl to her before she retched into it.

Thank heavens for the bowl and towel. He held his breath and carried both to the bathroom, where he emptied the bowl, rinsed it, and set it back in place along with a clean towel. Then he dampened a washcloth and carried it to her.

She whimpered as he wiped down her face. And then he heard words along with the moan. "Mommy... I want my mommy."

He felt the crack in him widen. "I know, honey. I know."

The problem was, he did. Her words opened him up, and he saw himself curled on his bed and crying piteously for his own missing mama. Mama Bea had been there, crooning to him, but his mommy hadn't been. Nor had his daddy.

No, sir. Daddy Evermire had come back into his life only to milk the talent he'd heard about. Must have been from one of Darling's uncles. Wouldn't have been from Mama Bea. Never from her. She'd despised what her son had done with his life and fought him trying to take Darling away.

But Darling had gone willingly enough, hadn't he? The promise of glamour. The promise of riches. The promise of anything he wanted.

Brisa clutched her stomach. She was going to be sick again. He saw it in her movements and readied the basin. Easier that way than hauling her to the toilet.

When she'd finished, he wiped her face with the cloth and carried the bowl off to empty it again.

He was going to kill his brother. Fire the band. All of them.

---

"They could have killed her," he said when his manager finally responded to his message the next day. "Alcohol poisoning. Of. A. Child. And they were filming her with girls who were stripping. And RJ was snorting cocaine in front of her. Oh, and I smelled pot. At *my* house." He was fuming. He couldn't help it. And his smug manager kept coming back with the same lame excuses.

Arthur cleared his throat. "I repeat. They didn't poison her, you got rid of the stuff, and you destroyed the phone."

"Yeah, great news. Thanks. My twelve-year-old daughter was saved from dying only because I got home in time. Also, good for me, I got home in time to keep her from showing up all over social media. Great job, everyone." He laced his words with as much sarcasm as he could dredge from a rage that Arthur's half-baked apologies weren't touching. How could he make the man realize the severity of what had happened?

"Look, I'm sorry, Darling, but no one knew they'd all head to your place."

"I was up all night with a puking child. A suffering, very sick kid. Not good, Arthur. Not good at all."

"Wow, man, that's awful."

"I want them fired. Every single one who was here last night. Fired."

"Oh, great, now you're going to try a solo act?"

Arthur's thoughts leaped in that direction? Who cared what kind of act he had? Were those musicians—including his brother—the only people willing to work?

"Better," he finally said, "than running with crazies who are bent on ruining my reputation—and helping me lose my daughter."

"You think so?"

Darling held his cell phone away from his head and stared at it. Was the man even listening?

"Can't fire them," Arthur said. "Contracts. Besides, Daddy wouldn't allow it."

Darling's anger pulsed in his neck. His heartbeat had sped

up. If he didn't do something now, this moment, he'd explode. He slammed his finger on the *End* button and pressed. Hard.

---

Brisa looked like a scared little girl, this daughter who'd captured his splintered heart, a heart he hadn't realized even functioned—not until she came into his life and he experienced the innocent delight of having a child, *his* child, smile at him in adoration.

She lay in her bed, her big eyes regarding him as if he were miracle worker enough to fix the pain she felt. He held out two acetaminophens along with a glass of water.

"These may help the headache." He waited until she'd swallowed them. "I'm so sorry you had to go through this."

"What happened? Do I have the flu?"

"No. Someone spiked your juice. With alcohol." He tried to keep his tone gentle when gentle was the last thing he was feeling. Rage at the culprits would be closer to the truth.

"You mean I was drunk?" Her eyes widened. "I've seen drunk people in Jersey City. They smelled."

He nodded. "It seems you were."

"I thought they were my friends. One of them is my uncle." Tears brimmed again. "How could he?"

"He doesn't think about anyone except himself." He blew out a breath. "Self-absorption seems to be rampant in this neck of the woods."

"I thought life here was glamorous."

"Big word."

She tried smiling, but it came across as a grimace. He smoothed her hair back again and sighed. "Yeah, well, parts of the life are glamorous."

"Like your life. You know, your house, your cars, your music."

And not his wife.

Mama's Bea's voice surfaced again. *"You put your trust in them worldly things like fame and fortune, honey, you gonna be disappointed. 'Member that story you learned in Sunday School, about the rich man who died afore he could enjoy the harvest he'd laid up? All on account of he'd trusted in his riches and not in God."*

Darling'd been sucked right into the life his father'd promised. He'd made his choices, but Brisa? Before he'd known this incredible girl, he'd imagined swooping in and doing the same thing for her that Daddy'd done for him. But he hadn't known, had he? He hadn't known what having a child of his own meant, the responsibility it carried.

She trusted him to do what was best for her, and he had to man up.

He smoothed his hand over the bedspread Lisette had picked out for this step-daughter who'd held her interest for a few measly days. Lisette's faux affection had lasted until Brisa began to capture the attention his wife thought should be hers.

"Working for other people requires sacrifices, and one of those comes in your freedom to choose those you'll have as associates. After what they did to you, I'd like to fire everyone who was here last night."

"You can't?"

"No, honey, I can't. It appears that only my father can, and he's not willing to do that."

"Because he doesn't care about me."

"Because he only cares about himself." And now Lisette, although he didn't imagine either of them knew the meaning of caring for others. Maybe he didn't either, but, as he sat there with Brisa, he thought he was beginning to.

"I'm thinking we ought to take a little trip, maybe to see my grandmother. Would you like that?"

Brisa's eyes brightened in spite of her physical misery. "When I'm better?"

"You rest now. I'll make the arrangements for us to leave tomorrow."

"Will I be well tomorrow?"

"I should think you'll feel a lot better by tonight."

He wasn't sure she would, but it would do him good to get away. Let Lisette miss him for a change. And he'd been wanting to show off Brisa to Mama Bea, hadn't he?

This would be good. Make Mama happy and get Brisa away from here until he could figure out how to protect her.

It would probably be something as simple as hiring someone to take care of her when he had to be away—someone with more authority than Todd. And she'd need a teacher or a school. He really ought to look into that, too.

A radical life change had to include professional as well as personal revamping, which meant taking back power to himself. He drew out his phone and dialed his agent—or was Jett his former agent? Arthur now dealt with the normal agenting requirements, but back in the day, back when he'd first come into the business, he'd been introduced to Jett Loren, the young go-getter of Jacobs and Loren Associates. Without Darling even realizing it, Jett had been pushed out of the way by Daddy Evermire to be replaced by Arthur.

Darling, in his eagerness to please and be pleased, had imagined Arthur his best friend. He'd been a fool.

He was put through to Jett, who seemed both surprised and pleased by the call. "I need your help," Darling said. "I want to figure out my contractual obligations to my father and my manager."

"Really?" Jett's surprise escalated. "Your lawyer would be better able to do that, I think."

"My lawyer seems also to be my father's lawyer. I need a new one. And I need a new manager."

"Why?" Jett sounded wary.

"Because I find I have no control over who is in my band or how they behave, and several of them just put my daughter in jeopardy."

"I heard you'd found a long-lost daughter. Congratulations."

"Thanks. I want to protect her."

"You thinking of striking out on your own?"

Was he? "Yeah. Yeah, I think I am."

"And you want my help."

"I do. You always played it straight with me. You think you can do anything?"

"Sure. There's a lawyer works closely with some of my clients. Let me call him and see what he can uncover for us."

"As soon as we know what I'm free to sign, we'll talk contracts. If your lawyer friend needs to talk to me, have him use this number. As far as I know, all the signing was done by others, but I may have some contractual agreement with my manager. Maybe with my father. And I want out—or at the very least, I want control of my life and who gets allowed into it."

"Got it." Jett paused. "It's good to hear from you again, Darling. Thanks for reaching out."

Darling smiled. It was a beginning. Maybe he'd form a new company with a new name. Instead of being known as Darling, he could go with his real name. Darlington.

It would declare to the world that he'd grown up. He was his own man. A father.

## DARLING

Mama Bea waddled into her small living room and took a seat next to Darling on the big green velour sofa. Everything looked the same, the same doilies on the chair arms and tables, the same frilly lamps. And Mama? Goodness, but she looked barely a minute older, except that her hair had gone completely gray, and she wore it closer cropped. Her daughter-in-law Delia, wife of Daddy's older brother, Eli, brought in a pitcher of iced tea along with cake slices in two kinds—vanilla and chocolate. She served the tea, then asked what kind of cake each wanted.

"Oh, give 'em a slice of each. Darling likes both—or used to —and that child looks like she would, too. I been baking ever since you called to say you was comin' and bringin' your baby for me to meet. I can't tell you what a delight it is for these eyes to look upon you again, darlin' boy, and to meet this precious girl."

Darling accepted a plate of cake and the fork Delia offered. "Thank you, Delia. And Mama, thank you for being so gracious, welcoming this prodigal back like you're doing."

"Oh, stop it. What else would I do for the boy of my heart, huh?"

"Yeah, well, you ought to be ashamed, Darlington," Delia said, easing herself down onto a chair on the other side of Mama. "It 'bout near broke Mama's heart, you never seein' fit to answer her letters, so many as she wrote, too." She scowled at him. "You shoulda leastways answered, all Mama Bea did for you."

He'd wondered, hadn't he? Now he had proof. He reached for Mama's hand. "I didn't get a single letter, Mama. Not a single one. I thought you were glad to see the back of me. Because I certainly figured you'd have written when you got the money I sent."

"No money came here for nobody," Delia said, hands on her hips, her chin jutting forward.

"Daddy promised." Darling shook his head. "I'm so sorry."

"Another thing on his record," Mama Bea said. She'd started out looking ready to bawl, but that changed to anger pretty quick. "Honey-lamb, you shoulda knowed I never in my life wanted you gone. I didn't care nothing about money."

"Daddy must have gotten rid of your letters, like he stopped the money. That was wrong on so many levels, but I should have known. I would have written. You know I would have written."

She lifted his hand to her cheek. "Sweet boy, I surely shoulda knowed the truth of it. That son of mine never cared for any but himself." Blowing out a long sigh, she squared her shoulders. "Water over the dam, that's what the past is. We gonna start from now."

"We are."

"How long you stayin'? Will you come to church with us? Sing for the people who was once your family?"

She took him by surprise with that one. He hesitated.

"Brisa, honey, you need to meet the people helped raise your daddy. And they need to meet you. Darling, you'd make me mighty proud, you do this."

"Brisa?" He looked at his silent daughter. "Would you like to go?"

She nodded her head and smiled at him, then glanced shyly

at her great-grandmother. "I'd like to come. I didn't grow up with any family. Only my Mom."

"Honey, you got yourself a passel of kinfolk right here in Georgia. And I hear you got the same gorgeous voice as your daddy. Maybe you can sing with him tomorrow. Grace us all."

"But... but I don't know any church songs."

Mama Bea wagged a finger at Darling. "You haven't taught this child how to praise the Lord?"

"I'm remiss, Mama. How about you get over to that piano, and we'll take care of that now?"

"It's Delia does the playing now my fingers are full of that arthritis. You just tell her. I'll sing with you."

Darling slid onto the piano stool and shuffled through the song books lying on top. Mama'd never needed written music. She only had to hear a song and out it came, her fingers to the keys, words and tunes on her lips. Delia needed song sheets. And Brisa might, too.

Darling let a smile settle on his lips. Singing with his girl in this place he'd fled and now come back to? Yes, sir. This was good.

He swallowed back the sudden lump that clogged his throat, shut his eyes on the damp gathering there. Mama Bea and Brisa. Imagine.

———

Mama Bea asked Delia to take Brisa outside and show her around. "First, you let her see where she can sleep tonight, please."

"Yes, ma'am," Delia said, offering her hand to his daughter. "Happy to."

"We can go to a hotel, Mama," Darling said. "No need to put yourself out."

"You hush with that, son. Your old room is there, with just a few sewing things to be moved aside. And Delia knows which will be for that sweet girl. I want that child to wake up tomorrow right here. You, too."

They'd practiced their music and shared the meal of meatloaf and potatoes Delia'd set before them, and now Mama'd asked for time alone with him. He took the seat Mama pointed to next to hers.

"I got a few questions for you," she said. "One, I want to know how come you didn't know 'bout that child when she was born? And now you got her? Where's her mama in all this?"

He'd been hoping this wouldn't come up. He couldn't lie to Mama. But before he could speak, she continued. "Brisa was speaking to Delia. Heard her myself when Delia asked about her mama, and Brisa, she said she missed her mommy, but she didn't think her mama even wanted her back." Mama looked pointedly at him. "What'd she mean by that?"

"Agnes didn't tell either of us about the other, and Brisa wanted to know me." He was about to say more.

"So she run off to find you? How'd she manage that? You had to of fixed it so. And why hasn't she talked to her mama since? Or gone home? What you plannin' to do there?"

Oh, man. "It's my turn to have her with me. It wasn't fair her mother wouldn't let me be part of her life from the beginning."

"Then you tell me, Darlington Evermire, why that was? You do something made her believe you wouldn't be a good daddy for her girl? Made her not want you there? Or you gonna try to tell me that child's mama is no good?" Mama wagged a finger at him. "That won't fly, son. Not when that child's grown as sweet as she is." A momentary pause, and then, "You tryin' to do to her what your daddy did to me? Steal her to your life and away from her mama? Because that child loves her mama, and she needs both a mama and a daddy."

He hung his head, studied his feet, dangled his hands and shifted his focus to them. Seemed he didn't need to answer anything. Mama Bea had it figured out, and he wasn't going to win in her court of opinion.

"I raised you better than that, son. Much better. I ain't gonna see you be like your daddy. I ain't. I don't care how old you be."

"No, ma'am."

---

He couldn't say the Sunday service was exactly as he remembered because then he'd been an innocent boy, and now he was a man grown and with all the innocence rubbed off. But seeing it from Brisa's eyes, standing up front and singing with this incredible girl-child who was his own blood, standing among a church full of other folk carrying some of that same blood, about filled him up with something fine.

Making music, making joyful music as if he really meant it, made him imagine he might get some of this life back. His heart felt too big for his chest, standing there, his voice drawing out hers, hers improving his. This was a taste of... well, of something.

Mama's hankie got a workout, and he had to admit, he had a moment or two when he had to bite his inner lip to stave off an emotional leak.

After church, Mama Bea rode with them to her youngest son's house. Uncle Jase and his wife and five children were going to host everyone for a picnic dinner on account of Darling being there with his girl. Everybody brought something to contribute. They feasted on fried chicken and ham, greens and beans and potato salad and cakes and puddings and Jell-o until all anyone wanted to do was pass out from over-indulgence.

The cousins, most of them grown with kids of their own, complimented him on his well-behaved daughter and were unbelieving that he hadn't known of her until recently.

"Her mama done good," his cousin Isaiah said.

"You're mighty blessed with that one," Isaiah's wife said.

Darling pulled a chair over next to Mama Bea's. "Hey, Mama."

"Sweet boy, I can't tell you how full this makes my heart, seein' you and your girl here. Means the world, it does."

"I'm gonna fix things, Mama, and I'm so sorry it took me this long to come back."

"You remember I once told you how God put each of us here on this earth to learn things? It's our purpose to experience life and learn 'bout ourselves and 'bout him? We face the hard things and the easy things, but it be the hard things teach us the most. Somehow, it's all pointin' us to Jesus, only not everybody listens, do they? And when they don't, they get to learn it again and again. God's always hopin' we get it right." She patted his cheek with one gnarled hand. "See, it's the choices we make, the hard choices that determine who we turn into. Seems you had a tough one back there in that place you chose to live, a tough one I see you makin' with that girl of yours."

"Yes, ma'am."

"I see how that girl's changin' you. Makin' you into a real father. That girl's daddy."

Darling bit the side of his cheek again. Seemed he was doing it a lot. "You... you think?"

"I see it. I do. And best of all? God, he sees it."

He drew her hand to his cheek and then to his lips. "I love you, Mama."

"I knows that, sweet boy. I knows that."

If only what she said were true. If only it could be real.

He stared out over the crowded back yard, past the fire pit his uncle'd set up, to the children racing around through the trees. Brisa had found friends in the cousins' children, especially two girls close to her age.

Would he have been like this, with kids, a wife, a fire pit in the back yard? If he'd chosen differently. If he'd not followed his father and the siren call of fame.

Would he have wanted this?

Or his real life.

Mama looked into his eyes now and patted his cheek. "You made plans for her, son? I see the sadness in you."

Of course she did. She'd always seen through him.

"I don't know. I want to keep her with me. I've missed so much."

"But you know you got to fix that, too." Mama turned to watch the children again, and he shifted his focus there, too. For the first time since he'd been in her company—except for that trip to Santa Monica when she'd laughed on the carnival rides—Brisa was acting like a joy-filled kid. The way she was supposed to act.

"She's got sparkle, she does, on top of that angel voice. What you gonna do about her talent? You and that father of yours." She shook her head. "Yeah, I knows he's my son, but he won't own it. It's a shame, it truly is."

"I'm sorry, Mama. But I won't let him stay between us any longer. And I'm making arrangements to keep him out of Brisa's life."

"Now you've found your way home, I'm hoping you'll follow that way a whole lot more."

"I will."

"And if you can, you bring that sweet baby. Maybe her mama, too." She looked at him slyly. "Brisa's old grannie's going to want to keep lovin' up on her, you know?"

"And no one can do it better than you, Mama."

They had to leave soon. He had obligations, appointments, practice sessions, and plans to make. He didn't know how all this was going to work out, except one day at a time. "I've a concert coming up here in the fall. At least, I think I do. If I sent you all passes, would you come?"

Her eyes brightened. "All of us?"

"Well, not the little ones. You'll have to send me a list."

She pretended to slap his wrist. "You come more often, you might remember your family and who's in it."

Grinning, he leaned forward to kiss her smooth cheek. "You get Delia to put a list together so I don't forget anyone, and I'll get the tickets sent."

"Front row?"

He laughed. "Yes, ma'am. Front row."

## 48

## HENRY

Henry climbed from his bunk that Sunday morning, stretched, and then quickly pulled on a sweatshirt and wool socks against the chill of a rainy day.

"First things first," he said to the empty cabin.

Yes, he talked to himself.

He ducked into the salon and opened the diesel heater's door before flipping the switch to start the fuel drip. A couple of minutes later, he lit a long match and held it until the flame caught. While the heater worked its magic to dry out the boat, he quickly finished washing up in cold water and headed to the galley. The kettle waited on the propane stove, the coffee in its airtight canister, and his mug hung neatly above the galley sink.

As he prepared his coffee, he checked the time. Father Stanley would be finished with his devotions in another couple of minutes, which meant Henry had time to fill his mug and find his phone.

When he put the call through, his mentor answered with, "And how are you this brilliant day?"

It was raining outside here, but perhaps not everywhere. "Hoping this is a good time to catch you."

"I've twenty minutes before I leave for chapel, so it is a very good time."

"I've been thinking about my friend Agnes."

"The one whose daughter ran away." Interesting that Father Stanley picked that to mention and not Henry's feelings.

"It was the daughter's birthday on Wednesday, and I went to try to be a comfort. Within minutes, her housemate wandered into the room, belting out a hymn."

"Which you knew."

"You can guess what happened. I didn't even think, just opened my mouth and joined in. The harmony was perfect. Becca—the housemate—is a big woman with a powerful voice, and she slid from that song into another and another."

"It must have been glorious. Did Agnes join you?"

"No."

"I'm surprised you kept on."

"Well, I got zinged by the power of it. Maybe it's just that Agnes isn't comfortable singing."

Father Stanley chuckled. "I can picture it."

"And then Becca started waving her hands and praying for Brisa and Agnes and me, then for her daughter and her church and even for Brisa's father. We had what amounted to a revival meeting right there in the wide hall, with Becca asking God to step in and change them and this situation and to bring Agnes's girl home where she belonged."

"I wish I'd been there."

"I do, too. I made arrangements to go with Becca to visit her church today. It should be interesting." Henry paused. "I'm sorry Agnes felt she had to leave the room when Becca started asking God to work on Darlington's heart."

"Ah," Father Stanley said. "Forgiveness seems to be a stumbling block for a lot of people."

"Even receiving it."

"Yes, son, even receiving it. Look at your own walk."

"I know."

"You're spending a lot of time with Agnes."

Henry didn't comment. He didn't want to mention the kiss, the attraction.

"I'd like you to remember that you need people surrounding you who can keep you focused so you don't stumble," Father Stanley said.

Henry sighed and nodded his head. Because it was true, wasn't it? "The voices come," he admitted, "but I'm trying to recognize their lies and get help when it's hard."

"Good. And surrounding yourself with people who can pray for you is part of your defense."

"Will the voices ever stop?" Henry raked fingers through his hair.

"You tell me."

Another sigh and another bit of truth. "No," he admitted. "Probably not."

"We all have to deal with them coming at us. It's warfare. The enemy changes tactics when he sees one doesn't work. In moments of weakness, we'll hear the lies in our head, but we must grow strong enough to overcome them. With God's help."

"There've been a lifetime of lies," Henry said.

"But at least you know now they were lies."

"I kissed her." Way to go, blurting it out like that.

"Ah."

"I think I'm in love with her."

"Is this a relationship that's likely to help or hurt you? And if you think it will put you in jeopardy, can you stop it from going further?"

Henry sighed once again. "I don't know."

"You've raised expectations in her."

And in himself. Although Father Stanley couldn't see him, he bowed his head. "I have."

"Perhaps it's time for some truth speaking. Before you both have lasting regrets."

Oh, man. This was going to be tough. How on earth could he

have such a conversation with her? What sort of questions was he supposed to ask?

"God can help you through it, Henry. But you'll have to trust him, even if he wants the doors closed. Can you do that?"

Could he? God was bigger, greater, mightier.

"Because of the Cross, my son. The Cross has already given you a way out. And it's given Agnes a way to victory over everything she faces. If she'll take it."

"If."

"I must go. I'll be praying for you."

"Thank you. Thank you for being there."

"Talk to God. He's got your back. He'll give you the right answer for your circumstances."

Henry closed his eyes and remembered the psalmist's promise that God had heard and given heed to the voice of his prayer. God had not turned away from him—and would not.

He recited the words of Psalm 66 to himself as he dressed for church and remembered them as he retrieved his foul-weather gear. He was ready for whatever came his way. But as he pulled the dinghy to the boarding ladder, the rain stopped and the sky cleared.

---

Henry hadn't even known what he was missing before yesterday. When he'd relocated to Beaufort, he'd picked a church within walking distance of the marina, but it seemed that Becca Barnes knew more about prayer and worship than he'd seen in a long time.

He rowed in, left his jacket in an underseat dinghy bag, and tied up. Becca was at the end of the dock, waving from the driver's side of a small Ford. "Mornin'," she said as he slid in beside her. "Seat belt's a little tricky. Sorry about that."

He had to pull and release a couple of times before he got it to go all the way across him, but he managed finally and gave her a smile. "Thank you for picking me up."

"Got to be a bit limiting, not having your own car."

"A bit. I can walk most places, though."

"You all set to have another glory fest?" she asked.

His stomach did a little flip, because, glory fest or no, walking into a church where he might be the lone white face rattled him more than he wanted to admit. What if they resented him? "What's the congregation like?"

"Happy."

That didn't exactly answer his implied question. "Anything I need to know before we get there?"

"We probably make a little more noise than you might be used to, on account of all that happy needin' a way out of us and up to the good Lord, you know?"

Both loud and happy were interesting concepts when used to describe a church service. He was used to solemn, which meant quiet. Nothing wrong with quiet, of course.

They entered the white clapboard building and were met by two ushers ready to seat them. Henry asked to remain near the back. "I'm so tall," he said by way of excuse to the usher. To Becca, he whispered, "And I want to be able to see everyone."

She grinned and slid into a convenient pew.

He scanned the faces. Yes, he'd been right about being the only white congregant, but as soon as the music started, he no longer gave his differentness a thought. Because, oh, man. The swaying choir, the congregation clapping on what seemed to be the off-beat, voices crying words like "O Lord," "Yes, Lord," and "Amen." When the preaching began, Henry was riveted to his seat, because the man's words seemed real and powerful... and perfect for him this day. *In everything give thanks. In everything...*

And wasn't that a word he needed, and one he had to live? For his trials, give thanks. The word had been *in*, hadn't it? Not *for*. So, *in* his addiction, give thanks, *in* his trials, give thanks. In his aloneness, in his neediness, always and evermore give thanks.

How was he supposed to do that?

Because he wanted to rail against his birth defect, rail against his father's brutality, rail against his mother's addiction and suicide. Rail against it all.

*Give thanks.*

Really?

He bowed his head and whispered, "Really?"

The congregation soared into another song, but he remained bowed, bent and low. And with bowed head, he imagined doing something that would actually help Agnes. He imagined stepping in and rescuing Brisa.

If he had the money to go. If he had the guts to confront Darlington on his own turf.

Why not? He could do it.

*God, will you show me how? Part this sea for me?*

"Go in peace," the pastor said. "And remember the psalmist's words as you enjoy this beautiful day. Remember to 'see the works of God, Who *is* awesome in His deeds toward the sons of men.' Let him be awesome in all you do and say and are today. Rejoice!"

"Amen!"

Henry let the meaning bubble up until all he could say, albeit quietly, was "Amen."

He turned in the pew to see if he'd left anything, and a voice intruded. "Henry, hey." Rita grinned up at him. "I'm so glad you could join us."

"Hey, Rita."

She pulled a little white-haired lady forward. "You remember my mama, don't you? From the picnic at Tadie's?"

"I do. How are you?" Although he couldn't remember her

name.

"Elvie Mae Whitlock," Rita said. "And my daddy, just behind her, James Whitlock."

"Pleased to see you both again," Henry said with a rapid lift of his brows to thank Rita for bailing him out of awkwardness.

Rita's mother beamed at him. With his hands resting on her shoulders, her husband looked just as welcoming. "Glad you could make it, son."

*Son.* A quick smarting at the back of Henry's throat and a sudden need to sniff followed the sound of that word, a word his own father'd never used for his second-born.

Recovering, Henry said, "I'm glad, too. You all know how to do church."

"We do at that," Elvie said. "And Becca, well, honey, she lights up the place with her voice, don't she?"

"I heard you right there with her." Rita's words brought the heat up his neck to his face.

"Thought there was a new tenor in the mix," James said. "We could do with more men folk outside the choir who can carry a tune."

"James." His wife scowled at him. "You do just fine yourself. And there's a half-dozen other men with talent enough to add to the choir up front."

"I'm thinking she's tone deaf," James said, his eyes twinkling.

Henry laughed, figuring he was supposed to. Nice folk. Certainly friendlier than those at the church he'd been visiting. It took all kinds, he guessed, but he sure felt more welcome here, among faces that had nothing in common with his except their smiles.

And wasn't that what it was supposed to be about? Happy, smiling faces reflecting happy, smiling folk? Folk who loved each other and their God?

Rita touched his arm, glanced from him to Becca. "We're meeting Tadie and her crew back at the big house for lunch. You and Becca want to join us?"

Becca shook her head. "Can't today. I'm supposed to spend a couple of hours with my daughter, helpin' her figure out what she can still wear from all those clothes she brought home. Girl's lost herself a good thirty pounds since she left that man, and we've got to decide how much we can alter and how much she's got to give away."

"I know'd she wanted to lose some of that weight. Good for her," Elvie said. "How's Miss Agnes doin'?"

"It's hard on her," Becca said, "having her baby so far away and not knowing when she'll get her back."

And turning back to Henry, Elvie said, "You know we've been praying, all of us here at the church and also the folk at Tadie's church, including the Morgans—Hannah, Matt, and their kids—and the Dougherty family. You remember Clay's wife and step-children?"

"Met them at Tadie's."

"We're all praying for that child and her mama. And for the daddy, who seems to need a lightning bolt or two."

Henry grinned. "That's a nice way of putting it."

"Not too hard for God, though," Elvie said.

"Maybe not. I suppose if he got hold of me, he can get hold of anyone."

James nodded. "That'd be true for all of us. Nary a body escapes the need for God."

Elvie patted Becca's arm. "We'll pray together this afternoon, every one of us."

"Thank you, Elvie. I'll be back over to Agnes's right after I see my girl, and I'll tell her. Agnes, she needs our prayers. Don't think she knows how to speak them for herself, but we who do, well, we can just carry her for now."

"Yes, ma'am. We can sure do that," James said.

"And maybe while we pray, we can beseech the good Lord to grab ahold of her," said Elvie.

The church had emptied around them, and Rita spoke up, looking right at him. "Why don't you come on with us then? Let

Becca go see her daughter. We've got room in the car, and I know Tadie and Will would love to see you again. Martin's on call, but he'll be free by two or so."

Going with them would keep him from racing over to see Agnes and repeat the mistake he'd made with that kiss, which he had wanted to repeat since it happened. Keeping his focus on prayer wouldn't hurt him at all because he still hadn't gleaned the wisdom he needed. "If you're sure."

"Absolutely."

"Then I'd like that."

Elvie put herself in front of her daughter. "Honey, why don't we get Tadie to call Agnes, get her over to the house? Seems that girl could use being there. What do you say?"

"Mama, I think it's a great idea." And to Becca, "Why don't you stop by on your way back to Agnes's place? See if she's agreed to join us. That way she won't be home alone more than she's been already."

"I'll just do that."

Henry grinned. Seemed to him Agnes was going to have a hard time standing against all these people. And he wouldn't be alone with her.

In the car with Rita and her parents, he thought of the last picnic he'd gone to and his empty hands this time. "I don't have a dish to share."

"Oh, you've seen us gather. Never a shortage of food," Rita said.

He grinned because he remembered tables laden with more food than any twenty people could finish in one meal. "I guess not."

An extra person didn't seem to make a bit of difference when Jilly met them at the door, and her parents welcomed him. No doubt about it, these were good folk, and the food did smell enticing, but it was the laughter, the talk, and the prayers that cemented his conviction he wanted to be part of this group. He'd never wanted to belong somewhere more than he did right then.

And that feeling was only enhanced when Will answered the doorbell and ushered Agnes into the kitchen. Tadie rushed over to hug her.

Agnes glanced around and nodded when she saw him but turned back to Tadie as their hostess said, "We were about to grab plates and find places to sit, so you got here just in time."

Elvie Mae pulled a couple of baking trays out of the oven. "Biscuits are ready. I brung my fig preserves for folk who like those, and Tadie's set out molasses for the others."

Will filled a plate and suggested the men take their food to the back porch. "It's perfect weather, and there's just the right amount of breeze." He called to James. "You coming?"

"Y'all lead the way," James said. "I'm gonna pause for some of Elvie's jam."

Agnes hung out with the women folk, which he figured was something she needed, friends and conversation to take her mind off missing Brisa. Maybe Tadie and Rita, even Elvie Mae, would have some counsel they could give her.

And maybe they'd pray with her. Maybe she'd open up to them. To God.

He had a lot to consider. A lot he needed to understand about himself and his motivations.

Back on *Harmless,* Henry settled in with a glass of water. He'd lit the kerosene lamp in the salon, and its golden glow soothed him. Soon, though, he climbed out to the cockpit to watch night take over the anchorage.

As the wind dwindled to nothing and bare ripples showed on the water's surface, he thought about his conversation with Father Stanley that morning. What was truth for him? Should he be afraid, constantly afraid, of what failure would mean? Was he meant to avoid certain relationships—specifically his relationship with Agnes?

Or, had God led her to him for a purpose? For her or for him —or perhaps for them both?

"Whoever dwells in the shelter of the Most High will rest in the shadow of the Almighty." He spoke aloud the words he'd memorized and remembered the next bit that said God would save him from the fowler's snare and... the deadly pestilence. Fowler's snare sounded a lot like addiction. Pestilence, too.

The Creator of all things—including him, Henry Donato Houston, as well as Agnes Jones—wasn't one to mince words. So when the whisper came, Henry wasn't really surprised.

*Wait. Trust. Believe.*

And if that was only his imagination speaking, Henry figured he was safe following those orders. Not much was required in waiting, unless you were the sort who got antsy without action.

Hadn't Agnes said that about herself?

As if to save him from too much reflection, his phone rang. Eric's voice spoke when he answered. "Just checking in. And wondering how Ms. Jones is handling everything. Rita's been the contact person, so I haven't talked to her personally, but I know you two are close."

"Agnes. Real name, Agnese."

"Yeah, I saw that. Only, I didn't know how to pronounce it."

"Now you do."

"What's with you?" Of course Eric had noticed the sharpness of his tone.

Henry sighed. "Sorry. I've been wrestling with a few things."

"Like?"

"You wouldn't be interested."

"How do you know?"

"Bible related."

"Ah. But I am interested in how you think, Bible or no."

Eric had always been his best friend. Twins were like that, he supposed, even when one was perfect and the other a mess.

"Okay." He took a deep breath, wanting to explain in a way that would make sense to his brother. "Okay," he said again.

"Scripture says that God is the protector of those who call him their refuge. And I'm wrestling with what that means for an addict. If I call God my refuge, will he actually vanquish all my enemies? Even if the one trying to destroy me is myself?"

"Interesting question."

He might as well tell Eric the rest. "If I believe that God is there for me, fighting my battles, and if I believe he has delivered me, then I have to believe I've been freed from addiction, too, don't I?" Either he'd been freed from his addictions or he hadn't. Either God had delivered him or he hadn't. Either Henry could trust in God's promises—or he should quit now. Unless his reasoning was facile and self-serving because he wanted it to be true.

"It sounds as if you believe there's the possibility of change, of growth between the point where addiction rules and the point where freedom does." Eric's words sounded measured, thoughtful. "What was true when you first became clean may not be true for you now."

"Maybe. And, it seems, the scripture about being double-minded, reprimanding those who say they believe but don't act like it, may be speaking to my worries."

"Ah," said Eric. "That's a subject you'll need to discuss with your sponsor. He'd be a better person to debate it with you."

"He would be. We've begun the discussion."

"Great. Good. Sorry I'm no better help. But I do want you free, so whatever it takes, Hen. Whatever."

"Thank you." That meant something, didn't it? That his brother had his back. Always had, even when Henry had pushed him away.

"So, how's Agnes?"

"She seemed okay when I saw her at Tadie's. Not great, but okay."

"Let me know any way I can help, in spite of my biblical ignorance." Eric spoke with enough humor that it brought a smile to Henry's lips.

## 49

## HENRY

He stood under the spray from his onboard solar shower the next morning, his head full of questions. He'd wrestled most of the night, and he kept asking himself—and God—what it meant not to walk in fear. He was still asking.

"Okay, God, here's the deal. If I believe, I shouldn't fear falling back into my old ways, right?"

Silence. Well, he hadn't expected a booming voice.

"Look, if I'm wrong and the once-an-addict-always-an-addict mantra is right, suggesting I need to tiptoe through life, afraid of failure, let me know, okay? Doesn't sound like you, at least not from what I've read in your book, but I could be wrong."

After he'd toweled off and dressed, he speed-dialed Father Stanley.

"What's up?" the priest asked.

"I have a question."

"Shoot."

"It's a follow-up to our discussion yesterday morning, and it has to do with fear, specifically what's discussed in Psalm 91."

"That's a good one."

"Remember how the Narcotics Anonymous meetings always suggested 'once an addict, always an addict'?"

"Yes."

"Well, how does that work with the idea of being free in Christ? I mean, I get that my actions have consequences, but the once and always part has me worrying that if I'm not vigilant enough, I might fail. Bam, back in my addiction."

The priest waited.

"Remember the link you sent me to that recovered addict's blog? Nick Patchen? He just wrote about an experience he had in Southeast Asia where God worked a miracle among his fellow missionaries. He told how the miracle—protection from poison —got the attention of the witchdoctor who'd administered the potion, and when it failed to work, the witchdoctor wanted to know more, figured his victim had been protected by a mightier God than the ones he served. Now he's a convert and a missionary himself."

"I haven't read that one yet. Nick has certainly had some interesting experiences in his short life."

Henry asked, "Did you send me his information because of how he looks at addiction?"

"I did. It's a different perspective from what we'd heard in the NA meetings."

"The timing of all this seems like a God thing—my discovering that he sees himself not as an addict, but as a man freed by God for a relationship with him, which is the same argument that came to me as I was reading scripture. I can't help but ask, if I'm really free, shouldn't I act that way? Like Nick does?"

"He's certainly being effective in his ministry, isn't he? But I think before you declare yourself ready to head off to Asia for missionary work—"

"Not in my immediate future, thank you."

Father Stanley chuckled. "I don't know Nick's full journey, but I imagine he had to deal with the things that made him crave oblivion in the first place before he could find the freedom he knows now. I think you must do the same thing."

"You mean, like feeling sorry for myself because I wasn't as good as Eric—as perfect?"

"And your father?"

"Yeah, he was a—" No, better not use that word. "Well, you know."

"We've talked about this many times, the importance of forgiveness."

Henry sighed audibly. "I know. And I've said the words."

"But have they come from your heart or your head?"

"I don't know."

"And your mother? Your brother?"

He felt another sigh coming on, a deeper one, because really? Did he need to do that? "I'm not angry at them."

"Your mother wasn't willing to hang around for you."

Nor had she been willing to be there for either one of her sons while she'd been alive. "Fine. My mother, too."

"And Eric?"

"You mean because he was born perfect."

Father Stanley didn't answer. Henry figured the priest was smart enough to recognize a question that wasn't a question at all. Still, he felt compelled to say, "Not that it was Eric's fault."

"Do our unconscious thoughts separate the intentional from the actual?" Father Stanley asked.

Had his? "I guess not."

"Think about it," Father Stanley said. "There are hooks we've allowed to remain stuck in us, and those are the ones that have the power to snag addiction."

"We're back to talking about freedom."

"Yes. You want to be really free, then you need to dig the hooks out and leave them with God."

Easier said than done.

After they disconnected, Henry climbed back into the cockpit. Ahead of him was the island, but he didn't really focus on anything specific until a pair of banks ponies ambled into view.

Man, they were gorgeous, their heads bowed over the grasses as they grazed. They had the place to themselves, but there were probably others, checking out some other ground, maybe looking for fresh water.

He was so incredibly fortunate to live here, like this, on a boat he owned outright, no rent to pay. Free.

But not all the way.

What had been killing him was the whole feeling sorry for himself thing he'd had going for more years than he could count. The confession that he'd always be an addict had presumed the possibility of failure, which brought along the fear of not being vigilant enough and of ultimately succumbing.

Father Stanley had spoken of his broken places, the ones that had made him vulnerable to drugs in the first place. That festering wound implied the need to forgive his family.

Just thinking of that made his skin crawl, and the need to do something physical almost overwhelmed him. Was he seeing clearly or deluding himself?

He tucked his cell phone in his pocket, got out a fresh bottle of water, and pulled his dinghy close in. Then he climbed down the ladder, settled himself, untied his tethering line, and took up his oars.

This was good, he decided as he rowed himself away from *Harmless* and down the creek. He'd go until he wore himself out. Exercise, that's what he needed.

He hit his stride, and by the time he'd rowed past any houses he recognized, his muscles were ready for a rest. He let his little boat and his thoughts drift.

He might as well admit he'd carried anger toward God. Because he'd been the maimed one while Eric had been perfect. And then he'd been angry with Eric for being perfect. Henry dropped his head forward.

He sucked in a deep breath and pulled his oars in the boat. Yes, he was a mess. But God had said there was a way out, hadn't He? Repentance, forgiveness, freedom?

There was no one around who'd hear him. He could speak to the water, to the sky. "God, I'm sorry. I should never have blamed you or Eric. I'm sorry, and I forgive…"

*Whom?*

"I forgive everyone."

*Name them.*

"Name them?"

He sighed. It sounded so ridiculous to be having this conversation with… himself? And yet…

"Fine. I forgive… Do you know how hard this is?" He took another deep and, he hoped, cleansing breath. "Okay, okay. I forgive my father. I forgive him for…" He felt like puking as the memories surfaced. He slammed shut his eyes as he tried to mean the words he spoke. As he tried for more than obedience.

"I forgive him for being cruel and violent and for pushing my mother to kill herself." Once the words started flowing, they didn't stop. "For rejecting me. For preferring Eric. For… Well, I forgive him for… everything."

*Next?*

"I forgive Eric. For being what I wished I could be."

*And?*

"I forgive my mother. For not being strong enough, for not loving us enough, for giving up. For leaving us with him."

He didn't wait for the next reminder. "I forgive you, Lord. I forgive you for making me an imperfect, maimed baby."

*Did I fail in my creation? Do I see you as imperfect? Did I ever?*

He wasn't sure he had an answer for that one. He shook his head. He'd skip that one for now.

*And?*

"That's the hardest."

*But it's necessary. Say it aloud.*

"Okay, okay. I forgive…"

Could he? Could he actually mean it?

He let himself drift on the current for another few minutes, and then he drank most of the water he'd brought, picked up the oars, and turned the boat around.

---

The tide must have been at slack because the trip back took no longer than the trip out. He tied up, climbed out, and took his sweaty self below to wash off. He was holding out on part of it, but that's the way it had to be, at least for now.

He called Eric's phone. "It's time," he said when his brother answered.

"For what?"

"I'm working on forgiving him, and I need to let you give me something of his."

Money would give him the ability to help Agnes. To be the rescuer he'd longed to be. To think of someone other than himself. To take the next step in his quest for freedom.

The silence was only momentary. "Took you long enough."

---

Phone calls kept him busy that Monday evening and into Tuesday. Plans were for Eric to take him to the rental car agency that afternoon so he could drive to Raleigh and catch the Wednesday morning cross-country flight. Much better than trying to leave from New Bern and having to change planes in Charlotte or Atlanta.

Chef wasn't thrilled, but he finally said, "Take what time you need. I'll square it with the owners."

"Thanks, man." He was already in Chef's debt. He kept quiet about this adding to it.

Rita said she'd let everyone know to add him to the prayer list. "You're the perfect person to go since Agnes can't. Call me if you hit a snag. I'll see what I can do to help from this end."

"Don't get Agnes's hopes up—or worry her. If things go as

planned, I'll call with the good news. If I fail... well, we'll deal with that when and if it happens."

"You'd better warn Clay, too."

He had, and Clay had offered to put Henry in touch with someone he knew out there. "Ex-LAPD. Good guy, originally from here."

"I'll let you know if I need him," Henry said.

He'd booked everything. Now he just needed to get the job done.

With the time difference, he'd be at the L.A. airport by nine on Wednesday. As he drove to the hotel in Raleigh, he tried to keep a clear head and keen vision. The last thing he needed was an accident or something else to stop this rescue mission.

And so he prayed. For safety, for grace, for mercy.

For Agnes, fretting at home.

# 50

## AGNES

Agnes hadn't seen Henry since the picnic on Sunday, and he hadn't called yesterday or today. She didn't understand his silence or Rita's. Becca'd stopped in for a few hours, Tadie'd called to check up on her, but other than that, there'd been nothing but her empty house and empty hours and Link barely lifting his head when she spoke to him.

When Billy the postman came whistling up the porch steps, she headed downstairs, expecting Link to follow, but he didn't budge. Sighing, she continued outside, thinking maybe, by some remote chance, a letter might have come from Brisa.

Her only correspondent was the gas company. She remained isolated, a mother with a hole in her heart, an empty place in her world, and no answers from anyone about anything.

And suddenly, she'd had enough. Enough of moping, enough of pining, enough of sitting around waiting for the courts to bring some relief. Without thinking of the consequences and motivated by a panic she couldn't explain, she climbed to the third floor, found one of her mother's carry-on suitcases, took it to her room, and started packing.

She didn't need much because she wouldn't be able to stay long. Before she called the airlines to book her ticket, she'd give the universe one more chance to direct her steps and fix things. She carried the suitcase downstairs, picked up her cell phone, and punched in Rita's number. It usually went to voicemail, but this time Rita answered and said, "I'm in your driveway. I'll be right in."

What did this mean? Did Rita come bearing good news? Bad news? No news?

She opened the front door and waited for Rita to climb from her car and walk up the sidewalk and to her steps. Agnes didn't speak; the prolonged silence had dammed up her words. She ushered the other woman toward the living room.

Rita's eyes widened when she saw the suitcase, but she only said, "I'm sorry I haven't been available. How are you holding up?" She eased down at one end of the sofa.

Agnes sat at the other end. Her legs were jittery, and she had to focus to keep them still. She pleated the hem of her shirt between her fingers. Finally, words came. "I have to go and get her. I can't sit here another day hoping something will happen and having no control over any of it. My girl's been gone eleven days, Rita. I should have left as soon as I knew where she was."

"I'd feel the same way if she were my daughter."

"You won't try to stop me?" Agnes waited and then stared hard at the other woman, who no longer seemed calm and in control. "What?" she asked.

"I only wanted to come and encourage you, to tell you it would all work out, but staying silent isn't fair to you."

"Silent about what? Has something happened to Brisa? Do you know something I don't?" Agnes heard the panic in her voice, the raised pitch she couldn't control.

"No, nothing like that. It's Henry…"

"What?" Did Rita think these half-finished thoughts were helping? "What about Henry?"

Rita curled the fingers of one hand inside the other as if trying to warm it. "He knew it would be risky for you to go to

California to get Brisa, and he knew, we all knew, that someone had to go. He flew out there this morning."

"Henry went to get my baby?" The panic wasn't gone, but Agnes could feel the intensity of it dissipating as it was replaced by a sense of relief so profound she almost burst into tears. She stifled them with a sniffle and finally was able to speak. "Why didn't he tell me? Why didn't someone tell me?"

Rita reached over to lay her hand on Agnes's. "He didn't want to worry you. He knew if he failed it would be worse for you, and he said he'll call just as soon as he sees her."

"When? When will he see her? When will he get there?"

"He boarded a direct flight out of Raleigh early this morning." She checked her watch. "He should be getting to Darlington's sometime in the next hour."

"The next hour. We'll know something in the next hour." She'd flattened her voice against the ricocheting emotions that wouldn't settle.

"We should. Assuming Darlington and Brisa are there, and assuming they let him in. I found out the process server has been turned away often at the gate by some male employee, so there are a few hurdles Henry will have to jump over before we'll actually hear from him."

"But she might be coming home."

"She might. At least we'll know something from someone who has actually been there. And knowing Henry, he won't come home until he's talked to her. Probably until he can bring her with him."

"Will you stay with me until we know? Until he calls?"

"I plan to."

51

# DARLING

At just past ten the next morning, Darling was seated in the sunken area of his living room with a cup of coffee and a bran muffin. Brisa was still asleep. Poor baby had to be exhausted, all she'd gone through in the last week.

The front door opened, admitting Lisette, who was dressed in a tight little suit, one he'd bought for her. She didn't close the door but instead waited for a companion to join her. Darling recognized the man's ring as his fingers curled around the edge of the door. Daddy entered, a smile playing across his face as his attention remained on Lisette. It wasn't a nice smile.

Darling lifted his cup to his lips and watched them. Eventually, his father noticed him and said, "Good morning."

Lisette turned toward him. "Ah, Darling. How is *la petite?*"

"Fine." He assumed she was still asleep, exhausted from travel, although it was after nine.

"Did she enjoy her trip into your past?" his father asked. "Did Mama fawn all over her?"

"It was good to see Mama again and learn she'd written letters I never received. I also discovered she hadn't gotten any of the money you promised to send."

His father fluttered fingers at him as if the letters and money

310

weren't worth mentioning. Of course he'd play it that way. Like he did with anything that made him look bad.

Darling pictured the scene that had prompted his trip to Georgia. "The mess I found here after the party couldn't have been worse."

His father's brows lowered in a scowl. "I heard your accusations from Arthur. I don't believe them."

"She was given glasses of juice laced with alcohol, I'm guessing vodka. I walked in during the filming. And RJ was snorting cocaine."

"We'll just have to keep it quiet." Daddy's nonchalance made Darling want to hurl something his way.

"Is that your final word on it?"

"It is."

"What about you?" Darling turned to Lisette. "You claimed you wanted to be her mother. You're not acting much like one. You weren't even here when we got home."

His father straightened his spine and puffed out his barrel chest, but the old man's bluster came across as weakness, which made Darling want to laugh out loud. Instead, he schooled his expression to one of polite interest.

"What is that supposed to mean?" his father said. "You left your wife at the after-party to run home after your daughter. You then took your daughter across country without mentioning the trip to either your wife or to me. What was Lisette supposed to do? Stay here alone? No! She stayed with me."

Darling focused on his father, ignoring Lisette who seemed not at all bothered that they discussed her. "She's been doing that a lot lately, hasn't she?"

"You live up here in the hills. It only makes sense for her stay nearer the city."

"And the night of Brisa's birthday?"

Daddy shrugged. "You left. We took the party elsewhere."

"My wife"—he glanced over at her and noted her inappropriate grin—"stayed elsewhere."

"You left her then, as you have so often, without considering her needs. You don't put her feelings first, and she's your wife, the one person you should be considering before all others." Daddy leaned in and said quietly, "I made you, Darling, both by fathering you and by bringing you into my world. I made you, and I can unmake you." Daddy snapped his fingers. "Just like that. If you come up against me, you won't know what hit you."

Funny how those words no longer had the power to wound him, Darling thought.

Daddy turned to Lisette. "Hurry it up."

Darling said, "What now?"

"Oh, did we forget to mention that while you were gallivanting around the country, Lisette signed with Drexel and Weatherman? I'll be working with her, which will make her move to Beverly Hills much more convenient." Daddy waggled his fingers in Lisette's direction as if to scoot her along.

Darling let his gaze follow her retreat. Once, he'd adored her tinkling laugh. And then she'd spider-cracked that love by coming home smelling of sex with someone else—his father?—and by not coming home at all some nights. Oh, he'd tried to inject resin in to stabilize things, a resin made up of money, fame... and Brisa. It had all been self-delusion on his part, an imaginary once-upon-a-time shattered like a hammer to glass by his father's hand on his wife's backside.

He hid behind his coffee mug, sipping the now-cold brew with the blandest expression he could muster. He wouldn't move. He'd sit here until they left, and then he'd... well, he'd follow Mama Bea's advice. "Do what your hand finds to do, son, and do it as best you can."

He merely had to be patient a little longer. He was in full rebellion mode now, even if it meant breaking a contract or two —and facing the resulting lawsuits... He hoped it wouldn't, of course.

He had regrets aplenty, but they didn't include calling Jett Loren or putting things in motion with him. He couldn't wait to hear back from Jett or the lawyer Jett had contacted. He checked his watch. It wasn't too early to call the bank and make certain all was secure for some money to head Mama Bea's way. And to make certain no one else had access to what was his.

Then he needed to set up a trust fund for Brisa. And Agnes? Mama Bea's admonition continued on replay. One step at a time.

---

He didn't want to talk to anyone, certainly not anyone who might be trying to get in the front gate today, barely thirty minutes after his father and Lisette had left. Todd was very good at getting rid of the riff-raff.

Soon, Todd came in and cleared his throat. "Someone named Henry Houston's here. Says he's from Beaufort."

"Police?" Darling asked without turning from the window.

"No. A friend of the family."

Darling sighed. "You think I need to see him?" He did turn then. Maybe this Henry Houston would go away if he refused. Not likely, not if he'd come from North Carolina. The airlines had been doing a brisk business this month on flights from that nothing little town to this nothing tinsel city.

"I think you'd better." Todd sounded mildly apologetic, although he didn't explain his reasoning.

"Fine, let him in." He wished he could have a drink. Surely it was late enough somewhere.

It took about five minutes for the man to enter, park, and walk up the stone steps to the front door. Todd opened it for him and waved him toward the living room and Darling.

The man was tall, about his own age. He'd obviously had some work done on his lip. Darling had never met anyone with a cleft lip before. Nice to know it could be fixed as well as this one had been, leaving only a slight lift and a small scar. Now that he thought about it, that imperfection made the man seem interesting.

Well, fine, he couldn't keep staring without saying something. He stood, walked forward, and extended his hand. "Darling Evermire. How can I help you?"

"Henry Houston." The man accepted his hand and shook it. It was a strong clasp with a workman's calloused hand. Even more interesting.

"Nice place you have here. Probably very attractive to a young girl," Henry Houston said, "but I would really like to speak to her. Brisa, that is."

"I imagined you might, but the question is, why?" Darling waved toward one of the couches. "Please, have a seat."

The man lowered himself onto the leather and waited a moment before speaking again. "It's her dog, Link."

As a conversation opener or a reason for being here, the man's words had Darling's mouth gaping open. He quickly shut it. This Mr. Houston had come all this way to talk about a dog? "What about Link?"

"Brisa is his person, and, since she's been gone, he only leaves her room under duress. He barely eats, won't go for walks. He's waiting for her. Pining, actually."

A plane trip across country because Brisa's *dog* was unhappy? Not to threaten him or whine about her mother, but to say the *dog* misses her?

Darling stared at him. "You've got to be kidding."

"I'm not."

"And you think Brisa should leave all this because of her dog?"

"It's one reason."

"And the others?"

Henry spread his arms along the back of the couch. "I bet you can guess those."

Darling pushed himself up with his hands on his knees. "You want something? Tea, coffee, a drink?"

"Tea'd be great. I had wretched coffee on the plane."

Darling called through the door to Todd, who was hovering

nearby, and asked for two teas. It wasn't long before Todd returned carrying a tray of fruit and Cook's raisin brownies along with the tea. "Cook made these for Brisa," his man said, "but I know you like chocolate."

"Thanks, Todd. Don't wake Brisa just yet."

"Right."

"Try one." Darling passed the plate to Henry and picked up his mug of tea, then slid the tray closer to his guest. "I have a little story to tell you, but first, I'd like to know more about you and how you fit into Brisa's life."

---

Darling turned at the sound of Brisa's footsteps in the hallway, and now she stood at the entrance to the living room. He saw the moment she connected with their guest.

"Oh, Mr. Henry! Mr. Henry!" She darted forward and straight into his arms.

Well, that answered one thing. The man had a relationship with his daughter.

As Henry's arms tightened around her, she burst into tears. Tears!

"Oh, sweetie, it's okay. You're okay," Henry crooned as he patted her back, a little awkwardly, Darling was pleased to note. At least the man wasn't used to a little girl's hugs—*his* little girl's hugs.

He got up and went in search of tissues. By the time he returned with a wad of them, Brisa's sobs had slowed. She took one and blew into it.

"Mommy? Did Mommy send you? I thought she never wanted to see me again! She never called or anything. I thought she hated me. I thought… I thought she was so mad she didn't care if I stayed here." Another choked sob, and she dashed the back of her hand across her eyes.

"Why would she hate you?" Henry sounded shocked. "She loves you!"

"But"—and here the tears threatened again—"it's on account of me she had to quit school and doesn't have any money. I figured she was happy I was gone on account of not having to remember the bad that happened."

Henry looked over at him and raised his brows. Darling wasn't about to admit his culpability to this man he didn't know.

Henry sighed. "It's okay, honey. Your mom loves you more than you can imagine. You're her life, and she's been frantic with worry."

"How come...?" The sobs were back. "How come she didn't call me?"

"Brisa, listen to me. Your mom has been calling out here every day, trying to talk to you since you left, to tell you how much she misses you. Two phone numbers. She called two phones, and no one bothered to get back to her or let you talk to her." He turned a scowl in Darling's direction. "One of those was your phone. And," he said with emphasis, "your wife promised to have Brisa call. I assume she didn't mention it to Brisa?"

Brisa frowned and turned her gaze to Darling. He raised one brow. "Or to me," he said. "I knew Lisette had spoken to Agnes. She told me Agnes was furious, but that's all. She certainly never mentioned daily messages."

"You didn't get any?" Henry said.

"Well, eventually, but the lawyer told Arthur it would cause legal difficulties if I spoke to Agnes."

"But..." Brisa looked stricken. "You let me think my mommy didn't care!"

"I'm sorry, honey. I really am. I shouldn't have listened to Arthur." Darling wished he were the one holding Brisa, comforting her. It appeared instead that he was particularly adept at making bad decisions.

Henry pulled Brisa closer. "Everyone misses you. And Link

won't leave your room except to go outside when he's desperate. I think he's going to waste away if you don't come home."

"Link? Oh, my sweet boy, my poor sweet doggy." The tears started again.

Henry had tissues at the ready this time.

As he watched the two interact, Darling knew this interlude, this time-out of the real world where he'd held his daughter as his own, was coming to an end. The choice had been made for him.

It always had, hadn't it? Been made for, not by, him. Had he really had a choice at seventeen, a boy in need of a father? A boy who wanted to please that father?

He supposed he had and had made the one that seemed best to him then.

And, of course, he'd made the choice to try out that drug and then to believe Arthur that everything was fine for Agnes. He'd made the choice not to find out for himself if there'd been repercussions for her. He'd made the choice to marry Lisette without looking at her motives, believing her words instead of her actions. He'd made the choice not to call his grandmother, not to make sure she had everything she needed, to believe his father.

To be like his father and think only of himself. Yeah, that had been his common denominator, hadn't it?

It was too late to change the early choices. Too late for do-overs. Too late to be the father he wished he could be, the father he wished he'd had.

One thing remained, though. One choice he could make that would be motivated by love. He could choose not to let his world screw things up for his daughter. He could let Henry save her.

## 52

## HENRY

Henry withdrew his cell phone from his pocket. "Shall we call your mommy now?" he asked Brisa, not bothering to look at Darling.

"Can we? Oh, please, can we?" She stood a little away from him now, her small body tightly wound, her clasped hands near her lips. Her lashes still held traces of the tears she'd shed.

"Of course we can."

He had Agnes on speed dial. He let it ring, and when he heard Agnes's voice answering, he handed the phone to her daughter, but he put it on speaker. It wouldn't hurt Darlington to hear these two talk to each other, to hear their pain and love.

"Mommy? Oh, Mommy." The tears were back, streaming down her face.

Agnes's voice came through clearly. "Brisa, oh, Brisa honey... Baby, are you okay? Are you really okay?" There were tears in Agnes's voice, along with hope and joy.

He withdrew a handkerchief from his pocket and passed it to Brisa, but she only clutched it in her free hand as she told her mother, "I was so afraid."

"Of what? Of me?"

"That you didn't want me anymore. That maybe I'd been so

318

awful and so bad you were glad I was gone. I wanted to talk to you so badly, but you didn't call."

"I called every day, and I kept hoping someone would tell you so you'd call home, or you'd do it on your own. Didn't you have your own phone? Or a house phone you could have used?"

"They took the one Daddy gave me. It was that man Arthur. He said I wouldn't need it. And I was too scared to ask anyone if I could call you. I thought they'd be mad at me."

"Even your father?"

Brisa lowered her head and nodded, then she glanced toward her father and mumbled something at the phone.

"What, honey? I didn't hear you."

"He was so happy to see me. And Lisette seemed to really like me at first."

"And then?"

"Not so much." Her child's voice sounded puzzled and hurt.

"I'm sorry. I wish I'd known."

"I'm okay now, but I want to see you. Why didn't you come with Mr. Henry?"

"He surprised us, sweetheart. I didn't know he was going to get you for me."

"Is he here to get me?" Brisa looked from Henry to her father, but Darling stood at the long window, his back to the room.

"Do you want to come home?" Agnes asked.

Brisa swiped at her wet cheeks, one at a time. "I miss you so much."

"Will you put this on speaker so I can talk to Henry, too?"

"We're on speaker," Henry said. "I'm here."

"Thank you, oh, thank you. When can you bring her home?"

Darling turned then. "I'll make the arrangements for tomorrow morning. I have a plane available."

"Did you hear? Tomorrow!" Brisa was bouncing now. "I'll see you by—when will we get there?"

"Around five," Darling said, and Henry heard something in

319

his voice that sounded very much like resignation. "You can
update arrival time from the air."

"I'm going to take us off speaker, Agnes, and let Brisa talk to
you for as long as she wants."

He suggested Brisa take the phone with her to her room. "Go
on, honey, visit with your mama. I'll talk to your dad."

Brisa grinned at him and ran off down the hall.

And then Darling turned, a rueful expression on his face. "I
have a few things to take care of before we leave," he said.
"Banking issues and a phone call to my lawyer."

"Friendly fire?"

Darling grinned. "Ah, but no. This is a new lawyer. I won't be
working with the old one again. The plan now is to set up a trust
fund for Brisa."

"And you're coming with us, why?"

Henry's suspicious question, meant to rattle the other man,
only enlarged Darling's grin.

"Because," Darling said, "I'm also going to negotiate a truce."

And with that Darling called in his manservant—whatever
the man was to him—and said, "Todd, would you please show
Mr. Houston to the blue guest room? He will be keeping us
company tonight, and tomorrow we'll all be leaving together."

"Yes, sir."

Darling said to Henry, "My soon-to-be-ex-wife liked the idea
of color coordinating rooms. It's a little frilly in there, but I'm
sure you'll manage well enough. Feel free to make yourself at
home this afternoon. I have work to do, but Todd will make sure
you have what you need, and I'll see you at dinner."

"Thanks," Henry said.

"*Mi casa es su casa* and all that." And then Darling excused
himself, and Henry allowed Todd to show him his room.

"Do you have a suitcase?" Todd asked.

"I do." It wasn't a big one, but he'd brought supplies in case
he'd had to lay siege to Darling's castle.

"I'll bring it to you if your car is unlocked."

"Thank you," he said, and Todd opened the door to a bedroom big enough to fit ten of him.

"The bathroom's a shared one," Todd said, "But there's no one using the far room, so it will be private."

"What's that one called?"

"The yellow room," Todd said.

Ah, blue and yellow. Henry wondered, but didn't ask, if there was a red or green one.

Todd returned with his case and offered to serve lunch whenever he wanted it. "Intercom, line two, will ring me."

"Thanks. I'll talk to Brisa." Henry left his door open after Todd left. He imagined Brisa would come looking for him when she finished telling her mother all about her adventures as the daughter of this oh-so-genial superstar.

He kicked off his shoes and lay back on the bed, studying the room and hoping eventually his eyes would close. He'd been so wired in the last days that he hadn't let himself even think of what awaited him at home. He'd merely bought a ticket and a superman cape.

Did he imagine himself the hero of this piece? Well, la-dee-da, here he was, his role pre-empted by the villain-turned-good-guy.

Maybe Hollywood could do something with the story, because how often did this happen? The mega rich, mega famous, self-absorbed you-know-what has a miraculous change of heart and becomes daddy of the year.

Oh, yeah. That would sell.

---

He'd had actually fallen asleep on that comfortable bed, and when he'd woken a couple of hours later, he'd wandered out to the living room. Brisa had been sitting with Darling, singing along as he strummed his guitar. Henry'd taken a seat across from them, moved by the obvious tenderness the man showed his daughter.

Over dinner, Darling had told him some of the story of their time together, and all Henry could do was give thanks to the God who had obviously been at work answering prayers. Surely Agnes would have to admit the Lord's intervention here, because only God cared about changing hearts as well as outcomes.

Now they were Beaufort-bound in a Cessna Citation, a luxurious small jet the likes of which he'd never encountered. The co-pilot pinch-hit as a steward to take care of whatever the three of them wanted or needed, which tickled Brisa. She sat up straighter whenever he asked if he could get her something to drink. "A snack, maybe?"

Henry watched the landscape pass until there were only clouds below, and then he closed his eyes and let the sounds in the cabin become background to thoughts that were soon smothered by sleep.

A change in engine noise woke him as they descended into the Beaufort area. He'd never flown into Michael J Smith Airfield. The experience of being delivered by jet only a few miles from *Harmless* would be worth repeating if he ever had somewhere to go that required a fast flight instead of a slow sail.

There wasn't a terminal here, only hangars and what looked like an administration building. The plane taxied in, the engines shut down, and the plane's door opened. Henry stepped onto the boarding steps. In the lingering daylight, he could see Eric's arm shooting up in a wave from other side of the fence, Agnes at his side.

As Henry reached back to help Brisa navigate the steps, footsteps pounded on the tarmac toward them. And then Brisa jumped down and was racing into her mother's arms, and the two of them were hugging and bawling and pawing each other. The co-pilot helped him carry suitcases from plane to car, and Henry introduced Darlington to his brother Eric.

To his credit, Darling offered none of the famous-entertainer swagger Henry'd watched during the televised introduction of Brisa to his adoring fans. "Glad to meet you," Darling said. And then he hung back.

"Where can we take you?" Eric asked him. "I understand we have an appointment tomorrow."

Darling shook his head. "I made a reservation at the inn. Agnes may prefer I get a taxi."

Agnes, who still held on to Brisa but had moved with her to the car's back door, nodded agreement. Henry stepped forward and addressed her. "There's some talking that needs to be done, Agnes. You mind if we give Darling a ride to town? You can choose when to have the conversation. But it needs to be had."

Agnes didn't respond. She drew Brisa to the car's backseat when Eric got behind the wheel. Henry motioned for Darling to ride shotgun, and he slid in on the other side of Brisa.

They were headed into town when a beep signaled someone had a message waiting. Darling checked and then held the phone to his ear to listen to his voicemail. Maybe it was the quiet engine and no road noises when they stopped for a light. Maybe Darling had his volume all the way up. Whatever it was, they could all hear the voices coming through his phone's speaker.

"Hey, Darl, what's up?" was the first, a masculine voice, deep and resonant. Henry didn't recognize it. Then the same voice said in another message, "Todd said you've taken Brisa to Beaufort. What on earth are you thinking?" The third, a different voice this time, was gruff and angry. "Darlington, turn that plane around and bring that child back here. I'm already negotiating her next appearance. The reviewers used words like 'magnificent voice,' 'stellar performance,' 'she may surpass her father in talent and charisma.' Get her home now."

"Daddy?" Brisa said, her voice worried.

He turned in his seat to smile at her. "Don't you worry, honey. I told you, he's no longer going to have control of either of us."

"Are you going to get in trouble on account of me?"

"No, of course not. He'll be angry, but none of that matters. I'm going to tell them that as proud as I am of you, the decision to pursue a music career will be yours when you're an adult. I will not allow either of them to ruin the sweet young girl I had the privilege of fathering."

Agnes had her eyes shut in what looked to Henry like a wince, but Brisa didn't seem to notice. She spoke from the comfort of her mother's arms. "You mean it?"

"What?" Darling asked. "The privilege thing?"

"Yeah."

"More than you can know." And then, as if to himself, "More than you can know."

Finally, Agnes spoke. "Henry said we needed to talk. I agree. When and where?"

Darling shifted so he could see her. "You name the place and the time. I'll be there."

"My house. We need to keep this private." She checked her watch. "In one hour?"

Darling nodded. When Eric pulled up in front of the inn and popped the trunk, Darling thanked him, alighted, and grabbed his bag. Then Eric turned the car down Front Street and headed to Agnes's house. He parked in her driveway and helped Henry carry Brisa's bags to the house. To Agnes, he said, "Would you like either Rita or me with you?"

"Let me hear him out first. But I would like Henry to stay." She looked at him. "Will you?"

"No place I'd rather be."

## 53

## AGNES

Link's whine as he wiggled up to Brisa nearly broke Agnes's heart. He jumped and nuzzled and licked his beloved human with the adoration only a dog can give. "I'm home, sweet boy, I'm home," Brisa said, over and over again, as she laughed and hugged and found a few more tears.

The hanging lamp above the front hall illuminated her daughter's long dark curls, stealing Agnes's breath. Her girl. Her Brisa. *Home.*

She, like Link, didn't want to stop touching her daughter. She reached over and drew Brisa close again. "I've missed you so much." If she wasn't careful, the tears would spill into more sobs. Her sweet baby was home.

Brisa's arms encircled her. "I am s…so sorry."

And that set them both off.

Finally, Agnes set her daughter down and brought tissues from her pocket, one for each of them. "I can't believe I can finally touch you again."

Becca was drying her hands as she came from the back regions of the house. "Hey, there, sweet girl. You done come home." She held out her arms, and Brisa walked into them.

"My daddy and Mr. Henry brought me."

Agnes looked toward the stairs as Henry descended after taking Brisa's suitcases to her room. He was smiling. "I'm very glad to be back in Beaufort, I can tell you," he said. "Interesting place out there, but far too many people for my comfort."

"And some of them aren't nice at all," Brisa said, looking worried.

Agnes wanted to ask for details, but perhaps not yet. Henry set a hand on Brisa's shoulder. "I think that's why your father wanted to bring you home, don't you imagine? To protect you from them?" He glanced over at Agnes with an expression that obviously held a warning, even if she wasn't sure what he meant by it.

"What can I get for you, little missy?" Becca asked. "You be wantin' something to drink? Eat?"

Brisa shook her head. "We had stuff on the airplane. It was a fancy one."

Naturally. Agnes controlled her features so her daughter wouldn't notice how hard that was to hear. She checked her watch and then glanced over at Henry.

"What do you want me to do?" he asked.

"I don't know. Maybe you could keep Brisa company?"

"I can do that."

"First off," Becca said to Brisa, "let me take you upstairs and help you unpack. I 'magine you got yourself some new clothes you can show off to me."

"Mr. Henry, you want to see them, too?" She sounded so eager.

"I wouldn't miss it for anything." He winked at Agnes and followed the other two up the stairs. "You need me," he said over his shoulder, "just shout."

When she had the downstairs to herself, she went into the small bath to brush her hair and wash her face. That was all she'd give the occasion. And then she waited.

Darlington arrived on time with a minute to spare, and she ushered him to one of the big chairs in the living room, perching primly on the couch across from him. She wished he weren't here—or anywhere else on earth.

"Okay," she said. "So talk."

"Nice place you have here."

She merely hiked her brows.

"Well," he said, the faintest hint of a smile on his face. "When Henry arrived at my doorstep, I expected pistols at dawn. Instead, he said Brisa had to come home to keep her dog from expiring."

Darling could drop his voice into a drawl or shift to cultured in a moment. She'd heard it when they met at that bar. She'd heard it on the recordings Brisa played. Elocution lessons, or had he come from money? She hadn't known. Now he used his amused, sophisticated voice. A mimic's voice.

She didn't trust it—or him—for a minute.

"You didn't get on that plane because of Link. Why, then?" Agnes asked, all hackles and suspicion back in force.

"Things change. People change."

"You exploited her. Your own daughter." A knife to his carotid artery would be too swift a justice. "She's only twelve."

"I got to know her." He shrugged. "She's special, but that's from how you raised her as much as from genetics. I allowed her to perform because of her talent, because she loved it, and because it was a safe venue, a benefit for kids with cancer. She was carefully monitored and kept away from the crowds. It was after the concert that things fell apart." He stared at his hands and then at the floor.

"What happened?" Breathe, she told herself. Just breathe.

"The after-party... they wanted to take her there. I shouldn't have given in. It got rowdy."

"A party for adults." Booze, maybe drugs, and her daughter there?

"I was about to take her home, but before I could get back to where she was standing, my father sent her to my place with one of the female band members. Once I found she'd gone, I followed." He rubbed his palms against his knees as if to dry them. "I was too late to keep someone from giving her booze-laden juice."

"Someone got her *drunk*?" She had to work on controlling her voice. She really was going to call her great-uncle Massimo. A cement block in the deep Pacific was too good for Darling. Forget the river. Make him shark bait.

He raked fingers through his hair. "I wouldn't have had that happen for the world, Agnes. When I told my father and manager I wanted every one of them fired, they said it was impossible. So I called in another lawyer. I'm leaving the band, no matter how many contracts I have to break."

That stopped her. "You're going to stop singing? Quit performing?"

"No, but I'm no longer going to let my father and my ex-manager run things. I will not let them use that precious girl for their own ends. I'm sorry, Agnes. Sorry for everything except that child. You've done a spectacular job."

So he'd said. She stared at him, trying to read between the lines. "What do you want from me now?"

He sighed. "You have every right to hate and distrust me. I was a stupid kid when I accepted that drug from my brother and took advantage of you. I was selfish and rotten, and I'd go back and undo it if I could, except then there wouldn't be Brisa. I'm hoping she'll never have to know how badly I acted, and that you'll allow me to see her occasionally." His voice had softened. Was it an act, or did he mean what he was saying?

She had no idea how to process all this new information. It was like night had suddenly become day and day night. As if the man she'd hated all these years had been transformed and some other man sat before her. Some guy who pretended to be nice, but who might actually be manipulating her once again.

"After she sneaked out," Agnes said, "I told her what you'd done to me. Only, she didn't believe me. I'm sure it will come up again someday."

He rubbed his forehead again. "And she still came to see me."

"She wanted a daddy."

"I'm so sorry, Agnes. I wish I could undo what happened."

"Yeah. I do too."

"But now there's this incredible daughter, as if that night has been redeemed." He leaned forward, his gaze intense. "I got to know her while she was with me. And it was a whole new experience for me, having this beautiful girl-child think I was something special. It was as if her faith in me made me need to be better than I'd been."

"I hope so."

He nodded. "My wife," he said with a hint of disgust, "was supposed to put together a great birthday party and invite a bunch of kids for Brisa. Instead, she used the party for her own ends and left the birthday girl standing on the sidelines. So I took Brisa for some kid time at the Santa Monica pier and amusement park. Brisa thought it was magical. And she thought I was, too." His expression seemed filled with regret.

Agnes watched him closely. "She'd have enjoyed that."

"She enjoyed it so much that I did, too. And someplace along the way, when she held my hand and laughed, when she fell asleep in my car, I realized I'd fallen for her. I, who probably had never loved another human after my father took me away from my grandmother, had fallen in love with my daughter. All I wanted was to make her happy. And to protect her." He leveled his gaze at her. "Even from me."

She squinted at him, because a person didn't shift personalities and behavior overnight. "Are you telling me the truth?"

"Why else would I have brought her home, Agnes? I did it because she needs you, not me. She is too special to be thrown to the wolves like I was."

"Well... thank you."

"I don't want to lose her completely. I've spoken to your lady lawyer, who, by the way, is tough, and tomorrow I meet with her and the other guy, the one who drove us, Eric Houston."

"Henry's twin."

"Really? I didn't know." He scanned the room as if expecting Henry to be hiding nearby.

"Upstairs, with Brisa and Mrs. Barnes."

"Ah. Anyway, I have asked Mrs. Levinson to draw up a document that will allow me to visit periodically. It seems we can each drop the civil petitions with voluntary dismissals, which we'll both have to sign. Rita has drafted a Consent Order, where I admit paternity and agree to pay support, which I've already begun. I have set up a trust fund for her, with you as executor—"

"I don't need your money. We're doing fine on our own."

"I get that. You're thinking of that letter I sent."

"Sounded a lot like trying to buy her."

"I'm sorry. My motives weren't innocent, I grant you. But you'll have to accept something, even if it's contributions to a trust for her. And a college fund. I truly didn't know anything about Brisa until my manager, Arthur, broke the news to me a couple of months ago. I'd like to make up for all those years of neglect."

"I'm no longer destitute."

"That's neither here nor there. I need to give the money. Payments will go into the trust monthly to make up for all the child support I didn't contribute over the years. And visitation either here or with my Georgia relatives will be on the condition that I don't mess up again—in any way. Rita's going to write it up as a temporary agreement. If I ever endanger Brisa again, I lose visitation, or if I fail to make the regular payments to the trust." He sighed. "As I said, Rita's one tough negotiator."

"You and your world are bound to look enticing again, especially when there's been time for her to forget the effects of being drunk. By the way, how did you manage that?"

"Her getting sick?" He grinned. "I remembered how Mama

Bea used to take care of me when I had the flu, with a big bowl and a towel near my bed."

"*You* took care of her?"

"Held the basin and cleaned her up."

"I can't picture it."

"I told you, I fell in love with her."

She felt as if her head were filled with cotton. How was she supposed to process this? Maybe he'd done an about-face, but she was going to have to set aside thirteen years of hatred. How did one do that?

"Why did you leave your grandmother's?" she finally asked.

"I was seventeen, and my father swooped into my life with promises of fame and fortune. I believed him."

"And now? Because it looks to me like that's what you were trying to do with Brisa."

"That's what Mama Bea said. She was furious with me. Told me I had to make this right, although by then I'd already begun the process."

So he'd gone back to his roots. Maybe that explained some of the shift in him. "Your grandmother sounds like an admirable woman."

"She's probably the most loving and wisest woman I've ever known, but you can't expect a stupid seventeen-year-old to have understood that, not when he'd missed having a daddy all his life. See, I get it. And when Mama accused me of acting just like he had, it hurt all the way down to my gut. Because I'd seen him for what he was, soul-less and heartless when it came to me and mine. And I didn't want to be his replica, not with Brisa."

"I admire your grandmother's forthrightness."

"She said she wanted to meet you someday because you've done such a fine job with Brisa. She and my whole family took to Brisa completely. They were pretty angry with me for not having been in contact, but that was just another instance of my father's manipulation. It seems he destroyed all their letters to me and stopped the payments he'd promised to send Mama Bea. I thought she had turned her back on me because she was angry I'd left."

"Like Brisa felt when you wouldn't let her talk to me."

"I'm sorry about that. I really am. I listened to Arthur when I shouldn't have. It's all about choices, and mine have been terrible."

His voice held such regret that she had to believe him. No wonder he'd broken things off with his father. She said as much.

"He's about to find out how completely I did break away."

She had to grin at the hint of ruthlessness she heard—or maybe that was pride in finally getting it right.

"Please, Agnes, I love our daughter. I don't deserve anything from you or her, but I think she needs me in her life, just like she needs you. You've done a fantastic job with her—yes, I know, with no help from me, but you know why that was."

"You didn't deserve—"

"I admit it. I didn't." He plowed his fingers through hair that was so much like Brisa's.

"And now you do? Have you truly changed enough to give up the things that go with that lifestyle? The drugs, the drinking?" This time she squinted at him. "Because now that Brisa has tasted the high life, she may want more of it. How do you plan to protect her from that if I let you see her?"

"I don't drink very much, and I never do drugs. Haven't for years. And now that I have some reason to do things differently, I will. I'm not sure what form it will take, but there will be a change." He sighed. "I do have to figure that out."

"You'd better figure it out fast, because she's not going anywhere with you until you do."

Darling stood and wandered to the front window. He wouldn't be able to see much—street lights, dark water, shadowed islands on the far side. Neither of them spoke until he turned back to the room. "I trust we'll come to some sort of understanding that will work for you in that meeting tomorrow. Throwing up all night should have soured Brisa, at least for now, on fame and fortune." His eyes twinkled, as if some benign uncle had taken over and pushed out the taking, grabbing, self-absorbed Darling.

"Have you made any promises to her? Anything that's going to entice her to run away again? I've never been so scared in my life as I was when I found her missing."

He grinned. "She's resourceful, isn't she?"

"I wanted to kill the boy who drove her all the way to Raleigh," Agnes said. "And kill you for your part in giving her that phone and credit card. That was underhanded and mean."

"If it's any consolation, I about died when I heard she'd taken a ride with a kid no one knew. I'd given her the card so she could buy things for herself."

"And so she'd get the idea of coming to find you."

"Probably. I didn't think it through very well. I'm just grateful she survived and got to me."

"Yeah. Well, I'd like you to take that credit card and phone back."

"Maybe we can compromise on the phone? I brought it back with me, but you keep it and let her use it to call me when she wants? You may want her to have one for emergencies."

"I can pay for one if she needs it."

Shrugging, he said, "She changed me, Agnes. Maybe you don't think that's possible, or certainly not possible in so short a time, but it happened. I may not have had her for long, but knowing her has truly made me a different person." He rubbed his temples and sighed. "She made me want to become the father she needs me to be." He waved away any protest she wanted to make. "I know I missed the chance to be present. Circumstances, choices... and, yes, selfishness got in the way of that. But for what it's worth, I'd like to start from now. If you'll let me."

If what he said was true—and bringing Brisa home instead of using her to advance his career gave credence to his words—he might, eventually, prove worthy of being Brisa's dad. Maybe.

There were some big ifs in that equation. "I'll go to the meeting tomorrow," she said.

"Good."

He returned to his seat and leaned forward. "As for the future, what Brisa does with her voice is completely up to her. She needs to grow up before she even considers making that choice. Our daughter is incredibly talented. I think you will need to find an outlet for it, or she may find it herself in less acceptable ways."

"Like?"

"I don't know. I haven't thought that through, but the glamor of that stage may one day override her memories of being sick. I'm thinking maybe she could find a way to use her voice like I did, in a church. Maybe in school. And we could arrange for her to have some classical training. Point her in other directions than the life I followed."

"This is hard for me to take in, you know?" She shook her head. "It's hard to believe you've changed this much."

His chuckle sounded more self-deprecating than laced with humor. "Yeah, I know. I'm struggling with it, too."

That choked out an involuntary bark of laughter. "You?"

"I've spent a lot of years thinking only of me. I had my father behind me, my manager, everyone telling me how great I was. And this beautiful wife I wanted to please." He sighed. "Like any of that was real."

"I don't get that. Suddenly they all changed?"

"No, they all suddenly showed their true colors in a glaring enough way that even I, who'd been turning a deaf ear and a very blind eye, couldn't fail to notice. I don't know what the turning point for them was. Maybe instead of liking the idea of Brisa—as Lisette had claimed to—she was actually jealous of her. I had no idea that my manager had been taking all his orders from my father. I thought he was my friend and employed by me. And I had no idea that my father was the man behind my wife staying out all night until Brisa's party. "

"Hard lessons, especially about your wife."

"Very." He paused. "It's hard having your eyes opened like a slap in the face, but when they did open, the knowledge that those three wanted to spread their filth over the sweet child who believed in me hit like a lightning bolt."

"I'm glad." She was, if she could trust it.

"Mama Bea suggested God had a hand in letting me know Brisa—which brought me back to my roots. She claims God has been tugging on me for a while."

That got Agnes's attention and made her blood start to hammer behind her ears. She clasped her hands tightly. First Becca and then Henry and now Darlington? "God?" It came out just above a whisper, but he heard her and nodded.

"I was raised in church, singing there every time the doors were open. When Brisa and I got to my grandma's house, Mama Bea pronounced God had done this 'cause He comes after those who've known him and doesn't stop until he has them back," he said. "What do I know? I've been running from that background for… what? Eighteen years? Kind of hard to justify the change without some outside force, but it's even harder for me to accept the idea of God butting in all of a sudden because he wants me back." His words had a bristly quality. "I mean, I don't like imagining a puppeteer and me the puppet."

"But wasn't that how your father was with you?" Yeah, that was snarky, but it was also real.

"You could say that." He spoke with a self-deprecating expression that wasn't quite a smile. "Maybe I just don't want to exchange one puppet master for another."

"I get that. This town is full of Jesus people who've been having prayer meetings for Brisa to come home. Seems they were also praying for you." She shook her head. "It just shocks me, you giving God the credit."

"Not me, necessarily. My grandmother."

"But you said…"

"Look, I don't know what I believe or how I handle any of

this. Maybe God's at work, and maybe there's some cosmic merry-go-round I jumped off of for a moment." He dashed a hand across his forehead. "I don't have a clue."

They were silent for a couple of minutes, taking it in, she guessed. Finally, he spoke again. "I hurt you, Agnes. I did a despicable thing to you. And I'm sorry."

She kept her expression neutral, as if his apology didn't matter. But it did. His words made her want to weep. How could she let go of years and years of blame and anger... and, yes, hatred? Did he really mean it, or was he playing the manipulator again?

She had no idea what to do with a nice Darlington.

"I'm hoping you can forgive me, but if not, think about letting me at least do this thing by helping financially. I'm loaded." His smile was a little lopsided, but his eyes... well, they seemed sincere. But then they'd seemed sincere all those years ago, too.

He continued. "I think it's important for her to know I care. And if I'm not part of her everyday life, which we both admit would be impractical and probably unhealthy, I can best show her by setting things right for her future. When she's ready, if she ever is, I'll help her get the proper training to use that voice of hers in whatever way she'd like."

"You need to say something to her. She knows what happened, how she was conceived."

He covered his face with his hands. "I deserve that, but, man, that's going to be the hardest—"

"There also need to be consequences for her, because she ran away. I'd like to lock her in her room for the rest of her life."

He snorted. "Yeah, I get that. Mama Bea never spared the rod when I was little, then she made me do things for other folk when I was too old to spank. Maybe something service oriented?"

"That sounds good. Mrs. Barnes might have some ideas. She's always doing things for people."

"I think I should get this said to Brisa now, while my courage is high."

She stared at him. The idea of letting him near Brisa again sucked the air from her, but she had to do it. She walked to the bottom of the stairs and called up to Henry.

He came out. "You ready?" As if he'd read her mind.

———

"Come sit down, honey." Agnes waved Brisa toward the couch as Henry settled himself in a second leather chair.

"Henry knows everything?" Darlington asked.

"I do," Henry said, obviously not needing anyone to speak for him.

Darlington stood and moved to stand in front of his daughter. Then he stunned Agnes by getting on his knees. "Brisa, honey, I've already asked your mama's forgiveness, but I need you to hear this from my lips. She told you how badly I behaved years ago, which is why your mama never told either of us about the other. I especially didn't deserve to know about you, although I wish I had. I wish I'd been able to be around for you and to have made things easier for you both." Brisa leaned forward, but he said, "No, don't interrupt. You've got to hear this. I was rotten and selfish and I did a terrible thing to your mother. An evil thing. I deeply regret what I did to her. But—and this is something you've got to believe—neither your mama nor I regret that you came from that night. You are the best thing that ever happened to either of us. The *best* thing. We love you more than anything else in this life. You, Brisa. You."

He had tears in his eyes, but they were nothing to hers and Brisa's. It only took a moment for her precious daughter to fling herself into her daddy's arms and weep all over him. He patted her and crooned in her ear, and it just about killed Agnes.

Not because she was jealous. No, this time it was because her

337

daughter was getting some healing. Her daughter had finally gotten a daddy, and that was a powerful thing.

Agnes swiped at her eyes and sniffled. Becca walked in with a box of tissues, and Henry grabbed enough for them all. He passed some to Agnes and put another handful in Darlington's hands.

Darlington shifted Brisa and dabbed at her face. "Come on, honey," he said. "Your old dad needs to stand up."

Brisa backed up onto the couch again and into Agnes's arms. "Oh, Mommy." Agnes tightened her hold. "I'm sorry for all the bad things I said to you. Are you still mad?"

"No, sweet girl, I'm not." She rubbed a hand up and down Brisa's back.

"Then," and now Brisa was all eagerness, "can Daddy come for Easter? Becca said you've planned a nice dinner, and wouldn't that be wonderful, all of us together? Please, Mom. *Please.*"

Easter? Darlington here? For *her* Easter fun? *Theirs?* The one she wanted to spend with Henry? She didn't know what to say. The kind feelings she'd begun to have started to leak out.

Darlington cleared his throat. "Honey, that's several days away, and maybe your mom already made plans. You're putting her on the spot here."

Yes, absolutely. Perfectly correct. She'd assumed he would go away and let them get back to their own life, no matter what he'd said about wanting to see Brisa. He'd had Brisa, he'd *taken* Brisa and *fought* about Brisa. And now she was supposed to invite him to a family celebration?

"But," Brisa said, her voice plaintive. "You're here, and who knows when you'll come back? I mean, why not? And if Mom won't let you come here"—she turned an unhappy glance Agnes's way—"then you and I can hang out someplace and celebrate by ourselves."

"Brisa..." Agnes glowered at her daughter.

"That's manipulation." Darling said. "Maybe not the nicest

way to go about this. As it is, your mother and I have been discussing the consequences for you of running away. Perhaps you ought to be very careful how you behave from now on."

Brisa's jaw looked like it might scrape the floor, but she was no more stunned than her mother. Who *was* this man?

"We have indeed," Agnes said, clearing her throat. "And your father suggested something service oriented." She looked over at Becca, who'd settled in one of the straight-back chairs on the periphery of the room. "I'm sorry. I haven't introduced you."

Darlington turned toward Becca and loosed *that* smile on her housemate. "We've seen each other but never met properly."

"Becca Barnes, meet Darlington Evermire," Agnes said.

"I'm pleased to meet you, Mr. Evermire, 'specially when I hear you actin' the parent for this sweet girl."

"Agnes thought you might be able to offer a suggestion for some way Brisa could help the community to make up for her behavior in running away."

"Yes, sir. I know just the way." Becca laced her fingers over her belly. "There's this family, four little ones with the mama about to go into the hospital. She's gonna be needin' help for several months. I been plannin' to give her some on Saturdays and a couple mornings."

"There you go." Darlington nodded toward Brisa. "Sounds like something Mama Bea would have made me do. Reason I put this notion in your mother's head, Brisa, is because I agree, you need to know that all behavior has consequences. I learned that young and then forgot it for too long. Meeting you, learning to love you, has brought me back to those roots. The biggest—the worst—consequence of my early selfishness has been not knowing you for twelve years. I missed so much. I have other things I'm sorry about, and I'm going to do my best to make up for them. But I don't ever want to be someone who entices you to do wrong again." He smiled sadly. "You're too valuable, honey. Much too valuable. Your mother and I want you to keep on growing up to be a fine young woman. So whatever your mama says do, that's what you have to do."

Agnes entered the fray again. "You'd be willing for Brisa to go with you, Becca? Help with housework and childcare?"

"I would. She could be a big help to me."

"But, Mo-om! Saturdays?"

"Absolutely. And maybe a few other days, too, when you're out of school. Speaking of which, you have some apologizing to do to your teacher, too."

Brisa kicked the toe of her shoe on the rug. "But I can't work all that time," she said, ignoring the comment about school. "When would I get to play with Jilly?"

"Afternoons when you don't have homework."

She stuck her lower lip out, a gesture that made her look very young indeed. "You're mean."

"Brisa," Darlington said in what Agnes would definitely call a fatherly voice. "It's possible that those consequences aren't severe enough if you're going to speak to your mother that way."

Brisa glared at him, but he didn't back down.

"Apologize, please," he said.

Agnes checked out Henry's expression. He seemed as surprised as she.

"Sorry." But she mumbled the word.

"Brisa?" Darling said, one eyebrow arched.

Brisa lowered her eyes. Agnes could see she was nibbling on the inside of her lip, putting off the inevitable. Finally, with a sigh, she said, "I'm sorry, Mom."

Darling smiled at her. "Good girl."

"Becca, thank you," Agnes said. "We'll work out the details this week."

"Yes, ma'am. As the child is off school Monday after Easter, you think maybe she could go over with me then? Get a feelin' for the house and the family? I'd normally go this Saturday, but someone else is takin' that day, and I promised Monday."

"That sounds great."

Brisa put on what Agnes liked to think of as her "best" smile. "Now do you think Daddy can come for Easter?"

Hadn't they'd buried that one? She glanced helplessly at Henry, but got nothing from him. She said, "Let's see how tomorrow goes. Your father and I have a meeting to go to. If that goes well, we'll talk about it."

"But, Mom…"

"You'll have to be satisfied with that. You spent your birthday with him, and you've had a lovely holiday. You have school you'll have to make up, too."

"But it's spring break."

"Which only began Monday. You have all of last week's homework to face."

Becca intervened. "Sweet girl, you come on upstairs with Becca now and let's finish putting away all your pretties so you can get ready for bed. It's getting late."

"Do I—"

"Yes, ma'am, you do," Agnes said. "Now hug your father and Henry goodnight. I'll come up and see you soon."

Brisa gave Henry a quick hug and thanked him for coming to get her, and then she moved to her father. He pulled her into his arms and kissed the top of her head. She said, "You'll come tomorrow?"

"I'll see you again before I leave."

"You promise?"

"I promise."

## 54

# HENRY

Henry knocked on the hull of his brother's boat, waited, and then knocked again. A moment later, Eric poked his head out the companionway hatch and grinned. "Hope you've got news. Come on aboard."

Henry stepped into the cockpit and waited until Eric joined him before handing over the car keys. "Thanks for the lift."

"You want anything?" Eric asked. "Tea, water, dinner?"

"I'm fine. My body's a wreck from all that travel, but at least there's a happy ending."

"Good for you."

"Not so much me. The prep work had already been done."

"Tell me."

He did, giving him Darling's take on the events that had changed him.

"You think it's real?" Eric asked. "That's a pretty big leap, from threatening Agnes to conceding defeat and returning a runaway."

"A huge leap."

Darling seemed to love his daughter and want the best for her, in spite of his past actions. So maybe there'd been a real change. Maybe.

"I hope it's real," Henry said, "and that it will last, but it's hard not for me to want him gone."

"I get that. You want that piece of the pie you figure Daddy-dear's going to snatch."

Henry laughed without humor. He'd liked the man—until they'd gotten to Agnes's, and the demon of jealousy had gripped him hard. "Oh, yeah. The man's a mega star, rich, and now he's turning out to be repentant and nice. I, instead, find my motivations not at all nice." Nope, he was going to need a lobotomy to slice off the muck in his brain. Or intervention by the Divine Engineer.

"What are you going to do about it?"

"What can I do? Pray, I guess."

Eric headed for the companionway. "Come on down. You may not be hungry, but I am."

Henry followed his brother below and into the galley area. Eric waved him to a seat. "Thought you might want something, so I cooked up some fajitas. Already started on the salsa and chips."

"Chips sound good." Of course, once he started dipping them into that salsa, he couldn't stop.

"You're stuck on her, aren't you?"

"Who, Agnes?"

Eric only raised a brow.

Henry raised his right back.

"She feel the same?" Eric asked, amusement back in his voice.

With a slight huff, Henry said, "I once thought so."

"You imagine things shifted because the man who raped her is back in town? Is she that forgiving?"

Henry grinned. "Put that way, it sounds kind of stupid, doesn't it? The problem is, he even asked Brisa to forgive him. Made a big show of it in front of us all."

"You're kidding. I can't wait for our meeting tomorrow." His brother passed a plate across the u-shaped counter. "You've got to eat."

Henry settled at the dinette. Eric joined him, his own plate in hand along with two water bottles. They bit, chewed, and swallowed in silence until Eric said, "You worried about how this will play out in terms of your recovery?"

"Mind-reading again?"

"Of course."

"I suppose I am, but I've seen a softening in Agnes. I'm hoping it will mean we can be on the same page."

"Yeah, like you and me?" There was a gleam in Eric's eyes.

Henry matched it. "Blood supersedes ideas. Blood—at least for us—and being a twin makes the difference. I mean, I know you'd give your life for me. I'd give mine for you."

"In a heartbeat."

"But it's not the same in other relationships." Henry set down his fork. "There's enough stress in a romantic relationship, especially a marriage, without a division along faith lines to muck it up even more. I'm not talking church affiliation. I'm talking belief versus unbelief. I've had too many unbelievers scoff at faith. I can ignore that in a casual relationship."

"But not in a romantic one?"

"No, I don't think so."

They ate in silence for a few minutes. Then Eric carried their empty plates to the sink. "We didn't exactly have the perfect role models."

"I've seen some, though, in the couples I've met here. Attraction, yes, but also friendship and real pleasure in being together. That's what I want."

"Well, I know Rita better than I know Martin, and Clay better than Annie Mac, but we've talked, just things in passing, and I've watched them together. So, I'd agree with you. As for myself," Eric said, "I'm too busy with that great American novel and the struggling practice."

Henry upended his water bottle. "You interested in joining me for Easter service this year?"

"We used to do that, didn't we? Get dragged to church twice a year, as if it would seal our eternal destination?"

Henry remembered, but not with any fondness. "I'm enjoying the small black church in town. Who'd have thought?"

"You integrating the place?"

"They don't seem to mind my white face. Becca Barnes—you've met her, haven't you?"

"I think so. Big lady, always smiling?"

"That's the one. Anyway, she talks about them offering all their joy to the Lord, but she calls it their 'happy'. And that's what it's like. The preaching's good, too."

"Not what we ever saw, anyone feeling joyful in church."

"Exactly."

***

Agnes was on a roll. Henry wasn't sure what kind of a roll, but she'd told him she wanted to have a celebratory breakfast before Easter Sunday service and wanted him and Eric to join them. Maybe she wanted to one-up the after-church brunch Darlington had planned for everyone.

It all sounded awkward and like too much emotional work to Henry, but he couldn't tell her so. Instead, he got there early and volunteered to man the pans of egg and sausage.

"Thank you," Agnes said, pouncing on his offer as she pushed her hair off her face, her expression slightly harried. "Thank heavens, Becca left us a batch of her homemade biscuits and said she'd meet us at church."

Brisa had set the table, and Darlington placed a basket of plastic eggs in front of her seat. She kept eyeing it until they all sat down, when she pointed to it. "What's that?"

"A few fun things." Darling grinned. "Open them. There are notes inside."

Darling had gone over the top in buying for them, including a new GPS for *Harmless*. "State of the art. You mentioned one was on your yet-to-get list."

"Thank you," Henry said. "I had no idea we were gift-giving."

Darling's rush to fill the empty spots from the years when he hadn't been there for his daughter put her over the moon, especially when one of the notes sent her to a box containing a computer and another that held a printer. "It's for you and your mother," Darlington said. "I've had it set up with parental controls, so your mother will be able to monitor your internet searches. You've got to share." He winked at Agnes.

The wink made Henry's heart plunge.

Brisa hugged her dad. "Thank you so much! Jilly has those things on her family's computer, so it's okay. Miss Tadie said it's to keep her safe."

"It is." He nodded toward Agnes. "I asked your mother if you had one. So you can thank her, too."

Brisa climbed over empty boxes to reach her mother. "Thank you! And I'll share with you." The giggle was back.

"I appreciate that," Agnes said. "It's time to clean up and get ready for church if you want to go."

"Why don't we take my rental. It's big enough for everyone. Henry, Eric?"

Them, too. Oh, yes, the big man would include them, too.

*Stop it.* But stopping those thoughts might be more than he could manage.

"I've got my car," Eric said. "Henry?"

"Coming."

---

He and Eric pulled into a spot just behind Darling's SUV. As they all walked toward the small church, Brisa between her parents, Henry thought he'd never seen her happier.

He and his brother slid into a pew behind the other three, catching the attention of the congregation. Rita gave them an appraising glance. Henry caught the wink Eric returned. He wished he could see Agnes's expression, but she was probably trying to hold herself together. If he were sitting at her side, he'd take her hand, but there hadn't been enough room in their pew for both him and Eric.

The pastor rose and looked right at them. "Welcome to all our guests on this beautiful Easter Sunday. I hear from certain quarters you know how to praise the Lord, Mr. Evermire. We're a church likes to sing and give glory. Would you be willing to maybe sing for us during the offering today? Lead us in worship as we give gifts to him?"

Darling nodded with a smile. "It would be my privilege, Pastor, if you'd allow my daughter to join me."

"We'd be honored. You all be thinking what you'd like to sing, and we'll give you the time."

Darling looked down at Brisa, and she nodded up at him. Henry's heart did a little tap-tap. He couldn't help wishing for that kind of communion with Agnes's girl, but he was still thankful she had a father who'd changed enough to be there for her now. Yes. Thankful.

That was better, being thankful. Keep it good. Keep it right.

He hoped—he supposed he hoped—he wasn't just tamping the jealousy down, sticking it under a prayerful façade.

The question was, what would happen next week, after Darling returned to his old life? He'd suggested maybe Agnes would want to go with him and Brisa to Atlanta one day soon.

Sounded like a plan, didn't it? Was this the writing on the wall? Brisa wanted her parents to become a real family. Agnes would give in, wouldn't she, because look at the guy. She'd be a fool not to want him, gorgeous, rich, wanting to be Brisa's dad. Actually turning out to be a nice guy who regretted his past actions. A guy who'd asked for forgiveness.

No, he wouldn't gag. He'd pray for God's best for them. He would.

And he'd turn his thoughts to worship, *right now.* He would.

*Please. Help me accept. Help me worship now and forever, no matter what... no matter what.*

Eric nudged shoulders. "You okay?"

"Yeah. Yeah, I'm fine."

During the next hour, he did a pretty good job of shutting out his worries and focusing on the music and the preaching. With everyone else, he applauded the special musical bond Brisa and Darling shared and joined with the congregation for the chorus. As the praise swelled, a tide of love and longing for the Creator took hold of him. Happy, they called it. Becca said they were showing their happy. Well, he wanted to show his happy, too.

It was Resurrection Sunday. The Lord had risen. Indeed.

---

After the service ended, they were surrounded by groups of well-wishers. James and his wife singled him out, wanting to meet Eric. Henry made the introductions. "Glad you could join us. Hope you'll come again," James said.

"You all certainly give new meaning to making a joyful noise," Eric said.

Henry gave him a questioning look. "Where'd you hear that expression? It can't have been from our rare excursions into churchianity as children."

Grinning, Eric said, "Oh, no, but I read."

"Obviously more than I gave you credit for."

"Well, of course. There's your example to follow, brother dear."

Henry laughed. "Aha. Checking on my credentials."

"What else?"

They'd lost the others. "I'm sorry," Henry said. "Twin nonsense."

James slapped him on the back. "Don't look much alike, but you've got the same laugh in your eyes. Can always trust the eyes."

"And you can trust my daddy's discernment." Rita had come to join them, her hand at Agnes's elbow.

Agnes smiled, but she glanced over her shoulder at her daughter, caught in the circle around Darling.

"It's okay," Rita assured her. "You don't need to hover. Becca's nearby and Martin's right there, keeping his professional eye on things."

Oh, right. Martin was a pediatrician, although what that had to do with anything at the moment… Still, he was glad Rita had Agnes safely in tow.

James still hovered. He'd begun to whisper something, but he wasn't a tall man, and Henry had to lean down to hear him. "Don't you worry none. You sing just as good as him."

Elvie Mae swatted her husband's arm. "James Whitlock, you hush up. It ain't no contest."

By the time they'd thanked the pastor for his rousing sermon, which Henry barely remembered—*sorry, God*—and exited, all he wanted was to head back to *Harmless* and try to find some equilibrium. But there was still lunch at Darling's expense. He'd hang with his brother and the Levinsons. He'd like to get to know Martin.

As Eric buckled his seatbelt, he grinned. "That, brother dear, was an experience I wouldn't have wanted to miss. On so many levels."

"It's not over yet."

## 55

## AGNES

The brunch had been delicious and surprisingly convivial for such a diverse group. Or maybe the only diversity had come from the man who'd morphed from culprit to benevolent daddy and was doing his charming best to make the rest of them like him—or at least accept and enjoy his hospitality. Brisa, of course, had been radiant—a fact that had both blessed and worried her mother.

As did the diamond pendant Agnes had seen clasped around her daughter's neck that morning. She kept her mouth shut, not wanting to ruin Brisa's fun, but when they returned to the house and Brisa went up to change out of her pretty dress, Agnes asked Darlington if he could spare a minute to speak with her.

On the way out back to the porch, she tried to come up with a good opening line and ended up with "I think jewelry with diamonds is a little over the top for a twelve-year-old. I'm sure it seems like a mere trifle to you, but it could cause problems in a community like this if the other children see her wearing it."

He stood staring out at the back yard, one hand on a post, and kept his focus there when he said, "I'm new to this, Agnes. I only wanted her to have something really special from me."

"Yeah, I get that, but perhaps that sort of 'special' could wait a few years? Maybe even into adulthood?"

"I didn't think." He shifted his gaze to her. "Would you like me to speak to her about it? About keeping the pendant safe and maybe putting it away until she's older?"

She hadn't thought past being upset, but he was right. The words needed to come from him. "Thank you. That would be very helpful."

"I doubt she'll want it to be in a safety deposit box."

"Nope. Too far away."

"I'll take care of it." He touched her arm, and when she flinched, he drew away quickly. "Sorry," he said, looking as if he meant it. "I didn't mean anything by it."

She shook her head, embarrassed by her automatic response to him. "I know. I'm afraid it's going to take time for me to trust you."

His lips formed a slightly crooked half-smile. "I'm going to have to leave soon. May I go up to her room to speak to her?"

"Please."

He spent a good quarter-hour upstairs, and when Brisa came down with him, her eyes were red-rimmed, and she clung to his hand and then his neck as he said goodbye.

Agnes turned away to light the candles resting in their sconces on the mantle. They'd been unlit since Christmas. It was time, she decided, to light them again. Besides, the act of striking the long match and lighting the wicks kept her from watching Darling caress Brisa's tear-stained cheeks.

"We'll talk often," he said. "Really. And see each other soon."

"You promise?" Brisa asked.

"I promise."

Agnes turned back in time to see Darling extend his hand to Henry and say, "Thank you for everything."

"Sure," Henry said, shaking the other man's hand.

And then Darling looked at her. "Thank you for allowing me this time."

She nodded. "Just don't let her down."

"Or you. I won't let either of you down again."

She hoped his words were true.

"Stay, will you?" she asked Henry as he started to follow Darlington out the door.

"For a little while."

"Can I have some cereal?" Brisa asked.

"You're hungry already?" Agnes couldn't believe it. Brisa had eaten enough for three people. "Henry? Do you want anything?"

"No thanks."

Agnes waved her daughter off. "One bowl. And finish it before you get on the computer, please."

"Yes ma'am!"

Agnes watched her go a little anxiously. "I hope those parental controls he installed actually work."

"I can show you how to keep tabs."

"Good. I've read too many horror stories." She waved him toward the couch and sat down also, letting her head fall back.

"Exhausted?" he asked.

"Incredibly." She drew a cushion close and held it against her front as if to cocoon herself.

"Why don't you go lie down?"

"I will. But I wanted to thank you for everything. I don't think I've taken the time to say it, not really. Thank you for caring enough to go all the way out there. To bring her home to me." She turned her head to look at him. "It means a great deal, more than you can know."

He took her hand. "I'm glad. I couldn't stand watching you hurt like that."

She closed her eyes momentarily against the surge of memory and pain. When she felt in control enough to speak, she said, "It's been hard, all of it."

"But you've been amazing."

She felt anything but amazing. Wrecked, maybe. Half

awake, certainly. "I know having her father here—this new father—has been good for Brisa, but I can't quite wrap my head around the changes in him. I've hated even the thought of him for so long."

"That was an impressive lecture on consequences he gave her. And taking the blame in front of her? Powerful."

"I didn't expect it." And wasn't sure how to feel about it even now.

He cleared his throat. "You know, don't you, that Brisa's hoping you and he will get together. Make a real family."

The sound she made came out somewhere between a bark and a hoot. She sat up abruptly, coughing. "Henry, what are you talking about? Darling with me? *Together?*"

"Well, yes," he admitted.

She sobered. "You're too absurd for words."

He frowned and pushed himself up. "I should get back to the boat."

"Stay, please." She reached toward him.

He merely stared down at her. And then he sat again.

She touched his hand. When he didn't respond, she pulled away. "I'm sorry. I didn't mean anything by those words, but I can assure you, there will never be anything between Darlington and me except our daughter."

"Fine."

"I mean it. Really. He's not the one I want."

And then his gaze met hers, and she felt the heat rise in her cheeks. The stare lasted, and his hand lifted, and he touched her chin. She leaned toward him. His beautiful, wonderful face drew close, his lips touched hers. She let them. No, she was active here, not passive. She needed those lips on hers, and so she clutched the front of his shirt and tugged at him.

They felt so perfect, his full lips grazing hers, moving, and her yearning rose up to meet his. She moaned.

The moan must have broken the spell because he suddenly broke away. "I'm sorry," he said, drawing back so that her hands fell loosely against him. "I shouldn't have done that. I didn't intend to."

Why not? She'd shown him she wanted him to. What was wrong with a little kissing?

She stared at him. His anguished expression frightened her. "Henry? What's wrong?"

He didn't answer, except to repeat, "I'm sorry," as he got up and walked out of her house.

What on earth? He couldn't do that. He couldn't. "Henry!"

She ran to the door, flung it open, and barreled outside, ready to race down the sidewalk and make the foolish man stop to talk to her. But there he stood, both hands clutching the balustrade, his head bent. He didn't look up or move.

She lowered herself to the top step and waited, shivering, and not from the cold. Once her body recognized it was at rest again, she spoke. "Are we friends at all, Henry?"

He pushed off and lowered himself beside her on the step, dangling his hands between his knees. It was only dusk, but his face was enough in shadow that she couldn't make out his expression. She wondered if it mirrored her frustration or if he'd given in to some inner demon. Finally, he nodded and spoke. "I want us to be."

"And yet you're playing games with me."

"I don't mean to. I shouldn't have let my desire for you overrule what's best for each of us."

"And that is?"

"I've got issues. And it looks to me as if we want different things, need different things." He hadn't answered her question, which felt like another game.

"You want to explain what those different things might be? Because it sounds as if you're suggesting only clones should be romantically involved."

"That's absurd."

"Is it? Clones share the same goals, don't they? The same interests, the same wants. It's an interesting concept. I wonder if they'd be considered hermaphrodites." She pretended to give that some thought. "Although I suppose not."

He only sighed loudly. *Coward.*

"So, if not clones, then what do you have in mind? Don't men and women often have different goals and want different things? Or would you only consider a relationship with someone who listens to the same music, likes the same food. I suppose you could never be with someone who hated shellfish. I don't suppose I could be with a man who insisted I cook liver once a week, because I can't stand the smell of the stuff."

"It's more fundamental than that."

"I get it. I'm fundamentally unsuitable. Good to know."

"You're not even trying to understand," he said.

"And you're not even trying to explain."

"I don't want to hurt you."

"Oh, good, *this* is not hurting me. Telling me I don't cut it because of some fundamental difference that makes me unsuitable."

"That's not what I meant."

Yeah, well, she'd had enough. Standing, she brushed off the back of her slacks. "Fine, whatever. you just wander on back to your boat and your life and leave me and mine alone."

"Agnes…"

But she left him on her porch and walked into her house, then closed and locked the door behind her. She'd given Henry Houston enough of her energy and time. Too bad he was so caught up in his mistakes and his past that he couldn't see through the fog in front of him.

She fell back onto the couch in the same spot she'd occupied minutes earlier and stared blindly at the still-lit candles burning in their sconces.

Fundamental differences? What on earth did he mean?

Yes, they were different genders, but that was a plus, wasn't it? He'd been an addict; she hadn't, but so what? He was free, supposedly. He had issues, but didn't they all? It couldn't be their lifestyles, a boat versus a house. She flicked her hand in the air to show what she thought of that as an excuse.

Then what?

She chewed on the craziness of it all as she went to check on Brisa, who seemed engrossed in some sort of math game.

Math was good.

"It'll be time to turn that off soon," Agnes said.

"But not yet."

"Half an hour."

Agnes wiped water spots off the stainless sinks. Then she looked up, biting her lip as another thought shoved its way in.

Maybe it was the God thing.

But why would Henry care that she didn't believe with the intensity he did? She wasn't opposed to God. She'd enjoyed church that morning, and if he wanted to go, great. She might even give it another try, especially because Brisa liked it so much. No biggie, right?

Maybe it wasn't too late to call Rita, just ask her outright. She checked her watch and punched in Rita's number on her way back to the front room.

"Hey, Agnes," Rita said. "Happy Easter again."

"Same to you. Have you got a minute?"

"Of course. Let me go into the other room. Martin's watching a British mystery."

"I wanted to thank you for all you've done to help with this legal stuff."

"Sure. I'm happy it's all working out. Hard to believe, but miracles come in all sizes and shapes." Rita paused. "But I don't think that's why you called. Is something the matter?"

"Henry. It's Henry."

"What's Henry? Did something happen to him?"

"No. It's just… I don't get it. He… well, he kissed me, not for the first time, and it felt as if he meant it, but then he fled as if I'd burned him. He actually *apologized* for the kiss. And then, when I confronted him, he said there were fundamental differences between us."

"Ah."

She held the phone away from her ear and stared at it. Then she said, "What do you mean by *ah?*"

"I don't know quite what I mean, because I don't have enough information." There was humor in Rita's tone. That didn't help.

"Does this have anything to do with him being so into God? I mean, is that what he's talking about? Because I've tried to come up with some other reason for him to think we're too different."

"Do you think maybe it has to do with him feeling unworthy?"

Agnes dismissed that almost immediately. "No, I think it has more to do with him deciding *I'm* unworthy."

"Agnes, no."

"Well, yes. What else could it be?"

"You mentioned the faith issue. That actually might be a stumbling block for Henry."

"Why? I don't get it. Is it a really big deal? I mean, if I don't mind Henry going to church, why should he mind if I don't?"

Rita didn't answer immediately. "Agnes, what, other than Brisa, matters most to you?"

What else? Making a living? Supporting them? Friends? Did that include Henry?

"Brisa." There wasn't anything else.

"Okay, I get that. But for a believer, his or her relationship with God is paramount. Everything else pales next to that, and anything that might get in the way of that fellowship—or distract from it—is dangerous, especially for someone like Henry who's had to hang on tightly to that vertical relationship so he can remain free of addiction. It must be especially important that no horizontal relationship, no friendship, certainly no romance, gets in the way." She paused as if to let that sink in. "No matter how intent we are on keeping those separate, they do interfere.

Can you imagine being with a person who didn't value Brisa, didn't put her needs first?"

"It couldn't happen. She's my life."

"Exactly. And for Henry, his relationship with God is his life and his salvation."

"Which doesn't leave room for me."

"You misunderstand me. Think about it in terms of Brisa. If you were with someone who didn't value her—or with someone you wouldn't allow into the circle that includes her—what would that do to the relationship? Say you were with Henry, but he wanted only to spend time with you and never include Brisa? Or if you didn't want him to share in the close bond you have with your daughter? What would that make?"

"Two separate relationships."

"Exactly. There'd be you and Henry on one side and you and Brisa on the other, but never you, Henry, and Brisa as a unit."

"But I wouldn't do that."

"No, you wouldn't." Rita paused as if waiting for her to speak.

"You're saying that Henry's relationship with God would become an alienating relationship that would leave me out."

"Unless you also had a relationship with God, which would mean you and he would share that—as you'd share Brisa."

"Ah."

"Does that help?"

"Yeah. It does. It helps me understand, anyway."

"Happy Easter, Agnes."

---

Getting Brisa settled had been a battle. She was so wired from that day and the days preceding that all she'd wanted was to talk. She had no idea her mother's heart was breaking, that Agnes longed to be in her own room, under her own covers, hiding. Eventually, though, Link's leap onto the bed convinced Brisa to quit and gather him close.

Agnes headed to her room, closed the blinds and curtains, and waited for darkness to entice sleep. But her mind wouldn't hush.

The man she loved had some stupid idea that they had to agree on all things. Who lived like that? Had she complained about his world? Had she said, "We can't be lovers if you believe in God and call yourself a Christian?"

No.

What if one person in a relationship wanted to be a Democrat and the other a Republican? Was that a deal breaker? Did they have to walk in lockstep? Joined at the hip—or in this case, at the brain?

She got Rita's argument, but she wasn't convinced it applied to her. She listened to a quiet that was broken only by old-house noises and the occasional car's engine. No one seemed to be moving on Taylor Creek. She imagined boaters tucked in for the night, as Henry would be. Tucked in, silent, sleeping the sleep of the righteous.

And the lonely.

She knew he was lonely. And she'd imagined them easing each other past that.

What was so bad about her that he couldn't take a chance? Rita'd taken a chance with her husband, and that seemed to have worked well.

It wasn't as if she were an atheist. Or even an agnostic. She believed in God. She just didn't make him the most pre-eminent thing in her world. Was that a requirement?

Her mother's pre-death faith had changed her—yay, Mom— but not in time for her to work harder at reconciliation with her estranged daughter.

Still, what had her mother said?

Agnes switched on her lamp, climbed out of bed, and drew

the letter from her desk drawer. As she reread it, her throat constricted and her heart thurumped at a faster pace.

*I'm praying that, if you're reading this letter, you will find it in your heart to forgive me finally and to accept that your mother loved you with an imperfect love, one I hope you'll finally believe in. I hope you'll find the God who makes real love possible.*

She hadn't wanted to read her mother's words; they'd seemed too little too late. But, really, why hadn't she herself been the one to make a move without waiting for her mother to be the first to reach out?

That thought slid in and took hold. Then another truth piled on top of it. Yes, her mother had failed her, but her mother'd also admitted it, admitted to being human and imperfect. And she'd begged for forgiveness, which Agnes had withheld.

So, while her mother had judged the girl Agnes and found her wanting, hadn't she, Agnes, been doing the same thing— judging and holding onto her anger? Revealing human failings not much different from her mother's?

She hadn't wanted to let her mother off the hook for past mistakes. Or let Darlington off, for that matter.

She shut her eyes tightly against the truths that washed over her. They were each imperfect. What had Henry said? The only perfect person was Jesus?

Did that let her off the hook?

Probably not when it came to holding onto anger because there was that whole forgiveness thing. She'd learned the prayer; she knew the words. *Our Father…*

She had to forgive—and she had to ask for forgiveness. Darlington had been able to do that, and wasn't that thought a slap to the face?

She took another deep breath, let it out, in again, out slowly. And then she spoke to her dead mother's memory. "Mom, I'm sorry. Sorry I didn't take your calls. Sorry I didn't let us fix this before you died."

She was. She was truly sorry.

Faith had certainly changed her mother. And it had helped Henry find freedom. But...

She returned to bed and clutched her mother's words to her chest as she turned out the light. Then, lying again in the dark, she whispered, "I forgive you. I forgive you, Mom."

And the words that followed her into sleep were, *Forgive yourself, too.*

## HENRY

"Happy Resurrection Sunday," Father Stanley said when he answered the phone that night. "What's going on?"

"I know it's late. I'm sorry, but..."

"Tell me."

Henry sat cross-legged, a pillow plumped behind him, his boat riding easily over the gentle wake left by an old trawler chug-chugging its way out to sea. Otherwise, the anchorage was quiet. Stars flickered above, and the moon hovered on the horizon. He should be relaxed, at peace in the stillness. Instead, his leg muscles felt jumpy as if he needed to run a couple of miles to uncoil them.

"I thought it would be okay," he said, speaking softly, keeping his words here on board instead of traveling across the water. "Your warning. I mean, I really thought God was in this relationship, you know, with Agnes, but I kissed her, and it hit me, your words. The differences between us. What has to come first in my life."

"'Seek ye first the kingdom of God and His righteousness...'"

"'...and all these things shall be added unto you.'"

"Yes," Father Stanley said. "You went to church this morning, I take it? Cleared your focus?"

"She came, too. So did Brisa's dad."

"That's a story I'd like to hear. But how did Agnes react to the worship? You went back to the on-fire church you told me about?"

"And it was on fire again today. She sat in the pew ahead, so I couldn't really tell. I'm sure it was strange for her, and then Brisa and her dad sang together."

"And when you spoke to her about faith?"

"I never did. Not really. Oh, we all talked about God having been the catalyst for Darlington's change of mind and pretty much everything else. I mean, Becca Barnes certainly isn't quiet when it comes to praying or speaking."

"Ah. You're saying you made assumptions about Agnes's understanding without discussing the matter and then somehow ended up making a move on her. And then you changed your mind."

"I apologized for the kiss and walked away. I had a chance to mention fundamental differences between us when she followed me outside." Yeah, that sounded really lame. All of it.

"Mature of you." Father Stanley spoke without condemnation, but Henry sighed and heaped the coals on his head anyway. He deserved them.

"Yeah," he said. "Smart, too."

"You donning a hair shirt now?"

"I would if I thought it would fix anything."

"What do you think might?" The voice at his ear posed the question, but gently.

If only he knew. He raked his hair off his forehead and puffed out a loud breath before saying, "I guess I'd better talk to her. Apologize."

"For the kiss or for walking out?"

"For everything. Especially for not treating her like the friend she is. For being a coward."

"Why don't you try listening for God's voice tonight to see if you can figure out what he really wants for you and Agnes? He doesn't make mistakes, you know. And nothing catches him by surprise."

"I'm not very good at hearing him."

"I think you're better at it than you know, but recognizing his voice comes from practice, patience, and a heart willing to trust."

Henry felt an overwhelming love for this man who never seemed to tire of his messy self. Father Stanley, the master listener.

"You know," Henry said, suddenly ashamed. "I never ask how you're doing. I mean to and I think about it once I've hung up the phone. Now that I've paused my self-absorption for a moment, let me ask. How are you? Did you have a good Easter?"

Father Stanley laughed. "I did. I spent it with one of my girls, Bitsy, who's home from college."

"What about the other one? The older, Maggie, isn't it?"

"You remembered." He sounded pleased. "She still hasn't forgiven me for my failures as a father."

"I bet you miss her. How long's it been?"

"Well, I've been clean and sober for fourteen years, but there were the two before that when I let them all down. Bitsy was just a toddler during my bad years, but Maggie was ten when the troubles began, and ten-year-olds can have long memories. All I can do is pray that she'll find her way to forgiveness and one day allow me to try to make up for the lost years."

"I hope she does." Henry sighed. He certainly hoped Maggie found her way back to her father, because if anyone deserved to be fully happy, it was his mentor.

"God loves Maggie even more than I do, and I'm convinced he is working to bring her back to himself—and to me. Until then, I send my prayers and my love in her direction, every day, all day, all the time. And I trust in God's timing."

"It's time for me to let you get some sleep. Thank you again for being at the other end of this phone."

"Always."

When he hung up, he went outside to do his nightly check before heading to bed. Standing on the deck, the soft breeze blowing over him, he studied the stars and said, "Lord, you told me to wait until I know—or until you show me. How long did you mean for the waiting to take?"

He listened for a few minutes before going below to finish his routine. Then he lay awake for hours, sometimes talking to the night, sometimes listening to silence. He waited for a voice to answer, for some truth to hit him. For something.

Feeling desperate for answers, he finally climbed back into the cockpit and got on his knees on the hard deck. He was as close to the heavens as he could get, with the sky open above him. "I'm going to stay here, awake until you speak, Lord. I need you. I need to know my path ahead."

But the silence lengthened, and eventually his eyelids grew heavy. The next thing he knew, he was lying on the deck, aching in his hip, his shoulder, his back, cold and damp and miserable. Crawling to the seat, he murmured, "I'm sorry, but I can't do it."

He climbed down the companionway stairs and to his bunk, stripping out of his damp clothes and lowering himself to his mattress. He'd failed. Again, he'd failed.

---

With daylight streaming through the portholes, Henry took inventory. He felt surprisingly rested, and his aches had vanished.

Carrying a mug of coffee, he climbed out on deck. The wind had kicked up in the early hours, and while he and Beaufort were protected from the ocean's rages out beyond the barrier islands, he could imagine the sound and fury of those waves rising high above the sea floor, curling over, breaking in a huge rush of foam as they rolled toward the beach.

As boys, he and Eric had loved the beach in a storm. They'd

summered mere yards from the dunes that protected their family's Sullivan's Island retreat from the encroaching sea. They weren't supposed to venture near the water alone, which pretty much meant ever, but those tasked with watching them hadn't hovered. And so they'd gone searching for shells or sharks' teeth, for pieces of driftwood among the flotsam washed up by wind and tides. The dunes had been there for climbing and conquering, the flat areas for building castles, the sea for watching... and for dreaming.

Henry hadn't known much of God beyond the Sunday school images that didn't make the Lord very appealing. But there, at the edge of that vast sea, where clouds scurried from one end of the sky to the other, where storybook places could be reached one day if only he had the right ship... well, there he could speak to a God big enough to have created it all. While Eric brandished a driftwood sword to conquer the next dune, Henry'd stood barefoot at the water's edge and whispered his hopes and dreams in a prayer.

He'd thought of them as his sea prayers. And he'd believed the God who'd made that sea actually heard him.

What about now? Did he still believe God heard? And that God's purpose would be revealed to him if he waited and listened?

He'd poured out his heart. He'd begged and pleaded. But had he trusted? Had he believed?

Looking out over the islands toward the visible horizon, he imagined the one he couldn't see, the far horizon that was there, touched by the eternal even if never by him. God saw and touched and knew. And he whispered, God did, words like "'I know the plans I have for you... plans to prosper you and not harm you, plans to give you hope and a future.'" If God had plans for him as Jeremiah had written, then all he, Henry, had to do was put one foot in front of the other and do what came next. That wasn't an easy task for someone who'd been planning and organizing and neatly fitting things into place as a means of coping with his addiction recovery. But he wouldn't have made it this far without clinging to hope and clinging to the bits and pieces of faith that had been growing in him, revelation upon revelation.

He would take the next step. He would trust God to show him as he walked forward.

57

## AGNES

Agnes stood at her basin, smoothing cream over her face and neck. Whatever it took, that's what she'd do, and she'd do it with renewed strength. She'd aim for a healthy self-confidence, even if she had to live alone for the rest of her life. Perhaps she'd even find her way fully to the God who seemed to have been working in her life in spite of her level of faith. After all, God hadn't asked her how much she believed before bringing Brisa home, had he?

Henry'd made a choice, and that was on him, not on her. She'd toyed with the idea of being in love, but that's all it had been, an idea. If he could walk away like he had, he was lily-livered as well as being a cad. He didn't deserve her. And he certainly didn't deserve a relationship with her precious, miraculous daughter.

That whole addict thing must have warped and emasculated him, turned him into someone afraid to take a chance. In other words, a terrible risk when it came to romance.

She dressed with care, not because she expected to see anyone but because she was donning her renewed persona. The old Helen Reddy song, "I Am Woman" came to mind. Like the songwriter said, she'd been through pain, but it hadn't broken her. Instead, it had given her wisdom. She was strong, invincible, woman.

In her freshman—and only—year of college, one of her dorm mates, a woman's studies major, had a collection of recordings, including this one from 1972. The tune was catchy enough and she replayed it often enough that most of the girls could sing along. And here Agnes was, hearing it in her head all these years later.

But it fit, she decided, as she carried her second cup of coffee back upstairs and collected the shoebox holding the letters her mother had written to Brisa. She made herself comfortable in her cushy chair and began to read the letters, one at a time, before she exposed her daughter to whatever her mother might have said.

They were surprisingly benign. Perhaps her mother had purged any that had leftovers of her former spite—or perhaps she'd never held her grandchild—the grandchild she'd wanted Agnes to abort—responsible for the mess.

"Stop that," Agnes told herself. "Don't go there again."

She'd forgiven her mother, hadn't she? It was time to breathe out all that poison and find a semblance of peace so that she and her daughter could start again in this house that had been her mother's during happier times.

She sipped her now-cool coffee, waiting for her daughter to wake. And then she rested her head back against the chair, closed her eyes, and fell asleep.

That's how Brisa found her. "Mom?" she said.

Agnes opened her eyes. "Hey, sweetie. Good morning."

Her daughter was kneeling in front of the box of letters. "What are these?"

"Your grandmother's letters."

"My grandmother?"

"My mother. The grandmother who left us this house."

"Really? Can I see?"

"You may. She wrote to you from the time you were four. If you want, you can come sit in this chair and read them."

Agnes stood and let her daughter slide in behind her, the box on her knees.

"Come on down when you want breakfast."

But Brisa didn't seem to hear her.

---

"I wish I'd known her." Brisa paused with a spoonful of cereal halfway to her mouth. "She loved me."

Agnes didn't address that last statement. Her mother may have wanted—finally—to love Brisa, but she hadn't tried in time, had she?

Instead of digging out another bite, Brisa stirred the remaining cereal around and around in her bowl. And then she said, "How can she have loved me when she never came to see me? She didn't know me."

Ah, yes. Her daughter was no dummy.

"I imagine she wished she had. She was an unhappy woman until the last years of her life."

"Oh."

"Anyway, it seems to me we can think about her sometimes and enjoy this lovely house she gave us, can't we?" At least, here her mother had found some happiness. Here she'd changed.

"Do we have any pictures?"

"There are a few albums in the attic." She'd stuffed them all in a box when she'd moved into the house. If she remembered correctly, at least one held pictures of her own childhood. "I'll dig them out soon."

"Today?"

"Sure."

Brisa finished her breakfast and added her bowl to the dishwasher. Interesting that she didn't need a reminder.

"I promised Jilly I'd come play. Is that okay?"

"Did you forget that Mrs. Barnes is coming to pick you up at one to visit that family?"

"Aw, Mom."

Agnes put on the mom-face.

"Okay. But can I see Jilly before?"

"Straighten your room first. And then be home by lunch time."

"'kay!"

A half-hour later, Brisa was out the door and on her way, and Agnes was sitting at the kitchen table with only a glass of water in front of her, trying to summon the energy to do something constructive. Anything, really. Because she wasn't going to feel sorry for herself.

Not today. "Not ever again."

Strong words. Well, she needed strong words spoken aloud so she'd hang onto them. She'd managed for years on her own, and she could manage again. Maybe she needed to keep singing Helen Reddy's words.

She tried them out and then grinned, because she did *not* have her daughter's talent.

The knock came first, and then the doorbell. Someone wanted her attention, but she wasn't sure she wanted anyone's. She waited. Maybe whoever it was would go away.

But what if Rita had come to check on her?

She could tell from the profile and the height visible through the glazed sidelights that it wasn't Rita. She hesitated, but the knuckles hitting wood unnerved her. She threw open the door. "Go away. I don't want to see you today."

The expression in Henry's big eyes would have softened her at any other time, melted her, actually. Not today.

"I'm sorry," he said. "I had to at least come by to say I'm sorry."

"Yeah, well, sorry doesn't cut it."

"Please, may I come in?"

"Why should I let you in my house? So you can abuse me again? Frankly, I'm not up for that."

She began to shut the door, but he extended one foot to keep it open. She stared at him silently. He didn't back down or stammer another apology. He just waited, a rock of a man with a large foot blocking her door.

She would not notice his size or those muscles clearly visible under the cotton of his shirt. His eyes were a problem, so she focused on his chin. Too bad it was square and she particularly liked square jaws. She wouldn't look at his hair either, not at the dark waves in need of a trim. No, she was too angry to let anything about him affect her.

She opened the door and stepped back.

He stood in her hallway with the light playing on that hair and his eyes in shadow and said, "I've come to grovel. I didn't show myself much of a friend yesterday, and I've no excuse for my cowardice." He looked straight at her as he spoke. She'd expected instead lowered eyes and fumbling hands. She'd have despised those.

"Why did you do it? Why did you say such things?"

"I listened to a lie in my head. I owed you so much more."

"Yes, you did." Perhaps it was his stance that compelled her, the way he stood tall and strong even as he called himself a coward. He reminded her of a warrior at that moment, a gentle one, perhaps, even a humble one, if that made any sense. She wasn't sure it did, but her thoughts weren't exactly working in a linear fashion, A to B to C. They felt scattered, driven by opposing forces of attraction and hurt.

"Come on back," she said finally. "I can make tea."

"Water would be fine."

She filled a glass for him and refilled hers. "Let's sit on the back porch. I don't have chairs yet, but the view's much better since someone mowed the grass." She allowed a miniature smile to curve her lips.

"He'll probably need to do it again this week."

"Part of groveling?"

"Sure, why not? But also part of friendship."

Agnes led him out the door and patted a place beside her as she lowered herself to the stoop. She wasn't going to let herself need anyone, certainly not him, the faux friend. "I'm not so sure about the friendship thing. I've decided not to let myself be subjected to any more emotional manipulation." And as she said the words, she sat a little straighter.

Focusing her attention on the shed out back and the garden space that had nothing growing in it, she let the truth of that statement take root. Spring, after all, was the time to plant.

"I'm sorry, Agnes. I truly am."

"So you said."

"I shouldn't have—"

"What?" She whipped her head around and set her glass on the porch deck. "What shouldn't you have done? Kissed me? Walked out? Or declared there can be nothing between us because of 'fundamental' differences that somehow don't let us connect. I thought we connected very well."

He swiped a hand down his face. "Boy, I really was brutal. I don't blame you for not wanting to have anything to do with me."

"Really? That's the best you can do? Woe is you?"

He started to turn. "I'm thinking I should go in that door and come out again to start over. What do you think?"

"I think you should just say what you came to say, which had better include all those things you shouldn't have done."

"Okay. Let's start with this one: I definitely shouldn't have walked out."

"That's a given. Friends don't, only cowards." She had to stifle a smile of satisfaction once she'd said that.

He drained his water and set the glass aside. "I shouldn't have said anything that made you feel demeaned."

"True." Too bad she wasn't taking notes. That one deserved top billing.

"I shouldn't have kissed you if I wasn't ready to admit my feelings."

His words sounded promising. So, he had feelings... Did she want him to? Or did she still want to toss him out the door? "Another truth," she said, keeping the edge in her voice.

"I shouldn't have made assumptions about anything, much less how you feel about God."

"Well, hello, home run."

That surprised a laugh from him. "Home run?"

She kept her expression neutral, although she rather liked her word choice, too. "You assumed a lot and acted on those assumptions, didn't you?"

"I did. Faith isn't really quantifiable, not when Jesus says faith the size of a mustard seed can move a mountain. While our faith is meant to grow through use, it's God's faith in us and through us that does the miracles. I denied its power in you."

He'd interested her with that, but she kept quiet.

"Which," he said, "if you brush away all the trappings of rhetoric, means I showed even less faith than you did."

Whoa. She squinted at him, as if that might bring him into better focus. "Did you have some sort of divine revelation last night? I mean, the you who was here yesterday and the you who can say that don't even seem related."

He grinned. "Well, you might say something got hold of me. I was up a lot of the night, asking for guidance. Tried getting on my knees on the deck and woke up hurting."

"Served you right," she said, trying not to respond with her own grin. "Now that you've had this shift in understanding, what happens next? I mean, how do your revelations affect us?"

"I'm hoping you'll tell me we can be friends again. At the very least."

The least? "If friendship's the least," she asked, "what's the most?"

He waggled his eyebrows at her. Now she did laugh.

He tried to take her hand, but she held it palm up to stop

him. "Hang on a minute. All joking aside, the one thing you haven't touched on is the trigger that started things last night. It couldn't have been the kiss."

Henry brushed something invisible from his pant leg, his expression unreadable as she stared at his profile. Finally, he said, "Retreating from difficult situations is a pattern of thought —and behavior—I've been trying to overcome. I've been taking steps to be the man I was created to be, the man I've been called to be, but last night, I slid back into the old pattern. Jesus wants so much more for me. And for you." He turned and let his gaze move from her lips up to her eyes. She couldn't look away.

Those eyes, oh my, those eyes.

"I think," he continued, "the force of my feelings for you frightened me. And I'm sorry."

"Yeah, well, I find it hard to trust feelings like that, especially when you toss in God's name as some sort of justification for running. " She nudged at a pebble with her foot.

"I'm a very imperfect man."

"No kidding."

He grinned then. "You're not playing by the rules of polite conversation, Agnes."

"Nope. I got over polite when a supposedly strong and loving man showed me he doesn't deserve me—or my love."

"Ah." He rose and walked a few feet away. When he turned, his arms were crossed, his feet spread in that warrior's stance. "To call this our first fight would mean we'd have to acknowledge a relationship, wouldn't it?" His lips twitched as if he fought to keep the humor tamped.

She waited.

"I am the culpable one, Agnes." Her silence seemed to have sobered him. "I offered my heart and then I withdrew it. I wish I were more deserving of your love, but I am an admitted coward when it comes to interpersonal relationships." His expression seemed rueful. "While I may be strong enough and willing to defend you and Brisa, I seem to have failed in this most vital thing of convincing you to trust my heart."

He was killing her. She had no defense against words such as those. None at all.

"I will leave now, if you'd like. But I won't give up. Last night, I begged God for clarity and courage. I believe he has given me this love for you, and it feels right. It feels true. I ran from it yesterday because I let fear overwhelm me. But fear has been my *modus operandi* for too long, and I don't want to let it win again. I'm a very imperfect man, Agnes Jones, but I want to love you with God's love, which is perfect."

She was melting. Pretty soon she'd be a puddle at his feet. "Okay."

He looked surprised. "Okay, what?"

"Perfect isn't something I understand, but I can wrap my head around imperfect." Considering that was what she'd been discussing with herself during all those hours.

"So, it's a starting point?" He moved quickly to her side and sat next to her.

What she wanted to know was what it entailed, this starting point to some kind of love. Did he mean friendship-love or love-love? Romantic love. Did it include kisses? More than? Less than?

"I don't like games, Henry. And I'd rather have nothing from you than be involved with someone who can take fright and run off without really talking to me. It's going to take me some time to forget how horribly you acted last night and to let go all my mistrust."

"You have every right to feel that way. I'm hoping, though, you'll let me try to make it up to you. I'm not sure how I can do that, but I'd like to try."

"Was it a one-off?"

He laughed. "Oh, honey, very one-off. First, I've never felt for anyone what I feel for you. That scares me to death. I'm thirty-five years old, and I've never been in love. In lust, yes, I'm sorry to say. In bondage, yes. But never in love and never where I felt the Lord was leading me more deeply into grace through that love."

She hiked her brows. "Grace? What do you mean by that?"

"The place where God's love abounds—unmerited favor, true love." His eyes were doing that twinkling thing again.

"An unknown place for me, that sort of love."

He took her hand and drew it to his chest. "Do you want it for yourself? For us?"

She curled her fingers around his, loving the strength of them, the comfort he offered, even as she said, "I'm not certain what that would entail."

His expression softened, and he lifted their joined hands to his lips before speaking again. "I heard a teacher once say that God puts people together in a body—or in pairs—because they each need something the other has. He went on to talk about rough edges, how we each have them and can only be rid of them by rubbing against one another."

"Sounds very uncomfortable."

"It does, but he had a point. He used the story of David and Goliath to talk about the five smooth stones David picked up out of the stream. Only a smooth stone would have flown true and hit its target, and the stone could only be smoothed by rubbing against other stones in that stream bed."

She watched him as he spoke, his face expressive, his eyes gazing directly into hers.

"I'm hoping, Agnes, that you'll take a chance that my rough edges and your rough edges can rub together to smooth us both out and make us better people, the people we've been created to be. I've been a broken man; I was a broken boy. But the Lord God is in the business of rebuilding broken lives, and if I trust him with me, then I can trust him with us." His eyes seemed to glow, so alight were they. "He has given me a love for you that is more than I could ever have imagined. I've been frightened by it, but I know Jesus is faithful in all things, and what he has begun, he will complete."

This was a lot to absorb, but she'd been buffeted on all sides recently, hadn't she? With Darling's about-face, her mother's apology, and now Henry's admission of love along with a whole lot more. And God seemed right in the center of it all.

But *love*? Her gaze wandered as the word settled. On a resigned—albeit slightly puzzled—sigh, she admitted, "I've not only never been in love. I've never actually dated anyone."

He grinned and again lifted her fingers to his lips. "Aren't we a match made in heaven?"

His touch sent a shiver up her spine. "Are we?"

"You ready to trust?"

"To try." She might not know what that meant, but she wanted to. Oh, yes, she wanted to.

"To try, then" he said. "To see what it all means."

"I can do that. I need to learn to trust your words, Henry." And the words of God, she thought but didn't say.

"We'll move forward, one step at a time."

## 58

## HENRY

Henry drew her close. His lips touched hers, gently at first and then with growing passion. She was so perfect for him, everything about her. But if he didn't slow things down, he'd find stopping much more difficult. Finally, he broke away. "We're supposed to be taking this one step at a time," he said on a half-laugh.

The breathlessness in her voice encouraged him. "Yes."

Okay, distraction. They both needed to think of other things if those slow steps weren't going to become a race to the finish line.

"On a lighter note," Henry said, "I have good news. No, great news. I'm going to have access to money. Oh, not Darling-the-megastar money, but I'll be a whole lot wealthier than I've been in a long while."

"Rich, eh?" Her eyes danced. "That changes everything."

"You like the idea of stone-rubbing if mine is gold-flecked?"

"I do!"

He laughed out loud. "Brisa should be pleased. I'll be able to fix *Harmless* sooner."

"She will be, but did you rob a bank or something?" Her eyes were still twinkling.

"In a manner of speaking. Eric's been hounding me about taking some of my trust fund, and I finally told him I was going to. He and his co-trustee invested the money, and Eric says I have a tidy sum—a very tidy sum—waiting for me to draw the interest."

"I thought you were joking." She chewed on her lip and then said, "Really?"

"Yeah. I think Eric shelled out some for my last in-center treatment, but I haven't let him give me any to live on until very recently."

"What changed your mind?"

"A lot of things. Talking to my sponsor, to Eric. Thinking about unforgiveness and the hold it has on us if we don't let it go. I realized I'd never be completely whole or healthy until I forgave my father. I had a few others to forgive, too, including God. The big one was forgiving myself. I've probably got more work to do there, but I've spoken the words, and I'm trusting that the truth of it will take complete hold so I can find the freedom I crave."

"That's powerful stuff."

"Is it okay with you? We still on the same page? You can handle all this God talk?"

She remained silent.

He gave her a moment and continued. "It's only by God's grace."

"What is?"

"Forgiveness."

She stared out at the yard. When she looked back, her eyes were damp.

"I'm sorry," he whispered. "I didn't mean to upset you." And then he increased the volume as he spoke. "I'm sorry. It's too much. I know. Really. Imperfect, remember? I warned you."

"Kiss me, will you? I need a kiss right now."

"Ah. I can do that."

## 59

## DARLING

Darling had ignored the phone calls from Arthur and his father as Jett and his new lawyer, Ballantine Richards, set up a company using his full name instead of the old stage name. Initially, Arthur had been conciliatory, his father merely bombastic. These latest, though?

He'd told Todd to refuse entrance to any of them, including Lisette. "Oh, and we should change the passcode for the front gate. Can you do that?"

"Yes, sir. It won't be a problem."

"You and I will be the only ones who can access the new one."

"Yes, sir." Todd smiled as he nodded. "I think you're wise. Far too many could get in before."

"Indeed."

Darling had washed his hands of his unfaithful wife and had given permission for Ballantine to get one of the divorce lawyers he knew to take care of that end of things.

Now he picked up the phone. Arthur first.

"It's about time," Arthur said by way of greeting.

"I've been thinking about things."

"You need to—"

"No, let me finish. Friendship involves trust, and you have lost mine. You will soon be receiving a letter from my new attorney explaining things fully."

"You can't do that."

"Oh, yes, I can. Your contract is obviously with my father, and you may remain on his payroll—or not. But you and I no longer have a relationship. Goodbye, Arthur."

The shouts only ceased when his finger hit the disconnect button. Certain that he wouldn't have long to wait for his father's response, he sat back and looked over the contract Jett and Ballantine had drafted to send to Jeminy Buchanan, his songwriter. Brisa liked Jeminy, and Darling thought her enormously talented. He planned to offer her a lot more than she was probably getting through her boyfriend's management.

His phone rang. He answered.

"You cannot do this, Darling." He'd once admired that gravelly voice, his father's masterly way of command. "You have a contract."

"I can do it, and I have."

"I'll take you to court. I'll sue you for everything you have."

"Try it," Darling said, "and I'll talk about the drugs your son brought into my house and the video your people were trying to make to corrupt a young girl. I'll ask for a jury trial and see how well they like that your people—not mine, as you assured me the next day—your people got a twelve-year-old drunk and thought it amusing."

"You can't prove any of that."

"As a matter of fact, I have a witness. Todd. He also retrieved the data from the phones in use that night. Even without a witness, how do you think this will play in the media, considering that I was so concerned for the safety of that child that I took her back to her mother instead of subjecting her to your crew again?"

His father continued to bluster, but it was all hot air. Finally, Darling cut him off. "Enjoy your new star and your new girlfriend. I hope you make each other very happy. But we're over. You keep yourself and yours away from me and mine."

And then, with the depression of a button, he disconnected from that most toxic relationship.

Sitting back in his comfortable desk chair, he realized he had one more call to make. He punched in his grandmother's number and waited. When her voice answered, he said, "Hey, Mama. I did it."

## 60

## AGNES

Agnes felt like a giddy school girl—a giddy something, anyway—who'd caught the boy and couldn't quite believe in her good fortune. She and Henry had moved to the front porch rockers, which she'd never used, thinking how lonely it would seem to put only one in motion. Now there were two. Two feet pushing off the porch floor, two hands holding across the space between the chairs, two to smell the occasional scent of plough mud and the tang of salt, the sweetly perfumed wisteria, even sometimes the faint odor of diesel exhaust from a shrimper heading in or out.

The air was coolish, a spring evening cool that wiped away humidity. A slight breeze wrinkled the water's surface. Tourists had begun to return after their winter hiatus, and pedestrians wandered Front Street. Music blared from the occasional car radio.

She told Henry about her own foray into the realm of forgiving as she'd let go of her anger toward her mother. God, Henry assured her, never made mistakes, and he'd given them each other. "To keep us out of trouble."

"Me?" she said. "I never get in trouble."

"Me, then. He knew I needed you."

She shook her head. "No, we need each other. And Brisa needs us."

A car pulled into the driveway, and Brisa bounded out, waving to Mrs. Barnes as she dashed up to the porch. "Hey, Mr. Henry. Guess what? Mrs. Barnes taught me to make mac and cheese, and we all ate it for dinner."

Henry grinned. "Punishment turning out to be fun, is it?"

Brisa wrinkled her nose. "Not so much. The twins both had stinky diapers at the same time, and I had to learn to change them. Yuck."

"School starts up again tomorrow," Agnes said, "which means it's off to bed with you."

"Okay, but I was thinking…"

"Uh-oh, that's dangerous," Henry said.

Brisa giggled. "Mom, now that you're going to marry Mr. Henry—"

Agnes glanced in his direction as heat hit her cheeks. "What gave you that idea?"

"Give me some credit, Mom. It's obvious."

"How old *are* you?" What had happened to twelve?

"Smart girl," Henry said. "Told you."

"So." Brisa leaned slightly forward, her hands clasped against her chest, looking ready to burst with excitement. "Seeing as how you're going to be my step-dad—"

"We haven't gotten that far, honey," Henry said, saving Agnes the trouble. "Your mom wants to make me work for it."

"Well, I bet you will, and I think it's a great idea. You have your big boat, so I was thinking we can go sailing to some of the places Jilly and her folks went! Wouldn't that be fun?" Her gaze shifted from Henry to her mother and back. "And maybe they could go out on the *Nancy Grace* and we could all sail our own boats to the same place! You think we could?"

"It sounds great," Henry said. "But I'm still working on getting *Harmless* ready, and you and your mother need to decide if you even like sailing."

"We will! I know we will."

"So," he said in a rallying tone, "if someday we do get married, and if you both like sailing on *Harmless* once she's ready, we can certainly take trips. Maybe we could start by sailing to Cape Lookout."

"That would be fantastic!" Brisa said. "Jilly stayed a whole week at Cape Lookout once."

Enough was enough. Agnes shooed her daughter toward the stairs. "Time for bed. Take your daydreams with you."

"Okay!" Brisa snapped for Link to follow. "See you later, Henry. Don't keep Mom up too late," she said on a laugh.

"Yes, ma'am," he called after her.

As she let the screen door close behind her, Henry chuckled. "That's quite a precocious girl you have."

"It scares me."

"She'll be fine. And if we get both of you out sailing, maybe actually cruise for a while, she'll see a different aspect of life. It'll be good for her. And, it will distract her from thoughts of her father's glamorous life."

"I like that. I just hope we don't get seasick. You know, on the actual ocean."

He hooted. "Well, you didn't when *Harmless* bucked over the wake, so it's not likely, but there are meds if you need them. Think of all we can explore together, both here and beyond."

They watched the waterfront, and she dreamed of adventures, of going beyond the small life she'd led all these years into one of togetherness with this incredible man.

"One step at a time."

"The good thing about me accepting my inheritance," he finally said, "is that you don't have to worry I'm interested in you for your money."

Her laugh at his unexpected words sounded like a bark. "Good gracious, I don't, do I? Same for you. Should put Eric's mind at ease."

"He's a good guy. A little protective, but a good brother."

"Talk to me about where we can go and what we can do. I want to dream a little."

"Ah. To dream. That sounds perfect."

And as he spoke of seas and islands and turquoise waters, of dolphins and whales and wind propelling them to the back of beyond, she tightened her hold on his hand. "I know we're doing this slowly, but I'm pretty sure I love you, Henry Houston."

In the invisibility of the dark porch, he stood and drew her out of her rocker. "I don't have to wonder if I love you. Rubbing the rough spots right off me, are you?"

"Hoping to."

He lowered his lips to hers, and the thought hit her. With him, she felt beautiful. With her, he could feel whole.

And her heart sang, *Thank you. Oh, thank you*.

Then she broke away from his embrace long enough to speak the words aloud. "I believe."

She did believe. In the promises, in the hope, in what could be.

In so much, she thought as his lips captured hers again. In so much.

The End

# ACKNOWLEDGMENTS

So many people contribute to my writing world that it's hard to thank them all. First must be my husband who is always my greatest cheerleader, along with my mama who can't wait for my next book to release and will forgo my attention if I'm writing.

My vigilant critique partners prod me to dig and improve. Thank you, Jane Lebak and Jennifer Fromke, for taking the time out of your busy lives. I couldn't manage without you, and any accolades for this story will bounce back to you both. My editors, Ray Rhamey and Robin Patchen, catch my oopsies and push my stories to the next level. They make me work hard for every word, and I am grateful for their insight. Early readers Tracie Heskett and Jinx Gilmore found typos everyone else missed. Thank you both!

Without the brilliant help of Henri McClees, Esq., the legal bits and pieces in this story would all be a jumble. I am so very grateful for her willingness to answer my questions and to make sure I got it right. If I missed anything, the blame is mine.

If I look good on social media, thank the very talented Tanya Eavenson for her gorgeous memes and other help. I feel so privileged to have her on my team and as my friend.

And there are my encouragers without whom I'd be flailing

in a sea of a writer's worries: Susan, DeeJay, Carol, Becky, Jenny, Kimberli, Andrea, John, JoAnn, Bonnie, and Nicole. Thank you so much for kind words and lovely smiles.

For my tribe at Women's Fiction Writers Association, especially the talented Barbara Davis, Barbara Claypole White, and Laura Drake: You've shared your words of encouragement from the beginning and helped me believe. Thank you, thank you. Your talent inspires me.

And you, my readers: you mean the world to me. Your letters bless me and your continued support keeps me writing.

If I've forgotten anyone, it wasn't intentional. I love you all.

# ABOUT THE AUTHOR

Normandie Fischer lives in coastal North Carolina with her husband, her aging mother, their aussiedoodle, and two once-feral cats. If only her two adult children and two adorable grandchildren lived within hailing distance, life on land instead of on their cruising sailboat would be just about perfect.

Please feel free to contact me on social media or at my website. I'd love to hear from you.

www.normandiefischer.com

Made in the USA
Las Vegas, NV
02 September 2022

54570646R00233